W9-ABM-040

WITHDRAWN

Restoration

ALSO BY JOHN ED BRADLEY

Tupelo Nights

The Best There Ever Was

Love & Obits

Smoke

My Juliet

Restoration

A NOVEL

John Ed Bradley

DOUBLEDAY

New York London Toronto

Sydney Auckland

RODMAN PUBLIC LIBRARY

PUBLISHED BY DOUBLEDAY
a division of Random House, Inc.

DOUBLEDAY and the portrayal of an anchor with a dolphin are
registered trademarks of Random House, Inc.

Book design by Caroline Cunningham
Title page photo copyright © Ken Glaser/CORBIS

This novel is a work of fiction. Names, characters, businesses, organizations, places,
events, and incidents either are the product of the author's imagination or are
used fictitiously. Any resemblance to actual persons, living or dead, events, or
locales is entirely coincidental. Although there were several WPA artists in
the South who painted murals, many of which have been badly damaged or
destroyed, the mural depicted in this book and its setting are entirely the
product of the author's imagination.

Library of Congress Cataloging-in-Publication Data

Bradley, John Ed.
Restoration : a novel / John Ed Bradley.— 1st ed.
p.   cm.
1. New Orleans (La.)—Fiction.   2. Suicide victims—Fiction.
3. Art thefts—Fiction. I. Title.
PS3552.R2275 R47 2003
813'.54—dc21
2002031182

ISBN 0-385-50261-3

Copyright © 2003 by John Ed Bradley

All Rights Reserved

PRINTED IN THE UNITED STATES OF AMERICA

March 2003

First Edition

1 3 5 7 9 10 8 6 4 2

For Bill Thomas

38212004099971
Main Adult Fiction
Bradley
Bradley, John Ed
Restoration : a novel

WITHDRAWN
SEP 2003

Restoration

The buses have not yet begun to arrive: the garden club ladies in sandals and straw hats, the schoolchildren on field trips, the pale, weary northerners grousing about the heat. The least pleasant of the museum's visitors are the amateur painters from the local art academies. They shuffle from room to room dismissing the silence with cruel laughter and snorts of disapproval. They know everything. They take the guided tours only for the opportunity to humiliate the docents. Huddled before the Asmore, they stroke their chins and pose the same questions: Why did the artist kill himself? Was the subject of this painting his lover? What on earth compelled him to make her mouth a smear?

"Smug sonsabitches," says the man.

"Dad?"

"I'd like to give them a tour." And now he shakes a fist at the morning air.

Today the man and his son hike up the long, shady drive and climb the stairs to the great bronze doors at the museum's entrance. The man is a sport, and the sort one would not expect to find here on his day off. He wears a rayon shirt decorated with a diamond pattern, slacks with sharp creases from his wife's iron, a porkpie hat with a feather in the red silk band. He is a photographer by trade, specializing in French Quarter views which he colors by hand and sells as "New Orleans Originals" to tourists.

They are a team, the man and the boy. And they are early again today, and apparently alone outside but for a maintenance worker, some twenty feet away, sweeping leaves and candy wrappers into a dustpan. The boy wonders aloud at the morning's absence of visitors; the man hesitates to respond, not wishing to invite a stampede.

"What time you got, Jack?"

"Three more minutes."

"Oh, baby. And we'll have her all to ourselves."

This is church, this building with the names of dead artists carved into the façade, and so the boy, too, has come dressed as if for worship. "Mr. Woodward, I adore you, sir," says his little blue sport jacket. "Mr. Giroux, I think the world of you, as well," say his polished penny loafers.

Against the side of the building hang long, flowing banners advertising the latest exhibition: someone's collection of Early American paperweights. The show has entered its last week, and proved to be a miserable dud, a failure to museum personnel and patrons alike, with the exception of the man and his son, who, still alone now, cannot believe their miraculous good fortune.

"How much, Jack?"

"I have ten o'clock on the button, Dad."

"You have ten o'clock?" And before the boy can reply, the man is thumping a hand against the door. "It's ten o'clock. Ladies! Ten o'clock!"

The docents welcome them by name. It is no longer necessary for the man to show them his member's card. He removes his hat and gives a polite bow. Even though he has fallen under the spell of the hipsters he remains courtly and kind. He was humming Bobby Darin earlier. He has stopped that now.

"How are you, John?"

"I'm well, Mrs. Dupuy. Thank you for asking."

"And Mrs. Charbonnet?"

"Mighty fine, too, ma'am. I'll surely tell her you asked."

The volunteers all smell of their morning baths. They are as powdery as cream puffs in a baker's window. The boy is scared of them. "You want to be like your daddy when you grow up?" one of them says.

The boy looks up at his father to make sure it's okay to answer. Given a nod, he says, "I guess I do."

"You positive about that?" And the woman laughs to show she's only kidding.

They climb sugary brown stairs and turn toward the room with the Asmore. They have no use for so much of what resides here: the Fabergé eggs, the marble statues, the ecclesiastical portraits of men with flowing robes and gilded halos. Give them pictures of oak trees and the bayou. Give them French Quarter courtyards and clumps of jasmine on garden gates. Give them Creole girls with small mouths who seem forever on the verge of saying something.

"Where are the guards?" The man stops and spins around. "Jack, hurry, son, go stand by the door."

"By the door, Dad?"

"Tell me if you see anyone coming."

The boy does as he's told. At eight he is still too young to grasp the portrait's sexual content, although the sitter's breasts make him uneasy, flattening out his breath and provoking a tipsy sensation, like vertigo. He has wondered why the woman looks so sleepy, but somehow knows better than to ask his father for the reason.

"Anybody coming?"

"No."

"Nobody?"

"Still empty, Dad."

The portrait hangs at the center of the wall facing the doors and burns against a battery of spotlights. The man lifts a hand and spreads it wide and gently places his fingertips on the surface. He repeats the exercise with his other hand. Together now his hands explore the figure of the woman.

"Jack?"

"Nope."

It is when the man brings his nose to the surface and sniffs the paint that his hat falls off his head and lands on the floor, spinning a slow circle. The boy moves to pick it up but the man, raising his voice, tells him to stay at the door.

"I didn't do this, did I, Jack?"

"Do what, Dad?"

"Come over here, son. It's your turn."

By now tears are running down the man's face. Jack spots one of the old women coming up the stairs, putting two feet on each step, both hands on the banister. But this isn't why he shakes his head, no. Jack knows beauty. He is content simply to look.

ONE

When the old car pulled up, I was waiting by the gate, gazing past a colorful shroud of crape myrtles and wisteria at a plantation house I had long admired. The rent sign hanging from the finials on the tall, iron fence appeared to be hand-done, as the lettering was clumsily formed and running in streaks. YOU CAN LIVE HERE, the sign said, and provided numbers for a local business called High Life Realty.

I cracked a smile at the spectacle of the approaching car. Its exhaust pipe was dragging the ground and shooting sparks in a great, feathery arc. After parking against the curb in front, the driver made a furious attempt to open his door. It wouldn't budge, and so he slid across the seat and got out on the passenger's side. He was an odd-looking fellow with a flaming-red complexion, thinning blond hair and, today, a crust of dried shaving cream on the side of his face. Perhaps because of his company's name, he was not at all what I'd expected. In other words, there was nothing of the high life about him. Cat hair clung to his cheap navy coat. His shoes were brown brogans caked with mud. "You Jack?" he said, ambling toward me with a hand to shake.

"Yes," I answered. "You Mr. Marion?"

"Patrick. Call me Patrick, please." He was the agent representing the rental; I'd phoned him less than an hour before. "It's only eight hundred dollars a month," he said, "but it isn't for the main house, Jack. It's for the bachelor's quarters—the garçonnière—attached to the rear of the building."

"Does someone live in the main house?"

He nodded. "The owner, an elderly man named Lowenstein. I'd offer to introduce you to him but he's not well, I'm afraid. He keeps a maid and a nurse, and if you rent the place you're likely to see more of them than of him. Except for the occasional afternoon when he rolls out for coffee on the back gallery, he tends to remain hidden."

"He's in a wheelchair, then?"

"Well, part of the time, when the arthritis flares up. He doesn't exactly welcome personal questions, but that's how the nurse described his condition."

I followed Patrick to the back of the house and the garçonnière. The apartment was small, dark and cramped, and the floors were badly warped from water damage. Ceilings reached upward to a height of twelve feet and each of the three rooms had a fireplace. I checked to make sure the shower worked and the toilet flushed properly, and when I stepped out of the bathroom Patrick was waiting for me with a familiar look on his face. "Jack, have we met before?"

"I don't think so."

"Then how do I know you? I'm certain I've heard your name before."

"You read the paper?"

"Always."

"I'm Jack Charbonnet," I said, pronouncing it the French way, as we do, *Shar-bo-nay*. "I write a column . . . well, I did write one. I resigned last week."

"And how old are you, Jack? If you don't mind my asking."

"Thirty-two."

"Thirty-two and you've resigned? How wonderful."

"If I look familiar it's probably because the paper ran my mug shot with the column." I imitated my pose in the photo. "Maybe you've seen it."

He pulled a hand down his long face and gave me another look. He shook his head finally, and then pointed to the ground at his feet, no doubt intent on getting back to the issue at hand. "If you want privacy and seclusion, Jack, this is the spot."

"It does inspire, doesn't it? I'm almost embarrassed to admit this, but a moment ago I had a flash of déjà vu."

This seemed to please him, and he answered with an energetic nod. "You're perfect for the place, I can tell. Except for the modern conveniences like plumbing and air-conditioning, it's just as it was in 1830, when the house was built. Maybe you lived here in another life, Jack. Maybe you will live here in many lives to come. In any case, the garden in back is yours to enjoy. Every pink azalea and purple iris, every olive jar, the garden oak and the giant palm . . . even the ghost."

"A ghost, is there?"

"Mr. Lowenstein asked me to make sure to mention it, in the spirit of full disclosure. Unexplained footsteps in the middle of the night, the sound of someone weeping. You get up to see who it is and there's no one. Frankly it strikes me as a bunch of hogwash. But the old man insists it's real." Patrick slapped another hand on my shoulder. "I hope that doesn't kill the deal."

"Not at all. If you live in New Orleans, they can't be avoided, can they?"

"Who's that?"

"Ghosts," I said. "Ghosts and termites. They own this town."

We sat at a small table on the front gallery and he spread out a collection of papers in front of me. I began filling out an application form and paused when I came to the question of employment. Patrick raised an eyebrow as I wrote the word *Self.*

"If you have no job, Jack, how will you pay rent?"

"I've recently come into some money. By way of inheritance. My father left me some assets. My credit history's strong. I assure you I'm a good candidate."

"I ask only because Mr. Lowenstein will want to know."

"Of course," I said.

"I'd just returned to the office from putting my sign up when the phone rang and you asked to have a look."

"Then it really was meant to be," I said.

To finish the paperwork I wrote out a list of references, then Patrick and I walked across Moss Street and stood staring back at the house from the grassy bank of the bayou. The wind was blowing and pink and violet dust from the trees swirled in the dense, sun-bright air. I could see the windows past the second-floor gallery, in one a lamp glowing against the counterpane.

"Mr. Lowenstein collects paintings," Patrick said. "Has them scattered all over the house, from floor to ceiling in some rooms. He's a bachelor, never married. Probably gay. Or he was gay when he was younger and that sort of thing mattered."

"You mean when sex mattered?"

"Yes, Jack, I do mean sex." He touched my shoulder again. "But back to the paintings. It might interest you to know that Lowenstein even owns some landscapes by that fellow Drysdale." Patrick pronounced the artist's name this way: *Driz-dul.* "You'll have to get him to show you sometime," he said.

"Drysdale," I repeated.

"Maybe you've seen the stuff. He painted oak trees and Louisiana bayou scenes, most dating to the early part of the century. People today pay bloody fortunes for them. I was never one for the primordial—my idea of camping out, you understand, is staying at a Holiday

Inn on the edge of the woods—but these Drysdales are kind of inviting if you're only having to look."

Patrick was quiet as he inspected me once again. Immediately after scheduling the appointment, I'd shaved my face and trimmed back my sideburns, I'd combed the curtain of hair out of my eyes, and I'd put on freshly laundered clothes, a gray tweed jacket, and my best shoes, with socks. Still in all, Patrick seemed keen to my fakery. He saw past the shine. For a second I thought for sure he'd dismiss me as a rental candidate, but then a smile came to his face and he nudged me with an elbow. "I don't mean to be presumptuous," he said, "but are you a Chambers man, Jack?"

"A Chambers man?" I had never heard of such a person.

"I'm referring to the stove, built by Chambers. Mine dates to '29 and is the rarest of all colors." He seemed to be waiting for me to say it. "That's right, a red one. We Chambers men must stick together, Jack. Remember that."

How do you respond to such an assessment of yourself? In the past people had judged me to be many things but never this: I was a Chambers man, of all things.

"Chambers men have little use for the present," Patrick explained. "The past is where their hearts reside. They are smitten with cobwebs and dust. Consequently they spend a lot of time gathered around the stove, and on barstools."

"Patrick, would you like to join me for a cocktail?"

"See there," he answered. "I knew I'd read you right."

We returned to the house a couple of hours later, as dusk was settling in, and Patrick, still pitching the place, offered another look at the rear garden and garçonnière.

"Doesn't it just drip with old New Orleans charm?" he said. "It drips, Jack. It absolutely *drips* . . ." He'd had a few more than I had, but it didn't show in how he carried himself. I was impressed by the fluidity of his movements, all the more so because I found it necessary to touch trees and statuary to maintain balance.

"I'm having guests over Friday night for supper," he said. "It promises to be great fun. I hope you'll join us. You'll meet a nice lady or two.
Better still, you'll have a chance to see the Chambers in action."

We'd already got halfway drunk together. I could think of no reason to decline. "Shall I bring anything?" I said.

He seemed to think about it. "Dreams," he said. "Bring your
dreams, Jack. And if you know how to make one, a nice big Jell-O
salad. I'm crazy for the stuff."

We sat on the garden bench and watched the house for a while,
then Patrick walked up to the back door and rapped on it with a fist.
I was standing next to him. When Lowenstein failed to answer, we
moved to the very rear of the property. Here we could see the place
more clearly and observe the full length of the upper windows as well
as the lower ones.

I put my hands around my mouth and called out Lowenstein's
name—I shouted it repeatedly—and at last he showed himself, his
seated form pausing at a window downstairs. He came up out of his
chair and stood gazing at us. I lifted a hand and waved, but he offered
no response. I thought it only polite that I introduce myself—we soon
would be sharing the property, after all—but when I started walking
in his direction he dropped back into the chair and vanished just as
suddenly as he'd appeared.

"Ghosts," Patrick said bitterly, as if we'd just seen one.

I'd learned many things during my time at the paper, none more important than the importance of keeping people's secrets. It was a rule
that extended to my own interests. The truth was, I could recognize
the hand of A. J. Drysdale long before Patrick Marion told me how
to pronounce his name, having grown up in a home crowded with
paintings by the artist. My father had been a collector, chasing antique
pictures of the bayou the way other men chase Bourbon Street strip-
pers and sure bets at the Fair Grounds. Drysdale was Louisiana's answer to Claude Monet, his oil washes possessing the same ethereal,

haunting quality as the French Impressionist's portraits of lily ponds and flower gardens, but his prices being considerably more affordable. Dad found his at garage sales, junk shops, flea markets and consignment stores, rarely paying more than twenty dollars for a picture. At the time of his death he owned twenty-three Drysdales, one image barely distinguishable from the next, as well as twenty or so other paintings by long-dead Louisiana artists. After we buried him my mother found it difficult to live with the paintings, just as she found it impossible to open the armoire in their bedroom and keep from sobbing at the sight of his clothes still neatly hanging. On a Friday morning I loaded my car with Dad's clothes and donated them to the Saint Vincent de Paul thrift store on Jefferson Highway. In the afternoon I consigned his paintings to the New Orleans Auction Galleries on Julia Street. It hurt me to let the paintings go, knowing how he'd loved them, and the weekend when they came on the block neither Mom nor I were on hand to watch them being sold.

Although Dad famously steered clear of auctions, in the end he would've been pleased with the results of the sale. The John Francis Charbonnet Collection, assembled over thirty years of picking through junk, netted his family nearly $200,000. I offered the entire sum to my mother, but she insisted we split the money. As I was waiting in line at the bank to deposit my share, it came to me that every story I'd ever written had been for the old man. And if they were all for him, I wondered, then who would I write for now? When I arrived at the office later that morning I found my editor outside, where she was permitted to smoke. "I'm quitting," I said.

"You're not quitting shit, Jack," said Isabel Green, then flicked ashes at me.

"I'm telling you I quit, Isabel."

"Jack?"

"I'm going," I told her.

"You can't leave me like this. *Jack?* Jack, you bastard, come back here."

I saw her cigarette fly past my head. "Too late," I said.

I'd given ten years to the job, and I frankly was tired of words—tired of speaking them and having them spoken to me, but also tired of writing them. My fatigue had intensified during my father's long ordeal with lung cancer. I'd sit by his bed and read newspaper stories to him. My column appeared three days a week, and they were always the toughest to get out of my mouth. I wondered why he didn't grab me by the throat and rip out my voice box. "How do you tolerate such torture?" I asked him one day. The only good thing about Dad's dying—for both of us—was the end of my lousy readings.

I don't claim to be the first of my generation to face the crisis of professional burnout before he'd succeeded in paying off his college loans, not to mention finding a wife and buying a home. But I probably differed from most quitters in that I was leaving at the top of my game. Giving it up when you still have some good years ahead isn't a concept that most people would dare apply to their own experience. Readers mailed in letters to the editor pleading with me to stay. My friends said I was being stupid. To judge from their reactions, one might've thought I'd publicly torched a winning lottery ticket. My last column appeared under the heading "To Your Own Self Be True," and it basically was a finger shot at those who would keep me employed. I might've been the paper's "award-winning humor columnist," as my obit was certain to read one day, but I couldn't remember the last time I had any fun at the job. More than anything I longed for the freedom of observing a day without having to reduce my observations to eighteen column inches of wit and jocularity. I'd had it with wit and jocularity.

To show its gratitude for my dedicated service, the paper's management threw a going-away/early-retirement party in my honor at a pasta restaurant out by the interstate. Attended primarily by my department's lower-echelon support staff, I sat and listened as copy aides and summer interns lifted toasts wishing me well in my every future endeavor. Except for Isabel, who wept delivering an obscenity-laced send-off, there were no staff heavyweights in attendance. Come to think of it, even the middleweights stayed away—the writers and editors with whom I'd worked for nearly one-third of my life. At last there came the bright tapping of flatware against wineglasses, and shouts for me to speak. I shoved my chair out from under me and confronted them at last. "Thank you for your kindness," I said, "and good luck to all of you as well. I'm moved not only by your presence here tonight but by your generous and heartfelt sentiments. I apologize for not knowing more of you by name. You seem so nice and I recognize the possibility that, given more time, you might have become dear to me. No hard feelings, anyone, but I'm off to do something altogether historic. That is, I'm off to see if I can arrange to take a nap each afternoon for the rest of my life. Isabel, I'm sorry, darling, you have every right, as you said in your very moving remarks, to hate me and wish catastrophic ruin on me. . . . Anyway, well, drink up everyone. And good-bye."

The party lasted until the restaurant closed its doors at 2:00 A.M., and then I found myself alone with Isabel in the cold backseat of a cab. I loved the taste of smoke and whiskey on her mouth, and she felt truly amazing when I slipped a hand under her skirt, but Isabel was married and all that sort of thing was behind me now. I kept hearing my father's desperate, labored breathing and my own voice as it had sounded when I read to him. Now Isabel was sneaking her hand down my skivvies, and I forced my eyes open and pushed her to the other side of the car. "Pull over. Cabbie, pull over."

"We're on the interstate," he protested, meeting my eyes in the rearview.

"Pull over anyway."

Isabel was screaming at me when I threw a fist of cash at the driver and scrambled out of the car, but she'd screamed at me before and better the verbal abuse in the short term than the specter of her soft, ravaged form in my morning bed. It took me more than an hour to walk home and once there I sat out on the front stoop and drank from a carafe of day-old coffee and waited for paper delivery. When it came I read each section from front to back, thrilled beyond telling that I was nowhere in it.

Some days after the sale of my father's collection I returned to the auction house to retrieve those paintings that had failed to attract buyers. There were only a few of them, and as I was loading the trunk of my car the company's consignment director came outside and regaled me with stories about other Drysdale collectors in town. If I bothered to park one night in front of Roger Houston Ogden's house on Broadway and look in his windows, she said, I might see paintings by the artist hanging on the walls. Other big Drysdale collectors were Gig and Mabel Jones in Lakeview. They owned sixty bayou landscapes, all of them similar in appearance, and once when a plumber finished work in their home he looked around and said, "Mr. Jones, I like your painting." Yet another Drysdale collector, and perhaps the most renowned in the city, was someone named Lowenstein who lived in a spooky old house at Bayou Saint John. Lowenstein was a shut-in, the woman told me, and no one knew exactly how many Drysdales he owned, but estimates put the number at no less than a hundred.

As it happened, I was living only about a mile away from the Lowenstein house, in a rented cottage by Whole Foods Market on Esplanade Avenue. And I knew the place well because I ran in front of it every afternoon on my jog along the bayou. After learning that a vast collection of Drysdales resided there, I made a point of stopping each day and looking up past the trees. I ran in place and studied the windows, but I never saw a thing—never a painting, let alone a human face. Then the day came when something at the house did engage my eye: a High Life Realty sign hanging on the fence.

I'd endured so much change recently that a move didn't seem like a bad thing. Dad was dead, I'd quit my job, and the latest girlfriend had decided I wasn't her soulmate. Others might've been paralyzed by so much upheaval, but I was beginning to find adventure and romance in challenging the bounds of my own comfort. How much could one retired newspaperman take? Welcoming the opportunity to find out, I sprinted home and called High Life as soon as I got in the door.

❋

Patrick was famous around town for his dinner parties, or so he told me just minutes after I arrived at his apartment. "They don't call me

Hurricane Patch for nothing," he said. "We'll eat and drink and then, for your added viewing pleasure, I'll tear the place apart."

He lived in a big Queen Anne Victorian at Coliseum Square in the Lower Garden District: the Loeber Mansion, architectural historians call the place. Patrick prepared the meal himself, and his long-time girlfriend, Elsa Dodd, a CPA from a nearby town, poured the drinks. There were twelve of us—not counting Boots, Patrick's cat— and everyone crowded in the kitchen and watched as Mr. High Life himself cooked on his old red Chambers. Tonight's menu included fried hush puppies and sweet potato wedges, fried shrimp, fried oysters, and fried soft-shell crabs covered with lump crabmeat. "Dessert won't be fried, too, will it, Patrick?" Elsa said.

"Since when you got something against fried?"

Rather than a Jell-O salad, I'd brought a bottle of Jägermeister, the same stuff Patrick and I had enjoyed a few days before. "Oh, man," Patrick said as he inspected the gift. "Hurricane Patch has now officially been promoted to a Category Five. It won't be only my apartment that gets flattened tonight. Elsa, go warn the neighbors, sweetheart."

As was his custom, he didn't start cooking until each of his guests had consumed a few cocktails, and by the time he finished, everyone was so miserable with hunger it didn't matter that half of his dishes were either burned, undercooked or unrecognizable.

"God, Patrick, it's so good I could cry," I stated in too large a voice, after biting into one of his fat, crusty oysters.

I'd been drinking Scotch from a plastic go cup emblazoned with a picture of a Carnival parade float, and it was only the first of many declarations I would make this night. One couldn't overstate the amount of pride Patrick took in his cooking. His eyes watered as he thanked me for the compliment, then he bounced to his feet, retrieved my plate and stumbled into the kitchen for another large helping.

"Jack, better be stingy with the praise, my friend," Elsa said. "If you're not careful, he'll have you over tomorrow night, too."

"Dinner on Saturday, as well?"

"Yes, and like tonight every bit of it fried on the Chambers. For the continued good health of your heart you would be well advised to keep your enthusiasm in check."

It was a struggle to consume the second serving, though not because the quality of the food had slipped. I found that I couldn't stop looking at the woman seated directly across the table from me. I'd hardly paid attention to her earlier when we were introduced, and I couldn't recall her name. But now candles were burning in the space between us, and I was having a devil of a time resisting an urge to reach between the flames and place my hand on her lovely, golden face.

I leaned forward, my shirt absorbing grease from the plate, and waited until she surrendered and acknowledged me with a glance. "I'm sorry," I said, "but I forget what you said your name was."

"I don't remember telling you my name."

"Was it Roberta?"

"It's Rhys," Elsa said. "Rhys Goudeau. Now be a gentleman, Jack, or we'll demand that you eat another plateful."

Like me, the woman had come without a companion. The threat of more to eat worked to snap me out of my spell, but I did watch her when she walked to the buffet for another bottle of wine. And I watched her when she returned to the table. It struck me that she was the only one of the guests who was not dressed entirely in black. Rhys was a mix of colors: yellow turtleneck, pink skirt, red clogs. Her hair, a dizzying assemblage of whorls and corkscrews, shone a brassy gold. Hard as I tried, I could not determine whether her eyes were blue or green, as they seemed to change as the night went on, and as the light in the room changed.

"Jack," said Patrick when he and Elsa were clearing the table, "it might interest you to know that Rhys recently worked on one of your landlord's paintings."

"One of Mr. Lowenstein's paintings?"

"Rhys restores damaged artwork. Have you heard of the Crescent City Conservation Guild? Rhys is the director, aren't you, darling?"

It seemed to pain her to have to nod. She cleared her throat.

"Paintings, frames, pottery. People bring me their broken things. I fix them."

Hoping to improve on the impression I was making, I didn't speak again until Patrick and Elsa returned from the kitchen. This time I was careful not to slur. "Rhys, was the painting of Mr. Lowenstein's a Drysdale?"

"Yes, it was, as a matter of fact."

"And how was it damaged, if you don't mind my asking?"

"He put his foot through it."

"You mean it?"

"He'd taken it off the wall for dusting and placed it on the floor." She laughed for some reason. "An accident, he said."

"The Guild amazes me," Patrick said. "Put your foot through a sheet of canvas and when they're done, you could never tell it underwent such trauma." Now he was addressing the rest of his guests. "Ready for a story, everyone? My great aunt dies and we're settling up her estate, dividing property. In a closet there's a cardboard box holding what once was a piece of pottery. The thing—whatever it was—is broken in a million pieces. Well, I look up 'Art Restoration' in the Yellow Pages and find the Guild's number and give the place a call. Next day a fuzzy, tattooed boy pulls up in this antique van with magnetic signs on the doors advertising the Guild. He takes the box and leaves. Weeks go by and I've pretty much forgotten about it. Then I hear a knocking at my office door and I open it to this ravishing young woman. This is how Rhys and I meet, the first time. She's holding a large Newcomb College vase: the pieces from my cardboard box, restored so that you could never tell it had been broken."

"Marvelous," said someone at the table.

"Marvelous until she gave me the bill," Patrick said. "When I learned the charge was fifteen hundred dollars I nearly smashed the vase to pieces all over again. You remember how upset I became, darling? My face was the color of the wine I'm drinking." He held up his glass. "But then I placed the vase for sale with the Neal Auction Company and the most incredible thing happened." Patrick paused and sipped his Merlot. "Twenty thousand dollars," he said. "That's what it fetched—this box of *garbage*. Rhys, what was the guy's name who bought the vase?"

"Tommy Smallwood."

"Yes, Tommy Smallwood."

"He's the most voracious collector of southern art of his generation," Rhys said. "And by southern art I don't mean southern California or southern Indiana or southern France. But the South, the real South." She looked at me. "The *American* South."

"The underbidder," Patrick said, "was one of those dotcom billionaires who only yesterday shaved his face for the first time. I talked to him after the auction and he said he was out shopping for something to buy his girlfriend. He's driving along Magazine Street and he sees a sign that says AUCTION TODAY. They'd just given him a paddle when my Newcomb vase came up."

"Two people who possess as much ego as they do money and who insist on owning the same item," Rhys said. "This is what creates the perfect climate for a runaway auction. And that is what happened to you, Patrick. That vase, in mint condition, is worth fifty thousand dollars. None of the museums or serious collectors wanted it, however, because it had repairs. To them it was worthless. They want the pristine item, the undamaged one. But you were lucky. Two determined and like-minded individuals with more money than sense just had to have it."

"A runaway auction," Patrick said. "I do like the sound of that."

"Yes, and they're more common than you might think. At the right auction even the most common lot can sell for many times more than its appraised value. When a bidding war erupts, logic is the first casualty."

"Hold your hands up," I said. "Let us have a look at them."

Rhys sat glaring at me. She never did show us her hands.

※

For dessert Patrick served Angelo Brocato's lemon-flavored Italian ice, a local favorite, along with meaty chunks of overripe mango. By now my tongue was so saturated with grease and whisky I could barely taste what I was eating.

Elsa invited us to move to the living room, and once there I lowered myself to the floor and lay flat on my back gazing at a chandelier. I recall hearing the music of Louis Armstrong on the stereo, and Patrick's laughter as he and his guests proceeded to dance around me. Someone fell after tripping on my leg, and this was greeted with a loud, happy roar. I don't know how long I slept; it might've been hours.

When I awoke, the house was quiet but for the sure, deep voice of Rhys Goudeau. Despite the mix of throbbing and ocean sounds, I managed to lift my head off the floor, and there she sat with Patrick on the tufted red leather of a Chesterfield sofa. Nearby Elsa was sleeping in a plantation chair, a leg draped over each arm, her short skirt failing to protect her from view. Everyone else had left. A group of candles was burning, their deep yellow glow repeated in the high polish of the mahogany-paneled walls.

On the floor between Patrick and Rhys a painting was leaning back against the antique cypress tool chest that served as a coffee table. It was in such bad shape that at first glance it was hard to tell much about it, other than the fact that it was dark and dreary and looked ready for the trash pile. "Patrick, did the canvas come from your great-aunt's estate as well?" Rhys was saying.

"Yes, it did. From the attic."

"What a great eye she had. Patrick, tell me her name again."

"We called her Aunt Dottie," he said.

"Dottie Marion?"

"You got it . . . well, her real name was Dorothy, Dorothy Marion. She was my grandfather's baby sister. She also was an old maid who lived alone in a big, weird house on Ursulines down near where it intersects with Broad. She used to talk about being a flapper and shooting pigeons for supper with her boyfriend William Faulkner from the roof of his French Quarter garret. Sometimes, when she'd had a few, she'd talk about rejecting Faulkner's marriage proposal, but it was only the crème de menthe talking. I'd done the math, you see: Faulkner had lived in the Quarter in 1925, when Aunt Dottie was all of three years old. She was never a flapper—she was still in diapers when the flappers were having their day. She'd made it all up, but then she made everything up. By the time I knew her she was an eccentric, wig-wearing old bat who lived alone in a house full of cats."

Rhys seemed mesmerized by the painting, which, now that I inspected it closer, looked to be a portrait of a woman. "I won't be able to authenticate the painting before I run some tests at the studio," she said, "but I think . . . Patrick, I'm very excited because I think you've discovered something very special here."

"Oh, Rhys, I love you for saying that."

"It's too dirty to locate a signature, but I think . . . I hope you're ready for this. Patrick, I think your painting could be the work of Levette Asmore."

I sat up and felt my head clear suddenly, even as my heart began to hammer away at the walls of my chest. I squinted trying to see the painting better.

"Levette Asmore," Patrick said. "Of course. Who else would've painted it? She's my favorite artist of all time. Rhys, I absolutely adore the woman." He cleared his throat in a dramatic, everyone-look-at-me fashion. "Rhys, who is Levette Asmore?"

"Levette Asmore was a man," I said.

They both turned and looked at me, and for the first time tonight I saw a spark in Rhys's eyes.

"Yes," Patrick said, "and I adore him, too."

Rhys smiled. "Jack, what else do you know about the artist?"

"Besides the fact that he was the greatest painter the South ever produced, do you mean?"

"That's a matter of opinion, of course."

"I'll give you that, but it's one you share with me, isn't it?"

She didn't answer. Instead she turned her attention to the painting. "Levette Asmore is so rare to the market," she said, "that I've never seen one for sale in a gallery, nor have I ever encountered one at auction, although I do know he's been dealt privately for large sums of money—for *crazy* money. Museums all over the South have him, but he's in only a score of private collections. Demand for Asmore far outdistances supply, and his popularity never seems to wane. These two factors, taken together, make him extremely valuable. Every collector of important twentieth-century southern art would kill to have an example, and those who do own an Asmore would not pass on the chance to acquire another. But where does one find an Asmore?" Rhys glanced at Patrick. "They simply don't turn up."

"You're damned right they don't," Patrick said. Triumphant, he threw his hands over his head and kicked his feet like a swimmer treading water. "I have a question," he said, after calming down.

She waited.

"If Asmore's paintings are so popular, why didn't he paint more of them?"

Rhys shot a look my way. "Want to take that one, Jack?"

"The reason Levette Asmore wasn't more productive," I said, "and this adds to why he is so coveted by collectors . . . Asmore died young and under mysterious circumstances. It was 1941, a few months before Pearl Harbor, and he was only twenty-three years old. He didn't live long enough to assemble a large body of work."

"How'd he die?" Patrick said.

When I didn't immediately speak up, Rhys took over. "He threw himself from the Huey P. Long Bridge, a suicide. Searchers dragged the river for days but his body was never recovered. You know the Huey P., don't you, Patrick?"

"I know I wouldn't want to *leap* from the dang thing, let alone jump. My God, at that distance there couldn't have been much left of him. It would be like smashing into concrete. No wonder he was never found. His body was probably obliterated."

"If you thought Tommy Smallwood was aggressive in his pursuit of your Newcomb vase," she said, "just wait until the greedy buzzard lays his eyes on this thing. He'll bleed big green puddles all over the auction house floor. Smallwood is relatively new to collecting, and it's the new ones who will pay virtually any price to acquire the artist they don't yet possess."

"The way you sound," Patrick said.

"And how is that?"

"As though by owning an Asmore painting this Smallwood guy would own an actual piece of the man."

"Do you think he wants only pretty pictures to hang on his walls? Tommy Smallwood is a cannibal, Patrick, a flesh-eater. When he sees something he wants he has a violent biological response to it. His heart rate and blood pressure skyrocket, and his brain releases neurotransmitters called serotonin and norepinephrine. They induce in him a sexual response, and he begins to feel good all over. He can't control himself—he's a slave to desire. His appetite swells and his penis becomes engorged."

"It does what?" Patrick said, seeming alarmed.

"Look, earliest man performed two basic activities that neither time nor evolution has erased from the gene pool: he hunted, then he went out and collected his kill. A caveman like Smallwood won't be content until he's bagged everything there is to get."

The room was quiet and I flashed to an old picture of my father's hat slowly turning on the museum floor.

"How can you be certain it's by Levette?" Patrick said.

"Several ways," Rhys answered. "My staff and I worked on one of the Asmores that belong to the Historic New Orleans Collection. And there are strong similarities between that painting and this one."

"Such as?"

I scooted closer for a better look. Rhys gave me a nod and I said, "Asmore didn't have a whole lot of money, so he often had no choice but to use inferior materials, such as burlap and house paint, which are what he appears to have used in this case. To finish his paintings Asmore almost always used shellac instead of varnish, because he could get it for nothing at the shipyards. Rhys will have to confirm this, but this surface glaze looks like marine shellac, the kind you'd cover the hull of a boat with. It's the same texture, and it's orange, the color marine shellac would be at this age. You probably have some incredibly vibrant colors underneath this awful stuff. Asmore was known for his bold, inventive use of color."

Rhys stopped running her fingers over the surface and faced me again. "Looks like the discovery of this painting is only the first of the night's surprises. Who are you really, Jack?"

"Just the son of a guy who liked Levette," I answered.

Her mouth was open a crack and in the candlelight you could see her tongue tracing over the inside of her teeth. "The surface is so filthy you can barely make out the subject matter," she said, "but it looks like a young woman. This is good, Patrick. Levette Asmore was the classic romantic bad boy, and apparently irresistible to women. He laid waste to whoever came in his path, or so legend has it. At his funeral several of his female admirers threw themselves at his empty coffin. He'd painted some of these women in a series of portraits that art historians today refer to as his *Beloved* paintings. *Beloved Marie, Beloved Claire.* All of his paintings are valuable, but the real trophies are his *Beloved* girls."

"*Beloved Rhys,*" Patrick said. "Now how does that one sound?"

"I don't want to get your hopes up," Rhys said. "In this condition it's impossible to tell who she is. See how badly the paint is cupping? See how it's lifting off the burlap? Asmore's paintings often have this condition problem. He rarely primed his surface with gesso, and in all likelihood he painted this image directly on top of another painting—or on top of several others. This baby will start flaking and losing paint if we don't do something soon. It's already pretty sick."

"Sick, did you say?" said Patrick.

"Critical condition, barely hanging on, in need of emergency surgery."

"I was afraid you were going to say that. Maybe I should've left the thing in the closet. I'd ask for an estimate but the night has gone so well I'd hate to ruin it now."

"Ask her what she thinks it's worth," I said to Patrick.

"I would do that, Jack, but I can't seem to get up the nerve."

"Rhys, tell him what it's worth."

Her tongue played with her teeth again and her fingertips continued to caress the painting. "Okay, then, for Patrick's edification, let's explore a theory of value. In New York City, ground zero in the world of art, paintings originating in the American South largely went ignored until recent years, when collectors started to pay serious money for them. The big auction houses like Sotheby's and Christie's had little respect for Asmore, but New York tends to take a negative view of most things southern—unless, of course, the artist has moved up North and established himself there. The most money a southern painting ever fetched at auction in New Orleans was just over three hundred thousand dollars. It was for a mural that once hung in Delmonico Restaurant on Saint Charles Avenue."

"Sure," Patrick said. "I used to go there when I was a kid. That's the place Emeril Lagasse turned into a steakhouse. Emeril's Delmonico, he calls it."

Rhys nodded. "The artist, John McCrady, was one of the most celebrated this region ever produced. And the painting had many of the rather hackneyed features that collectors of the genre like—the Mississippi River, a steamboat, a plantation house ringed with columns, oak trees. And all this contributed to its result. But a McCrady, though widely sought after, isn't as uncommon as an Asmore, nor is it as sexy." Rhys exhaled and leaned back on the couch. "A conservative estimate?" she said. "On a bad day when it's raining buckets outside and the stock market is taking a dive and the air is thick with talk of economic recession . . . ? Even on the worst of days I'd say at auction in New Orleans this painting would bring no less than three hundred and fifty thousand dollars."

"Jesus Christ," said Patrick, jumping to his feet. He moved to the middle of the room. "Jesus Christ, Rhys. Did you . . . ? You have got to be kidding me."

She was shaking her head.

"Did you just say three hundred and fifty thousand dollars?"

"And that's on a bad day. On a good day I could see it going for as much as half a million. I say this because it's that rare and that important and that desirable, and because it's a portrait of a woman, perhaps even one of Asmore's *Beloved* paintings."

Patrick staggered back to the couch and threw his arms around Rhys. I could hear him crying and so, obviously, could Elsa. She woke up, brought her legs together, and asked if anything was wrong. "Darling," Patrick said, "your boyfriend of seventeen wonderful years is going to be rich."

Elsa had been hitting the Scotch, too. "Oh, wonderful," she sighed, then promptly went back to sleep.

※

Six weeks later I received a call from Patrick inviting me to attend the unveiling of the newly restored Asmore at the Guild's studio in Central City. Rhys Goudeau had phoned him only minutes before, with news that the painting was fully restored and ready for his inspection, and he thought it good karma to invite me along, since I'd been there when the painting's identity and potential value were revealed.

The Guild leased an old brick firehouse on Martin Luther King, Jr., Boulevard, in a depressed area known as Central City. A hundred and twenty years ago Rhys's neighborhood had been one of the better addresses in the city, but now it ranked among the least desirable, despite the many examples of Victorian, Greek Revival and French Colonial architecture still lining the streets. Though long ago targeted for renewal, Central City had managed to repel the run-of-the-mill urban pioneer who idealistically sacrifices security for a posture of hipness in a large, inexpensive space. It took someone with a death wish to stake a claim in this spot, mainly because to live in the district too often meant to perish there as well.

"Sorry, old sport, but I forgot to tell you to wear a bulletproof vest and my spare happens to be at the cleaner's," Patrick said as he parked in front of the firehouse.

He killed the engine and fitted an antitheft device on the steering wheel. Next he placed an antitheft collar on the steering column. As a final measure he reached under the dashboard and flipped a hidden switch that cut off the flow of fuel to the car's engine. "Just for the record," he said, "by taking these precautions I do not in any way mean to insinuate that this is a bad neighborhood."

"If not, then what are you doing, Patrick?"

"I'm stating emphatically that it's a bad one. I'm shouting it from the rooftops. Jesus, help us, Jack." Hands gripping the top of the steering wheel, he took in a deep breath. "Now who's first to make a run for the door?"

We rang the bell and several minutes passed before anyone answered—minutes that found Patrick nervously watching in every direction for potential trouble. A number of rusty locks were disengaged, a large door was pulled open and finally a scarecrow appeared in a second door's thatch of iron bars. "We're here to see Rhys Goudeau," Patrick said, a slight tremble warping his delivery.

"And who should I tell her is calling?"

"I own the Asmore."

"Oh, Mr. Marion. It's Joe, Joe Butler. Please come in."

Butler wore eyeglasses with tortoiseshell frames, each stem patched with electrician's tape, and a badly stained lab coat with his name in red script on the left breast. He seemed to be trying to cultivate a goatee, although the growth on his chin as easily could've been acne. You meet a person this undernourished on the street and you lead him to the nearest diner for a plate of fried eggs and ham. You give him ten dollars when he's done and include him in your prayers at night.

"I'm Jack Charbonnet," I said.

"So, you're . . . oh, okay, nice to meet you, too, Mr. Charbonnet."

The ground floor was where the Guild built reproduction frames and repaired old ones. Half a dozen worktables stood in the open space. The walls held corner samples of frames and antique mouldings hanging from ten-penny nails, with old mirrors scattered about and an occasional nineteenth-century portrait bringing color to the room. Each portrait had an ID name tag, such as the kind conventioneers are known to wear: "Hello, My name is . . ." The obese woman in the black, scalloped church veil was called Gertrude. The old man with bushy whiskers and a greasy, lascivious grin was Carl. "We spend so much time with them," Joe Butler explained, "that after a while you feel as though you know them. They're all dead, most of them forgotten, and so we give them names. People collect these old portraits for one of two reasons: either as shabby-chic decorative items to dress up antique homes or because they want instant ancestors."

"Instant ancestors, did you say?" asked Patrick.

"The nouveaux riches like to pretend they come from something. They have the money, they have the manse with the historic designation in the right Uptown neighborhood, they belong to a prestigious Carnival krewe. The only thing they're lacking is the pedigree. Rhys can provide that. She buys these things at auction for next to nothing, then restores them and sells them as ancestral portraits to clients eager to say their family's been in the city since it was founded."

"When in fact the family was living in a trailer park in Chalmette only a generation before," said Patrick.

"Ah, so you know the type, Mr. Marion."

"What are you talking about, Joe? I *am* the type."

I walked the length of the room, driving my boot heels hard against the red cypress flooring, freshly washed with mint oil. The walls had a nice patina created from orange brick and layers of desiccated paint, but much to my disappointment there were no firehouse poles or blaze-weary Dalmatians asleep in the shadows. Hanging alone on one side of the room was a portrait of perhaps the most unattractive person I'd ever seen. A broad, flat nose dominated his face, and his skinny lips were pulled back in a grin, revealing gray, diseased teeth. His skull, pocked and dented, sprouted a tuft of frizz over each shrunken ear. Unlike that unfortunate street person who looked like Joe Butler, when you happened upon this man you did not take him out for fried eggs and ham, and at night he did not rate a mention in your prayers. Instead, you ran from him screaming for 911. Another of the Guild's name tags had been applied to the portrait. "Hello," it said. "My name is . . . Jack."

"Hey, bro, you weren't supposed to see that," Joe said.

"Then Rhys shouldn't have put it there."

"Rhys didn't put it there, Mr. Charbonnet, I did. I should let you punch me out. My apologies. I mean it."

"Am I missing something here?" I said. "We've never met before, have we?"

"No, we haven't. But Rhys told me about Mr. Marion's dinner party. How you had too much to drink and rolled around on the floor looking up skirts and everything. Also, Mr. Charbonnet, about how nice-looking you are in person, unlike the little picture they used to run over your stories in the paper."

"Rhys knew me? She knew I wrote for the *Picayune*?"

He shrugged. "What can I tell you?"

"I don't know, Joe. What can you? Is there more?"

"Just that you were up on the subject of Levette. I don't mean to leap to conclusions about you, Mr. Charbonnet, but they always try to get to Rhys that way. They fake it. They try to get her to the museum because they think that's the quickest route to get her in bed. I've seen so many come and go by now, shit, bro, maybe I'm cynical. The last one pretended to be related to Picasso. Uncle Pablo, he called him."

Patrick stood studying the hideous face in the painting with his hands held together behind his back. "Others might need instant ancestors," he said, "but not you, Jack. This man has got to be the real thing. The resemblance is . . . well, shall I say it?"

"Go ahead."

"Uncanny."

"Can we see the Asmore now?" I said to Joe Butler.

They were still laughing as he led the way up a narrow oak stairway to the second floor. Joe banged a fist against a door, and after a couple of deadbolts were unlocked, Rhys stepped forward and greeted Patrick with a hug. I was hoping for the same treatment but all she offered was a handshake, and a less than enthusiastic one at that. It was at this moment that I understood how she felt about me. Rhys was interested. Otherwise she would've embraced me as she had Patrick.

"Jack's my good-luck charm," Patrick said to Rhys, misreading the slight. "Plus, I thought I could use some protection traveling to your 'hood."

"Good, keep thinking that," she said. "I've run a studio and lived in neighborhoods all over this city and I've had fewer problems here than in all of the others combined. I'll keep the studio in Central City until this new generation of Goth kids and computer geeks finds us. I see a Bill Gates wannabe, or a boy with dyed black hair in ponytails, and wearing black clothes and jackboots, and quoting from Anne Rice—when those people come snooping around I am definitely a gone pecan."

The second floor, decked like the first with shiny old boards, was where the Guild repaired paintings, porcelain and pottery. Rhys introduced us to her staff of artists, two of them young women who sat on plastic lunchroom chairs before easels holding paintings, the third an older man in a lab coat who stood at a worktable cleaning a picture of a riverboat. "You gentlemen have met Joe," Rhys said. "He's the Guild's resident jack-of-all-trades, as proficient at building an exact replica of a Newcomb-Macklin frame as he is at filling in paint loss on a Martin Johnson Heade still life. Sarah and Morgan, like Joe, are retouch specialists who also patch and line paintings in need. Leland here is the one who does all our cleaning. Patrick, Leland cleaned your Asmore. How many cotton balls did you say you used to get rid of that miserable shellac?"

"Three thousand one hundred and twenty-seven," Leland said, "give or take a few."

"That was only the first problem we had to overcome. Termites did such a job on the strainers that when you pressed on the wood it crumbled and turned to dust, and there was all that tunneling, more evidence they'd been there. It's a miracle they didn't eat the painting."

"They wouldn't dare," Patrick said.

"Sure they would," she said. "Termites will eat most anything they encounter. We've seen valuable paintings that were eaten to bits. Termites track upward from the soil munching away as they climb. In the wall of a house they devour the wood and the wallpaper and then whatever happens to be hanging on the wall. Paintings don't stand a chance."

"Tell them what else," said Leland from his perch.

"Well, roaches love to eat paintings, too. Actually, they love the rabbitskin glue and wheat starch on the reverse of paintings that have been previously lined. Patrick, your dinner party the other day was nothing in the feast department compared to some of the meals I've seen roaches enjoy. Rodents like glue, too. People set rat traps with cheese, but they'd get more takers by pouring glue on the traps. There's a world-famous antique store on Royal Street whose name I'd better not divulge. One morning the owner called and said he'd discovered that his most valuable painting had a huge hole in it. He couldn't understand how this had happened. The painting was secure on the wall and hadn't been moved in weeks, and the damage wasn't a tear or a rip that would indicate it had fallen against anything. No, there was a jagged hole, as if it had been cut out with the serrated edge of a knife. The painting was a huge thing worth about a hundred thousand dollars. When we moved it to the studio Leland and the girls and I studied it under a loupe. You could see the teeth marks where a rat had supped on it. He'd come in from behind and eaten out a hole six inches in diameter, and the hole was in the most unpleasant of places."

"Unpleasant?" said Patrick, in the exact moment when it occurred to him which part of the anatomy she meant. He looked down at the spot on his own person. "Thank you for that story, Rhys. Thank you ever so much. Of course I won't be able to sleep tonight fearing a rat assault. You know those athletic cups baseball players fit into their jock straps to protect against stray balls? From here on out I sleep in one of those."

"Sometimes I can't get over the problems we're asked to fix," Rhys

said. "Your Asmore is nothing in comparison. As for the termite damage, we ended up replacing the strainers with stretcher bars made of
poplar. Also, we played it safe and lined the burlap with Belgian linen
and consolidated the painting to prevent against future losses. By con-
solidate I mean we massaged the surface with a mixture of beeswax
and damar resin to readhere loose paint pieces and flakes. Joe did the
retouch."

"Did you have time to make a frame for it?"

"Yes. And you're going to love what we did. It's really beautiful:
twenty-three-and-three-quarters-karat gold leaf with a gesso ground
and yellow bole. Joe gets credit for that, too. He did the water gilding.
And he carved the moulding by hand, working from a design that was
popular with the American Impressionists."

"Sounds expensive," Patrick said.

"It's *damned* expensive," Rhys answered. "But don't think about
the money yet. You've taken the most important step by electing to
conserve something that potentially could change your life. Even
more significant, you're doing a good thing. We don't just patch old
paintings here. We give them new life. We save them so that future
generations can enjoy them. I'm proud of you, Patrick."

We followed her into another large room, the first yet without
worktables. It was Rhys's office. Along one wall shelves bent under
the weight of art history books and massive tomes with titles such as
The Preservation of Santos and *The Structural Conservation of Panel
Paintings*. A pair of partners desks held computers and digital camera
equipment, along with small bronze sculptures, terra-cotta forms and
more whatnots than the eye could absorb in a glance. Behind the
desks stood racks for paintings in various stages of restoration. Some
of the paintings, I would learn later, were worth as much as fifty thousand dollars, while the value of others couldn't buy you a corn dog for
lunch. Antique vitrines held Rhys's pottery collection, one devoted to
rare Van Briggle pieces, a second to vintage Shearwater, a third to creations by contemporary New Orleans potters such as JoAnn Green-
berg and Charles Bohn.

There was much to see, and to take it all in one had to dodge a brass display easel standing in the middle of the floor bathed in light from a pair of strategically positioned photoflood lamps. A bedsheet, appropriately splattered with a rainbow of paints, covered the rectangular object on the stand.

"I'm being unusually dramatic today," Rhys said, "but the occasion calls for it. When will I have the opportunity to unveil an Asmore again? Patrick, say hello to your Aunt Dottie. Or *Beloved Dorothy*, as Levette Asmore called her."

The sheet came off and there it was suddenly, so different from the thing we'd seen on the floor at Patrick's house. The portrait showed a young woman in a simple white dress holding a small book and a clutch of purple irises. Her brown hair was pulled back and held by a ribbon, and her eyes radiated a dark shade of blue that was nearly cobalt. It occurred to me that they were just like Patrick's eyes. In the background Asmore had provided a Louisiana landscape with oak trees clotting the horizon and a red wash of sun reflecting off a winding river. But it was the subject of the painting that made the strongest impression. Dorothy Marion was so exquisitely beautiful that I felt an ache of sadness recalling Patrick's story about how she had survived to be an old maid chasing garage-sale finds.

How does it happen? I wondered. We are young without a notion of how we'll end up, stupid to the truth of what will come. Had someone told this girl she was destined to live her life alone in a dusty house full of cats she would have laughed herself silly.

Patrick's hand went up. He reached to touch the painting.

"Better not," Rhys said. "The varnish needs more time to dry." She pointed to the upper-left corner. "Asmore's signature is there, clearly visible. Leland and I screamed when it turned up during the cleaning."

Both Patrick and I stepped closer, squinting to see it. Just beneath the name, Asmore had added the words "Beloved Dorothy," and the date, "December 28, 1940."

You poor bastard, I thought. Dead in less than a year.

"It's very difficult for me to believe," said Patrick. "I mean, Aunt Dottie? I knew this woman. She would sit at her kitchen table with her wig on backward, like how kids wear baseball caps. There'd be cats eating scraps from the dinner plates stacked in the sink. When she'd start on the old days I'd roll my eyes. She never even mentioned this Asmore character, but obviously they were a couple once. You look at this and it's undeniable. She looks as if . . . okay, to put it bluntly, she looks as if he's just had his way with her. They've made love, haven't they?"

"Have either of you noticed the river in the painting's background?" Rhys said. "When that came up during the cleaning, Leland and I screamed a second time. You can't overstate how significant that is to the value of this painting. It portends Asmore's terrible destiny. It also echoes an experience of his childhood: his parents drowned in the great flood of '27, when Levette was just a boy. Patrick, I might have to ratchet my estimate upward another twenty thousand."

"Really? Another twenty thousand?"

"They're going to fight for this one," she said. "The museums, the collectors, the dealers. There's going to be a brawl on the auction house floor."

His face was wet with tears. I might've offered warm words of congratulations, but I found that I, too, was on the verge of sobbing.

TWO

At least once a week I made a point of driving Uptown and visiting my mother. She still lived in the house where I grew up, over on Hampson Street near where Saint Charles Avenue, following the path of the Mississippi River, makes a hard turn and becomes South Carrollton Avenue. More than a hundred years old, the house is a big, wood-frame thing that stands behind a broken wood fence and a yard crowded with too many trees. It's the kind of place people tend to feel sorry for, a feeling that only deepened when they learned that its only occupant, a widow three months out, still wept each day at the reality of life without her husband.

Mom had plenty of friends, and she had her church, but I was her only child. I took care of the yard work, brought her car in for servicing, changed out the air-conditioning filters. Every Sunday I drove her across Lake Pontchartrain; she liked the water and the smell of the air. Other days we cooked supper together in her little kitchen, and ate on trays in front of the TV. My visits cheered her up, and I always left feeling as though I'd accomplished something. Besides the help, I'd given her what she needed most, that being family.

It was Tuesday night and trash collection came in the morning, so I dragged her cans out to the curb for pickup. Next I helped her rearrange the furniture in the living room. She wanted her favorite chair situated closer to the bay window in front so she could read her paper by the morning light, rather than by the floor lamp she had me place in a guest bedroom. "I don't like the paper as much without you in it," she said.

"It's not any good anymore, is it?"

"No, it's not, Jack."

"I was the only writer there who could write. There isn't a good writer left."

"That's what I said when I called and threatened to cancel my subscription unless they hired you back."

"They really should hire me back. Pay me a lot more money."

"You said you wouldn't go back for any amount of money."

"Then I guess it's their loss, isn't it?"

"You're a young man, Jack. I don't understand you. Your father and I did not bring you up to be this way. You need a life, something to do with yourself."

"I have plenty to do with myself."

"Oh, do you? What?"

"Whatever I feel like," I said. "It keeps me hopping."

And so went another day at Mother's. We drove over to Foodies on the avenue and bought takeout and ate directly from the paper cartons while watching reports about Tom Cruise's latest love interest on *Entertainment Tonight*. Dad had kept one of his Drysdales behind the TV, and my eyes traveled from the screen to the shadow of a rectangle that still remained on the wallpaper. I glanced around the room and counted half a dozen other places where his beloved Drysdales had hung, each of them a shade lighter than the wall surrounding it. I could've become awfully depressed had I let myself, but now we were learning about the rash of pregnancies among Hollywood starlets, and my mother was saying, "Oh, how fascinating," and I understood that I had no reason to despair. If everything wasn't right with the world at least it was the same as it had been the day before, and as it would be tomorrow.

I waited until a commercial came on before I told her about Patrick's Asmore. "Your father would be so jealous," she said. "And to think of all the times we pulled into the parking lot at the Salvation Army and he said, 'Today we find one.' And you say your friend had never heard of him?"

"He never had."

"Why couldn't your father have discovered one?"

"I've wondered that myself and I've come up with an answer. Dad never found one because we would have lost him earlier than we did."

"I don't think that's it at all. How ridiculous."

"It kept him alive, Mom, kept him searching. Without the Asmore to dream about the cancer would've taken him much sooner than it did."

"I'd rather think he fought so hard because he didn't want to leave you and me behind." She settled in deeper in her chair. "Jack, the man liked paintings but they were only *things*. He didn't take any with him, did he?"

She was sad most of the time but she still had a way of making sense. I brought our cartons to the kitchen and folded the trays and put them away. When I returned to the living room I sprawled out on the sofa and closed my eyes and shut out the TV. He had wanted me to be an artist and enrolled me in a drawing class, but I'd shown not a whit of talent and he'd grudgingly let me drop it. One didn't have to understand how a picture was made to appreciate it, he said, almost as an apology to the world for producing a son so devoid of creative talent. Dad had the good sense to marry right: he not only loved his wife but he loved a woman who inherited a big house and enough money to let him have a go at being an art photographer. He followed in the tradition of N. M. Swinney, C. Bennette Moore and Eugene Del-croix, shooters from the first half of the century whose romantic images of the Vieux Carré made for popular souvenirs. Dad never hung any of his own pictures in our home, and he was always embarrassed when he found them among the offerings at weekend garage sales. One usually could be had for ten cents or a quarter, framed. The hardest I ever heard him laugh was when he found one marked for a dollar. It also was the only time I ever knew him to buy one of his pictures, but then he threw it away before we got home, stopping by a can in Audubon Park. "Don't tell your mother," he said, a warning I had to listen to almost every day of my childhood.

"Don't tell her you paid a dollar for something and then put it in the trash?"

"No. Don't tell her your father is such a failure he's turning up at yard sales."

I opened my eyes and she was still watching TV. She didn't look at me, but she somehow knew I was awake again. "Do you remember the day . . . God, when was it?"

"When was what?"

"When your father drove us across the bridge trying to decide on the spot where Levette had gone to jump. Do you remember that?"

"Sure do. I was in the backseat, scared to death. That was a traumatic thing for a young kid. I thought Dad was going to stop and jump from the span himself."

"It wasn't traumatic, Jack. It was educational. You learned that there's nothing wrong with being sensitive and loving beauty."

"I'm glad one of us remembers what I learned."

To show that she was enjoying my silliness, she tossed a copy of *Reader's Digest* at me. "You didn't cry when you first saw your friend's Asmore, did you?"

"No, I didn't. I was being very brave."

"The only reason your father cried in front of great paintings was because he *felt* more than other people do."

"I'll give him that," I said.

I got up and kissed the side of her face. The tears had started to fall again, but I pretended they weren't there as I headed for the door. "Call if you need anything, Mom."

⁂

The Williams Research Center stands on Chartres Street adjacent to K-Paul's Louisiana Kitchen in the heart of the French Quarter. It houses the bulk of the Historic New Orleans Collection's curatorial archives, including photographs, microfilm and clip files for artists, writers, architects and others who contributed to the city's history and culture. Today the doors to the old Beaux Arts structure were locked, so I rang a bell for admittance. Several minutes passed before a receptionist buzzed me inside. Without once looking at me, she instructed me to fill out a form stating the purpose of my visit. "Asmore," I wrote, and left it at that.

I climbed a broad flight of stairs to the second-floor reading room. It was a cool, vast space with a high glass ceiling and shelves crowded with books bordering the dozen or so cherry tables occupying the center of the floor. Each table came equipped with writing pads and cups holding pencils. On one end of the room there was a wall of enormous multipaneled windows looking out on the old district, on the other a desk staffed by a research assistant. "I'd like to see any materials you have on the artist Levette Asmore, please," I said to the woman.

When she hesitated before responding, I wondered if I'd said something wrong. I nearly sniffed the body of my sweatshirt to make sure it was clean. She allowed a smile, but not after first giving me a look over her reading glasses. "Did you say Asmore?"

"Yes, ma'am. The artist." Then for some odd reason I added, "The one who jumped from the Huey P."

"Is today his birthday?" she asked. "Or perhaps the day he died?"

Even as I tried to stare it away, she would not quit with the condescending smile. "I don't know much about him," I answered. "That's why I'm here."

"I haven't pulled the Asmore file in months and already you're the second person this morning who's asked for it."

I wheeled around and immediately spotted her. She was sitting alone at the opposite end of the room, photographs and news clippings and other ephemera spread out on the desk in front of her. "Thank you," I said to the librarian.

Head lowered in a pose of intense concentration, Rhys apparently hadn't noticed me either. I pulled back a chair and sat across from her. "Mind if I join you?" I said, and leaned forward on my elbows.

She still seemed loath to acknowledge me. She glanced up, then hurriedly scribbled on one of the writing pads, *"Jack, are you following me?"*

"God, no," I replied, my voice loud enough to lift heads in the room.

The librarian rose to her feet and glared in my direction. I mouthed the word "Sorry" and lowered my head.

"God, no," I wrote on my own pad. I showed Rhys, then added, *"I wanted a look at the Asmore file. My father used to come here."*

She looked at me. *"Huh?"*

"He had a small collection of southern paintings, swamp scenes mostly, and liked to read about the artists. Look, I will leave now and come back later if you like."

She seemed to be trying to decide whether to send me off. I pointed to my chest, then the door, to show that I was prepared to leave.

"No. Just keep quiet. They're real funny here about talking."

"I promise."

Another nod. And a smile, or the cool, quivering fragment of one.

The first thing I reached for was a photograph. It was one of those soft-focus portraits that cast the subject in a veil of gauze—the sort of high-handed, diaphanous treatment Hollywood used in the old days to glamorize movie stars. It was my first glimpse of Asmore, and rather than provide understanding it added to my confusion about the man. He had a thick sweep of dark hair and dark eyes that stared intensely rather than simply looked out at the world. His face possessed a feminine aspect in that it appeared carefully tended to, carefully fussed over: the eyebrows, for instance, were so perfectly straight they might've been plucked with tweezers, and his mouth was full and expressive, the lips perfectly formed. It was a mouth you wanted to kiss—or rather the kind someone else might want to. Boys this pretty catch hell growing up and spend much of their time brushing the dust off their jeans; bullies, finding them easy marks, take it upon themselves to teach them that not everything will come easy. From the photograph you never would've imagined the terrible end that awaited Asmore. You'd have thought, rather, that the future would run on forever and deliver nothing but the best: the best wife and kids, the best house in the neighborhood, the best galleries to support his career, the best collectors to pursue him, the best seat in the museum hall at the banquet honoring him for a lifetime of achievement.

A block of ecru matting had been fitted over the photograph, and it bore a photographer's stamp. "Whitesell," it said. It was a name I recognized. Crossing over the stamp was the photographer's signature with a bouquet of flourishes.

"Levette was quite the dreamboat," I wrote on my notepad.

Rhys smiled and wrote, *"Yes, but strongly resented emphasis on looks."*

She slid another photograph across the table and turned the page on her pad. *"Asmore with the artist Alberta Kinsey, his friend and teacher at the N. O. Art School. Like a mother to him. Called her Miss Bertie."*

It was a small snapshot showing the young man and older woman painting together on location in the French Quarter. In the photo the artists are sitting on campstools with paint boxes open on their laps. Each has an arm extended with a brush in hand, as they appear to be painting the same view. Asmore is wearing a white shirt and white pants and dirty half boots without socks. He is painfully thin, his face gaunt with shadows around the eyes, hair tortured by a breeze. He is situated a few feet behind his mentor. The brim of a straw hat partially obscures Kinsey's face, but she looks old enough to be his grandmother.

There is a third figure in the photograph. It is the blurry form of a young woman standing just over Asmore's shoulder. Is she a curious onlooker? Yet another admirer? Because her face is too distorted to make out, she would have spotted the photographer with camera raised and turned away just as the frame was being shot.

When I finished with the picture Rhys was waiting with another notation: *"Who do you imagine the girl is?"*

"Could be anyone."

She shook her head. *"Don't think so."*

"Another Aunt Dottie?"

"Lover," she wrote, pressing the point of her pencil down hard on the pad. She leaned across the table for another look at the photograph. *"Notice the old car with the La. license plate?"*

I smiled and nodded and she shook her head again. *"Look!"* And then I saw what she was getting at. The plate was dated 1941. *"He died in September, same year. Age twenty-three!!!"*

Next she slid over a batch of newspaper clippings, including a few of his obituary published in New Orleans papers. They were yellowed and brittle and stamped with the dates when they appeared. To judge from the accounts, Asmore had been doomed from the start, with tragedy breathing down his neck every step of the way. He'd spent his childhood on a farm near the town of Melville, hard by the west bank of the Atchafalaya River in Saint Landry Parish, and today about a two hours' drive west of New Orleans. His parents were sharecroppers who drowned in the great flood of 1927 when the levee near their home ruptured, creating a crevasse, and their bodies and belongings were swept away in twenty feet of silt and water. In the stories Levette's survival was portrayed as a miracle: he clung to a small house floating past and climbed up on its roof, which already was carrying nests of angry water moccasins. Stranded by the rushing tide, nearly two days would pass before a sheriff's deputy chanced upon him while out surveying the devastation. The house had traveled several miles from its original location before becoming stuck in a small tupelo swamp. Levette was still on the roof. Although the boy had avoided being bitten by the snakes, he was dehydrated and badly sunburned, and he would spend weeks recuperating. *"Poor kid,"* I wrote. This time when I looked up at Rhys there were tears in my eyes.

"Yes," she whispered. "Poor kid."

Asmore had been an only child, and his parents' lone surviving family member, an uncle on his father's side, could not afford to keep him. With no other options, the boy was shipped to New Orleans and placed in an orphanage run by Catholic priests. Nine years old now, he was too traumatized to speak, and he became hysterical whenever it rained or the sky grew black with clouds. A teacher, recognizing how much Levette liked to color with crayons and to sketch portraits, gave him a kit containing paints and brushes and challenged him to make a picture. The result was stunning: a detailed panorama of the flood that had claimed his parents' lives. Asmore didn't paint the scene on the paper provided by the teacher, but rather on a canvas blind removed from one of the windows in his dormitory. A collector would pay the orphanage a hundred dollars for the picture, at the time an unheard-of sum for the work of an amateur, let alone a child.

That same year priests from the orphanage enrolled Asmore in the children's classes at the New Orleans Art School. He became a sensation. By the time he was thirteen he was taking advanced classes with adults at the French Quarter establishment and winning drawing and painting competitions. One of Asmore's most influential teachers was Paul Ninas, a modernist who would become famous for the murals he painted in 1938 in the Sazerac Bar of the Roosevelt Hotel, today known as the Fairmont. According to the clippings, Asmore assisted Ninas on the Sazerac project. The two artists completed the work at Ninas's studio in the Pontalba Buildings at Jackson Square, and they installed the four large panels during the bar's off-hours, beginning at two o'clock in the morning and working until noon.

"I know those paintings," I wrote on the pad. *"Former hangout, back when I wrote for the paper. Gorgeous."*

"Of course you'd know them!"

"Barfly that I am, you mean?"

She made her head bob up and down in an exaggerated nod.

"Beautiful in the candlelight," I wrote.

"Yes. Beautiful any time."

Early in his studies Asmore was regarded as a child savant. Later on, though still a teenager, he had matured to a point where he had no peer either among his classmates or instructors. Ninas, who often complained about having to teach to make a living, said he would gladly give classes for free "if they all came like the amazing Levette." Alberta Kinsey referred to her young pupil as "our exciting master." One newspaper story, titled "Local Prodigy Wins Scholarship," quoted Kinsey as saying, "In describing Levette I hesitate to use the word genius—that is quite a large statement—but he is like no one else. He is unique, he is special, he awes us to no end."

In another story a school administrator said, "We have in our midst the greatest talent of our time and his name is Levette Asmore."

Despite the long roster of testimonials, when Asmore was twenty-one the Arts and Crafts Club held a solo exhibition of his paintings at its Royal Street gallery and succeeded in selling only seven of the thirty works offered for sale. The poor result was attributed to a newspaper review that ran on the morning of the opening. Its critic wrote, "Thirty years ago Mr. Asmore's carnality might have appealed to the depraved clients of Tommy Anderson and Lulu White, Storyville flesh peddlers, but in today's more sophisticated climate the art patron deserves a respite from such obscenity. His emphasis on the Negro figure strains the viewer's patience while simultaneously assaulting him with an exaggerated use of color. Even Mr. Asmore's still life of magnolias looks like a woman in the throes of childbirth, and a colored one at that. I would warn any and all mothers of impressionable young girls to lock them inside. Gentlemen, protect your wives. Levette Asmore has arrived."

"Can you believe this crap?" I wrote.

"Don't want to," Rhys replied.

It would be the only sales exhibition of Asmore's career. At the time of his death two years later he was sharing a tumbledown Creole cottage with a friend in a tough, racially mixed block of the French Quarter. Unlike today, when an address in the city's oldest neighborhood is widely coveted and considered chic, to live in the Vieux Carré then was often a proposition of last resorts, and usually meant you could not afford better accommodations in an Uptown neighborhood. A midcentury photographer named Clarence John Laughlin had published a picture of Asmore's last residence in a large limited-edition book called *New Orleans and Its Living Past*. The photo appeared as plate 24 with this caption, written by the book's author, David L. Cohn: "An eighteenth-century house in Saint Philip Street. It is of the earliest type of construction, brick between posts. Note the fine dormer window.

"It is said in the neighborhood that this house is haunted. Certainly it presents a sinister aspect."

A copy of the Laughlin photo, reproduced on a sheet of crumpled Xerox paper, was clipped to a story about Asmore's funeral, which ran to a length of a thousand words. A mortuary, the House of Bultman, had handled the well-attended service for the "infamous young firebrand," as the artist was described. A portrait of Asmore, lovingly painted by Alberta Kinsey, stood next to an empty and closed coffin adorned with a single magnolia blossom, the flower the artist most liked to paint. "I feel as though I shall never laugh again," said one young woman as she wept.

"But why exactly did he do it?" I wrote. *"Booze? Women? That bad review? WHAT MADE HIM JUMP?"*

Rhys slid another clipping across the table, dated September 1941, less than two weeks before Asmore's death. The byline belonged to the same newspaper critic who'd so mercilessly ridiculed Asmore's gallery showing two years before. CONTROVERSIAL ARTIST TO UNVEIL PUBLICLY FINANCED MURAL, read the headline.

For days now, visitors to the Magazine Street post office have noticed a dark, ruggedly handsome young man in their midst. He wears the stained overalls of a house painter but in fact he is a creative artist, one Levette Asmore, 23, a product of Warren Easton High School and currently a student at the Arts and Crafts Club, 712 Royal Street.

Asmore studied with Paul Ninas, Enrique Alferez and Alberta Kinsey, among others, and in recent years he made a memorable debut when his erotic paintings, predominantly of Negroes, were featured in a one-man exhibition that this writer had the opportunity to review.

Asmore has installed a mural in the station that he completed at his French Quarter studio. The work measures eight feet tall and twenty feet wide, and it now hangs on a large expanse of wall in the lobby. Scaffolding cloaked in tarpaulin reaches to the ceiling, blocking the view for visitors curious for a look.

The subject of this creation presumably is the history of transportation in America, according to both WPA officials and agents with the U.S. Treasury Department's procurement division, which gave Asmore the commission. The official unveiling next week normally would be an event of great civic pride for area citizens, but it is this writer's unpleasant duty to report that there is nothing normal about Asmore's mural.

Trains, planes and automobiles, ostensibly the painting's subject, have been substituted with the young man's perverted preoccupation with our baser selves. Once again the American Negro is featured in the Asmore composition, and in poses even more scandalous than those presented in the artist's inflammatory easel paintings. Is perverting the nation's youth the goal of the New Deal artist? Is miscegenation another aim? The answers are yes, if one is to judge from the raucous Asmore production.

Reached at his home last night, New Orleans district manager Charles F. Dodge reacted strongly to the report that Asmore had elected to explore subject matter other than the one to which he had been assigned. "Immediate steps will be taken to remedy this unfortunate situation," vowed Dodge, who added, "I am saddened and chagrined."

Angela Gregory, consultant for the WPA art project in Louisiana, also voiced an objection. "Mr. Asmore submitted sketches showing the history of transportation in America," she said. "Subsequent visits to his studio revealed that indeed he was developing the project. He followed procedure. In one private conversation he allowed as to how he hoped to show space travel as a future possibility, perhaps in the form of a rocket ship. I thought he was under the spell of Jules Verne and requested he dismiss with fantasy and stick to reality. That he has chosen the subject you describe is a mockery not only to the government agency that so generously supported him but to the American people whose moral integrity is under attack and whose tax dollars are being squandered."

Dodge has ordered the station closed until the matter can be investigated.

Asmore refused to comment when approached last night as he was walking home from a Frenchtown jazz club. He became agitated when questioned about the mural's content. "I am an artist," he said before racing off. "I have no interest in the history of transportation in this or any other country."

I had barely finished reading the article when Rhys slid another clipping in front of me. The story appeared under the heading "News in Brief."

Federal and city officials convened yesterday at a post office on Magazine Street and determined that a mural by controversial artist Levette Asmore was obscene and ordered the painting destroyed.

A large crowd, estimated at several hundred, gathered at the station, demanding to be allowed entrance. "We want to see how our hard-earned tax dollars are being spent," said David Parker, a service station attendant from Biloxi. "It isn't right they won't let us see it. I drove three hours in traffic to get here. Plus, I need stamps. This is an outrage."

Asmore provoked negative criticism earlier in his career when his inaugural sales exhibition proved to be "pornography disguised as fine art," as a reviewer for this newspaper reported. The mural reputedly depicted Negroes.

A WPA official called police to the scene when a supporter of the project became unruly. Order was restored when the artist himself volunteered to whitewash the twenty-foot-long painting. Asmore has been ordered to return the government funds he received for the work. He refused comment when contacted later at his home in the French Quarter.

"What do you think was in those paintings?" I wrote.

She hitched up her shoulders. *"Not sure what you mean."*

"The subject matter, the scene he painted. Miscegenation means breeding between races—whites and nonwhites."

"Ahead of his time, no doubt. Way ahead. Even for THIS time."

I stared at her and shook my head.

"To some people," she added in a fast scribble.

"Are there any pictures of the mural? Any sketches? Anything to show what it looked like?"

"None."

I nodded, then wrote, *"They made him whitewash his own painting. How terrible."*

Rhys shrugged her shoulders again.

"Too bad it was destroyed."

She waited a long time before writing, *"If whitewashed, not necessarily destroyed at all."*

"What do you mean?"

She didn't answer and I wrote again, *"WHAT DO YOU MEAN?"*

From the notepads she removed the pages with our scribbling and tucked them in a sweater pocket. I helped her gather up the Asmore material and place it back in the file. "Let's take a drive up Magazine Street," she said, speaking out loud at last.

THREE

The building stood about fifty feet from Magazine Street, its wooden façade scabbed with flaking paint, the lawn in front a patch of smooth brown earth bisected by a narrow cement walkway. Plastered on the windows were broadsheets showing women either having their nails done or sporting elaborate hairdos. An electric sign standing out by the curb, and burning even in daytime, said HAIR NAILS SKIN. Another over the entrance said WHEELER BEAUTY ACADEMY.

I checked the address again to make sure we'd come to the right place. The post office, apparently, was no more, replaced with a school for aspiring hairdressers and cosmetologists. It was a dumpy, neglected building in an Uptown district crowded with dumpy, neglected buildings. To imagine the young Asmore bounding up the stairs and pushing past the wide double doors, on his way to install a master-piece, required more creative steam than I was able to muster at the moment. "Nothing beautiful about this beauty school," I said and is-sued a low whistle.

I drive a nice car, a late-model Audi sedan with a leather interior and power everything. But it was so nice as to draw attention, so ear-lier, when Rhys and I left the French Quarter, it was in her van: the ancient, rust-ruined one with an expired brake tag and magnetic signs on the doors advertising the Guild. We were sitting in the van now, parked on the street that ran alongside the school. "Can I trust you with something, Jack?" she said. "You think I can do that?"

I turned and faced her. I didn't answer.

"Let me make a proposal," she said. "Whatever we've learned so far today about Levette Asmore—and whatever we learn when we go in the building—is privileged information that stays between the two of us. It's to be shared with no one else, not even Patrick Marion. Can we agree on that?"

"I hear you, Rhys."

"But can we agree on it?"

"Sure. Sure, we can. Let's agree on it."

It was around four o'clock in the afternoon. Classes must've just let out, ending the day, because about a dozen young people suddenly came charging out of the building, most of them African-American women of college age or older. They were lugging books and knap-sacks and talking in animated voices. Some headed for the bus stop, others for the pizza restaurant across the street; a few more sped off on bicycles. Every good-bye seemed to inspire more joyful noise, more grab-ass.

The last person to leave the building was an elderly white woman who came down the stairs sucking on a cigarette, sucking so hard that her face appeared to cave in on itself. She was wearing a loose-fitting polyester arrangement with her skirt hiked up near her chest, forming ripples along the beltline. Her stockings hung like flab at her knees, and a crocheted sweater rode her shoulders attached by a single pearl button at the neck. As she slowly made her way to the sidewalk she stopped to pick up gum wrappers and flattened potato chip bags. At the bottom of the stairs she dropped the trash in a can and stood gazing up at the building, the cigarette sticking straight out from her mouth. She cleaned off her hands by patting them together, then she made loose fists and propped them against her hips. Her eyes tracked from one window to the next, and her thin lips moved as she mumbled something I couldn't make out for the distance. Finally she lowered her head and walked over to a car parked on the street in front of us.

Passing in front of the school, she braked and came to a stop and leaned across the seat and once again stared up at the building. Maybe she was checking for damaged flashing where the gutters hung from the roof, or for broken windowpanes, of which there were plenty. Or maybe she was looking at all the pigeons roosting in the eaves, or for roof tiles that had blown away in a recent storm. But her expression suggested something else. It was only a building, and a dilapidated one at that; and yet she looked at it with expectation and longing, as though, in a window upstairs, she hoped to find the face of someone she loved.

"Tell me what you think about when you imagine Levette's mural," Rhys said.

"How's that?"

"Do you think about what Patrick said to Elsa at his dinner party, that he was going to be rich? Do you want the painting to make you a lot of money?"

"Money?" And I laughed. "Slow down there, Rhys. Since when did it become mine to sell? Why would you ask me such a question?"

"What if I told you that in some instances a painting on canvas, one that's been whitewashed, can be restored to its original condition? What would you say to that?"

"I'd say, 'How nice.' Or maybe I'd say, 'Well, I'll be damned.' But I don't think I'd get too worked up about it, if that's what you want to know."

"I don't believe you," she said. "I think your response would be quite different. I think you'd try to convince me to help you remove the mural from this building. Are you going to propose that, Jack? That the two of us, having discovered it, work out a deal together to save it and place it with a wealthy collector for a king's ransom?"

"First of all, Rhys, I'm not a thief. And, second, aren't you getting a little ahead of yourself? I really just want to see the thing, if it's even there. In all likelihood it was removed some time after the authorities forced Levette to paint over it, perhaps during a renovation. Have you considered that? Or that some enterprising collector or dealer came around before we did and got his hands on it? So many things could've happened. It's incredible to believe we're the only people who know about it."

"I think we are the only ones," she said. "Those newspaper stories said the mural was destroyed, and to most people whitewashing an existing painting amounts to destruction. But I'm a restorer. I encounter paint on paint every day, and I remove one layer to get to the next, and it isn't easy but in many cases it can be done. Remember what the newspaper story said? It said the artist himself whitewashed the painting. Now what does that tell you? I know what it tells me."

"It tells me he must've been one strong, stout-hearted son-ofabitch, to cover up what he'd probably spent months working on."

"Yes, it does say that. But it also says he was a smart man, and a clever man, and maybe even a conniving man. The painting was still new, and so the oils Levette used hadn't had time to oxidize yet. In other words, the mural's surface was still wet—the paint was wet. He had to know he couldn't cover the painting with an oil-based wash because that would've made for an irreversible situation. The oils used to paint the picture would've cross-linked with the oils used to cover it, essentially making their chemical composition one and the same. You also have to remember that Levette wouldn't have had time yet to coat the painting with varnish. As a rule you don't varnish over oil paint for at least nine months after application. So while varnish might've offered some protection to the surface from a whitewashing, Levette wouldn't have been able to go that route."

"Rhys, you've lost me."

"Okay, let me go at it from a different direction." She sat up in her seat, raised a finger to her face and pulled at her lip. "What artist in his right mind would volunteer to destroy a painting that he'd just created? None would. But an artist, faced with a mob bent on seeing him punished and ridiculed, might've thought of a way to save his painting even while giving the appearance of destroying it." She was smiling now. "Rather than allow others to round up buckets of oil paint to cover up his painting, and to effectively eliminate any chance of saving it in the future, the artist himself finds a material that doesn't pose a threat to his painting. He uses something that, quite the contrary, works to *preserve* the painting. He covers it with a material like distemper or casein paint so that it can be restored."

"Casein and what is the other one?"

"Distemper. Casein and distemper. They're types of paint, and they're both water-soluble, which means they wouldn't cross-link with the oils he used to make the picture. Either one would've given the mural a kind of barrier or skin that's dissolvable and could be removed later without much trouble."

"You think Asmore did that?"

"I do. And I intend to prove to you that he did it."

"Prove to *me?*" I said. "Why prove it to me?"

She leaned forward against the steering wheel and stared up at the building. When she'd seen enough she looked back at me and held my eyes with hers. "I want to trust you," she said. "I do. I'm not going to pick up the newspaper tomorrow morning and read about the discovery of a lost masterpiece, am I?" She reached over and gave my leg a poke. "Jack?"

"What?"

"Will I read about the mural in the paper tomorrow?"

"If you do, I won't have been the source and I certainly won't have been the writer. Rhys, I have to tell you, you're starting to make me nervous."

"It's not about what they're worth," she said, lowering her voice so that I had to strain to hear. "It's about what they are. Will you prom-ise never to forget that, Jack?"

I didn't promise, I didn't say anything. I was only starting to get to know Rhys Goudeau, but already I believed she was too intense for her own good. To begin, she could not distinguish between what she did for a living and what she valued most in life.

"You think whoever owns this place now—this Wheeler guy—even knows the painting's there?" I said. "Or that it once was there?"

"Only one way to find out," Rhys said, then shouldered her door open and stepped out on the sidewalk.

※

We'd timed it just right, without even meaning to. When we entered the building everyone but the janitor had gone for the day.

The doors opened into a small reception area that in turn led to a hallway that spilled into a much larger room holding rows of beauti-cian's chairs, each of them covered in pink vinyl lined with black pip-ing and standing on chrome pedestals. The janitor was cleaning the floor with a rag mop, and though he trained his eyes in our direction he didn't stop working to greet us. Instead he placed a warning cone next to his bucket cautioning to step carefully. Though stooped over, he was still half a foot taller than I was, and nearly twice my weight. Music poured from the headphones of his portable CD player, the tinny whisper of which I could make out from across the room.

"Hello, there," Rhys said, as though he were a stray tabby that had crossed our path. But clearly the man was busy: busy mopping, busy listening, busy avoiding having to acknowledge us.

Photo composites showing former students crowded the walls, each arranged with individual head shots fitted into identical ovals. The same four teachers stared out from the top row of most of the groupings, as did the woman we'd seen outside earlier. Her oval and one other were twice as large as everyone else's. The name under her picture said Gail Wheeler. The name under the other photo said Jerome Wheeler. It showed an unhandsome man with eyes that peered out in different directions, one looking left, the other right. Thirty years ago student enrollment had run about a hundred, but the numbers began to decline sharply beginning a decade ago. Last year, if the composite accurately represented the student population, there were only fourteen people enrolled in the school. The faculty also went from four to two instructors, and Jerome Wheeler's photograph wasn't included in the most recent collection of photos.

"Think they divorced?" I said to Rhys.

"I don't know what to think," she answered. "Maybe he died."

The room also came equipped with antiquated vending machines for candy, cigarettes and soft drinks. Yellowing posters from another era said, "Learn to gratify a multicultural clientele" and "Don't hesitate, dear, for an exciting career awaits." But there was no evidence of Asmore's mural, nothing high on the walls to indicate that a canvas lay hidden under coats of paint. The room had probably served the post office as a foyer, while my guess placed the lobby in the large open space with the beautician's chairs.

Rhys sidled up to the janitor, bravely depositing footprints on the freshly cleaned floor. She pulled at imaginary headphones. "May we have a minute of your time, sir? May we have . . . *sir*, may we have a minute?"

The man continued mopping, making bigger circles than before.

"Okay, then," Rhys said, "what about *half* a minute? Is half a minute too long? How about fifteen seconds? Would you allow us *ten* seconds?"

He tugged at his headset and let it drop to his neck, and I could hear the music better: seventies R&B.

"Hi, there," Rhys said, flashing a smile. "We were hoping to have a look around in that room there." She pointed to it. "Would you mind?"

He might've been fifty years old, but his body was cut with slabs of muscle that padded his gray, work-stained coveralls. His head was shaved and scars stood out on his shiny, copper-colored scalp. He glanced back over his shoulder and acted as if he'd only now noticed the room with the beautician's chairs. His mouth formed a circle, as if to say "Oh." "I take it you talked to Mrs. Sanchez," he said.

"Mrs. Sanchez? Yes, well, we have talked to Mrs. Sanchez, as a matter of fact. And she said it was fine with her. Would you mind?"

That was all it took to get him to move out of the way: permission from Mrs. Sanchez and far more obsequiousness than I thought Rhys Goudeau capable of. "Watch your step," the janitor said. "Those tiles tend to get slippery." As we were moving past him he said, "Mrs. Sanchez in Admissions, right?"

"Right," Rhys said.

The man dunked his mop back in the bucket, intentionally splashing water on the floor; I had to step quickly to avoid getting my shoes wet. "There is no Mrs. Sanchez in Admissions," he said. "There was a *Mr.* Sanchez who taught hair weave, but he was only part-time and hasn't been around here in ten, twelve years." He was gripping the wooden mop handle with both fists, holding it close to his waist. "State your business," he said, with nostrils flaring. "You two from Baton Rouge?"

"Baton Rouge?" Rhys said.

"I can spot you people a mile away."

"What people?"

"You know what people." He paused, wiped the sweat off his face. "You're inspectors with the government, aren't you?"

"Inspectors?" Rhys said. "Why would you say we're inspectors?"

"And why would you want to torment Miss Wheeler?" he shot back. "You oughta be ashamed. You really should."

"What are you talking about?" I said. "We've never even met Miss Wheeler. How can you torment somebody you don't know?"

He started mopping again. He erased our prints and reached to where we were standing. It was my impression that he would've erased both Rhys and me had he been able to extend his mop that far.

"We're not them," Rhys said. "I swear to God we're not them."

"You look like them."

"Listen to me," she said. "We heard this building was once a post office and we came today because we're curious to learn more about it. That's all. We're amateur historians who appreciate fine old architecture. We were doing research and we read about the building in some newspaper clippings in a museum archive. The truth is, we came to snoop around. We're snoops, all right? I'm not ashamed to say it."

He was looking at her the same way I was. It was a look that communicated as much bewilderment as amusement.

She stepped up closer to him, leaving more tracks. "We're no more the government than you are," she said. "And I think you know that. Why would inspectors be coming around here, anyway?"

"That ain't my place to say."

"Do you have a name?"

"I never met 'em."

"I meant your name."

"Cherry," he said. "Rondell Cherry." He put the headphones back on. "Go see what you want, just keep me out of it."

We walked past him and entered the room with all the chairs and slowly made our way to the center. The only light came from a couple of fluorescent panels high up on the ceiling. Although it was dark in the room it didn't take long to locate the mural. It was right where it should have been. That is to say, it was directly in front of us, some ten feet off the ground, and up above a run of mirrors and sinks for washing hair. The canvas, though covered with paint, was a different texture than the wood paneling and drywall that built out the rest of the room.

I glanced over at Rhys. I might've anticipated the tears, but not the intensity of her crying jag. The woman wept. She wept just as those young women probably had wept sixty years before at the House of Bultman when Levette Asmore's empty coffin was laid out with a single magnolia flower on the lid.

"You want a Kleenex or a handkerchief or something?" I said.

She shook her head.

The paint covering the mural—corn yellow streaked with dirt and water stains—also covered the rest of the room. The painting itself, from what I could see of the outline, was about the size of a small outdoor billboard. The corners were curling and in other areas bubbles were lifting on the surface. A couple of air-conditioning vents had been cut into the canvas and one of the vents had leaked. You could also see seams running between each of the four panels.

"He used some kind of glue, probably wallpaper paste, and tacks," Rhys said. "See the tacks running along the edge? They just painted right over them, too."

"It's really there, isn't it?"

"It really is," she said.

I supposed you could look at any wall with nothing on it and see the same thing, but the space possessed a power that was unexpected. The power came from imagining the image that resided beneath the grime and paint, the one Asmore had put there.

Wholly unprepared for any voice but Rhys's, I jumped when one sounded a few feet behind us. "That used to be a picture," Rondell Cherry said.

"What was a picture?" Rhys said, making sure to keep her back to him. I had to give it to her: she was good, she could turn it off as quickly as she turned it on.

"That place up there on the wall," Cherry said.

"No kidding?" And still not even a sniffle.

"The beauty school's been here thirty-one years, that's since 1970, and before that they had an insurance agency here. The insurance people bought it after the old post office moved and the government sold the building, and they were the ones that redid all the insides like you see here. They had all their desks in this room. It was one of the insurance people who told the Wheelers about the painting."

"My name is Rhys Goudeau," Rhys said, offering him a hand to shake. "And this is my friend Jack Charbonnet."

He nodded at us both.

"You been working here long, Mr. Cherry?"

"I started in '87. I'll make fifteen years next January."

"You really think there's a picture under there?" Rhys said. "When did Mrs. Wheeler tell you that?"

"Oh, whenever it came to her, I guess, a long time ago. I never knew her to lie. On top of that, we had some new air ducts put in and the electrician had to cut bigger vents. He made his cuts and I took out my pocketknife and scraped off the paint that covered the piece of board and cloth and whatnot and you could see it was something under there. Just too bad it's all ruined."

"What sort of person is Mrs. Wheeler?"

"What sort of person?"

"Yes, what sort? Is she a nice lady? A good lady?"

"Miss Wheeler is an *interesting* lady, let me put it to you that way. We get along handsomely and always have, since day one. Also, I think she's very funny. She likes to keep you laughing."

"What about Mr. Wheeler?"

"Mr. Wheeler passed away from a stroke or a heart attack, something like that."

"Does Mrs. Wheeler come to the school every day?"

"Yes, she does. Every day up until the bell rings. That is not counting Wednesdays, when people come by after classes to get their hair cut and Miss Wheeler stays late to supervise. She likes to be here in case something happens. We get people getting upset and screaming sometimes, seeing the job the students do, but what you want for three dollars? I mean, come on." His laughter sounded like an animal running across a tin roof. "You know what I'm saying?"

"I sure do," said Rhys, adding a laugh of her own. "Mr. Cherry, do you remember the last time this room was painted?"

"The last time it was painted?"

"Yes sir."

"Only once since I been here."

"And when was that?"

"Maybe a year after I started. No, it was more like six months. The color before was kind of dark, a kind of blue, and the Wheelers wanted to brighten things up."

Rondell Cherry seemed to like Rhys and to trust her implicitly, but for some reason he felt differently about me. He looked at me again the way he had earlier in the lobby. "You one hundred percent positively certain you're not a government man?"

I took out my wallet and flashed a press credential, the ID card the paper had issued me years ago when I was first hired. It was the wrong thing to show him. "You not intending to write a story about us, are you?"

"I'm not with the paper anymore. I quit a while back."

"Miss Wheeler like to die she knew I let the *T-P* in here."

"When you scraped the paint off that piece of cloth from the wall," Rhys said, "what did you see? What was underneath?"

He looked up at the spot on the wall and pointed. "Came from that vent there. I can't say it was anything you could make out. It was just some colors that weren't the blue before it. It was some reds, some greens and some whites."

"And Mrs. Wheeler will be here Wednesday when people come and volunteer to have their hair cut?"

"Three dollars and they'll do yours, too. Not that I recommend it."

Rhys kept staring at the wall and the feeling that had made her weep came over her again and I could see her fighting it, trying to keep it away. A beautiful old post office was now a run-down beauty school. A monumental work of art was painted over, then further desecrated to accommodate air-conditioning vents. The vents were too small, so they'd been replaced with larger ones. The larger ones had leaked. The government was investigating the woman who ran the school. The government would seize the beauty school and once again possess the painting that it had ordered destroyed.

"You're a very nice man," Rhys said to Rondell Cherry. "Thank you for accommodating us today."

She walked out of the room without another word, leaving Rondell Cherry and me to follow. As we were heading down the hallway he stopped and grabbed me by a sleeve. "Listen," he said with a tug, "you sure you're not a government man?"

FOUR

Rhys was quiet on the drive back to the French Quarter. I noticed her hands shaking as she held the wheel. She would look at me and start to speak, then stop herself. At an intersection she braked to a complete stop even though the light was green. From behind us came car horns and shouted curses. I sat rumbling with laughter. Rhys was oblivious.

"What do we do now?" she muttered, glancing at her reflection in the rearview mirror. "Come on, honey, what do you do?"

"You snap out of it and go," I replied, then pointed to the signal and slipped lower in the seat.

Rather than return to the parking lot where I'd left my car, she did an illegal U-turn on Poydras Street and headed back Uptown. I said nothing in protest, figuring we were returning to Wheeler for another look. But she passed the school without slowing or saying anything and drove another mile or so before stopping across from a building that looked like a well-tended warehouse. Painted high on an exterior wall were the words NEAL AUCTION COMPANY. "Hope you didn't have plans for the evening," she said.

"Me? Never."

"I just remembered it's Thursday night. Do you know what that means?"

"Maybe I did in a previous life but the significance escapes me at the moment."

"Thursday night is when auction houses in New Orleans traditionally stay open late and host preview parties."

"You're taking me to a party, are you? My God, we're on a date."

She cut me a nasty look and pushed open her squeaky door. She paused before stepping outside. "No, Jack, this is not a date. This is a preview party, with the emphasis on preview. In New Orleans auctions are held on weekends, and Thursday night is the only time a lot of buyers get a chance to see what's coming up for sale. Unlike you, Jack, they have real-life commitments like nine-to-five jobs and families and they can't come here during the day. Neal is the oldest auction business in town, and it specializes in all things southern. It's where I'm going to recommend Patrick consign *Dorothy.*"

As we were crossing the street my body reacted noisily to the smell of fried chicken issuing from the Popeyes on the corner. I hadn't eaten since breakfast, and the aroma stopped me in my tracks. "I'm starving," I called out. "Come on, Rhys. My treat."

She shook her head and waved me on.

"Rhys? *Rhys?*" When she looked back at me I said, "I truly believe I'd sell my soul for a biscuit. That's how bad it is."

"How can you think about food when there are paintings so close by?"

Double glass doors, tinted gray and stenciled with the Neal logo, opened into a space that seemed entirely removed from the present. Old rugs layered the gallery's wood floors, and mirrors and paintings

papered the walls. From the ceiling were suspended crystal chandeliers and vintage light fixtures, some of them ablaze and radiating
heat. Antique furniture crowded the large open rooms. The smell of
fried chicken now was replaced with those of furniture wax and pep-
permint oil. People of what seemed a genteel class circulated among
the pretty things: men in suits and jackets without ties, women in
pearls and neatly pressed outfits. I followed Rhys to an office area in
front where jewelry and pottery were displayed in big glass cases. She
retrieved a catalog with a label on the cover that said "House Copy."

"Take this," she said, and slapped the book against my chest. She
then took one for herself.

The cover illustration, wrapping from front to back, showed a
painting of a working cotton plantation, its fields crowded with
African-American laborers. "Well, I'll be," Rhys said. "Check this out,
Jack. They've got a giant Walker for sale."

As in the case of A. J. Drysdale, a collection of southern art wasn't
complete without a Walker. "Even my dad the junk-shop picker
owned one of these," I said.

"Get out of here. Your dad had a Walker?"

"He really did. It was small, though, not much bigger than a post-
card. It was a portrait of a laborer standing on the edge of a cotton
field. A black man."

"Of course the subject was black. What else would it be? Walker
made his name exploiting the image of the poor black."

"It was just a little picture, Rhys."

"You're very naïve," she said. "Now come. I want to show you
something."

I followed her into the main room of the gallery, where it was so
crowded with people and furniture that it was hard to get around. An
enormous dining table, not an inch short of fifteen feet long, stood in
the center and held magnum bottles of wine and supermarket party
trays loaded with vegetable sticks, cold cuts and cheeses. I paused to
spear a slice of ham, but in the instant before eating it Rhys yanked
me forward. The ham landed on the table with a splat. "God, Jack.

Are you still thinking about food? The Louisiana Room is right over there."

"The Louisiana Room?"

"Leave the ham alone and let me introduce you."

It turned out to be a small exhibition room decorated from floor to ceiling with oil paintings, most of them by southern landscape and portrait artists of the nineteenth century. Few of the paintings looked to be less than fifty years old and none was contemporary. The most impressive of the offerings, the Walker plantation scene, was hanging at the center of the wall facing the open double doors. That made it the first thing you encountered upon entering. At the moment Rhys and I were alone in the room, so she was free to talk. "I don't like it," she said. "No, I actually feel more strongly about it than that. I *hate* it. I abhor it."

"I like it a lot."

"Yes, well, in this case my opinion represents the minority, I assure you. I suppose I'm way too sensitive to Walker's use of demeaning racial stereotypes. The mostly white collectors of southern art covet his sentimental renderings of enslaved or indentured African Americans at their toil. 'Country blacks,' I hear collectors call them. These cotton kingdom images evoke feelings of nostalgia, though not the sort anyone but a real shitbird would admit to."

"A what kind of bird?"

"A shitbird, Jack. A *shit*bird."

"It's a nice painting. Come on, Rhys. What's so hard to accept about it?" When she didn't answer, I said, "Why does it always have to be so personal with you?"

"Why? Because all art is personal," she said matter-of-factly. "Otherwise it isn't art—it's *decoration*. Now move out of the way, Jack. You're blocking my light."

She stepped up to better inspect the painting, and I stood a few feet behind her. Men, women and children populated the scene, along with mules pulling covered wagons and dogs snoozing in deep puddles of sun. Everybody seemed to be working hard; the burlap sacks hanging from the men's shoulders were stuffed, as were the tall cane baskets balanced on the heads of some of the women. In the background there stood a gin house with stacks belching smoke, as well as the big house and assorted outbuildings, one of them a rustic cabin complete with animal pelts tacked to the wall. The blue expanse of sky suggested good times.

These people might've been serving their white master, but they appeared more than happy to do so. The catalog listing dated the painting as circa 1885, two decades after the Civil War and the emancipation of the American Negro.

Rhys was still studying the image when she said, "One of the unspoken truths about Walker collectors is that they're buying pictures of people they would never allow in their own homes, except on those occasions when their houses need to be cleaned."

"So you're calling anyone who owns one of these things a racist?" I laughed but not with any feeling. "Aren't you being a little unfair?"

"It's fine to hang pictures of African Americans on the wall," she continued, "but don't let a real one walk through the front door."

"What a load of crap. I don't believe that at all, Rhys."

"You're wrong not to," she said. "As a rule the more poor black people there are in a Walker, the more valuable the painting. And a painting depicting poor blacks is always more desirable than one showing poor whites. If it weren't so insidious, Jack, I might be as amused as you are."

"Amused? No, Rhys, I'm not amused. You just called my late father a racist because he owned a painting by this artist. I'll have you know he was nothing of the kind. We had black people visit our home quite often when I was growing up, always on social calls. Not one of them did the housekeeping."

"I was trying to make a point. I didn't mean to impugn your father's integrity."

"But you did, Rhys. You did that exactly. And all because he owned a little picture by an artist you don't happen to like."

She stepped back from the painting and looked around the room.

She might've been wrong—and dead wrong, at that—but there would be no apology. "Have you noticed by chance anything curious about the paintings in this room today?"

"No."

"Not one of them shows blacks and whites together. Not one, Jack. See that painting there of the French Quarter, circa 1932? Every figure in it is black. The nun is black, the child is black, the washerwomen are black, the man pushing the cart is black. But in this painting—it's by the Impressionist Clarence Millet—the people are all white. Every one is white. Why is that, Jack? Were all the artists back then racists who believed in segregating the human race by skin color?" I didn't answer and she said, "Of course they weren't all racists. Until the sixties artists in many areas of the Deep South were *forbidden* to paint images showing blacks and whites together unless the blacks were depicted in attitudes of subservience to the whites. Oh, you had plenty of pictures showing black maids waiting on their white employers and nursing their white children, and white foremen lording over crews of black laborers. And you might've had some showing famous black entertainers entertaining white crowds. But you never saw a picture where the races were integrated and treated as equals. Granted, segregation was a fact of life. But to look at the paintings in this room today," she said, "you would think that in the old days blacks and whites occupied polar universes."

She pointed to a painting of a popular French Quarter location called Pirate's Alley. It showed the area crowded with white people. She then pointed out another painting of the same location. The second painting, which looked to have been painted at the same time as the first, counted half a dozen African Americans but no whites. "Did whites have their hours when they could walk down the alley?" she said. "And did blacks have theirs? Didn't they ever walk down the alley together at the same time? If indeed they did happen to walk down the alley at the same time, why wasn't there ever an artist there to capture the moment? Think about it, Jack. Most of these paintings were done for tourists, and many thousands were painted. How could it be that artists failed to find an occasion when both black and white people were strolling down that alley together?"

"I don't know."

"I don't either. Want to hear a story? There once was an artist from a small town in Mississippi who entered a painting in an art-club contest. This was some time in the late fifties, and the painting showed a large public swimming pool crowded with both black and white people, all of them mixed together and enjoying the water on a hot summer day. The painting was beautifully done, and it won the contest, beating out a portrait of a long-dead Confederate general painted by the wife of the local sheriff. The woman complained about the content of the winning picture to her husband, and that night he and his deputies showed up at the artist's doorstep and told him he had a choice to make. He could paint the figures black or he could paint them white but he couldn't show blacks and whites swimming in the same pool together. The blacks had their pool on one side of town and the whites had theirs on the other side. He said the painting was subversive and anti-American."

"What did the artist do?"

"He refused to alter the painting and the deputies dragged him outside and beat him until he listened to reason."

"Did the artist fix the painting?"

"He made all of the figures white, if that's what you mean by fixing it."

She was upset and I knew better than to push it any further. I opened the catalog and turned to the description of the Walker painting, spread out with color photographs over two pages. The high side of the painting's estimate was $200,000. According to the description, the size of the painting—twenty-eight by forty-two inches—was monumental for an artist best known for painting on a small scale, and its provenance was impeccable. It had belonged to the same New Orleans family since the date of its creation, when the original owner bought it personally from the artist.

I could feel Rhys looking over my shoulder at the catalog, and I closed it and wheeled around and faced her. "Look at your own copy, won't you?"

"I don't mean to take it out on you, Jack. But sometimes I could just scream. Am I the only person who sees it? If others see it, why don't they say anything about it?" She stood in front of the Walker again and held her hands behind her back. "Now let me broach another sensitive subject," she said, "off the subject of race this time."

"Thank you, Rhys."

"Why would the consignor of the Walker choose to betray his legacy, break his family's long history of ownership and place the painting up for sale?"

"How many guesses do I get?"

"As many as you need."

"Money," I answered, then recalled my own experience with my father's collection and offered another possibility. "Or maybe it belonged to somebody who died. And maybe the people who survived him couldn't look at it without seeing him and missing him and wishing they were dead themselves."

"Your second guess is less likely than your first, although by the tone of your voice you could be sharing a personal experience. While I don't discount it, I've noticed an alarming trend lately, and I have a theory that conforms to your first answer."

"Are we in school, Rhys? You sound like a damn professor. Dr. Goudeau."

She ignored me. "Ever since the Louisiana legislature legalized gambling in the state there have been more rare and fine items appearing at auction. It's my guess that the city's aristocrats enjoy playing craps and poker at Harrah's and the riverboat casinos as much as the city's white trash do. It's also my guess that their luck at the games is no better. In the Deep South, in times of a depressed economy, the first things sold off usually are Grandpa's favorite Colt pistol, his prized Confederate saber or his cotton kingdom painting by William Aiken Walker."

"Will that be a question on the final exam, Dr. Goudeau?"

"Shut up, Jack."

Minutes later a tall, attractive woman with long red hair joined us in the room. Her name was Lucinda Copeland, and she worked at the auction house as the consignment director for paintings and fine arts. It had been her job to catalog the offerings now featured in the Louisiana Room. After Rhys introduced us to each other, Lucinda turned her attention to the Walker. "Well, what do you think?"

"It doesn't matter what I think," Rhys answered, "I won't be bidding it. What do Tommy Smallwood and Mary Lou Cohn think? That's the question."

"Mary Lou's crazy about it," Lucinda said. "She's already gone on record saying they have to have it. If you can believe it, she asked me yesterday how to approach Mr. Smallwood and persuade him not to pursue it. I told her I didn't have a clue."

"Mary Lou Cohn is acquisitions director for the Historic New Orleans Collection," Rhys told me. "She and Tommy Smallwood have had some nasty battles in the past."

"Nasty is an apt description," said Lucinda Copeland. "So are ugly, bloody, vicious and murderous. But Mary Lou's never outbid Mr. Smallwood, to my recollection."

"Never?" I said.

"Never. In fact, now that I think about it, I've never known Mr. Smallwood to finish as the underbidder. What I mean by that is, he has never lost anything he's gone after. I've watched him bid against museums as large as the National Gallery in Washington, D.C., and as small as one in the rural town of Lawtell, Louisiana, and in the latter case he was as ferocious in his bidding as he was in the former one. The lot is introduced and Mr. Smallwood's paddle goes up. It stays there until the hammer comes down finalizing the sale. It's reached the point where he usually gets things at a good price because he intimidates other buyers. Figuring they can't beat him, they concede after a few bids. Years ago, when he first started to collect, everyone here at Neal would become excited by his pursuit of things because it meant he would drive the price up. Now we dread it."

"You dread it," I said.

"The auction house doesn't own the lots that are sold here—the people who consign them are the owners—but we do receive a commission, a percentage of what things sell for. If they go cheap, we're not making as much money as we would if they were going at higher prices. And if they go cheap, the consignors are unhappy."

"So you're hoping Smallwood doesn't want the Walker painting?" I said.

"We're hoping he won't be the only one competing for it. Let me put it that way."

"Will he be here tonight?" I asked.

"Oh, that you can count on," said Lucinda. "Mr. Smallwood is a regular at previews, storming in just long enough to announce which lots he intends to buy, and just long enough to frighten away any other buyers who might be considering the same items. He's very shrewd. Dogs mark their territory by lifting a leg and spraying the periphery of that area which they designate as home turf. Mr. Smallwood, to my knowledge, has not yet watered the gallery floors, but he's done his share of posturing. Unlike others of his financial standing, he has never sent a proxy to do his bidding. And he's never bid by telephone. Some wealthy buyers prefer to remain anonymous—'stealth bidders,' we call them. But Mr. Smallwood not only grasps the importance of being seen, he exploits it. When it comes to the psychology of winning at auction, Tommy Smallwood is a master."

No more than ten minutes after Lucinda Copeland had completed this pronouncement a commotion erupted in the gallery. Rhys grabbed me by the arm and led me out of the Louisiana Room. "Speaking of Beelzebub," she said, then lifted a hand and pointed toward the entrance. "Movie and rock stars and other celebrities come through Neal all the time. But no one jazzes up the place like that horrible monster."

Smallwood was standing with a young woman in the front of the gallery. A throng had rushed up to greet him; I had to stand on the balls of my feet to get a good look at him. Smallwood was a big man, big enough to fill up the double doors and crowd out light from the Popeyes sign across the street. He had about him the air of the champion athlete who expects even those who don't like or follow sports to kiss up to him. His pumpkin head rode his shoulders without the apparent benefit of a neck, and he had one of those trendy haircuts that made him look as though he'd just held his head against a box fan. His looks were disturbing, but I did like his clothes: an off-white linen suit and a light blue Oxford shirt with an open collar, shoes that looked English and handmade. As for his companion, she was the sort of woman one often sees positioned at the entrance of an upscale French Quarter gentlemen's club, pretending to have come out for a breath of air when in fact her aim was to lure gullible men inside. Every gesture was a pose. Not wishing to objectify the woman, I will refrain from describing how she was built, except to say she had the largest breasts I'd ever seen in my life.

"How'd he make his money?" I said to Rhys. "Had to be oil."

"No, as a matter of fact it was real estate," she answered. "He began by pioneering blighted neighborhoods, fixing up abandoned houses and selling them or renting them to people who couldn't abide living in housing projects any longer. For years he was known around town as the 'Section Eight King,' which means he ruled the market for federally subsidized housing. But then Smallwood started buying up old office buildings downtown and in the French Quarter and putting luxury hotels in them. He recently sold one of his properties in the Lower Garden District to a strip mall developer for a cool two million after Wal-Mart announced plans to build a Supercenter in the neighborhood. Only the year before, Smallwood had invested all of ten grand in the weedy, trash-strewn lot. People hate him, no one more than the city's preservationists who've fought to stop him from razing important historic structures and replacing them with giant chain stores and discount hotels. I look at Tommy Smallwood and one word comes to mind."

"Cheesy piece of shit?"

"Sure, that works," she said. "But that's four words, Jack. No, the one that always comes to me is *motherfucker*."

As Smallwood and his companion drew closer, I happened to get a whiff of the man. He smelled powerfully of roux, that muddy blend of flour and vegetable oil used as the foundation for gumbo. This surprised me. All things considered, in particular the girl, I'd anticipated a scent more on the order of musk oil.

Suddenly Rhys was upon him, thrusting out a hand for him to shake. "Mr. Smallwood," she said. "How nice to see you again. Mr. Smallwood? It's Rhys Goudeau, with the Crescent City Conservation Guild."

"Rhys Goudeau," he said. "Are you the one that keeps sending me letters?"

"One and the same, sir."

"You need to cut that shit out," he said, then quickly moved past her on his way to the Louisiana Room.

"Mr. Smallwood . . . ?"

But he was gone, talking to someone else now.

"What on earth was that about?" I said.

"I'd rather let it go," she said.

"No, Rhys. Tell me what just happened."

She looked at me. "It's simple, really. I've been trying to get him as a client. And he's avoided me. I've mailed him at least two dozen personal letters and he's answered none of them. About a month ago I sent him a press packet complete with copies of stories about the Guild that have appeared in local and national publications. Smallwood returned the package unopened, with the words 'Leave me be,' printed across the envelope's seal. Did that stop me?" She shook her head. "I asked some of my clients—the ones who see him socially—to speak to him on my behalf, but even their intervention failed to bring him onboard. His conservator is someone named Mary Thomas Jones. Mary is my competition. She's also rumored to be one of his girlfriends."

"I'm a little confused here, Rhys. You've been courting the man's business, even while personally despising him."

"Please don't think it's his money I'm after. Sure, an account as big as the Smallwood collection would pay a lot of bills and help raise the Guild's profile. But that's not what keeps me chasing after him. It's his *stuff*, Jack. It's what he's got. From all reports he owns examples by every major southern artist but one."

"Asmore?" I said.

"Asmore," she answered. "Don't you dare ever mention this to anyone, but I'd do the work for free just to get my hands on his paintings."

⁂

The commotion died down, and Rhys led me back to the Louisiana Room. Smallwood, now, was standing in front of the Walker, and his girlfriend was using an index finger to count something in the painting. It wasn't long before I understood that she was trying to determine the number of workers in the cotton field. Her lips moved as she ticked off each one. "How many?" Smallwood said when she seemed to finish.

"I can't tell if this one's black."

Smallwood took a step forward and bent at the waist to see. He squinted as he tried to decide. His face was inches away from the canvas and a figure standing off to the side. "Looks white to me. Well, Mexican, maybe."

"There are three dogs, one cat and four mules," the girl announced.

The number of animals didn't impress Smallwood. His focus remained on the person of indeterminable race. "You think he's the boss man who runs the plantation?"

"Maybe the artist ran out of white paint."

"Well, he painted all that cotton white."

"If you think about it," the girl said in an apparent moment of clarity, "even white people aren't really white. They're more *pink* than they are white."

"He should've painted the man pink, then," Smallwood said. "In my paintings, I like as many Negroes as I can get. I thought I made that understood already."

"You got thirty-nine in this one," the girl said.

Smallwood came back up to his full height and resumed his wide-legged pose. "Then why on the phone did Lucinda make it sound like a hundred?"

By now Smallwood and the girl had the room to themselves. He glanced back over his shoulder and let on a smile when he saw how many people were standing at the entrance watching him. Rhys and I had joined a group of perhaps forty—approximately the same number, it occurred to me, as were shown in the Walker painting.

"I like how peaceable everybody looks," Smallwood said. He meant the people in the painting. "I don't see a militant in the group—nobody trying to make it difficult. Those were the days, huh, Dusty?"

"Everyone knew their place," Dusty said.

"Damn right," said Smallwood. "Knew it and liked it."

Rhys came up on her toes and put her mouth next to my ear. "Tommy Smallwood is a racist pig," she said, intentionally speaking loud enough to be heard.

Someone behind us coughed a nervous laugh, and I figured Rhys had just destroyed any chance of ever landing Smallwood as a client. I also figured she was in for a fight. "Tommy," said Dusty, "that girl over there just called you an ugly name."

He faced the knot of observers gathered at the door, but before he could say or do anything someone pushed past us and entered the room, diverting his attention. She was a small woman, small but for her hips, which seemed to occupy the entire area between her breasts and her knees, and to do so in the shape of a butcher's block. She fearlessly positioned herself next to Smallwood in front of the Walker, and mimicked his pose by spreading her legs out as he'd spread his, fists on hips.

"Well, if it isn't Mary Lou Cohn," he said.

"Is that you, Tommy?"

"Have you met my friend Busty Dusty?" he said.

Mary Lou Cohn smiled at the woman. "Your name is Busty Dusty?"

"My stage name. My friends just call me Dusty."

"Mary Lou," said Smallwood, "we've been counting, me and Dusty. We don't get past thirty-nine. How many did you count?"

"You counted thirty-nine what?"

"Blacks in the picture. We couldn't make out if he was one."

Mary Lou Cohn was staring at Smallwood now. She waited until he looked at her before saying anything. "When it's the property of the Historic New Orleans Collection you'll have to confer with Mrs. Thibodeaux, our curator of paintings. I'm sure she'll be able to answer any questions you may have."

Smallwood laughed so hard he sprayed saliva on the surface of the painting. "You've got a lot of nerve, Mary Lou, coming at me with that."

"Yes, you're right. I do have a lot of nerve. I don't think you know how much, especially at auction when I'm bidding on an item that belongs in the Collection. Tommy," she continued, "can we come to an understanding today?"

"An understanding," he repeated.

"I'm going to make a proposal, an offer you can't refuse."

"I own ninety-two Walkers," he said. "I'll quit collecting the man when I reach a hundred. After that I'll listen to your proposals, Mary Lou. Not before. Besides, I got a place over my commode that'd be just right for this picture."

Of course Smallwood, being Smallwood, pronounced the word this way: *"pitcha."*

Mary Lou Cohn raised a knuckled finger to her nose and sneezed.

"Most of mine are little things with a single black standing at the edge of a field. Some are bigger, though, with two or three blacks and chickens and a dog and some cats. Some are your *natures mortes* with dead birds and rabbits hanging from nails. One I have shows an old boot with a baby kitten playing inside. Little children really like that one."

"Meow," said Dusty.

"But my best," said Smallwood, "has thirty-five of your blacks in it. I'm always looking to upgrade, and this painting will help me do that. If I can prove somehow that this old boy here—" Smallwood plucked the canvas with a finger—"if I can show he isn't a white or a Mexican . . . well, I would break out of my rut."

Mary Lou Cohn was still staring at Tommy Smallwood with a look mixing amusement and disbelief. "Tommy," she said, "I'm here tonight to ask you a favor. I'm here to appeal to your sense of fair play and to that altruistic spark in each of us that inspires philanthropy."

"It does what?"

"Tommy," she said, resolve still evident in her face, "as you may have heard, both the New Orleans Museum of Art and the Louisiana State Museum were interested in acquiring this painting. So was the Morris Museum of Art in Augusta, Georgia. The country's top Walker collectors—the Jewells of Baton Rouge, the Hunters of Birmingham, and the dealer Alfred West of Charleston—also expressed a desire to purchase it. Tommy, in the past we at the HNOC have backed away from items that we've coveted but that other institutions and important private collectors, for whatever legitimate reason, have appealed to us not to compete with them for. Today we're taking our turn and asking these institutions and collectors to return the favor and let us have the painting."

"Dusty, count, sugah," Smallwood said. "Ignore her and count."

"Tommy?" said Mary Lou Cohn. "Tommy, listen to me."

"Count loud, Dusty. Count *loud*."

Dusty started to count, though not loud enough to drown out what Mary Lou had to say. "Tommy, in consideration of your backing off this painting, I'm going to give you a voucher that you can redeem at any time in the future. This voucher would eliminate the HNOC from competition for one object of your choice, to be determined at your discretion, at a future sale. Anything you want, and you return this voucher and we don't bid on it. Now, Tommy, the voucher is invisible, but nevertheless I'm going to make a point in front of all these witnesses of handing it to you. I give it trusting that you will keep your end of the bargain. There is always the next great thing to buy, Tommy. Who knows? Maybe at the next auction there'll be a William Aiken Walker with a *hundred* workers in it. Have you considered that?"

Although Smallwood seemed to have stopped listening, Mary Lou Cohn took his hand and placed an invisible voucher in it. "Redeem it, Tommy, and we go away."

Smallwood lifted his hand and looked at his empty palm. Mary Lou Cohn sneezed again. Smallwood's hand slipped into a pocket and retrieved a handkerchief. "Mary Lou," he said, "I do believe you're allergic to me."

She reached for the handkerchief, but Smallwood brought it up to his own face and spat into the silky fabric. Mary Lou Cohn lurched backward. Smallwood cleared his throat and spat into the cloth a second time.

"I just got to know," he said, then began rubbing the painting's surface with the wet handkerchief. He was squinting as he lowered his face and studied the mysterious figure. Squinting as the Walker seemed to resist him and repeatedly banged against the wall. "Nah, he's a colored boy, all right," Smallwood said. "Dusty? Here, sugah. I'm giving you Mary Lou's voucher."

The girl pinched the invisible item between her thumb and forefinger and held it out in front of her. "What do I do with it?"

He waited until Mary Lou Cohn had recovered and was looking at him again. "Save it for later," he said. "You can clean me with it when we're done."

FIVE

Two days later we were back in the auction house, sitting on metal folding chairs and following the action in the house-copy catalogs we'd pilfered at the preview. We sat so close together that our thighs touched and our forearms rubbed together, and I had to focus on the auctioneer lest my growing feelings for Rhys wipe out the purpose of our being there. I tried to recall if I'd felt such an attraction for the last girlfriend, or for any of them, but with Rhys so close by all memory eluded me.

To keep focus, I wrote down the hammer price of each item as it was sold. Buyers who looked as though they couldn't afford the three-wing special at Popeyes casually dropped thousands on silver tea-spoons. They moved this money simply by blinking their eyelids. Lots came and went so quickly I had a hard time keeping up, and whenever I failed to record a sale Rhys brought her mouth to within an inch of my ear and whispered the figure. After a while I began to lapse at my job for the chance to hear her voice speak a number.

It was around one o'clock when contents from the Louisiana Room came up for sale, and the intensity of the action immediately picked up. Porters trotted out the offerings and held them under spotlights that made the paintings burn with color. Now applause could be heard when the hammer came down, and winning bidders pumped their fists and hugged spouses and friends. I wondered why buying a painting inspired such passion when bidders who were buying furniture reacted with hardly more than a yawn. But then I flashed to something Rhys had said when I first met her: art collectors were hunters, enslaved by desire that swelled their appetites and engorged their private parts. At the time it had seemed an incredible claim, but now I knew it was true. Short of scouting around and checking crotches, I did notice that many of the bidders looked as though the competition was taking a physical toll on them. They wrung their hands together, chewed their lips, beat their shoes against the floor and squirmed in their chairs. Nerves had some gorging on the jambalaya, poboys and muffulettas for sale in the rear of the gallery, and others chain-smoking cigarettes outside.

As the sale of the Walker approached, the place grew more crowded. Except for a reserved section in front, the seats filled up and suddenly it was standing room only. People were three deep lining the back wall, and past the gray glass I could see dozens more loitering outside. The painting was exactly ten lots away when a wave of excited whispers swept the gallery and Tommy Smallwood came striding up the middle aisle. The girl from the preview followed close behind him. In recognition the auctioneer nodded and gestured with his gavel.

As Smallwood neared the front of the room, a woman in a yellow dress came up from her chair and stepped out into the aisle. Her black hair hung down to her shoulders in a dense, brittle sheet, and she wore a mustache almost as heavy as a man's. She planted noisy kisses on both sides of Smallwood's face, then proceeded to trip and fall as she started on her way back to her chair.

Rhys put her mouth against my ear. "Hairy Mary," she whispered.

I shrugged.

"Mary Thomas Jones, Smallwood's conservator."

The auctioneer's hammer cracked against wood. "Lot number three hundred eighteen is the monumental William Aiken Walker cotton kingdom painting in the hand-carved, hardwood exhibition frame. Ladies, do we have the phones ready? Everybody ready on the phones?"

Seconds later the bidding had already eclipsed the painting's estimated value. Mary Lou Cohn, sitting in the row ahead of us, put up a spirited battle but dropped out when the money shot past $160,000. She lowered first her paddle, then her head. Up to this point she and Smallwood had been the only bidders, but now three others, all on telephones, entered the fray. A gaggle of young women seated at a table near the auctioneer's lectern communicated with the phone bidders, and served as conduits to the action, their voices crying out "Bid!" and pushing the money upward. For his part, Smallwood simply sat with his paddle raised. He showed no expression except perhaps of boredom. The girl, whose perfume I could smell from thirty feet away, sat studying her fingernails. The bidding climbed in increments of $10,000. At $200,000 one of the bidders dropped out, leaving the contest to Smallwood and two others. At $230,000 a second was gone, and now it was between Smallwood and one other. The shout of "Bid!" was slower in coming, as the buyer on the phone seemed to deliberate each step upward. The auctioneer tried to coax the competition to continue the fight, saying things like "You'll rue the day" and "A once-in-a-lifetime opportunity shall surely be lost," but finally, at $280,000, the gavel came down and Tommy Smallwood the victor stood to wild applause. He bowed and waved and shook hands as he made for the exit, the girl following.

"Have you done the math?" Rhys whispered to me.

I shook my head.

"With the nine percent sales tax and ten percent commission for a hammer price over fifty grand, he just paid more than three hundred and thirty-three thousand dollars. That's double the previous auction record for the artist. If my numbers are right, he's paying about eight thousand three hundred dollars per field hand. Just think, Jack, real slaves didn't cost that much." She gathered up her personal items and nodded toward the door. "Come on. Let's get the hell out of here."

We stepped outside as Smallwood came roaring down Magazine Street in a Jaguar convertible with the top down. He was wearing a touring cap and mirrored sunglasses, and a long blue scarf—the same blue as the car—trailed in the cool air behind him. The girl sat next to him, her face tilted upward to catch the afternoon light. "I hope you crash and die," Rhys shouted after them. She caught the look on my face and said, "He'll get *Beloved Dorothy,* too, Jack. It makes me sick. He gets everything." She raised a fist and waved it at him. "You get everything, you bastard!"

"Come on, now. He can't get everything."

"He gets everything he *wants.* That makes it even harder to take."

After a long walk uptown we stopped in at Casamento's Restaurant, an old seafood eatery near the corner of Napoleon Avenue. We sat at a booth in the front room and ordered beer and oysters on the half shell. Rhys was still talking about the auction and the sale of the Walker. "Because Mary Lou had promises from local museums and collectors not to chase the painting, the phone bidders likely would've been from out of state. Attend enough auctions and you learn who's on the phone just by how they play the game. That last bidder *felt* like Alfred West, the dealer from Charleston. The way he hesitated before each bid? That's typically his MO. You think he's struggling to keep up with the action—that he doesn't have the money—and that's what he wants you to think. You think he won't answer and then he does, often at the last second when the auctioneer's about to drop the hammer. It demoralizes the competition, except of course when the competition is Tommy Smallwood."

"Alfred West plays possum, does he?"

"Possum is a pretty good way to describe it. Other buyers bid quickly because they want the competition to think they're prepared to answer at any price. That's the most common strategy. But the truth is, most bidders have a set amount in mind and don't go over it. Anybody can get carried away and pay more than they intended to, but for big-ticket items most of the bidders are pros who rarely make mistakes. In the case of Alfred West, he went as high as he could on the Walker, knowing that to go higher was foolish because it meant eliminating the likelihood of making a profit on the painting for a very long time. West is in business. Tommy Smallwood is in love."

"Love makes him stupid."

"Yes, exactly. In Smallwood's mind, paying too much is not nearly as painful as losing a painting because he offered to pay too little."

Our order came and Rhys prepared dipping sauce in a couple of soufflé cups, mixing ketchup, horseradish, lemon juice and Tabasco. I poured the beer into glasses, the frosty heads rising up and tipping over the rims. We ate for a while without saying anything, then Rhys pushed her plate to the side and leaned back in her seat. "There's something I need to talk to you about," she said.

"Okay."

"It's personal. It's not about paintings or auctions or anything like that. It's about me, Jack."

"Okay," I said again.

"My mother's mother . . . my maternal grandmother?"

"Yeah, what about her, Rhys?"

"Jack?"

"Go ahead. What is it?"

"Well, she was African American."

"Your grandmother was African American?"

"Right. She was black."

"That means you're black, too."

"Right. I'm black."

"You're black? Get out of here."

I looked at her, appraising her every feature, including, this time, the color of her skin. It was crazy. The woman was fairer than I was.

Put our forearms side by side and mine was darker than hers. It had to be a joke, and an unfunny one at that. Blame the beer, I thought. Blame the auction. Blame Tommy Smallwood. There was no way. "Sorry, Rhys," I said, "but you're white."

"I'm black, Jack." She was staring at me now with an intensity that made me uncomfortable. It was as though she was looking for evidence of rejection or disapproval on my part. "Want to see my birth certificate?"

"You carry around your birth certificate?"

"No, but I could get it, if you need proof. You don't believe me, do you?"

"No, I don't. How can you be black, Rhys? I mean, look at you. It's ridiculous."

"My grandmother was a little darker than I am, but she wasn't really black, either. And yet she was still black, if you know what I mean. She was a person of color. Or what some would've identified as an octoroon, which by definition means one-eighth black. The truth is, she had even less black blood than that. I think if you broke it down she was like one-sixteenth black, and even at that percentage she didn't look it. When she was seventeen years old she gave birth to my mother. The father, as I always understood it, was white. And they weren't married. Laws in Louisiana at the time forbid interracial marriage. Follow me so far?"

"Yeah, I follow you."

"My grandmother lived her life as a black woman, and without the requisite identity crisis that often tormented people who looked like she did. She wasn't one of these *passe-blancs* you hear about who move away and integrate into society as whites. She was a strong person—a strong *black* person. And she raised an equally strong person in my mother."

"Is your father white or black?"

"He's neither and he's both. He's what my mother is and he's what I am."

"In other words, he's a black guy with blond hair and green eyes."

"They're hazel," she said.

"Hazel eyes."

"They still live here, in Tremé, if you're interested in seeing them for yourself. Robert and Beverly Goudeau. Big French Colonial that's been in my dad's family for something like two hundred years."

"Rhys, I'm not sure what to tell you. A part of me still doesn't believe you."

"A part of you? What part would that be? Obviously not your head."

"You're black?"

"I'm black."

"I could give a shit what race you are. What if I put it to you that way?"

"You would make a mistake not to care about race," she said. "There is no bigger issue in my life."

"There are far bigger issues in mine."

"That's because you're white," she said. She let a minute pass for the words to penetrate. "Jack, did you notice how many African Americans there were in the auction house today? Every one of the porters was black. Every one of them. But count me out and there wasn't a black person in the gallery."

"I didn't notice. I wasn't thinking about what color everybody was. I was more concerned with how much money they were spending. Besides, maybe there were blacks in the crowd like you, Rhys. White people who are actually black but don't look it."

She took a sip of beer and the head left suds on her upper lip. "My grandmother died when I was eight years old, but my memory of her is vivid. She was a pretty lady, always wore gloves and a hat, flowery dresses, all this colorful Bakelite jewelry. She definitely had a style about her. She'd come over sometimes and sit in the kitchen with my mother and drink iced tea. She always brought me a present—a box of crayons or a picture book, something to encourage 'creative expression,' as she called it. One day I overheard her tell my mother that I took after my grandfather. My mother hadn't known him either. She said, 'Does she look like him?' And my grandmother answered, 'No,

Beverly, she looks like *me*. But she's sensitive and she has talent, like
he did.' That was as much as she ever said about him, that he was sensitive and had talent. Well, what kind of talent did this sensitive man
have, Grandmother? Was he a surgeon who could repair broken
bones? An accountant who could balance somebody's books? I never
knew his name, and neither did my mother."

"That doesn't seem fair."

"Yes, I guess it doesn't. But it was never a huge factor in my life
because it's just how things were. My grandmother felt compelled to
protect his identity for some reason. And because of that I knew she
loved him. I used to ask my mother about him and she would say, 'Sure,
it might've been good knowing who he was. But it might've been bad,
too.' Then she'd say, 'Rhys, darling, you have to know for certain that
you're ready to accept the bad if you intend to go chasing after the
good.'"

"Maybe when your grandmother said you had talent like he did it
was her way of saying he was an artist."

She smiled and took another sip of beer, capping it off with a sigh.
"Interesting you would say that, Jack. Because sometimes when a New
Orleans painting comes into the studio by an artist from the time
when my grandfather would've been a young man I wonder if it came
from his hand. I want to assign it to him, especially when the painting's beautiful."

"What was your grandmother's name?"

"Jacqueline. Jacqueline LeBeau."

"Beloved Jacqueline," I said with a laugh.

"Find that one and I'd kill to get it. Tommy Smallwood would
never make it to the auction preview. I'd have snipers on the rooftops,
ready to pop him as soon as he came cruising along."

We paid the bill and started walking back toward the auction
house, pausing along the way to look in the windows of antique stores,
junk shops and art galleries. We stopped at one and I waited until
Rhys turned away from the window. "You ever go out with a white
guy?" I said.

"I'm not sure I should answer that, Jack. It'll only lead to something else, to the next question."

"To the one where I ask you out, you mean?"

She moved back from the window. "Now let me ask you a question: Have you ever gone out with a black woman?"

"No, I haven't."

"Why not?"

"I don't know why not. Maybe I never really knew any."

"You never knew *any*?"

"Not really. Not like I've come to know you. I went to Jesuit, an all-boys high school, and the girls I knew at Tulane were all white. I was in a fraternity and so they were mostly sorority types. I just never had the occasion to get to know any black girls. They didn't seem interested, anyway."

"Maybe they didn't seem interested because you didn't seem interested."

"I don't know what to tell you, Rhys. I wasn't making a judgment about their desirability. My path just never crossed with theirs."

We moved on again, silent but for an occasional groan from Rhys when she spotted something she liked in a window. We were a block away from the auction house when I said, "I'm going to ask you, anyway. Rhys, would you go out with me? I don't mean beer and oysters some afternoon after an auction. I mean a real date where I show up at your place with a bouquet of flowers and we have a nice, candlelit dinner in the French Quarter, then go for a walk by the river holding hands. One of those dates two people go on when they're interested in each other. Where I kiss you good-night at the door when it's over and then ask you out for a second date. Where you say yes."

She opened the door to the van and got in and lowered the window. "I like you, Jack. I like you a lot. But I have to be honest with you even at the risk of hurting your feelings. I will not date you."

She started the engine and shifted to Drive, and when she looked at me again, and began to mutter her good-bye, I leaned my head in the window and brought my mouth against hers. She didn't resist, but neither did she respond as I would've liked. Her lips were cool and soft against mine, but so, I supposed, would most anyone's have been. When I pulled away her eyes were still closed, her mouth slightly parted. "Go out with me, Rhys."

She shook her head. "No, Jack."

I stuck my head back inside and kissed her again, and this time it was for real. I started to pull away but she brought her hands up to my face and led me back close. It had been weeks since I kissed a woman, and now I realized I'd been only half alive in all that time. She was as hungry for me as I was for her. But then I put my left hand on her waist and she grabbed my wrist and pushed me away. "You need to go," she said.

"Why?"

"You just do, Jack."

"I don't understand you," I said.

"There's nothing to understand."

"Sure there is. I wish I knew what it is you want, Rhys."

She raised the window about halfway, to make sure I was kept out, and I could feel the van nudge forward. Now she was talking through the glass, but traffic passing by made it difficult to hear. I watched her lips move.

At first I thought she was saying, "Somebody likes me," which, though not exactly a promise of great things to come, still offered reason for optimism. But then it occurred to me that she might've said, "Somebody like me." And I thought, *Somebody like you? Somebody like you, Rhys? Somebody black like you?* And I felt utterly hopeless.

I could do many things to improve myself to live up to her expectations, but changing who I was wasn't one of them.

⁂

Every night when I went to bed in my damp apartment I thought about the ghosts Patrick Marion had mentioned on the day I first met him. I listened for footsteps on the floor, but if I heard anything it was the imagined sound of Formosan termites eating out the studs in the walls around me.

I removed what remained of my father's art collection from the trunk of my car and hung the canvases on the walls of my bedroom. None was a Drysdale, and none had a recognizable signature. But they were nice enough, if you liked the swamp.

After living for years on noisy Esplanade Avenue, I relished the quiet of my new home. And I quickly established a routine. I would sleep until midmorning, then walk up to a coffee shop for a café mocha, a bran muffin and the paper. That was breakfast. Next I went for a long jog along the bayou. For lunch I visited a restaurant in the area or grabbed a sandwich at the Whole Foods deli. Occasionally friends from my former life joined me, but I stopped seeing them when none seemed able to complete a meal without quizzing me about my plans for the future. Did I intend to go back to work at the paper soon? Was I dating anyone? What did I do with all my time now that I had no obligations and nothing to do? I rarely walked home afterward without feeling like the world's biggest slacker, which was exactly how they wanted me to feel, and perhaps how I was.

In the afternoon I napped on the bench in the shade of the garden oak, oftentimes with a book open on my chest. I still liked an occasional murder mystery, but most of my reading these days went to southern art and the monographs, pamphlets, auction catalogs and books on the subject that I'd inherited from my father.

I was particularly drawn to the coffee table tomes published by museums and individuals to promote their collections. In these Levette Asmore was often featured. The books tended to follow the same format: on the left page a brief biography of the artist and description of his work, on the right a color plate showing the painting in the collection. One publication, brought out in 1958, featured portraits from the Louisiana State Museum and showed an Asmore painting whose composition was strikingly similar to the one Patrick Marion owned. A young woman—*Beloved Christine*, she was called—stood before a fiery Louisiana river landscape, looking as if she'd just been ravaged. "Asmore, you horny dog," I said when I encountered the image.

The bulk of the artist's bio added little to what I already knew about Asmore, but then came the last line:

> No artist ever to paint in the American South produced a more compelling story than Levette Asmore (1918–1941), an orphan raised by Catholic priests whose life was marked with tragedy from beginning to end. Asmore moved to New Orleans after his parents died in the Great Flood of 1927. A decade later, his teachers were calling him the most innovative and exciting artist then at work in the Vieux Carré. Asmore's sexually frank portraits of young women have drawn comparisons to the provocative nudes of his idol, Amedeo Modigliani. Asmore's apparent suicide ended a brief but brilliant career rife with controversy.
>
> Wiltz Lowenstein donated the portrait in the museum collection.

"Wiltz Lowenstein," I said out loud. "Wiltz Lowenstein? How do I know . . . ?" When the name finally registered, I nearly fell off the bench. *Lowenstein?* The painting's donor was named *Lowenstein?* I scrambled to the apartment to try to figure out what to do next. "Lowenstein," I kept saying.

My rent check went to High Life Realty, Patrick Marion's company. I'd never thought to inquire about my landlord's first name.

In minutes I was standing at the front door of the main house, beating a fist against the whitewashed cypress that formed the frame. A woman appeared past the screen, the rubber soles of her shoes squeaking as she approached on the high-polished parquet. "Hi, hate to disturb you, ma'am. My name is Jack Charbonnet. I rent the apartment in back and I was wondering if I could speak to Mr. Lowenstein, please?"

She sniffed and brought her eyes together in a tight squint, then shook her head as if I'd asked the impossible. "Mr. Lowenstein expressly asks not to be disturbed today. I'm sorry, Jack. If there's a message I'd be more than happy to deliver it."

"Are you his sitter?" I asked.

She was wearing pale blue house pants and an oversized T-shirt advertising the Cat's Meow, a Bourbon Street karaoke club. Even though I stood about six inches taller than she did, she outweighed me by no less than fifty pounds. "I'm his nurse," she said.

"Ma'am, would you by chance know Mr. Lowenstein's first name?"

"Charles."

"It isn't Wiltz?"

"It's Charles. Charles Howard Lowenstein."

"Will you ask him if he's related to Wiltz Lowenstein?"

"Wiltz Lowenstein," she repeated, then shuffled up closer, staring at me through the screen. She sniffed again. "Wait here, please."

After she left, I pressed my face up close to the screen and looked in the house. It had a large center hall holding an antique buffet. On both sides the walls were crowded with paintings, the space so thick with them that frames touched and in some instances overlapped. There were several dozen Drysdales, large and small, as well as five or six French Quarter courtyard scenes by Alberta Kinsey.

The nurse came striding toward me. I gave a grateful smile as she approached, figuring an invitation was sure to be offered, but instead she checked the latch on the screen door. "Jack, I'm sorry but Mr. Lowenstein says he isn't related to a Wiltz Lowenstein. Is there anything else?"

I heard a clattering from behind her in the hall, and the metal wheel of a wheelchair poked out in the darkened doorway before creaking back out of view. The woman glanced over her shoulder.

"Did you ask Mr. Lowenstein if he knows anyone named Wiltz Lowenstein?"

"No, I did what you said and asked him if he and Wiltz Lowenstein were related. He said they weren't. Jack, please, Mr. Lowenstein isn't feeling well today. Why don't you come back some other time when he's doing better?" And with that she took a step back and closed the double French doors in my face.

In the White Pages for Greater New Orleans there were three listings for Lowenstein. I immediately ruled out the first of them because it belonged to a suburban funeral home. A second listed Charles H. of Moss Street, and the other was Lawrence David, whose address wasn't listed. I dialed the number for Lawrence David, using a French Quarter prefix, and asked for Mr. Lowenstein. "Speaking," said the person who answered.

"Sir, are you by chance related to someone named Wiltz Lowenstein?"

"No, I'm not. Who the hell is Wiltz Lowenstein?"

"What about Charles Howard Lowenstein?"

"He's my late father's uncle, my great-uncle. Who is this?"

I told him who I was and why I was calling, then added, "I found your name in the phone book. I hope I'm not disturbing you."

"Not at all, Charbonnet. Uncle Charlie has kept a low profile for years, and so we don't talk much. But I can't recall his ever mentioning a Wiltz. Have you asked Uncle Charlie about this man?"

"The nurse who sits with him spoke to Mr. Lowenstein on my behalf. He told her they weren't related."

"Well, he would know. When he lived here in the Quarter he ran with that bohemian crowd—the writers and the artists and the gals with hairy armpits. Tell me, Charbonnet, how is Uncle Charlie? Treating you well, I hope?"

"I'm enjoying the apartment. But to be honest I haven't met your uncle yet. He doesn't seem to want to leave the house."

"He can be a real pain in the ass, that's for sure. I could blame the arthritis—you'll notice it's crippled him, disfiguring his feet and hands—but the truth is I never knew him to be very friendly, and he resigned from what you might call life long before he was ever diagnosed with the disease. Come to think of it, he resigned before I was even born. If he gives you any crap, don't hesitate to call again, you hear?"

"I'll call again if there's a problem."

"Well, all the best in your hunt for Wiltz Lowenstein."

Next I called Rhys Goudeau at the Guild's studio. I didn't mention our kiss the other day on Magazine Street, or any of what we'd talked about. Instead I told her about the odd coincidence connecting the name of my landlord to an Asmore portrait, a subject that I was sure would excite her. "They've got to be the same guy," I said.

"If you have any time today," she said, "you should go by the Williams Research Center and see if they have an artist file for Wiltz Lowenstein. Maybe something will turn up. You might also visit the State Museum—the place you want is the Old U.S. Mint at the foot of Esplanade—and find out if they have *Beloved Christine* on display. While you're there ask for Dr. Gilbert Perret, the curator. I've done some work for him and we have a good relationship. He's a decent-enough fellow and he's certain to have information about the painting's provenance. Hey, look, Jack," and now she paused, long enough to catch her breath, "are we still on tomorrow for your haircut?"

"Oh, right. My haircut."

"Meet me here at the studio at four o'clock. There's something I want to show you, something you need to see."

"This wouldn't have anything to do with your boy Levette, would it?" I said.

"Four o'clock," she said, and before I could respond, she put the phone down.

❊

Sorry, said the elderly docent, but I would need to schedule an appointment with the curator to view the Asmore portrait, and unfortunately Dr. Perret was traveling in Europe and wouldn't be returning for two more weeks. Could I come back at a later date? Or perhaps call and arrange a meeting?

"Yes, ma'am," I answered. "I'll do that. Thank you."

"It's a beautiful painting," she said. "It's in Gilbert's office. I know you'll be thrilled to see it. It gives me goose bumps every time I go in there. You know what else it does? It makes me smile. It really does. It makes me smile."

She was probably eighty years old but her voice sounded younger,

almost like a girl's. "Do we know each other?" I said. "You look familiar to me."

"I don't think we've met," she said. "I only know a few people under the age of fifty and we're all related. Isn't that terrible? Shows you
how old I am."

"Any way you could show me the painting now, ma'am? I won't
touch it or anything. All I want is to have a look."

"Funny," she said, "another gentleman asked me the same thing
only about an hour ago." She laughed and shook her head. "It's not
possible. Gilbert keeps his door locked."

Another man was there? I wondered about this person, this other
seeker of secrets, this *fool*, as I walked up to Chartres Street and the
Williams Research Center. Was he like me, someone with way too
much time on his hands? Or did Rhys Goudeau and I have competition in our pursuit of Asmore?

I checked in at the desk, climbed to the reading room on the second floor, and requested the files for Wiltz Lowenstein and Levette
Asmore. The librarian returned with only the one for Asmore. "I'm
sorry, but we don't have anything for a Wiltz Lowenstein," she said.
"Are you sure you have the spelling right?"

"Pretty sure," I said, then wrote out the name on a slip of paper.

She shook her head. "Nothing on that one."

I sat at the table near the big windows in front and spread out the
clippings and photographs. Although I carefully read over every news
account in the file, I could find no reference to Wiltz Lowenstein. A
housemate of Asmore's, who himself was identified as a former student at the New Orleans Art School, was mentioned in a couple of
stories, but in none did his name appear. I studied the Laughlin photograph of the Saint Philip Street cottage the two men had shared,
imagining the collection of paintings that must've once resided past
the old doors and shuttered windows, and also imagining the life that
Asmore and his housemate must've lived there. Before World War II
rich young Americans from the East Coast journeyed to Paris for adventure in neighborhoods like the Latin Quarter, Montparnasse and

Montmartre. But in the Deep South, where people had less money and fewer privileges, the young had sought their freedom in the bohemian district of old New Orleans. I quickly grew frustrated by my search for information about Wiltz Lowenstein. Had such a person really existed? In none of the photos was Asmore shown with a young man who might've qualified as a housemate. In fact, from the pictures one easily could have concluded that Asmore was a loner suffering from a social phobia. There were fewer than ten photographs, and in each of them he was the only figure in the frame. But then I recalled that there had been another, a small snapshot showing him painting on the street with Alberta Kinsey. I searched the file, turning over every page and scrap of paper, but the photo was nowhere to be found.

"May I have your file on Alberta Kinsey?" I said to the librarian, as I filled out yet another request form. Perhaps, it had come to me, a duplicate of the photo was included in the information on Kinsey.

Minutes later the librarian returned with an accordion file twice the size of the one for Asmore. I returned to my desk and sorted out the material, first examining the photos, none of which was the one showing her with Asmore, and then reading the newspaper and magazine profiles about the artist and reviews of her exhibitions.

In a story published a year before her death in 1952, Kinsey had broken a long silence and spoken on the record about Asmore. "It's very painful to talk about Levette," she was quoted as saying. "I loved him so and I was hurt by his passing—I tell you, I'm still not recovered, ten years later. Levette told me once that he felt as though he was born in the wrong time, and although I argued with him then I believe it to be true now. Most of us dream about going back in time to when things were simpler. Levette dreamed of leaping forward. He thought the world would accept him there—not only his work but the kind of man he was."

I returned the file to the librarian and asked her to make copies of some of the stories. "They're twenty cents for each sheet of copy paper," she said. "This is at least ten dollars here."

"I'll pay it."

"Fine, but I'll need a few minutes."

She collected the material and left the reading room, disappearing past a door leading into a hallway. There was a window shaped like a diamond in the door and I watched her walk to the end of the hall and turn the corner. I looked back at the reading room. Only two people were there today, both of them seated at tables on the other end.

The librarian's station was neat and orderly, and squarely centered on the surface of her writing desk were a pair of index cards listing visitors who'd checked out the Kinsey and Asmore files. I glanced over at the door for another look at the hallway past the glass. Finding no one in sight, I stepped around the desk and read the short roster of names and dates chronicling when the material was checked out and returned. My name, penciled in like all the others, was the last on the card. And just ahead of mine was Rhys Goudeau's, her most recent visit being the day before.

"Rhys, you thief," I mumbled under my breath.

As I was walking back to the other side of the desk a name on one of the cards suddenly came clear in my consciousness. It hadn't registered when I first looked, but it popped up now, as if to announce itself. One day last week, at ten o'clock in the morning, Tommy Smallwood had checked out the Asmore file.

"All done," the librarian said, cradling twice as many papers as she'd left with.

"Oh, wonderful," I replied.

❋

Next day at the studio of the Crescent City Conservation Guild, Joe Butler escorted me up the stairs to Rhys's office. He was no friendlier than the first time I met him, but no ruder either. I tried to beguile him with small talk but he would have none of it. He didn't even respond to my enthusiastic characterization of the day's weather. "Beautiful, isn't it?" I said, pressing him for the smallest utterance.

"Yeah, it's all right."

"I don't think it can get any prettier."

"That may be true."

I'd arrived half an hour early, intent on confronting Rhys about the missing photograph before we went for my haircut. But as usual she was way ahead of me. Joe shoved her office door open and poked his head inside. "Boss, it's Mr. Charbonnet."

The overhead lights were off, the windows shuttered against the daylight. In the middle of the room Rhys was sitting on a swivel desk chair with all four casters missing, looking up at a large screen holding the image of Kinsey and Asmore painting on a French Quarter street. On a table next to her stood a projector of some kind, throwing light that replicated the photograph. "Come grab a chair, Jack." She gave the one next to her a kick.

I studied the picture on the wall.

"What do you think?" she said.

"What do I think? I think you've lost your mind. That's what I think."

"What are you talking about?"

"You could've examined it under a loupe or a magnifying glass, Rhys. You didn't have to walk out with the thing."

"What thing?" she said. "And walk out of where?"

"Cut it out. You stole that picture."

"Stole it?" She looked back up at the image. "I did nothing of the kind. I had one of the librarians make me a photocopy. That's why it's so blurry. You think I'd steal from the HNOC? You're full of shit, Jack. They're good to me and they're one of my best clients. I'd never do that."

I took a seat and told her about my visit to the Williams Research Center and the purloined photograph and seeing Smallwood's name on the library card. "You think Smallwood stole it?" I said.

"You're making a leap in assuming it's been stolen," she answered. "Someone in the building, a staff member, might've been using it for research or some other purpose. Did you notice anything else missing from the files?"

"No, just the photograph."

"I'd worry more if you'd been unable to find the old clippings about Levette's mural. Did you notice if they were still there, by chance?"

I shook my head. "Didn't notice. But I wasn't looking for them. What is that thing, Rhys?" I pointed to the contraption on the table.

"Oh, it's called an episcope. Basically what it does is let you project a positive image, like a photograph, without having to first reproduce it as a slide or a transparency. Ever see a movie called *The Moderns*? It's about a struggling artist in Paris in the twenties who forges paintings— he makes fakes—and he does it with the aid of an episcope, just like this one. There's a scene in which he copies a painting by Cézanne by projecting the image onto a canvas tacked to the wall. Even today a lot of portrait painters use episcopes. Photorealists, too."

"You're not worried about Smallwood, Rhys?"

"No."

"Then I won't be either. But why aren't we worried?"

"Simple," she answered. "The mural's been there for somebody to pirate for sixty years. The odds that Smallwood would discover it now, at the same time we found it, are pretty remote. I think I know why he wanted to see Levette's file."

"Tell me."

"An Asmore is the one painting that's eluded him since he started collecting. He's been desperate to own one. From what I hear, he's contacted owners of Asmores and offered obscene amounts of money for their paintings. They've all refused him. He's also appealed to public and private institutions, in every case pleading with them to deaccession their Asmores. In consideration he's promised huge donations in the upper-six-figure range. None went for it. Although it still hasn't been consigned to an auction house yet, Patrick Marion has been talking around town about *Beloved Dorothy*. As you know, Patrick likes to entertain and when he entertains his tongue gets slippery— and not only about his Chambers stove, apparently. It's even come back to me," she continued. "Just yesterday a friend of mine who works at New Orleans Auction called and asked if I'd heard about a *Beloved* portrait that might be up for sale. I confirmed that I'd heard the report. She then asked if I'd had the occasion to see the painting, and my answer was the one I always give when presented with a question that might compromise an existing relationship I have with a client. I said, 'No comment.' Which in this business is the equivalent of saying, 'Yes. I not only saw the painting, I placed it flat on the floor and made wild, passionate love on top of it.' "

It was a good answer, but I still wasn't mollified. "Why would someone at New Orleans Auction be looking for the Asmore?"

"That's easy. The auction company that lands *Beloved Dorothy* stands to make an easy hundred grand in commissions if the painting performs as expected. The company also receives more valuable publicity and positive word of mouth than you could possibly calculate."

"So if your friend knows about the painting, then it's likely Smallwood does too?"

"A player that big? Come on, Jack. Smallwood probably was one of the first to hear about it. And that's why he went to the research center and checked out Levette's file. He's fired up, he thinks he's finally going to land an Asmore, and he's casting about looking for information. My bet is that he's already called Patrick and asked for a private viewing. It would be in Smallwood's best interest to buy it privately, without the involvement of an auction house. If it goes for sale at auction, there is always the chance he could lose it."

"Not from how you've described him. And not from what I saw when he went after the Walker."

"Shit happens, Jack. What can I tell you? Maybe some guy with twice Smallwood's personal wealth suddenly decides he's going to build a collection of southern art and he determines to start with an Asmore. Or maybe a *Fortune* 500 company wants the painting for its corporate collection, for the spot in the boardroom that heretofore was just a blank rectangle of shiny mahogany. In that event, Smallwood could come up short." She leaned forward and planted her elbows on her knees. Her eyes went to the image being projected on the wall. "Old Levette was a good-looking sonofabitch, wasn't he? No wonder all the girls were wild for him. But we've already established that, haven't we, Jack?"

"We both know you don't have that picture projected up there to look at Levette Asmore again, Rhys."

"Don't I?"

I shook my head. "You wanted a better look at the girl."

"At Miss Bertie?"

"No. The girl standing behind Levette."

She gave me a look that seemed to indicate she was pleased with me for making such an astute observation. She removed the photograph from under the episcope and replaced it with another, this one a black-and-white studio shot of a young woman who, but for her skin tone, hairstyle and manner of dress, could've been Rhys's twin. The resemblance was beyond uncanny—it was startling to the point of being spooky. "My grandmother," she said. "Jacqueline LeBeau, age seventeen. Kinda pretty, wasn't she?"

"More than that," I said. "God, Rhys, she's beautiful."

"That she was." She returned to the first picture showing Asmore and Kinsey, then she walked up close to the screen and lifted a hand and pointed to the woman's necklace. "See that, Jack? See this piece of jewelry?"

"I see it."

"It's a Spratling necklace, made with silver, rosewood and tortoiseshell. Spratling is William Spratling, the former housemate and friend of William Faulkner who left New Orleans in 1929 and moved to a place in Mexico called Taxco. He started out as an artist, architect and writer, but he had so much to give to the world he couldn't be satisfied with simply three important careers, so he launched a fourth, that being silversmith. Because of the city's former connection to the man, Spratling jewelry in the thirties was all the rage in New Orleans. Even during the Depression here, when most people couldn't afford such luxuries, they were buying Spratling." She took a step back and made sure I was looking at the necklace. "It was especially popular among the bohemian crowd of the French Quarter. Most of them couldn't buy diamonds and gold, but they somehow could scratch enough money together to buy Spratling. Now remove that picture and let's 'scope the other one. There's something else you need to see."

I did as I was told and the second image came up. Partially standing in the bolt of projected light, Rhys raised an arm and pointed again, now at what looked like the same necklace in the portrait of Jacqueline LeBeau. "The other one again if you would. Go back to the first picture." I put in the first picture and she pointed out the jewelry again. "Now the second one, Jack. Last time, I promise."

The necklace appeared to be the same in both images.

"This particular Spratling piece is very rare, mainly because it was heavy and uncomfortable to wear and, as a result, it didn't sell well. See how bulky it is? Imagine lugging that thing around on your neck. What materials appear to make up the necklace my grandmother is wearing in this picture, Jack?"

"I can't answer that for sure."

"Oh, yes, you can. Would you say it's the same Spratling piece the woman in the other picture is wearing?"

"How would I know that?"

"*How?* Jesus, Jack, from the pictures . . ."

I didn't want to give her the satisfaction of being right. I knew where this was headed and I was beginning to feel nervous and uncomfortable. I said nothing until she walked away from the screen and sat back down in her chair. "Rhys, you've proven that your grandmother owned a Spratling necklace and that the woman in the second picture also owned a Spratling necklace. That's all you've proven."

"No, Jack, I think I proved more than that. If it's the same necklace, then those two women are the same person. And if they're the same person—"

"For God's sake, don't say it, Rhys. Don't you dare say it." She was laughing when I brought both hands up in front of me as if to stop her. "Let me ask you this," I said. "How do you even know the woman in the snapshot has a relationship with either Levette Asmore or Alberta Kinsey? She could be somebody walking down the street whose curiosity brought her to watch a couple of artists at work. I know when I see an artist out painting I usually go and have a look at what he's up to."

She leaned back in the chair, creating a loud squeak. The portrait of her grandmother was being projected on the screen now. "She never finished high school, Jack, never graduated, but she was in line to be valedictorian, tops in her class. At this time, when this picture was made, Howard University in Washington, D.C., has offered her a scholarship, but then in the summer of 1941, not long before the start of her senior year in high school, she becomes pregnant with my mother. In September of the same year, Asmore dies in a fall from the Huey P. Quite a coincidence, isn't it?"

"A *fall*? I thought he jumped."

"Is it a coincidence or isn't it?"

"Rhys, Jacqueline LeBeau and Levette Asmore were people from different worlds living in the same city at the same time. Jacqueline's world was populated with black people, Levette's with white people. I might add there were half a million other people living in New Orleans in the summer and fall of 1941. I can't calculate the odds of their knowing each other, let alone their paths even crossing."

"Why do you think she turned her head away, Jack? Was she trying to hide her face? Did she want to obscure her identity?"

"Maybe she was starting to leave. She knew whoever was taking the picture was shooting the artists and she didn't want to intrude on the shot."

"That isn't it," she said. "She turned her head away because she was a young black woman in love with a white man in the Deep South at a time when people died for a love like that." Rhys's eyes shone bright with tears against the light from the episcope. "Levette Asmore was my grandfather."

"Oh, God, she said it," and I hopped to my feet. "I'm turning on the lights."

"Sit your ass back down, Jack."

"Rhys?"

"There's something else, another detail, you've failed to pick up on. Look closely, now, Jack. Come on. *Look*. Really look."

It took a while but she patiently went from one image to the other until I came up with it. I still wasn't ready to make the concession.

"The portrait of my grandmother is signed," Rhys said. "There's a signature in the lower-right corner. Have a look. What's the name you see there?"

"Whitesell," I answered.

"Whitesell," she repeated, talking to me now as though I were a child. "And why is that name significant to us today, Jack?"

"Whitesell was the studio photographer who also shot the portrait of Levette Asmore that's in the artist file at the Williams Research Center."

Rhys put another photograph under the episcope and suddenly the aforementioned picture of Asmore filled the screen, the photographer's signature identical to the one on the portrait of her grandmother.

"Big deal," I said. "They went to the same photographer to have their portraits made. So, probably, did scores of others. Yet another coincidence."

"You're an idiot," she said in small voice. "You're an idiot and I trusted you. Rhys," she said, "you've put your trust in an idiot. Worse, you *kissed* the sonofabitch."

"Why does kissing me have anything to do with it?"

"Boss?" It was Joe Butler, standing at the door. "Mr. Marion on the line."

For all her apparent anger with me, Rhys showed poise as she picked up the phone and greeted Patrick. As before, I was struck by her ability to change moods, or, more accurately, to disguise a troubled one. They were discussing the fate of *Beloved Dorothy*. Rhys flipped through her personal calendar, throwing out dates, until they seemed to agree on one.

"Did Tommy Smallwood call you yet?" she said and glanced at me. "He did, did he . . . ? Well, of course he wants to see it and of course he'd say that. But, Patrick? Don't do it, Patrick. Don't you dare do it."

She nodded and scribbled on a notepad. "Take my advice on this, Patrick. You're certain to make a lot more money by putting it up at auction. Let me tell you why . . . No, let me tell *you*, Patrick. Forget what you'll be giving up in commission to Neal. Forget that. Small-wood will tell you anything to get his hands on that painting. You let him in the door and he'll show you auction records for past Asmore sales and then offer you twenty-five or fifty percent more than the highest result. That's still not enough, Patrick. The last Asmore sold a decade ago, and the market for regional art, southern paintings espe-cially, has exploded since then. We can't possibly know what *Beloved Dorothy* is worth without letting everyone take his best shot at it. Do you understand? Right . . . Uh-huh . . . But the price Smallwood would offer to pay you is *not* his best, Patrick. He might say it's his best, but, believe me, it isn't. He won't really know his best until he's being challenged for that painting in the heat of battle, and that's at auction— when other buyers with as much money as he's got are challenging him. Sit tight, Patrick. It's all you can do now. Be patient. Check your Caller ID and avoid solicitations from Smallwood and any others if that's what it takes. Because this is just starting, Patrick. It's just starting . . ."

When she hung up, I said, "You guys schedule a date when you plan to consign the Asmore?"

She was writing in her calendar. "I'm sorry, Jack. But that's be-tween my client and me."

"May I join you when you do consign it, Rhys?"

She continued writing, eyes still focused on the page. "No, you may not. But you can come with me now to Wheeler. It's time for your haircut." She closed the book and walked to within inches of where I was standing. She tilted her head back and stared at me as if trying to make an honest appraisal. From her expression I concluded it wasn't a good one. "Levette Asmore was my grandfather," she said, "and I'm going to prove to you that he was my grandfather."

"Me? There you go again, Rhys. Why do you have to prove any-thing to me?"

She intentionally bumped against me as she walked to the door.

S I X

Those wanting haircuts were mostly relatives of the students and people from the neighborhood—poor people, I should say, for they certainly were that. Female guinea pigs outnumbered their male counterparts by four to one. All of the beautician's chairs were occupied, so a small line had formed in the hallway leading to the room with the mural. There Rhys and I waited. Still rattled by our showdown earlier at the studio, I made no effort at conversation. Had I felt like talking, however, I doubt that she would've responded. Even with the riot of activity in the place—the excited chatter, the buzz of electric clippers, a dozen faucets running all at once—Rhys seemed to see only one thing. "You in some kind of hypnotic trance?" I said.

Staring at the wall across the room, she made no reply.

The class of novice hairdressers included ten or eleven young African-American women and a couple of Hispanic men, all of them wearing identical blue smocks and white shoes with thick corrugated rubber soles. A single instructor was supervising the event. She stalked the room brandishing a pair of scissors and speaking words of encouragement to the students, most of whom looked determined though terrified. To those of us waiting our turn she offered a gently worded reminder that three dollars was still a bargain no matter how bad the result.

I'd been to many a barber in my day, but never to one who apologized *before* you sat in his chair.

"Government man," Rondell Cherry said when he saw me. The look on his face let me know he was only joking. To Rhys he said, "I can't see you letting one of our students practice on you, Miss Goudeau. You're way too pretty for that."

"We're actually here for Jack." And she looked away from the wall at last.

The janitor glanced at the top of my head and I could tell what he was thinking: *This one's already such a disaster a bad haircut won't make any difference.*

"Think you could introduce us to Mrs. Wheeler?" Rhys said.

"We can do that. She's in her office now." Rondell Cherry nodded toward the instructor with the scissors. "But it looks like they're ready. Hair grows back, government man. Remember that."

The instructor guided me to a chair near the wall lined with sinks. A young woman smacking gum covered me with an apron that clipped at the neck. She lowered my head into a basin and soaked my hair with warm running water, then lathered in a squirt of shampoo. Her fingers worked hard against my scalp—she might've been probing for worms, the way she dug—and I was confident suddenly that I'd lucked out and landed a good one. As she was rinsing me off, I said, "My name is Jack Charbonnet. What's yours?"

"Bonelle Louvrier."

"You seem to know what you're doing, Bonelle."

"My daddy's a barber. I guess it's in my genes to cut hair."

I closed my eyes and sighed in gratitude and relief. Perhaps it wouldn't turn out badly after all. But then an odd question came to mind: What was in my genes? Surely not to follow Rhys Goudeau wherever she would have me. Surely not to nap under a tree in the afternoon with an art book open on my chest.

When she finished with the shampoo, Bonelle combed my hair out and started clipping the ends. The more she clipped, the louder she smacked, and the heavier was the scent of pink bubble gum. She used an electric clipper to rid clusters of unruly hair from my neck, then she massaged warm dollops of shaving cream into the same areas and cut away the hair with a straight razor. She gave my sideburns the same treatment.

"Do you think everybody's got genes that lead them someplace?" I asked as she was dusting powder on my neck.

"Huh?" I'd broken her concentration, while at the same time returning to the subject of a conversation we'd had fifteen minutes before.

"What are genes for, Bonelle?"

She laughed. "Tell us where to go?"

To finish, she removed the apron and brushed off my clothes to remove any hair. I was standing now, and when I started to walk away she nudged me back into my seat and held up a mirror to let me look at the back of my head. "You've done a marvelous job," I said. She whirled the chair around. Now I could look in the mirror she was holding and see the view reflected in the mirrors on the wall. "Marvelous," I said again. I didn't realize how much I'd been worrying about having a student cut my hair until now. "Thank you, Bonelle. You've got a lot of natural talent."

"You were sweating it, huh?"

She let me up out of the chair and I gave her a tip, then walked over to the instructor with my payment. The instructor came up on her toes and studied the top of my head as I pressed three single dollar bills into the palm of her hand. "You got yourself a real talent in that Bonelle Louvrier," I said.

"Bonelle's got a future," said the woman, then marched off squeezing her scissors.

※

When I couldn't find Rhys inside the building, I went outside and checked to make sure the van was still parked on the street. "She's visiting with Miss Wheeler," Rondell Cherry said when I reentered the building. "Want me to knock on the door and tell them you're waiting?"

I shook my head. "Let them talk."

I went back out and sat on the steps and nearly two hours passed before Rhys appeared with the old woman. In the meantime the school had cleared out, with more than a few interesting hair results and as many hysterical victims. One girl looked as though she had a nest of snakes on top of her head, all of them alive.

"Jack Charbonnet, meet Gail Wheeler," Rhys said. "Mrs. Wheeler, this is my friend Jack Charbonnet."

I shook Mrs. Wheeler's hard little hand, surprised by her strength. "Nice to meet you, Jack," she said, without bothering to remove the cigarette from her mouth.

"Nice to meet you, too."

She was wearing the same outfit from the other day, and up close she looked even more fragile than she had when I first saw her coming down the stairs. Her skin was splotched with age marks and past the scratched, murky lenses of her glasses the whites of her eyes shone yellow. "Pleased with your haircut, young man?"

"Yes, thank you. Bonelle Louvrier took good care of me."

"Oh, Bonelle's a fine girl. Tonight when you say your prayers you need to make sure to mention Bonelle. You know what happened, don't you?" She gave me a wink and said, "You went and won the hairdo lottery, son."

Gail Wheeler was still waving—waving with a hand up over her head, and the cigarette poking out of her mouth—as we left and pulled into traffic, headed downtown.

"She even smelled old," I said.

"I didn't notice."

"You know that old smell that old people have?"

Rhys looked at me. "Not really. All I smelled was the smoke."

I shrugged. I no longer was so sure about it either. The only thing I was sure about was that everything I said was wrong. "What did the two of you do in there for so long?"

"We didn't *do* anything."

"You were in her office for two hours. Nothing happened in two hours?"

"The mural didn't come up, if that's what you mean. Mainly we watched TV."

"You watched TV for two hours while I sat outside on the hard cement?"

"I didn't tell you to sit on the hard cement. Mrs. Wheeler keeps this big Zenith console next to her desk—you know, one of those floor models from the seventies, with a plastic frame molded to look like some fancy baroque thing?"

"Yeah, I know the kind you mean."

"When I walked in, the lights were out and she was sitting in the dark watching Maury Povich—this little lady with her hands folded on her stomach. I told her I was with a friend who needed a haircut. She seemed glad to have the company. I liked her. I think I'd like her better if she didn't smoke so much, but she really seems like a good person. And she's funny, Jack, that woman is a hoot. She made a big scene of having me swear on a stack of Bibles that I wasn't one of those agents from Baton Rouge. But of course it wasn't a stack of Bibles—it was a dictionary and some old magazines. She's a tough old bird, Mrs. Wheeler is, but she's facing some serious shit. And she needed to talk. I want you to always be polite to her, do you hear?"

"I'll be polite, Rhys. I'm polite to everybody."

She drove on a ways and it seemed she was trying to decide whether to tell me the rest. She glanced over at me and I nodded. "You might as well say it."

"Some while ago," she began, "Mrs. Wheeler came up with a scheme to keep the school from going under. There are thousands of ways for kids to receive school funding these days, and she decided to explore a few of these options. She started applying for state and federal work-study grants, Pell grants, that sort of thing. She filled out the applications herself, and she used personal information from former students whose records were still in her files. Their Social Security numbers, for instance. She also started inflating enrollment figures with ghost students to qualify the school for extra funding. All along she says she saw it as a kind of loan and meant to pay it back."

"But she would say that, wouldn't she?"

"What do you mean?"

"She doesn't want to go to jail."

"I believe her, Jack. These agents just subpoenaed the school's records. It could take weeks or months before they decide what to do. But she's definitely in trouble. Apparently everything began to unravel after Mr. Wheeler died and another beauty school opened in Mid-City. Enrollment crashed, and Mrs. Wheeler had to let teachers go. Earlier this week she was going to fire Mr. Cherry but she couldn't go through with it. He has a wife and five children at home. You know what else? All of the students in this year's class are minorities—either Hispanic or African American—and several of the women are single mothers. 'What will my girls do?' Mrs. Wheeler kept saying."

"I'll tell you what they can do, Rhys. They can go to that other hair school." When she looked over at me I said, "Forgive my cynicism, but it sounds like a con job. And she confides all this to you, a total stranger? I'm sorry, Rhys, I don't buy it."

She considered this for a moment, chewing her lower lip, then said, "Ever sit next to a stranger on a plane and tell her intimacies about yourself that you'd never imagine sharing with the people closest to you?"

"Not really."

"Well, I have, Jack. And maybe I was that person for Mrs. Wheeler today. That person on the plane."

⁂

We reached Martin Luther King and she parked behind my car on the other side of the boulevard from the studio. The weather was starting to turn and the wind sent paper trash skittering past us. Even in the gloaming you could see thunderheads charging in our direction from out in the west. "When do you plan to tell her about Levette's mural?" I said.

She took the keys out of the ignition but made no move to leave the van. She sat staring off in the distance at the dark, boiling clouds.

"Are you going to tell her about the mural, Rhys?"

"No. No, I'm not, Jack. That wouldn't be wise at this time. And you're not going to tell her either. Do I have your word on that?"

"But if she's prosecuted, Rhys, and if the government shuts down the school or seizes the building or puts her in jail, what happens then? Any chance of recovering the mural will be lost."

She shook her head. "I'd never let it get to that."

I tried to hold her eyes with mine but there was something about her gaze that made me turn away. "What are you telling me?"

"We're going to help her," she said.

"*Help* her? Aren't we a little late for that? We can't fix her mistakes, Rhys. I mean, we can't change what she's done."

"But we can get that mural."

"Rhys . . . ?"

"We'll go in at night when nobody's there. I know how Levette hung the thing, it's all there in his file: four canvas panels attached to the wall using tacks and wallpaper paste. All we have to do is make a replacement mural to swap out with the original. Same awful color, same water damage, same holes for air-conditioning vents. It'll take a little work, but do you have any idea how easy this is going to be? We can do this, Jack."

"No, we can't, Rhys, and we won't. We won't do this at all."

"I'm not going to let the government have that painting. Listen to me. We can sell it privately, we can have a private auction. It's the only way. Don't forget, Jack: Levette's mural was a WPA commission. Do you know what that means?"

"It means it was a government job."

"Right, a government job. You ready for a little history lesson?" Before I could answer, she said, "Back during the Depression people couldn't afford to buy bread and soup much less paintings and sculptures, so the government created a number of relief programs to help people who were struggling to survive. The WPA, they called it. Stands for Works Progress Administration. Some of the greatest artists in our country's history were awarded grants to create works for the WPA, and they practiced every kind of medium imaginable— from immense murals like Levette's to small etchings the size of postage stamps. Most of these items went into public buildings—post offices, railroad stations, courthouses, college lecture halls, libraries, places like that. Nobody knows for sure how many of these artworks were created—the government bean counters didn't bother to keep track—but the number is in the hundreds of thousands. Well, World War Two ends and people go back to work, and what does the government do with its collection? The government sticks it in warehouses, puts it out with the trash and destroys still others it doesn't like. Imagine that, Jack. Some ignorant bubba down the road in Baton Rouge decides he doesn't like all the black people shown praying in a painting by Conrad Albrizio, so he takes out the same pocketknife he uses to pick his ugly, diseased teeth and he rips the thing to shreds."

"Did it really happen that way, Rhys?"

"It happened exactly that way. As a matter of fact, it happened that way every day for years. Murals like Levette's were routinely painted over, and magnificent bronze sculptures were sold off for scrap. It was cultural genocide, is what it was. It was nothing less than the artistic soul of the country being gutted, and those endowed with the public trust did little to stop it. No, let me rephrase that: Those endowed with the public trust were the ones *responsible* for it." She reached over and tapped me hard on the shoulder. "Forgive me," she said. "I get wound up sometimes."

"You've got a bee in your bonnet, all right. You've got a whole hive of bees."

"I'm sure you can predict what happens next," she said. "Years go by and those WPA art objects that did survive start to become popular with collectors. People discover not only the beauty in paintings produced during the period, but they learn to appreciate their historic significance. The paintings are *about* something. They're a specific record of a lost America and they possess an honesty and a realism that expose most other art movements as cheap, intellectual fakery. So, as objects from the WPA become more and more popular, their values start to climb. And as their values climb, the government suddenly decides that it still owns them. The government says, 'Yes, we allowed our artwork to pass into the hands of collectors and dealers. And, yes, we sat back and watched while these people took on huge financial risk to create a market for the stuff. But—guess what, everybody?—we want our art collection back.'"

"Have they been able to get it back?"

"A lot of it. Let me tell you how crazy it's become. The feds in Washington assign an agency, the General Services Administration, to start identifying WPA art. If this agency discovers that you, a private citizen, are in possession of something created for the WPA, it sends you a letter stating that you have the option of returning the object to the government or donating it to a public institution. It's still theirs, in other words. Want to hear how absurd it's gotten? You know eBay, the Internet auction site?"

"Sure."

"Lo and behold if WPA items don't start appearing for sale on eBay. And how does the government respond? This goes to show the gall of these people. The same government that gave these things away or locked them in warehouses for rats to eat or burned them in incinerators . . . this same government starts contacting eBay sellers and saying, 'Hey, wait a minute, friend, you do not have clear title to that work of art and we're ordering you to stop this auction.' Can you believe that, Jack? The federal government is monitoring art sales on eBay. Ask agents with the GSA and they'll deny it, but I'm telling you it happens."

"You're also telling me something else, aren't you, Rhys?"

"Yeah? Like what?"

"You're saying that Levette's mural still belongs to the federal government. Or at least that the government might well claim ownership if ever it were pulled out of Wheeler, restored and shopped around."

"You have been paying attention."

"Tell me if I got this right, Rhys. In '41 the government orders Levette's mural painted over, effectively destroying it. But if tomorrow the painting were offered for sale at auction, the government likely would intervene, stop the transaction and order that the painting be donated to a public institution. Either that or it would demand that it be returned to them . . . I mean, returned to *it*—to the same government that tried to get rid of the painting in the first place and, furthermore, that might've prompted Levette to kill himself."

"Good, Jack. Now let me ask you this question: Do you think the government gave a damn that Levette's mural was still in the post office when it decided to deaccession that old building?"

"No."

"More than just that, Jack. Shit no, fuck no and hell no. And the only reason the government would care about the mural today— notwithstanding its potential historic significance—is because it's worth a lot of money."

"How much is a lot?" I said.

She pushed her door open and stepped out in the street. "One million? Two million? We'll never know for sure until we put it out there and let the likes of Tommy Smallwood fight for it."

I followed her across the street, but when she reached the entrance there was no invitation to join her inside. She closed and locked the security door behind her and stood leaning against the bars, her face framed in the narrow space. "It came to me while I was in Mrs. Wheeler's office," she said. "I'm sitting there trying to figure out how to help this woman and I actually pray for an answer and you know what, Jack? I got one."

"God spoke to you," I said. "Is that what you're telling me?"

Rhys held me with another of her weird stares. "You know how we know things, Jack? How as human beings we just know things or at least intuit them? You might think I'm crazier than shit but all of a sudden I knew what to do. Levette's mural. We go in, Jack. We go in and get the sonofabitch."

That night the storm blew in and knocked out power all along Bayou Saint John. The wind blew the trees in the garden into odd configurations against the black sky and rain fell so hard it sounded as if the roof of the garçonnière was going to cave in. I stayed in my bedroom waiting for the electrical service to be restored. I read art books by the light of a lantern until it ran low on oil. Then I read by flashlight until the batteries went dead. I listened to weather coverage on my transistor radio. Local meteorologists were calling it a storm but it packed the intensity of a hurricane. I stepped outside for a minute and the air smelled of a briny sea and the birds weren't moving. It was so hot and damp the walls were sweating.

Toward dawn I fell asleep and when I awoke it was to the shift of the floor taking on new weight. Someone was in the room, stepping across the wood and making it creak. *You're dreaming*, I said to myself. But I listened more closely and there was no denying it. Either Lowenstein's ghost was checking up on me or a burglar was investigating the place. I'd kept a baseball bat near my bed in anticipation of just such a development, and it was what I reached for now. Raising the length of fire-tempered wood above my head, and pausing long enough to register Pete Rose's signature scripted across the barrel, I raced into the adjoining room and spotted the intruder advancing for the door. In seconds I was upon him, whooping in full battle cry. He wheeled around to confront me and I somehow stopped the bat's momentum and sent it smashing against the wall. Plaster broke off in chunks and a heave of white dust. "Jesus," I shouted, the word lost in the fount of obscenities spoken by my intruder.

It was Lowenstein. Although I'd never met the man, I had no doubt as to his identity, having glimpsed him enough times fleeing from windows to build an adequate physical profile. Rainwater streaked down his large, gray face and the few remaining strands of hair on his head clung to his scalp. He looked terrified. Flannel night-clothes, soaked, hung from his small, shivering form. He held a flash-light by his side, and he lifted it now, however late, to protect himself. "Don't you touch me," he croaked.

"God, man, you're the one who came uninvited into my apart-ment. What are you doing here? Why didn't you knock?"

"I did knock," he said. "I knocked repeatedly." He pointed to the French doors that led to the cloister and the garden. "My nurse left to make sure her home was safe against the storm. And, look there, a branch from the old oak came down. I was concerned about your well-being, Mr. Charbonnet."

I nudged past him and stood at the window. The branch had leveled the garden bench where I'd spent so many solitary hours nap-ping and reading my art publications. "Who was Wiltz Lowenstein?" I suddenly heard myself say. "Are you Wiltz Lowenstein, Mr. Lowen-stein?"

He reached a trembling hand for the doorknob. "I don't know why I should be expected to answer that," he said.

"Was it your nickname? Was it that, by chance? Was it Wiltz?"

"Good-bye, Mr. Charbonnet."

His wheelchair stood on the damp bricks of the cloister, and out-side now he sat in it and began pushing himself back to the house. I stepped out after him, into the swirling mist. "For a second I thought you were somebody else," I shouted after him.

"And you were right," he called out in response, never looking back.

※

I was sitting on a patio chair in the blue shade of the cloister, watching Lowenstein's team of gardeners remove the downed branch from the oak tree and replace the bench, when Patrick Marion surprised me with a visit. He came striding around the corner of the house, sweat running down his face and dampening his shirt. He seemed to be in a great hurry. When he saw me he signaled for me to follow him to the front of the house. "Awful loud here," he shouted over the noise of chain saws.

I slipped my bare feet into a pair of loafers and hurried after him, watching the windows for Lowenstein, although the old geezer never did make an appearance.

"The maid let me in," he said at the gate.

"What's wrong, Patrick?"

"Let's go sit somewhere."

His face was unshaven, his hair uncombed, his eyes shot red. Another rowdy dinner party with friends, I figured. He drove me over to the coffee shop on Esplanade. He was quiet until we took our chairs at a table on the sidewalk in front. He glanced around to make sure no one was within earshot. "Got a favor to ask," he said.

"Sure, man. Anything."

"Would you be willing to safe-house *Dorothy* for a few days? Rhys Goudeau and I have made an appointment with the Neal Auction Company to consign the painting on Monday, and until then the dear girl needs a place to hide." He lifted his steaming cup of coffee and rippled the surface with his breath. "Somebody broke into my apartment last night, Jack. I'm pretty certain he was after the painting."

"You're fucking kidding me," I said.

He shook his head. "I wish I were."

"Were you there when it happened?"

"I was asleep in my room. The painting was maybe ten feet away, propped up against the wall behind my chest of drawers. It was three o'clock in the morning and I could feel the bed vibrating. That's one thing about life in the Loeber Mansion: when one of your neighbors gets up in the middle of the night to pee you know it because the house shakes. Only last night it was a heavier vibration, closer. It felt like it does when Elsa stays over, and at first I thought it might be Elsa until I remembered she'd gone to Mobile on business. My door creaked open and in the darkness I saw the figure of a man. He was a big person, dressed all in black, with a stocking cap covering his head. Had it been like most burglaries in this city, he would've gone straight for my TV or stereo. But this guy was checking out the walls."

A waiter began cleaning off the table next to ours. Patrick waited until he was finished before continuing the story. "He might've been in the room for thirty or forty seconds—a minute at most—but I tell you it felt like forever. I pretended to be sleeping, but my heart was beating like a kettledrum and I was afraid he'd hear it. He spotted the painting behind the chest and moved toward it, then he lowered himself to a crouch and brought his face up close to the surface. He might've been sniffing the paint. I heard a small clicking sound and then a tiny beam of light was shining on the painting. He was holding a penlight to it, I suppose to make certain he was stealing the right one. He made a sort of gasping sound, as though he were trying to catch his breath, and that's when I came out of the bed screaming at the top of my lungs. I think I scared hell out of him. He tucked tail and ran, in any case. I'd have gone outside after him but I wasn't wearing any clothes. Later as I was getting dressed and waiting for the police I suffered a bout of extreme paranoia and convinced myself he was coming back. But then the cops arrived and looked around and made out a report. As soon as they were gone—it now was about five o'clock in the morning—I put *Dorothy* in the trunk of my car and left the building. I've been driving around since, trying to figure out what to do next."

"By all means leave her with me," I said.

"I was hoping you'd say that. And I thank you, Jack. I'd bring her to Elsa's house but as I told you Elsa's traveling. I thought about the Conservation Guild but the studio is too obvious a place for me to stash it, and my intruder's likely to go there next. I was trying to decide on a course of action when it came to me that you would be the right person to take her."

"This is pure coincidence, I'm sure, but the other day I had an intruder of my own, Patrick. It turned out to be Lowenstein, checking on me after the storm. But for a while I was certain it was a burglar."

"Yes," he said, "the old man told me. He called and explained, probably because he was afraid you were going to bail on the lease." Patrick laughed and sipped his coffee. "He said you nearly bashed his head in with a baseball bat. I hope you'll protect *Dorothy* the same way, Jack. You're a Chambers man. I know she'll be fine."

❋

By the time we returned to Moss Street all the workers had gone. Patrick, however, was still worried about carrying the painting to the garçonnière. I went inside for a blanket, and when he opened the trunk a splash of sunlight fell on the painting's surface and brought as much color to the face of Dorothy Marion as when Rhys had zapped it in her office with photoflood lamps. We covered the painting and each of us held a side of the frame as we walked along the path in the garden. Even in the privacy of the garçonnière Patrick looked uncomfortable. "It's safe here," I said, then gave his shoulder a squeeze. "No one's going to steal it."

"This painting is my future," he said. "It's my life. You understand that, don't you? I sell it and my worries are over."

"I won't let anyone near it. Trust me, Patrick."

"It's not insured," he said. "If someone takes it now it's gone and I get nothing. But it'll carry three hundred thousand dollars in coverage as soon as Neal takes it. If somebody were to steal it from the auction house I wouldn't mind so much because I could file a claim and get my money." He put a hand on my shoulder and raised a finger up to my face. "You can't let Aunt Dottie out of your sight, Jack."

Scouting my distressed and flaking walls for the perfect spot, I suggested we hang it on the old nail over the fireplace in my bedroom, but instead Patrick placed it on the bathroom floor with the image facing the wall. "Of course you're free to put it wherever you like after I leave," he said, "but a bathroom seems the last location a thief would think to find a valuable painting."

"The dampness in here might not be good for it. Have you thought of that? Maybe we should put it in a closet."

"Put her wherever you want, Jack. I have to leave now because I'm exhausted and I have to sleep or else I'll throw up. I'll call in periodically over the next few days to check and see how she's doing."

After he left I hung the painting over the fireplace and spent the better part of an hour observing the image from different vantage points in the room. The sitter's eyes followed me wherever I went, and I felt a passion growing in me for the youthful Aunt Dottie, her postcoital glow being the aspect of her appearance that I found most beguiling. Like many other *Beloved* portraits, her mouth was less finished than her other features, and for this reason my eyes kept returning to the smear that formed her lips. I studied the image with the intensity of a man who means to memorize the face of a departing lover. I really got to know the lady. Wondering if the ghost of my dead father had somehow invaded my body and taken possession of my soul (who but John Charbonnet ever acted this way, after all?), I went out in the garden to inspect the new bench, but I'd hardly reached the spot when I changed my mind and headed back for the garçonnière. "You weren't thinking about stepping out on me, were you?" I said to the painting. "Hey, you. Dottie! Talk to me."

I might've offered a response, in the imagined voice of Dorothy, but the phone rang and spared me the interlude with madness. It was Patrick, calling for a report. "She still in the toilet?" he said.

"No, she finished up and retired to my bedroom. She's waiting for me now with the most amazing come-hither look on her face. It might spoil the moment, but would you like to speak to her?"

"I'm glad one of us finds humor in this situation. That was humor, right?"

"She's in good hands, Patrick. Stop worrying."

"I'll stop when the money's in the bank," he said, then put the phone down.

At noon the next day I found myself standing at the front door of the main house, rapping against the frame. Lowenstein's nurse came squeaking down the hall in rubber shoes, and the old man appeared in his wheelchair in a doorway behind her. From the hall came the odor of rubbing alcohol and liniment oddly mixed with one of spicy boiled beef. Not pleasant.

"Didn't I already say he isn't related to that person?" yelled the nurse. She checked the latch on the screen door.

"I've got a painting by Levette Asmore," I said past her to Lowenstein. "It's hanging in my bedroom if you're interested in having a look."

He backed up out of the doorway, and deeper into the shadows, although his feet and the edge of a wheel were still visible.

"You can come see it. But you'll have to tell me who Wiltz Lowenstein was."

I left as the nurse unloaded with a verbal assault and returned to the garçonnière, certain that the collector of southern paintings who resided in Lowenstein would be unable to resist an audience with the single greatest painter ever produced by the region. As I lay in bed not ten feet away from the portrait, I flipped through one of my art books, entitled *Louisiana Painters and Paintings from the Collection of W. E. Groves*. The book was a slim paperback crowded with fuzzy, black-and-white images produced by mostly nineteenth-century artists who'd painted the state's agrarian scenes and portraits of its wealthy Creoles. The book did not include an entry for Levette Asmore, but it did provide a glimpse into the mind of the collector whose obsession always trumps the will of his better judgment. "Collecting is a vice that brooks no competition from other vices," I read in the Groves essay called "Notes on Collecting." "It is a passion that grows and dominates until you stand trembling before the object of your desire, determined to own it at all costs while earnestly striving to conceal your cupidity lest it affect the price."

I was all but certain, of course, that it was Tommy Smallwood who'd broken into Patrick Marion's apartment. I believed this to be so not only because of Patrick's physical description of the intruder but also because of his recollection of the man's behavior upon entering the bedroom. He had scanned the walls in search of something. Discovering the painting behind a piece of furniture, he'd dropped to his haunches to better inspect it. He'd then illuminated the thing with a flashlight, and this had provoked in him a gasp that could not have been voluntary. Having failed to persuade Patrick to sell him the painting, and unwilling to wait for the auction at which he risked being outbid, Smallwood's intention likely had been to steal *Beloved Dorothy*. In the end, however, after escaping Patrick's without being caught, he'd probably been pleased simply with having had a look at the painting. Only madness prompts a man of Smallwood's wealth to risk calamity for a moment such as that one. I wondered at the unforgiving power of a collector's desire, and made ready for a visit from Lowenstein.

It was a little past midnight; I'd turned the lights out an hour before. The door was unlocked because I'd left it that way. In the dark he moved past me wielding a flashlight that remained pointed at the floor until he was positioned directly in front of the painting. He moved the light to the girl's face, held it there for several minutes, then traced circles with it around the rest of the canvas. He let out a sigh and glanced back at me. He seemed to want to say something, but the image drew him back. Finally he shut off the light and sat in a posture of exaggerated defeat on a chair at the foot of my bed.

"After what happened the last time you visited," I said, "and you still haven't learned to knock. Who taught you manners, Mr. Lowenstein?"

He was still looking up at the painting when he said, in barely a whisper, "You're right to hate me. I only hope you'll stay on."

"Hate you? I don't know you well enough for that. And are you really worried I'm going to break the lease?"

"You spoke to Mr. Marion?"

"Yes."

I heard a click and his light found the painting again. A minute passed before he shut it off and the room returned to darkness. "Your rent helps me pay the nurse," he said. "I need the woman. My hips are finished and I suffer from rheumatoid arthritis. My hands and feet . . . I'm not well, Mr. Charbonnet."

"I won't break the lease, I like it here just fine."

"Thank you. Now what is the question you wanted answered, in exchange for allowing me to view your painting?"

"Who was Wiltz Lowenstein?"

"Oh, yes. Wiltz Lowenstein. Wiltz Lowenstein, Mr. Charbonnet, was a small law firm that once occupied an office in a building on Canal Street. It specialized, as I recall, in maritime law. Its founding partners were Joe Wiltz and Jonathan Lowenstein. I was not related to Johnny Lowenstein—he was from Boston, and much older than I—but I did know the man. In those days I lived in the French Quarter, blocks away from the Wiltz Lowenstein office, and often by mistake the post office would deliver the law firm's mail to my address and my mail to theirs. Mr. Lowenstein would come for his mail or I would go for mine, and I got to know him this way. We had lunch once, if I remember correctly, in the restaurant at D. H. Holmes. A fine man and quite the raconteur."

"He donated a painting by Levette Asmore to the Louisiana State Museum."

"You're mistaken there," Lowenstein said. "It was the Joe Wiltz estate that donated the painting, after Wiltz died in the early seventies, some ten years after his partner was killed in an automobile accident on the Airline Highway. The painting you're referring to is titled *Beloved Christine*."

"That's the one."

"Yes, but Joe Wiltz was the collector, not Johnny Lowenstein. After Wiltz's death the Wiltz Lowenstein law firm was absorbed by a much larger group—I forget the name—and its painting collection went mostly to museums in the area. The donations, you see, were tax deductible."

"Did you know Levette Asmore, Mr. Lowenstein?"

"Yes, I did. I knew him as well as anyone, I suppose."

"What can you tell me about him?"

"Nothing tonight. I agreed to tell you about Wiltz Lowenstein." He whipped the flashlight around and pointed the light in my eyes. "Levette Asmore wasn't part of our agreement. But I do thank you for the time with your picture."

The light went back to the Asmore, and it was a while before I could see again.

"Are you familiar with the term 'metaphysical desire,' Mr. Charbonnet? It concerns the pursuit of that which isn't available to us. The closer one hopes to get, the farther away he finds himself."

"Never heard of it."

"When it comes to love, we desire most that which will never want us in return."

"Sounds like an interesting concept."

Lowenstein looked at me and smiled. "You have a beautiful painting," he said. "I must go now." His face grew distorted with pain as he struggled to rise to his feet. I got up to help him but he gave his head a shake, stopping me. He turned on the flashlight and started for the door.

"What do you want in exchange for information about Levette Asmore, Mr. Lowenstein?"

"What do I want?"

"What if I paid you rent for three months in advance? That would go a long way with the nurse."

"Three months?" He shook his head. "No. That wouldn't do it."

I followed him outside. He was moving better now. He'd nearly reached the house when suddenly he turned back around. "Let me spend the night with the girl," he said. "In consideration I'll tell you all you need to know about Levette."

"The girl?"

"The painting, Mr. Charbonnet. Levette's beloved."

I might've let him have the painting had Patrick's voice not filled my head, reminding me that I was a Chambers man. It occurred to me that a fellow without a job or a woman needs to be something, and I had better keep my word. I'd lost most everything else lately. "I wish I could do that. But the painting doesn't leave my room."

He slipped into the darkness of the house without saying anything more.

❋

He came early Monday morning and knocked to be let in. I'd covered the painting with a blanket and placed it in the bathroom, in the spot where he'd last seen it. He came alone, which shouldn't have surprised me. He seemed to read disappointment in my expression. He bent down and checked the canvas for damage, and when he stood up again he said, "Sorry, Jack. She's set to meet me later at the auction house."

I didn't ask if I could join them. We carried the painting to the car as we'd carried it to the garçonnière three days before. Lowenstein watched from the front door, his seated form in the wheelchair visible past the screen. Behind him stood the nurse. "For a while she was mine," I said to Patrick, "and we got along beautifully."

"Rhys or Aunt Dottie?" he said.

"Aunt Dottie. Definitely Aunt Dottie."

We lay the painting flat on the floor of the trunk and I stopped him when he reached to close the lid. "One last look, please," I said.

He nodded and I had my moment and then Patrick, in his old car belching smoke, started on his way down the road that hugged the bayou.

※

Weeks would pass before I saw *Beloved Dorothy* again. In the meantime I agreed to do something I'd sworn off forever only a short time before. That is to say, I contracted with a magazine to write a story, this one about the tourism boom on the Mississippi Gulf Coast. I took the assignment because I needed to. The thought of having to place my fingertips on a computer keyboard was nearly enough to make me physically ill, but I recognized the fact that a break from my dark little cave on Moss Street would do me good, and the Gulf Coast wasn't a bad destination if one meant to reacquaint oneself with the world. The place was made even more attractive by the magazine's promise of a generous expense account.

The beach was wide open and there the wind blew. Even the light was different. My first day there, I called Rhys and invited her to drive down for a night out on the town. We could have dinner and take in a show, I said. If she liked, she could stay over in the hotel—not with me in my room, but in her own room. She was polite about it, but in the end she declined the invitation.

As long as it wasn't my money I was spending, I made sure to enjoy myself. I went out for meals at seafood restaurants. In huge, audacious gambling halls I played the slots and attended fight cards featuring flabby, washed-up pros who ten years before had been headlining in Vegas. One night an assistant publicity director for one of the casinos gave me a tour of what she called "my Biloxi." The woman's name was Cindy Fournier, and she was a twenty-something divorcée who'd become a PR flack after a brief career as a television reporter in Jackson. Her accent was pure Mississippi Delta, and the sexiest I'd ever heard. We drank beer and ate hamburgers in a dark little redneck bar by the water. Maybe she was only doing her job, that being to sell the area as the "Deep South's premier vacation paradise," as she kept calling the place, but it felt good to be with a woman who constantly looked at me as if she could eat me whole. "You're a very handsome man, Jack Charbonnet."

"Am I?"

"How come the men in Mississippi can't look like you?"

Cindy had a great line of bullshit—even better than my own. Between stories about the enchanting adventures that awaited travelers to the Coast, she talked about her on-again, off-again relationship with a blackjack dealer named Earl Chitty, who'd seemed like the sort of guy she wanted to settle down with if only he'd kick his horse habit.

"Earl likes the ponies, does he?"

Her eyes went wet with tears. "Horse is heroin, Jack. I would take the ponies any day over what Earl's gone and got hisself hooked on."

We held hands and walked the beach and sat in the sand under the stars and watched old men in hip boots cast for fish in the surf. At the end of the night Cindy drove me back to my hotel and followed me into the lobby. "Will you give me a hug, Jack?" she said. "I could sure use one."

She was small but strong in my arms, and the embrace awakened a feeling in me that until now I'd put on reserve for Rhys. Cindy and I should've ended it there, but an hour later we were lying side by side in bed, trying to understand what had just happened. "I can't believe you don't have a girlfriend," she said.

"I guess that's a compliment."

"I really do mean it in a positive way. When we were making love you made me wish I was someone else."

I lifted my head off the pillow. "Was that one a compliment, too?"

"That I deserve better than Earl Chitty, Jack. That's what I should've said. Because you made me wish that just now." She waited awhile, then said, "What did you wish for when we were making love?"

I couldn't tell her the truth—that I'd kept wishing with all that was in me that she was Rhys Goudeau—so instead I sank my face back in the pillow and said, "I didn't wish for anything, Cindy. Because my wish had come true."

I could've cut my own throat for being so sappy, but it scored big with Cindy. Thirty minutes later we were making love again, and doing so with an abandon that wasn't present the first time. She made so much noise I had to cover her mouth with my hand to keep my neighbors in the hotel from hearing.

On my way home I remembered something my father had told me when I was a kid. "Jack," he'd said, "be careful what you get good at. Most people aren't and live to regret it." With that in mind, I pulled over at the next exit and stopped at a bait shop with a pay phone out by the road. I was thinking about Cindy and her situation with Earl. I'd decided it was as important that we also be careful to fall in love with the right person, otherwise we grow to regret that, too. Cindy picked up right away but something in her voice told me she didn't want to talk. She seemed embarrassed to be hearing from me again, and it came to me that Earl was nearby, listening. I started to make a case for why she should come and visit me and see "my New Orleans," but then I dropped it. I probably could've continued the lie as long as she let me, but I knew that I might be smart to heed my own advice and let this one go. "Good luck with your story," Cindy said. "And, please, Jack, let us know when it's going to be running. I'll make sure to include it in our press packet."

When I got off the phone I needed to roll down the windows and play the radio loud before I felt halfway right again.

※

I returned to Moss Street to find a week's worth of the *Times-Picayune* scattered in the monkey grass beneath the crape myrtles, papers that neither Lowenstein nor his help had bothered to retrieve and save for me. An image in the Friday paper, set above the fold on the front page, showed Patrick Marion standing in front of Dorothy Marion's ramshackle house on Ursulines Street. His arms were open wide as if to embrace the whole world, and no doubt some of the money in it. LOCAL MAN DISCOVERS REPUTED MASTERPIECE, read the headline. I walked up the street to my coffee shop to check *Gambit Weekly*. I found a copy of the popular tabloid in the wire basket next to the door. A big color photograph on the cover showed Rhys and Patrick with the painting. THE MILLION-DOLLAR PICTURE NOBODY WANTED, went that one.

In both stories the Asmore legend was embellished to a point where the artist better resembled a Cajun Van Gogh than a troubled young man with a talent for scandal, and the hype didn't end with the print media. That night I turned on the TV and heard the voice of Neal's Lucinda Copeland seconds before her face came up on the screen. She was being interviewed for a segment about the painting on a six o'clock news show. "Finding a lost Asmore is like finding a lost Ernest Hemingway manuscript or the lost sheet music of a never-published Louis Armstrong composition," she said. "No, it's actually more significant than that. Hemingway and Satchmo lived long, productive lives. Levette Asmore died before the full flower of his gifts could be realized. I don't think I exaggerate when I tell you his passing was one of the greatest tragedies in the history of art in America. It is made slightly more bearable by the discovery of *Beloved Dorothy*."

The next day, taking a break from writing, I tuned to a popular talk radio program and encountered the voice of featured guest Patrick Marion. He represented himself well, although with perhaps too much candor, and he probably would've been wise to spit out the chewing gum. "I just wish Aunt Dottie had been prettier," he said. "Instead of a double with income potential, I'd be shopping now for a mansion at English Turn—you know, one of those marble palaces they like to put in coffee table books."

Because of a Friday deadline the magazine had imposed on my Gulf Coast assignment, I was pressed for time and had no choice but to skip the Thursday-night preview at Neal. But that Saturday there was no way I was going to sit out the event "that was sure to be as colorful as any Carnival parade that ever rolled," as an op-ed piece in the morning paper predicted.

Finding a place to park near the auction house proved to be a problem, and so I ended up in a pay lot nearly a mile away. The hike had me running with sweat, and I paused only once: to remove my jacket and loosen my tie. I spotted the painting as soon as I entered the gallery. It stood on an easel positioned next to the auctioneer's lectern, a blast of light hitting it from overhead. On a table nearby stood a huddle of Newcomb College pottery and a glass vase filled with Louisiana irises. It came to me that the flowers matched those depicted in the painting and that each of the Newcomb vases was decorated with the same purple blooms. I registered at the front desk and received a card with a number on it—Neal's version of a paddle— then I retrieved a house-copy catalog from the end of the glass counter, one of many hands grabbing at the stack. Upon spying *Beloved Dorothy* on the cover, I experienced a sensation that imposed on me physically. My spine tingled and a blanket of gooseflesh covered my arms. I could feel my breath go thin, and my body temperature went from hot to cold in an instant. I'd lived with the old girl for all of three days and yet we'd had our magic. These things really are alive, it came to me. And they really do belong to us, however brief their stay.

The only unoccupied seats were reserved, which gave me no option but to stand in the rear of the room, along with scores of others. I leaned against a giant secretary and marveled at the dexterity of the auctioneer ticking off one lot after another. When Rhys and Patrick finally made their entrance, accompanied by Elsa Dodd, it was to the sort of barely restrained excitement that had greeted Tommy Smallwood on my last visit to Neal. They'd timed their arrival for maximum exposure, as only about an hour remained before *Beloved Dorothy* was scheduled to be sold. A couple of news photographers, heretofore hidden in the crowd, stepped up with cameras raised and clicked off a barrage. Rhys and Elsa were wearing light summer dresses, white straw hats and platform espadrilles. Patrick wore seersucker, a bow tie and wing tips: the uniform of the quintessential southern gentleman. He strode up the aisle like a politician with nothing less than the world to save. In recognition the auctioneer gave a nod, the porters broadened their smiles and the female staff members manning the phones exchanged a chorus of sibilant whispers.

They went all the way up to the front row and removed the RE-SERVED placards from chairs sandwiched between Mary Lou Cohn and Beatrice Wolff, professor emeritus of art history at Tulane University. Although we'd never met, I recognized the elderly woman from recent news reports about the Asmore. In fact, Professor Wolff was the one who, in a TV interview, had spoken words that I later scribbled on an index card and stashed in one of my art books: "For a painter with immortality in him, Levette Asmore couldn't wait to die. I still can't cross a river without wondering why."

As his big moment approached, Patrick spent more time watching the rear of the room than the front of it. At the end of each sale he glanced back at the doors, then faced the auctioneer again only after the porters had brought out the next lot to be auctioned. By my count he checked the door forty times, and he still managed to go without spotting me. I was invisible to him because there was only one person he was looking for today. That was Tommy Smallwood.

Perhaps in anticipation of a large crowd, the auction house had turned up the air-conditioning, and the room was so cold now that it almost hurt. My head ached and my face felt fat and rubbery. We were about half an hour away when, unable to stand it any longer, I went outside to warm up and nearly bumped into Smallwood as he came rushing to the entrance. His face was burning with color, his eyes bulged and he was winded and gasping for breath. I stepped to the side to let him pass, but he threw his weight against me and collapsed in my arms. I gave a small burp of surprised laughter, and then we both groaned terribly. The man was in trouble. Recognizing that he was either dead or dying, I gently lowered him to the sidewalk and felt his neck for a pulse. Others came running to help. Someone removed Smallwood's coat, another his necktie. A young woman put an ear to his chest. "Mr. Smallwood?" she said. "Mr. Smallwood, do you hear me?"

Smallwood made a feeble effort to return to his feet but the woman pushed him back to the ground. "Mr. Smallwood? Mr. Smallwood, can you hear me? If you can hear me talk to me. Mr. Smallwood, talk to me. Talk to—"

"Levette," he muttered.

"We're going to take you to the hospital now. You just take it easy. Everything will be okay. Mr. *Small*wood? Everything will be okay."

"Levette," he said again.

The woman punched the keypad of her cell phone, identified herself as a doctor and asked that an ambulance be sent immediately to the Neal Auction Company on Magazine Street. By the time she finished, Smallwood was sitting up, although he still appeared to be in great physical distress. His general complexion had turned ashen, and sweat formed a milky film on his face. "Levette," he said a third time, shouting out the name, before falling to his side and flopping over on his back.

A small crowd had gathered outside. I could still hear the auctioneer and his gavel from inside the building. Time waited for no man, and neither, apparently, did the auction. My father had no use for spoiled, rich men like Tommy Smallwood, and Rhys surely held them in contempt, but as I gazed down on his large, defeated form I could feel only pity. The great pumpkin head, the expensive clothes stripped away to reveal mealy white flesh. Before, Smallwood had seemed a rude, bumptious ass, a mere caricature of a man, but now he'd proved to be as needy and vulnerable as the rest of us. I resisted an urge to kneel beside him and pillow his head in my hands, to speak words to console him. Finally an unusually large dose of cynicism kicked in, and I thought to myself, *You greedy hog, where's your money to save you now?*

After the ambulance took him away everyone went back inside— everyone but myself and one other, as it happened. I hadn't noticed her until now. It was Busty Dusty, or was the name Dusty Busty? She was leaning back against the front of the building with her arms crossed at her chest, and quietly weeping into a twisted rope of tissue. There was a large stain, shaped like a cloud, on her fancy cocktail dress. She was smoking a cigarette. "Miss?" I said, daring to step up close. "Miss, do you know what happened to him? Any idea what's wrong with him?"

When she looked at me her eyes seemed unable to focus. Each was smudged with mascara. "It's the pitcher," she said.

"The pitcher?"

"The Levette. That one by Levette. I stayed over last night and caught him crying in the bathroom at four o'clock this morning—he was sitting on the commode crying. Later I got him to eat some breakfast, but he threw that up on the way here." She looked down at her soiled dress. "If he dies," she continued, "it will be from want. All the man has got, and I'm telling you it will be from want."

"Do you need a ride somewhere? To the hospital, maybe?"

She shook her head. "I still have his car. He wouldn't stop vomiting and we were running late and so he made me drive. I let him out in front and went to park, and when I got here he was . . . well, you saw it."

The straps holding up the top of her dress had slipped over her shoulders, and her chest was almost completely exposed. She seemed to be waiting for me to say something. "I'd go in and bid for him," she said, "but they wouldn't give me a number. Not looking like this they wouldn't." She glanced down again at her stained dress.

I left her and returned to the gallery. There were even more people now than before, and a low buzz was coming up from the floor. As I pushed forward, squeezing past the crowd, I finally was able to catch Patrick's attention. I couldn't hear him, but clearly his lips said, "Where is he?"

I shook my head and shot a thumb at the door. He shrugged and made a gesture with his hands. "Sick," I said. "Smallwood is *sick*."

I had to say it a few times before Patrick understood, and then he left his chair and came running toward me down the center aisle. He fell against me with almost as much force as Smallwood had, and while I calmly explained the situation I thought he, too, would pass out in my arms. I finished and pushed him toward the front of the room, and he staggered to his place like a drunk on a day-long binge, bumping against those auction-goers who occupied aisle seats. Rhys and Elsa helped him to his chair, and then to the sound of his moans the sale of *Beloved Dorothy* commenced.

A couple of porters were holding the painting up high for inspection, turning it from side to side for all to see. From what I could tell, half a dozen bidders in the gallery and several on the phones were pursuing it. As usual, the auctioneer handled the charge with aplomb, deftly pushing the money higher even as numbered cards beat against the air and shouts of "Bid!" and "Here, man!" filled the room. All told it lasted three minutes, and then *Dorothy* was gone.

"Going once, going twice . . . *SOLD* for four hundred and ten thousand dollars to Jessica Wiley's phone bid."

At the sound of the hammer smashing down, I began to applaud and so did others in the room. Levette Asmore had shattered the auction record for a painting produced by a southern artist, outdistancing the previous mark by $100,000. In celebration Patrick stood and threw his arms up over his head, and both Elsa and Rhys wrapped him up with hugs and kisses. He had all of five seconds to enjoy the spotlight, when the next item, an old map, came up on the block.

I walked outside and waited for them on the sidewalk, momentarily forgetting that it was the sale of *Dorothy,* and not my being in Rhys's presence again, that made the occasion a significant one. Patrick was first through the door, stumbling past the gauntlet of admirers who slapped his back and grabbed and shook his hand. He embraced me while several onlookers whistled and cheered. "You did it, Hurricane. You did it, man."

"It must've been Smallwood on the phone, huh, Jack?"

"I wouldn't put it past him," I said.

"Me neither."

"I can just see it," I went on. "They're driving him to the hospital, medics are thumping his chest with those electric paddles, they're sticking him with needles and he calls in the winning bid on his cell phone."

Rhys was a few minutes behind Patrick and Elsa. "The phone bidder was somebody in town," she announced.

"Smallwood?"

"No, it wasn't Smallwood. I just talked to Lucinda. She says it was someone else. Some guy who asked to remain anonymous. She's disappointed. They all are."

"But it went for nearly half a million dollars," Elsa said.

"That's true," Rhys replied. "The damn thing is she thinks it might've fetched twice that had Smallwood been in the action. I'm sorry, Patrick."

"Can we go back inside and do the auction over again?" he said.

Rhys placed her hand on his face. "The sale's done, baby, it's final."

"What are you thinking?" Elsa said. "That they're going to get all the bidders back in the gallery and on the phone and make sure Tommy Smallwood participates this time?"

Patrick looked at her. "Yes, that's it exactly."

"We're leaving now," Elsa announced. "Rhys, thank you for the lift this morning. We'll call first thing on Monday. Jack, always nice to see you again."

They left in a cab. Past the car's rear windows Patrick looked as if he were joining a funeral procession, so dark and troubled was his expression. They turned the corner and disappeared. "He should be thrilled," I said. "God knows I would be."

"He'll buy a house and a car and then what?" Rhys said. "He already has a nice home and a car that runs and takes him where he needs to go. He'll never throw better dinner parties than the ones he's already given. And he'll have Elsa's love whether he's rich or poor. There's no doubt the financial security will make things better for him, but it's only for the short term. It won't be long—a year or two, maybe—when Patrick wakes up and everything will be as it was before *Beloved Dorothy* came into his life."

"What's your point, Rhys?"

"He should've kept the painting. I'd take an Asmore over a new house and a new car any day. The world is full of houses and cars, Jack. It is not full of Asmores."

Now that the sale was done, culminating the day's offerings of important southern paintings, a steady stream of people began to leave the building. Rhys took me by the arm and pulled me aside. "I'm glad you're finished with your magazine story," she said. She looked around to make sure no one was close enough to hear. "Maybe we can go get the mural now."

"Did you just say 'we,' Rhys?"

Her answer was the last one I expected. "I need you, Jack."

She drove me to the little pizza place across the street from Wheeler, and we sat at a table by the window in front and ordered beer and a large pepperoni, each of us throwing occasional glances at the school. That such a place held a forgotten masterpiece, an Asmore, would never let me look at another derelict building without wondering what kind of treasure was inside waiting to be found.

"How'd your story come out?" she said.

"Awful. It's an awful piece of crap, definitely not worthy of publication, and nowhere near deserving the money they're paying me."

"What did your editor say about it?"

"He loved it."

She laughed. "You sound like I once did about my painting, back when I honestly believed I was destined to be an artist. I was so self-critical that I couldn't stand to let anyone see my work. Before my first college exhibition I got so stressed I hyperventilated. I suppose it explains why some artists become painting restorers. They can't bear the new, especially their own. I have to admit, watching *Dorothy* being auctioned off today was a thrill for me. Even though Joe Butler did the retouch, I connected so personally with the painting that it might've been my own. Sometimes saving something is a more valuable contribution than making something."

"May I quote you on that?"

"Yes, you may," she said. "I might even have to quote me on that one day."

As we ate, Rhys debriefed me on her activities of the last few weeks. For the most part, she said, Gail Wheeler's situation remained unchanged, except for her decision to retain an attorney, the daughter of her late husband's sister. Alice O'Neil was fresh out of the Tulane University Law School, and while she had seemed capable enough to Mrs. Wheeler her professional experience was limited to representing former sorority sisters who hired her to write threatening letters to their landlords in apartment rental disputes. Apparently landlords quaked in fear upon receiving letters on stationery with a lawyer's letterhead. According to Mrs. Wheeler, Alice hadn't been admitted to the bar yet, having failed the exam on her one and only attempt.

"I'm trying to reserve judgment, but it isn't easy," Rhys said. "The one good thing I can say about the girl is that she's sensitive to her aunt's financial situation. The retainer, by the way, came to a handshake over cups of frozen yogurt at the mall."

"The mall?"

"They like to hit the sales. It's what they do."

Rhys's most recent meeting with Mrs. Wheeler had come a few days earlier at the school, and they'd shared another afternoon of soap operas and QVC, the home-shopping channel to which the old woman professed to be addicted. While Mrs. Wheeler recalled the details of every rhinestone bracelet sold on air in the last month, her recollection of the post office mural was vague. Her face went blank when Rhys asked if it was true about the painting. "What painting?" said Gail Wheeler.

"Didn't Mr. Cherry tell me something about a mural? I'm sure he did."

"Oh, that thing," said the old woman, when it registered. "Too bad they had to go and ruin it, huh? I'm sure the students would've liked having a painted picture to look at between botching hairdos."

"She's starting to wear on me a little," Rhys said now. "I mean, she's what you might call uncouth. And now that she's comfortable with me her language has become rather salty. She swears like a linebacker, Jack."

"And laughs like a seal," I added.

"The other day she asked me if I was dating anyone. I told her I wasn't, and she said she didn't know how I could stand not getting any. Can you believe that?"

"No, I can't," I answered, although the truth was I'd often wondered the same thing myself.

⁂

We paid the bill and she drove me to the parking lot where I'd left my car. She pulled up in the slot next to mine and killed the engine and squeezed into the space between her seat and the door. "Jack," she said, "I want you to be there when we take the mural out. I want you to help us." She was staring at me, making sure I saw the resolve in her eyes. "Are you with us or not?"

"Who's us?" I said.

"Joe Butler and me. Who else did you think?"

"Oh, God, not that dude." I feigned a cold shiver.

"You'll like him once you get to know him. He might look a little scary but he's a good man, and he's good at what he does. He's the best painter and materials man I've ever seen work. Believe me, we'll need him once we start pulling that canvas off the wall. Later in the studio the rest of the staff will help do the actual work on the painting but I've decided to leave them in the dark about its origin."

"Won't they know what it is?"

"How could they? Oh, they might recognize the hand of Levette Asmore, but they won't care where it comes from. We've restored several murals at the Guild—both from private homes and public buildings—and if any of them does bother to ask I'll say it belongs to a client who has a big house in town."

"Have you finished making the replacement mural yet?"

"Been finished. It's ready to go."

"How'd you pull that off?"

"Easy. I went to the school and took some chips off the wall for paint samples. I also shot some reference photos of the original mural, as it looks today. I'd fired off about two dozen frames when Mr. Cherry walked up and asked what I was doing. I told him I liked the quality of the light in the room. I said I was taking some art pictures of how the light looked streaming from the windows. He told me the most beautiful thing. He said, 'Yes, it does look churchly, doesn't it?' "

I opened the passenger door and stepped outside. "You've got it all figured out, don't you, Rhys?"

"I think I do."

"Have you figured out how you plan to get in the school?"

She opened the dashboard ashtray and retrieved a pair of shiny new keys. "One thing about Mrs. Wheeler," she said, "she's so busy running her mouth she doesn't notice half of what's going on around her. Somebody should warn that lady about leaving valuables out on her desk." Rhys laughed and put the keys back in the tray. "Don't worry, Jack. I made copies and returned the originals later in the day. She never even noticed them missing."

She started the engine and leaned over in the seat. She was holding me with another of those stares meant to convey her commitment. "It can't wait much longer, Jack. I had an interesting talk yesterday with Mr. Cherry. He says somebody was snooping around the building this week, asking questions about an old painting. Big guy in fancy clothes. Mr. Cherry had his accent down pat."

"Smallwood?" I said.

"Smallwood," she answered. "Are you in, Jack?"

"Hell yeah," I said, then gave her a wave as she drove away.

SEVEN

 Later that afternoon I left the city driving west on Interstate 10 and in minutes came to exit signs for the Huey P. Long Bridge. A cloverleaf led me around to Clearview Parkway heading toward the river. Past the usual suburban sprawl—the apartment complexes and strip malls, the donut shops and pay-at-the-pump gas stations—and suddenly there it was, blotting out the horizon.

Alone as I navigated a traffic circle and approached the on ramp, I straddled the center line and claimed both lanes as my own. The smooth ascent, tires thumping over reflector caps as I drifted from side to side. To my left a nest of gray steel suspended above a train track, to my right the river. More than six decades old and the bridge was no less an architectural wonder today than when the state dedi-

cated it to the former governor not long after he was shot by an as-
sassin in the state capitol some sixty miles upriver. In the months after the bridge's completion tourists had come from all over the South
for the simple experience of driving across it. New York City had the
Empire State Building, the Chrysler Building and the Brooklyn
Bridge. New Orleans had the Huey P.

"Where was it?" I mumbled out loud, slowing below the posted
speed limit. "Where, Levette? Where did you go to jump?"

The walkway to my right was barely wide enough to accommodate the body of a man. Had cars passed by as he climbed to the
bridge's summit? Had drivers blown their horns to distract him?

Descending now to the West Bank and the turnaround at Bridge
City, I recalled the day some twenty-five years ago when Dad took
Mom and me for the same drive, and I wondered now if a father must
die before his son can become the man he was meant to be. "Tell us
where to go," Bonelle Louvrier had said when I asked her what genes
were for. It seemed plausible. No, it seemed *right*. Bonelle knew what
she was talking about. I'd never understood my father better than at
this moment, as I made a U-turn and went back up, looking for Levette.

Before the bridge was built there would've been only a ferry boat
connecting one side of the river to the other, and rather than motor
inns and all-night package stores there would've been fields planted
with cotton and sugarcane and broken by stands of swamp trees. My
eyes were on the road and yet I kept seeing something else: the
picture of a beautiful, paint-stained boy leaping to churning brown
water.

I saw him throwing his body clear from the guardrail, his form a
black speck against the sky, legs pedaling and arms flailing as if for
purchase.

Why did he do it? What had compelled him to jump? Asmore's
suicide was made all the more difficult to understand by my own experience, and by my own good fortune. At his age I was way too busy
enjoying myself to contemplate the possibility that the party might

end one day. Nights when I wasn't covering a story for the paper I was out with friends, pursuing as many adventures as a young reporter's salary could afford. I went to movies and little-theater productions, attended gallery openings and rock concerts, drank beer wherever it was cheap, shopped the Gap for discounted chinos and pocket Ts. I worked out three times a week at the Lee Circle Y, kept track of my bench press in a daybook and played league basketball. The phone rang incessantly, mostly girls calling. My biggest worries involved issues that now, in light of how Asmore must've suffered, seem so insignificant I'm embarrassed to acknowledge them: which Carnival krewe to join, whether to rent in Mid-City or the Lower Garden District, who among my out-of-town friends to invite to stay over during Jazz Fest. Except for those days when I was assigned to write an obit about one of the city's leading citizens, death was never a consideration.

Crossing back over the river, I glanced in the rearview mirror and there he went over the side again.

※

I spotted the car as I was walking up Moss Street, returning home from my neighborhood coffee shop. In one hand I lugged an art book the size of a cinder block, in the other a *mocha grande* in a paper cup. The dark blue Mercedes-Benz station wagon was parked in front of the house with its rear door cocked open. I was about a hundred feet away when Lucinda Copeland came through the gate followed by Lowenstein's maid. Lucinda, dressed in a gray business suit and wearing her long hair piled on top of her head, walked to the open door and leaned inside. When she appeared again she was holding what looked like a painting wrapped in a padded blanket, the kind movers use. The maid grabbed one side, Lucinda took the other, and together they ushered the painting through the gate. When Lucinda returned a few minutes later she was alone. She folded the blanket and placed it in back.

"Lucinda, it's Jack," I said, striding toward her on the sidewalk.

She glanced up with a startled expression. "Jack Charbonnet," I said. "Rhys Goudeau's friend. We met in the Louisiana Room at the gallery some weeks ago."

"Oh, yes, Jack. Nice to see you again."

"Making a delivery to Mr. Lowenstein, were you?"

"Yes, making a delivery. The first of many today, actually."

"I live here. I rent the garçonnière in back—that is, the old quarters that connect with the house. The old man's got quite a collection, doesn't he?"

"Does he?" she said and bubbled out the nervous suggestion of a laugh. "If so, he certainly has the showcase for it. What a house. Well, it was good seeing you again, Jack. Take care, you hear?"

"Lucinda," I said, "was Mr. Lowenstein the one who bought *Beloved Dorothy?*"

She looked at me and smiled, the smile of one who recognizes when she's being led in a direction she had better not go, and lured there by a person she would be smart not to trust. "Jack, why don't you ask Mr. Lowenstein what he bought at the auction? It's really unethical of me to disclose information about purchases without a client's consent. I could lose my job. I hope you don't take offense."

"Sure, Lucinda, I understand."

"It's just that collectors are very secretive about what they buy."

"Really? I would think they'd be proud of it and want to show it off."

"Actually, the opposite is true. No one is more paranoid than a committed collector. He has insurance considerations, security issues, that sort of thing."

"Yes, you start advertising what you have, and there's no telling who'll be paying a visit." I let her have a big, toothy smile, then said, "Maybe even the thief you have living in your apartment out back."

"Jack, I hope you didn't think . . . it wasn't my intention to insinuate that you might want to *steal* Mr. Lowenstein's painting—"

"So it is a painting," I said.

"Well, it isn't an antique hobby horse, I will say that."

"Sorry for putting you on the spot," I said. "Good to see you again, Lucinda."

"You, too, Jack. Now have a nice day. And say hi to Rhys for me."

I cleared the gate and immediately went to the front door. Past the screen the only paintings I saw were those already hanging on the walls of the long hallway, and the few miniatures standing on photo easels on the buffet. I banged a fist against the frame and the maid shuffled to the door. Small and delicately built, she stood wiping her hands with a dish towel as she waited for me to say something. "Is Mr. Lowenstein's nurse here today?" I gave my coffee a careful sip to advance an appearance of insouciance and calm.

"May I ask who's calling?"

"Oh, I'm sorry. I forget we haven't been introduced. I'm the tenant who rents the garçonnière. Jack Charbonnet. Maybe you've seen me in the garden."

She stepped up closer to the screen and met my eyes with hers. "The nurse doesn't work here anymore. Can I help you with something?" Hers was a voice like Butterfly McQueen's, from *Gone With the Wind.* It was the voice of a child in the body of a woman, and an edgy, conspiratorial child, at that.

"What happened to the nurse?" I whispered, moving closer.

She looked back at the hallway, to make sure she was alone. "Mr. Lowenstein had to let her go," she said. "He told me that, anyway." She shook her head and shot another glance backward. "Things aren't good."

"Ma'am . . ."

"Sally."

"Sally, when you have a minute, please tell Mr. Lowenstein I send my congratulations. I'm sure he'll know what I mean."

"That you send your congratulations? Mr. Charbonnet from the apartment?"

"That's right."

"For what? I mean, he might want to know."

"For the painting, the one the lady from the auction house just delivered."

She blinked a few times, as if certain now that I really was out of my mind.

"The portrait," I said, "the pretty picture of the girl . . . ?"

"Yes, okay. I'll tell him."

"Also, if you wouldn't mind, please tell Mr. Lowenstein—"

"Tell Mr. Lowenstein *what*?" came a man's voice, so loud and unexpected that I nearly dropped both my book and coffee to the ground. It was Lowenstein, revealing himself in one of the doorways. His wheelchair clattered as he pushed out into the hall and charged toward me. "You've interrupted my quiet time, Mr. Charbonnet. What is it you could possibly want now?"

"Only to let you know how pleased I am that it was you who bought the Asmore, Mr. Lowenstein. I could tell from your visit how well you thought of the painting, and I'm glad she's back on Moss Street where she belongs."

Sally seemed to understand that she wasn't needed any longer, and perhaps that by hanging around she risked witnessing something she was better off not seeing. Lowenstein waited until she was gone before he said, "You assume too much. I would warn against that."

"You got a great painting, a masterpiece."

"Did I? Well, I'll accept that, if you say so. Is there anything else?"

"Just one more question, please. Mr. Lowenstein, if a portrait by Levette Asmore fetches more than four hundred thousand dollars at auction, my question is, how much do you think a twenty-foot-long mural by the same artist is worth?"

He was silent for a moment, then rolled up closer to the door, exciting a smell of someone who's been days since his last wash. "Is this a hypothetical question, or do you know of such a painting? If you're talking about the post office mural, it's a waste of time. It was destroyed before anyone but a few had a chance to see it."

"Anyone but a few?" I said.

"Yes."

"Mr. Lowenstein, were you one of these few, by chance?"

"Yes, as a matter of fact I was. Now allow me to ask you a question, since I was kind enough to answer yours. What were you doing with Levette's portrait, the one of the girl? Did it belong to you?"

"It was Patrick Marion's, something he inherited. The sitter was his aunt."

His mouth dropped open slightly as he pondered the connection.

"Mr. Lowenstein, did I hear you right? Did you say you saw the Asmore mural in the post office? The Magazine Street post office?"

"Is that where it was?" He looked down at his hands in his lap as if the answer lay there. "Well, if you say so. You know everything else."

"Do you remember what the painting showed?"

"What it showed." Not a question, but a statement: "What it *showed*."

"The subject matter. Asmore received a WPA commission to paint a mural showing the history of transportation in America, but he created something else, something so controversial that the community acted quickly to have it destroyed. What I'm curious to learn is what he painted to bring on such a response."

"You're like a child with all your questions. You know how children pepper you with questions? 'Why is the grass green?' 'Where do the stars come from?' That's you." He pushed back from the door and wheeled down the hall, making noise as he went. "Now excuse me, please. I have a masterpiece to hang."

※

First came footsteps crossing the brick walk of the cloister, then the sound of someone crying. I sat up in bed, pulled back the curtains and looked out at the garden. "Not you again," I muttered.

It was six o'clock in the evening, early for a visit from Lowenstein, let alone a ghost, and I'd just awakened from the most satisfying nap of my adult life. At the front of my brain floated puffs of cloud and gray matter, but at the rear, back there in all the fabulous cobwebs, a

small light shone on the fresh memory of a dream: Rhys Goudeau and
I in my Biloxi hotel room, making love with the windows open to a
Gulf breeze.

Head dull and heavy from sleep, I grabbed the handle of my
trusty Pete Rose and let it direct me outside. "Sally, what's wrong?" I
said. "Anything I can help you with?"

She had found her way to the garden bench. Her shoulders were
shaking as she wept into a wad of napkins. "He fired me," she said
with a shout, and the weeping came louder. "Oh, God, what am I going to do?"

"He fired you? That mean old bastard fired you, too?"

"He did it. Gave me my check and said there wouldn't be another.
Got me to give him my keys back."

I looked toward the house and the dark windows along the lower
gallery. "Wait here, Sally. I'll go have a talk with him."

"Ain't going to do any good." And the noisy tears came again.
"Why, he's the orneriest man alive, Mr. Charbonnet. The absolute
orneriest man alive." Coming from Sally the word sounded this way:
"Awnyeriest."

I went to him despite the warning, lugging the bat with me.
From behind me Sally called in that crazy voice, "You come back
here, Mr. Charbonnet. You can't talk to that man. That man is *awny-
ery . . .*"

I could feel heat dumping color in my face even before I shouted
his name past the screen. When he answered, he did so without the
aid of his wheelchair, shuffling across the polished floor with one
hand touching the wall for balance, the other gripping the pajama
bottoms at his hip as if to stave off pain. To complement the rumpled
flannel bottoms, he was wearing a white button-down dress shirt and
leather moccasins with fat winter socks. The shirt looked neatly
pressed, no doubt by Sally. "How do you live with yourself?" I said as
he came toward me, raising my voice in an approximation of rage.
"Now it's the maid you fire. Wasn't the nurse enough?"

"Since when are my affairs any of your concern?"

"Since your housekeeper ruined my nap with her crying, that's when."

"Mr. Charbonnet, I'm so sorry your nap was interrupted, especially at this hour of the day when all the rest of humanity is enjoying precious sleep. But I'm going to have to ask you to step away from that door." He pointed a finger. "You leave me no choice but to call the authorities."

"Go ahead and call them. You've kicked everyone else out. Why not add your sleepy tenant to the pile?" He now was only a few feet away from me, squinting as he checked to make sure the door was latched. "If you can afford to buy a painting as pricey as *Beloved Dorothy,*" I said, "I'm sure my paltry rent check can't mean much to you. But what about your obligation to Sally and the nurse? Not that I liked the nurse. You owed them something, didn't you?"

"Take a deep breath, Mr. Charbonnet. You're on the verge of apoplexy. And on my doorstep, at that."

He unlatched the door and nudged it open, and I hesitated before stepping inside, although I was probably no less surprised than he seemed to be at having invited me in.

"Leave your weapon at the door," he said.

I followed him, defiantly bringing the bat with me. We went into a large room crowded with books and paintings, and he pointed to the chair in which he wanted me to sit. "Would you like a drink, Mr. Charbonnet?"

"Nothing, thank you."

He was standing at a butler's tray holding liquor bottles. "I'm having cognac, my evening ritual. I was just sitting down to one when you . . . well, how shall I put it . . . when you came a-calling."

Snifter in hand, he lowered himself into a wing chair so old and worn you could see through its fabric to a subcutaneous layer of moss stuffing. He put the moistened end of a cigar stub in his mouth and chewed on it. "I recall this flaw in your character from the last time we talked," he said. "You like to make assumptions, don't you? You like to size up a situation and deliver your verdict, regardless of the facts."

"The facts?" I said. "Which facts are those?"

"The facts as you see them, not necessarily as they are."

"How about this for a fact?" Feeling absurd even as I did it, I lifted the bat out of my lap and held it out in front of me.

Hanging on the wall directly behind Lowenstein was a pair of nearly identical Drysdale landscapes depicting the Louisiana bayou, and randomly scattered next to them were New Orleans scenes by Robert Grafton, Louis Oscar Griffith, Clarence Millet and William Woodward. Yet another wall held more Alberta Kinsey oil paintings than I could count in a glance, the most impressive of them showing the interior of a Royal Street antique store, circa 1930. I took pride in being able to attribute the works to specific artists, my recent refresher course in southern art history having served me well. The one place that wasn't covered with either paintings or books was the most conspicuous of all.

"Something fall off the wall?" I said and nodded toward the vacant space above the fireplace. "Now that you have me here would you like some help in hanging *Dorothy*?"

"I didn't buy the Asmore. Whatever gave you that impression?"

"Don't do this, please. I know better. I clearly saw Lucinda Copeland—"

"Miss Copeland was returning a painting—a painting I've owned for more than twenty years. Not that it should be any of your concern, but I'd put it up for sale at the recent Neal auction and it failed to meet the reserve, and a modest reserve it was at that." He sighed in a way to show disappointment. "Again, Mr. Charbonnet, why would you think it was I who bought the Asmore?"

"Well, you liked it so much."

"Levette was brilliant, incapable of making a bad picture. But what does that have to do with anything?"

"Tommy Smallwood didn't buy it."

"Are Tommy Smallwood and I the only collectors who qualify in your estimation as potential buyers of important southern pictures?"

He choked out a laugh cloudy with phlegm. "You entertain me. You really do."

"Why is the space above the mantel empty?" I said. "What went there? Was it the painting you just tried to sell at auction?"

He sipped his drink and kicked the end of his cigar with a thumbnail. As before, when he came to see *Beloved Dorothy* in the garçonnière, Lowenstein was protective of every word that passed from his mouth, and he seemed unwilling to part with information, no matter how insignificant, unless I was prepared to give up something in exchange. "Six months' rent in advance," he said. "You offered three, as I recall."

"Six months? Six months and what do I get?"

"I'll take your questions and let the girl stay on."

"Sally?"

He nodded.

"In that case I'll drop a check off later tonight."

"Very good. And make it out to me this time. There's no reason to involve High Life." He waited a moment, then said, "To answer your question, Mr. Charbonnet, the painting I offered to sell occupied a place in a bedroom upstairs. That is until last month when I thought to see what it might fetch at auction. Do you know the artist Noel Rockmore, by chance? Or hasn't he rated an entry in your precious art books yet?"

"Noel Rockmore," I replied, practically reading text from memory. "Noel Rockmore, originally from New York, the son of artists, was best known for his portraits of the jazz musicians at Preservation Hall, painted in the early sixties."

"Your memorization skills are superb. And although every jot of this painting came from Rockmore's brush, it wasn't from his musician series."

"Was it the nude showing the woman with enormous fake breasts?"

Lowenstein smiled. "While you're correct in identifying the painting, I would strongly suggest to you that Saki's breasts, however large, were not fake. I knew the lady, you see. She came by her assets naturally."

I sat looking at him for a minute. "I was in the gallery at Neal when it came up on the block. It's a fine painting. I'm sorry it didn't attract a buyer."

"I'm not," he said. "I'd lost sleep the night before, upset about losing her. The odd thing is, I rarely even visit the bedroom where I've kept her all these years because I struggle to get up the stairs. It was wrong of me to offer to let the painting go—wrong at any price. I might have learned from previous experience." He glanced at the fireplace and the blank space above it. "Care to venture a guess?"

I walked to the hearth and stood staring at the wall. The color of the plaster where the painting once hung was a shade lighter than the area around it. The size was considerable: when framed, the painting would've come to about thirty inches by forty-four inches. I tracked back to recent auction sales and several possibilities came to mind. "Was it by a southern artist?"

"Of course. Look around you. Every painting I own is southern. Critics call it micro-collecting, when the collector can't see beyond his small purview. But what else, I ask, should I have hanging on my walls?" Another bout of phlegmy laughter. "Pictures of the California coast? Scenes of the Brooklyn Bridge? Old Mexico?" He shook his head. "You won't find any of that here."

"The painting you sold? Was it nineteenth or twentieth century?"

"Weren't there southern artists practicing the craft in the eighteenth century?"

I was becoming annoyed, even as I was closing in on the answer. "Would you just give me the century, Mr. Lowenstein?"

"Nineteenth. But late nineteenth."

"Were there people in it?"

"Yes, it was populated with several dozen people, although I never actually bothered to count. Animals, too. A mule as well, if my memory serves."

I returned to my chair and sat down. "So is it a fact that you were related to the painting's original owner, the one who himself bought it from William Aiken Walker?"

"Ah, yes, that would be my grandfather. Touché, Mr. Charbonnet. Touché." He put his cigar down, the snifter next to it, and gave me loud applause. When he was finished, he said, "I must say, that Tommy Smallwood bought my grandfather's cotton kingdom, and that it now hangs in his home, inspires in me a wild spirit of pyromania."

"Burning the man's house down seems a little extreme. Whatever happened to throwing eggs and wrapping the trees in toilet paper?"

He stood to pour another drink, the effort causing him to groan. He began to speak again only after he'd turned his back to me. "I've made some unwise choices of late, Mr. Charbonnet, choices that now threaten my security. Like many an investor I played the markets hard and recklessly in recent years. At some point I'm afraid I contracted the dotcom disease." He let on a rueful smile. "Most were start-ups. I bought into the fiction. Do you see where this is going?"

"I do."

"I'm quite a sizable chunk in arrears." His second glass contained twice as much cognac as the first. He disposed of it quickly. "I suppose it was inevitable that it come to this. I've been in decline—rapid, steady decline. First went my health, now the money. To be honest, I don't know which is worse."

"So you're selling off your collection to cover your debts."

"Yes, that was the plan. I offered to rent the garçonnière for the same reason. Nothing personal, Mr. Charbonnet, but it's nearly killed me to have to share my home. Obviously I'm the shadowy, private sort. Renting out the rooms seemed the least painful way to raise cash." He finished off the drink and placed the snifter on the floor at his feet. "The Walker performed well enough to keep some creditors away—I netted about two hundred and fifty thousand dollars. But the Rockmore disappointed. I could sell them all and easily wipe out my debt, but that isn't going to happen. Don't be alarmed if in the next few weeks you encounter a for-sale sign hanging on the front gate.

Given a choice between sacrificing the house or the collection, I give up the house."

"You'd give up the roof over your head before your paintings?"

"Sure I would. I won't let them go. They have been good company—the best company of my life. I will not allow them to be desecrated at more public sales."

"Where do you intend to live, Mr. Lowenstein? That is, if you do elect to part with this place?"

He seemed to have no answer. He shrugged. "A barn, a lean-to, an abandoned shack in the Lower Ninth Ward. I've even considered a large storage unit—but one that's climate-controlled, of course, to keep from exposing the paintings to the elements. I suppose it really doesn't matter where I end up, as long as my paintings are with me."

"Considering your financial problems this might seem like an insensitive question. But if you do sell the place . . . I mean, what about our arrangement? What about the rent I just agreed to pay you in advance?"

"Not to worry. I'll reimburse you with proceeds from the sale. Or you can contract with the new owner to rent the garçonnière. I can't imagine their not wanting to keep you. You would be taking a bite out of their mortgage, after all. Besides that, having you on the property has kept the ghost away."

I looked at him and his face showed no evidence that he was joking. On the contrary, he appeared to be quite serious. I cleared my throat. "I don't think it's smart to pay all that rent when I can't be certain I'll be allowed to stay on here."

"You're right. But you have no alternative if you intend to make your stand for the maid." Even as he spoke, I could hear a back door opening. It was Sally, returning from her interlude in the garden. Lowenstein glanced over his shoulder, in the direction of the hallway. "Mr. Charbonnet, this interview is over."

He was struggling to stand again when she entered the room, trails from her tears still marking her face. It occurred to me that I'd been set up, that she and Lowenstein had schemed to liberate me of advance rent. But Sally didn't seem capable of such deception. We exchanged smiles, sad ones, and I offered to let her have my chair. "I was just leaving," she said in a voice weakened by crying. "It was nice to know you, Jack Charbonnet."

I glanced at Lowenstein. He seemed to be waiting for me to make a decision. "Sally," I said, "there's good news. Mr. Lowenstein tells me he's changed his mind about your employment here. You've decided to keep Sally on, haven't you, sir?"

"As a matter of fact, I have," Lowenstein said, then lifted his empty glass to toast. "Sally, congratulations, darling, you're back on the payroll. I apologize if I've been . . . well, *unfeeling*. You go home now and I'll see you first thing tomorrow morning."

"Oh, thank you. Thank you, Mr. Lowenstein." She began to cry again, in her loud, theatrical way. She threw me a wave as she raced off down the hall.

"You're leaving now, Mr. Charbonnet," Lowenstein said. "But next time—and I'm sure there will be one—please remember to leave the baseball bat behind. All assumptions, too, if you would be so kind."

He rested a hand on my shoulder and guided me to the hall, then latched the door shut as soon as I stepped outside. "Drop your rent check in the mailbox. And do it tonight, as promised. If I consider another reduction in staff, I'll be sure to check with you first. Good evening, Mr. Charbonnet." He smiled now, exposing a set of dentures nearly as gray as his face. "As always, it was swell."

❄

It was hot outside, but Mom had insisted on making gumbo. A big pot of the stuff was waiting on the stove when I arrived at the old house in Riverbend and sat at the kitchenette table and drank from the glass of peach tea she'd poured for me. The air was heavy with the smell of roux and I thought of Tommy Smallwood and wondered what kind of man sat in his bathroom crying over a painting at four o'clock in the morning. It was seafood gumbo—Dad's favorite—and Mom served it from a ceramic tureen. She made sure I got plenty of shrimp and crabmeat and she served the rice on the side so that she could put more gumbo in the bowl.

I waited until she'd ladled a bowl for herself and was sitting down before I took my first bite. My dad had taught me to do that. He also taught me to fork some cold potato salad into the gumbo and let the salad absorb some of the thick brown juice, and when I did that now I caught my mother looking at me with a wash of tears in her eyes. I thought if I just didn't say anything maybe the feeling would leave her and it did after a while and then I began to eat.

We got through dinner and I cleared the table and told her I would do the dishes, to go wait for me in the living room. I didn't use the dishwasher; I did it all by hand. It took me twenty minutes and when I was done I went to join her. She was sitting in her chair crying and I sat on the sofa next to her and held her hand and neither of us said anything, we just let her cry.

I turned on the TV and we watched a couple of shows and I didn't once look at my watch, not wanting to have her think I wasn't enjoying myself. "That was a good gumbo," I said.

"It wasn't too salty?"

"No, ma'am."

Later I asked her if she needed me to take care of anything around the house. She said there was a lightbulb out on the back porch, if I didn't mind changing it. I had to use a ladder. When I was finished, I sat next to her again. "I met this girl," I said.

"Oh, Jack, you should've invited her over."

"Maybe next time I will."

There was more to tell her but I didn't think I could do it. She walked to the kitchen and threw away the paper tissue she'd been using. She seemed better now. "I've liked all your girlfriends so far," she said, sitting back down. "What's this one's name?"

"Rhys Goudeau."

"Oh, that's pretty."

"Mom, do we have any black blood in the family?"

"Any black blood?"

"Yes, ma'am."

"Why do you ask, Jack? Are you wondering again why your hair is wavy?"

"No, I was just wondering."

She looked at me and I could see that she knew what I was getting at, what I wanted to tell her had I been able to. She let out a sigh and settled deeper in her chair. "I just want you happy, Jack. It's what your dad wanted, too. We were never complicated people."

"Mom, I don't understand the world sometimes," I said.

"I never understood it, either, but then I never pretended to. Just do what you know is right, Jack. Good things will happen."

"Are you feeling better, Mom?"

"Yes, I am. Thank you."

I kissed the side of her face and she followed me to the door. When I was in my car driving off I slowed and looked back at the house and saw her through one of the windows in front. She had returned to her chair, and now the light of the TV was on her. I felt like pulling over and going back in and telling her that we were more complicated than she knew. But I got past the feeling and drove home to Moss Street, more sure now than ever that everything was going to be okay.

In the dark we covered the windows with sheets of brown contractor paper and used masking tape to keep them in place. Only after we finished did Rhys turn on a flashlight and light the Coleman lanterns. Her face, already damp with sweat, glistened in the cloud of yellow-green light. To make sure we weren't giving away our presence in the building, she sent Joe Butler outside for a look from the street. He returned through a back door shaking his head. "Darker'n shit," he said.

"Nothing? Are you sure?"

"Positive."

They were whispering, although it probably wasn't necessary. Earlier, when we'd arrived and parked on the side street, there wasn't a soul in sight. Magazine Street, which generally is trafficked at all hours, was desolate under the humming streetlamps. No dogs barked as we unloaded the ladders and supplies from the van. The key had fit perfectly; the door had opened without a sound. It was so easy that both Rhys and Joe had laughed when I said they should consider a future as art thieves.

Now they were raising an extension ladder and positioning it against the wall with the mural. "We'll start by taking the tacks out," Rhys said. "Joe, use these." She handed him a tack puller and a flat-head screwdriver. "Try to be careful not to dig into the canvas and damage the surface any more than it already is."

"I wish there was more light up there," Joe said. The light from the lanterns did not extend beyond the bottom edge of the painting.

"I'll keep a flashlight on you. Jack, come stand here and hold the ladder in place. Make sure it doesn't slip. We don't want any accidents."

"You got that right," Joe said, then started to climb.

He worked quickly and when he finished prying out the tacks on the side and bottom edges we raised the ladder higher and he began removing the tacks along the top.

"Joe?"

"What?"

"Make sure you leave some in up there, okay?"

"Remind me why I need to do that, boss."

"To keep the canvas in place in case the paste can't support the weight."

"Will do."

She kept the flashlight on him but it did little to cut the darkness. He was moving slower now and with more care and deliberation. He seemed to be almost finished when one of the tacks dropped from the darkness into the lantern light and whizzed right past me. The tack hit hard and skittered across the tiles before stopping near where Rhys was standing. "This isn't good," she said, leaning over and picking it up. "Joe? Joe, darling, this is unacceptable."

"One tack?"

"One tack might be all it takes."

"All it takes for what?" I said.

"For us to go to jail. And for Gail Wheeler to go there. And for the school to close. And for Mr. Cherry to lose his job. Want me to continue?"

"No," Joe said. "But you could relax a little. And point that light back up here."

As soon as he started working again I could feel dust falling and then a strip of canvas peeled off the wall and came flying past me and crashed to the ground. It measured only about a foot wide but the heave of dust extinguished both lanterns and left a powdery residue all over my clothes. This time Rhys didn't say anything, but as she was relighting the lanterns I noticed that her hands were shaking. "Hey, are you okay?"

"Just for the record," she said, "that wasn't anybody's fault."

"Fault?" Joe said, from the top of the ladder. "Who cares about fault? Of course it wasn't anybody's fault."

"I don't blame you," she said to Joe.

"Blame *me*? How about blame Levette? He put the damn thing up here."

"Rhys, what is wrong with you all of a sudden?" I said.

She looked at me and smiled, and in the light from the lanterns, with her hair showing different colors, I thought of the Whitesell photograph of her grandmother Jacqueline LeBeau, and marveled again at the likeness between the two.

"That dust is mostly dried paste," she said. "No big deal." She was trying to sound like her old self, the confident one who knows every-thing and never hesitates to share it. "Did you breathe much of it in?"

"It isn't toxic, is it?"

"It's just glue—rabbit glue."

"Thanks. That makes me feel so much better."

My attempt at humor didn't register. "Jack, do me a favor, honey," she was still whispering. "If you wouldn't mind, take the piece of canvas that fell and roll it up on one of those cardboard tubes. Make sure the yellow surface—the surface where the painting would be—is on the outside. You'll crush the paint if it's on the inside."

Joe came down the ladder and the two of them cleaned the residue off the floor, giving it more attention that it seemed to need. There was nothing left that I could see but they kept cleaning, anyway. Joe was first to stop and he stood watching her awhile. Finally he cupped the back of her arm with his hand. "Good enough," he said.

"You think so?"

"We don't want the sonofabitch *too* clean."

Next they positioned a couple of eight-foot folding ladders under the mural and ran matching two-by-fours from the top step of one to the top step of the other, creating a platform. The boards were new and Rhys tested them for strength, bouncing up and down. "This ought to do us just fine," she said. "Jack, you stay on the ground and watch the ladders and hold the flashlight. Joe and I will remove the panels. These things are pretty heavy and they're clumsy to handle and they're going to be a challenge, but we can do it. We'll hand them down to you, okay?"

"I'm ready," I said.

Working from the right to the left side, Rhys used a putty knife to scrape each section off the wall. As she progressed, Joe stayed close by her side with both hands on the canvas to make sure it didn't fall. When she finished scraping under the canvas Joe would reach up with his tack puller and remove the last of the tacks, then together they'd lower the panel for me to hold until they could come down from the platform. We rolled each section onto a tube and then Joe and I moved it off to the side. In the lamplight I could see the sinew of his small arms and streaks of perspiration cutting the film of dust on his glasses. His strength surprised me. Like his voice, it might've belonged to a much larger man. Rhys was always first back up the ladder, and then the residue came raining down again. By the time we got the last panel down my hair was powdered gray and dust sat a

quarter inch deep on my shoulders. "God, I'm sorry, Jack. I didn't realize there would be this much."

"You're hell with a putty knife."

"Just hang in there."

I checked my watch against the lantern and it was a little after
3:00 A.M. "What time does the janitor show up for work?" Joe said.

"Six," Rhys answered.

"I don't think we have enough time," he said.

"Don't tell me that. We have enough time, we have plenty of
time."

She started cleaning the surface of the wall with an iron brush,
more dust from the paste spitting out with each thrust. Joe went outside and brought the van over to the rear door and he and I unloaded
the replacement mural and carried it into the building one section at
a time. It was good to be outside in the night air, with stars fanned out
across the sky and the moon full and shining up past the trees. A truck
motored down Magazine Street, but there was no other sign of life,
human or otherwise. Joe lighted a cigarette and took a few long drags.
"Can I ask you a personal question?" I said.

"This the time you want to be doing that?" He removed a fleck of
tobacco from the tip of his tongue.

"Are you a black guy or a white guy, Joe?"

"Am I a *what*?"

"Are you a black guy or a white guy?"

"The first one." He looked at me. "Is that important, for some
reason? So important it couldn't wait?"

"The first one. You mean you're black?"

"Why is that important at four o'clock in the goddamned morning and we've broken into a building and we're stealing a painting?"

"It's not important," I said.

"You asked it."

"I asked it but it's not important."

"It was important enough for you to stop what you were doing
and make the words come out of your mouth."

"I was standing here watching you with your cigarette and the question popped in my head."

"That's right, that's what makes me wonder. Of all the things you could've asked me you asked me if I'm a white guy or a black guy. What kind of question is that?"

"I don't know," I said.

"It's a dumbass question from a dumbass motherfucker, that's the kind of question it is." He dropped the cigarette to the ground and crushed it with the heel of his boot. "What about you, Jack? You a white guy or a black guy?"

"I'm a white guy."

"Nice," he said. "Now you ready to go do some work?"

After we moved all four replacement panels inside he returned the van to the street and I took Rhys's place on the platform prepping the wall to accommodate the new canvas. She sat on the floor between the lanterns with her legs splayed and sucked hard on a bottle of spring water. I could reach higher than Rhys did but not high enough, so Joe and I raised the extension ladder and he went up and finished the job. We set up the platform again on the folding ladders and Joe and I lifted the first of the replacement panels onto the boards while Rhys lathered glue on the wall. The new canvas wasn't as heavy as the old one, but it was a bitch to hang. Rhys and I worked from the platform as Joe stood just behind us on the extension ladder. Except for the time I kissed her I'd never been so close to Rhys before and I could smell the shampoo in her hair and the smell of her sweat and I had to remind myself to keep working and not to think about it. By the time we'd hung each panel and hammered in tacks along the edges it was after five o'clock and I could see fatigue competing with panic for control of Rhys's expression. Panic was winning. "We'll make it," I said.

"I don't know. I think Joe was right."

"Why all of a sudden are you listening to anything I have to say?" Joe said. "I don't know shit. Now let's finish."

She went back up the ladder with a small can of paint and a small brush and began painting the heads of the tacks to match the yellow of the canvas. She had it all figured out. She'd been able to envision the heads needing that last touch of paint to make them look convincing. Joe removed the paper from the windows and I swept and cleaned the floor with a wet rag mop. "We can't leave anything behind," Rhys said. "Not a tack, not a piece of tape, not a mote of dust from the wallpaper paste."

Joe went out for the van and brought it back around. We loaded the panels for the original mural and then the ladders, supplies and bags filled with trash. The room looked as clean as we'd found it. Rhys, however, refused to leave before inspecting it a final time. She placed both lanterns on the floor and dropped to her knees and crawled around looking for evidence that we'd been there. "It's dusty here," she said, peering up at me with a look of recrimination. "You missed a spot."

"Did I miss a spot?"

"You missed it," she repeated, then started to wipe down the floor with a paper towel. "Missed it and with all we stand to lose. Goddammit, Jack."

"Let's go, we need to go," Joe said.

I was tired and sore and covered with dust and I could feel the twitching of the muscles in my arms as I stood in the middle of the room looking up at the wall where the replacement mural now hung. It looked exactly like the original. Rhys's work was so thorough that she'd remembered to put bubbles and other surface defects in the canvas. It also had water stains dripping down under the air-conditioning vents.

"Amazing," I said.

"To you, maybe," she said. "The real test will come when Mr. Cherry has a look."

"And Mrs. Wheeler."

"Nah, she's oblivious and half blind to boot. I wish the new tacks were identical to the old ones. The heads aren't exactly the same size, did you notice?"

"No, I didn't."

"And I'm afraid the new paint's too shiny. Do you see that, Jack? Does the paint on the heads look too shiny?"

"Let's go, we have to go," Joe said from the door.

We left as quietly as we'd come, and with daylight just starting to break. I sat in front squeezed between Rhys and Joe. It wasn't yet six o'clock, but as we turned the corner onto Magazine Street I spotted Rondell Cherry stepping off a city bus stopped a block away. We drove by him and watched in silence as he lumbered down the sidewalk carrying a lunch pail and wearing headphones connected to a small music box at his hip. "You remember what he was listening to that day we first met him?" I said to Rhys.

When she didn't answer I leaned forward to get a better look at her face. Her hands were tight on the wheel, whitening her knuckles.

"I think it was some Teddy," I said, in answer to my question.

"Who?" Joe said.

"Teddy. You don't remember Teddy Pendergrass?"

For a moment I thought Rhys was crying. But then she turned and faced me and a big powdery smile came to her face. "We did it," she said.

"Yes, we did," I replied.

Farther down the street, she lowered her window and stuck her head out, letting the wind blow the dust out of her hair.

EIGHT

Dr. Gilbert Perret, wearing a black turtleneck sweater and wool trousers even in summer, stepped out on the third-floor gallery and summoned me with a finger curling backward. "Here to see *Christine,* are you?"

"Yes, thank you for the opportunity."

He seemed to be trying to suppress a belch. It took a moment before I realized he'd meant to nod. "Always glad to show the old girl off," he said.

Perret wasn't much older than I was, and yet he might've been my superior by at least a generation. Perhaps it was the pair of reading glasses perched on the tip of his nose. More likely it was the rim of hair ornamenting a bald dome ridged with fat blue veins. He smelled like old books. "How was Europe?" I said.

"Cold and rainy but still Europe. Wonderful, in a word. Kind of you to ask."

We entered the administrative offices. The elderly docent who'd scheduled my meeting with the museum curator welcomed me with a wave as we approached her desk. "Appreciate your help, ma'am."

"Any time, Mr. Charbonnet."

The painting hung to the right of Perret's desk as you entered his office. To the left, and equally impressive, was a French Quarter Mardi Gras scene by Marion Souchon, a mid-twentieth-century Fauvist from New Orleans who also regularly turned up in books about southern art. "My first Souchon," I said, pointing.

"Ah. But you've seen other Asmores?"

"Yes, I have: most recently *Beloved Dorothy*, from the Neal sale."

"A real beauty, wasn't she? And a winning example of the series. But I prefer this one, if only because of the museum's familial connection to the sitter."

The lapse between his comment and my comprehension of it ran to about half a minute. I looked away from the painting. "I'm not sure what you mean."

Standing behind his desk now, Perret adjusted the blinds to lessen the flow of sunlight in the room. "What do I mean by what?" he said, in a tone to suggest he welcomed any intellectual challenge I might present him with. A sheet of glare had been reflecting off the surface of the Asmore, but now the painting's color glowed in soft, diffused light. Christine was a fair-haired, rather chesty girl standing before a river, with flowers in her hands. About her expression was the postcoital glow that identified her as yet another satisfied notch on the Asmore bedpost. In the background a circle of sun illuminated a stand of enormous oak trees.

"You said something about the State Museum having a familial connection to the sitter. What do you mean by that?"

"Christine," he said. "The woman you're looking at, as well as the one who welcomed you earlier with a wave as we walked by her."

I still refused to understand. "Forgive me, Dr. Perret."

"Come on, Mr. Charbonnet. My assistant, Christine Dalrymple, out in the hall." He pointed to the top of his head. "Don't you recognize her? The docent, Mr. Charbonnet, the one with the . . . well, with the curiously colored hair."

"Mind if I sit down?"

"Please." He came out from behind the desk and showed me to a chair.

I felt it in my chest. Someone had reached down my throat and was trying to yank my heart out. Perret walked past the open door into the hall. "Christine, if you have a few minutes, dear, I'm sure Mr. Charbonnet would enjoy hearing about Levette."

He pulled back a second chair and turned it toward me. I rose to my feet as the elderly woman entered the room, shambled past without a word and stood next to the painting. She held her head at the same angle as the girl in the portrait, and calculated her expression to mimic that of *Beloved Christine*. Obviously she'd practiced the pose many times before, and it seemed to delight Perret, who all but guaranteed future demonstrations by giving spirited applause. "Thank you," he said. "Mr. Charbonnet, I have a full calendar this afternoon, so if there are questions please ask them now."

"He's too shook up," said the docent, clearly pleased with herself. "Even worse than that other fellow. What was his name, Dr. Perret?" She put a hand up to her mouth. "We thought he'd throw up."

"I'll leave you with Christine, then," Perret said.

I cleared my throat and glanced back at the curator. "Someone else was here? To see the Asmore?"

"Only yesterday," he said. "Do you know Thomas Smallwood, by chance?"

"No, I don't. I mean, I know of him, of course. And I've met him. But I don't *know* him. He's a collector of this sort of thing."

"Yes, and a determined one. I must say, I admired his enthusiasm, exhausting though it may have been." Perret laughed. "He spewed out more hackneyed details about the Asmore myth than I've heard from even our least inspired museum guides. No, if you want to know the truth about the artist, Mr. Charbonnet—the man, the *real* one—then Mrs. Dalrymple here is your source."

"He took my picture," she said. "This Mr. Smallwood did. He had a camera and he took me with the painting, didn't he, Dr. Perret?"

"I saw him do it," said the curator, rocking back on his heels in a show of pride.

"Maybe I can get you a copy," she said to me.

"Pleasure to have met you, Mr. Charbonnet." He extended his hand. "And do make sure she tells you everything."

As soon as he disappeared past the door Christine Dalrymple said, "Fire away and don't be bashful. I'll sit here." With her descent into the overstuffed leather chair came the motherly scent of skin lotion and talcum powder.

"What did Dr. Perret mean by everything, ma'am?"

"Probably the sex. And maybe the body odor."

"Body odor, was there?" I laughed and looked back at *Beloved Christine,* as if for confirmation from the girl in the painting. "I suppose soap was hard to come by, for someone of Levette's limited means," I said. "You don't imagine how they smell."

"How who smells?"

"An artist. You see their paintings and that's the last thing that comes to mind."

She brought her hand back up and whispered again, "I liked it. Now want to hear about the sex?"

"Whatever you're comfortable sharing."

"The first time was in his studio. He wanted me to model without my clothes on. He asked all the girls to model that way. So you take your clothes off and he paints you but when he finished you always had your clothes on—in the picture, I mean. He just liked to look, I guess. He had a reputation, but I would have done anything for him. I was in love, you see?"

"Do you know why he jumped from the bridge, Mrs. Dalrymple?"

"Oh, did he jump from a bridge? I didn't know that. Why would anyone in his right mind jump from a bridge?"

"You don't remember how he died?"

"I think I remember reading something about it in the papers."

"The Huey P. Long Bridge? In Harahan?"

"Of course," she said. "I can tell you all about the Kingfish. He paved the roads and gave free schoolbooks to the children. Am I right?"

"Mrs. Dalrymple, please forgive me for asking this question. I don't intend to insult you. But you aren't really Christine, the girl in this portrait, are you?"

She squeezed her lips together and glanced back at the portrait, as if expecting the girl in the painting, whoever she was, to come to her defense.

"What color hair did Levette Asmore have?" I said.

"Hair?"

"What color was it? Levette's hair?"

Her eyes closed and she threw her head back. She seemed to be trying to concentrate. "Give me a minute, please."

"You recall how he smelled, you recall making passionate love to him in his studio, but you don't remember the color of his hair?"

Her mouth opened and she stammered a reply: "Was it red? That's right, I remember now. Levette was a redhead." She sank deeper into the chair. "That was a trick question, wasn't it?"

I walked over to the painting for a closer inspection. They were different people. They possessed similar facial features, perhaps enough to pass as sisters, but Christine in the portrait was not Christine in the room. "You didn't know Levette Asmore, did you? And you aren't the girl who sat for this portrait, are you?"

She seemed prepared to protest, but then resigned herself to a less likely tactic, that being honesty. "Dr. Perret is so proud to tell people I'm one of the *Beloved* girls. Promise you won't say anything. Please promise, Mr. Charbonnet."

I sat back down. I was disappointed, having already planned to drive to the Guild's studio to tell Rhys, but I also was embarrassed for the woman. "How did Dr. Perret confuse you with the girl in the portrait?"

"I don't get paid to work here, I volunteer."

"Yes, you're a docent."

"I walked in my first day and he did a double take. 'It's Christine,' he said. I nodded, because my name really is Christine. My *middle* name. He called everybody in, everybody he could find, and he started telling them, 'It's Christine, it's Christine, *Beloved Christine.*' The more he said it the more the stories came out of my mouth."

"And none of them true," I said.

"The only man I ever posed for was my third husband and his Polaroid. This was in the seventies when people did that sort of thing. I admit I enjoyed it."

Trading me step for step, she followed me out onto the gallery, then down the stairs all the way to the first floor and past the receptionist. As I approached a rear exit door I thought about Smallwood and wheeled around to ask more questions about his visit, and Mrs. Dalrymple and I nearly collided. "About Smallwood," I said. "The collector? Did he talk to Dr. Perret about Levette? Do you remember what he said?"

"Yes, now I do remember that. He said he'd been shopping for a painting by Levette Asmore for years, searching high and low, without any luck. He was thrilled, he said, because he'd finally located one to buy. He'd paid for it that day—yesterday, as a matter of fact—and was arranging for delivery."

"An Asmore?" I said.

"Someone here in town, willing to sell. When Dr. Perret asked him who the painting belonged to, Mr. Smallwood shook his head and wouldn't say. He was very secretive about it." She placed a hand on my arm. "You still haven't promised, Mr. Charbonnet."

"I promise," I said. "Don't worry, ma'am. Your pose is safe with me."

She let out a sigh. "I just pray God keeps the real Christine from ever deciding to make an appearance. Is it bad of me that I enjoy the attention? It keeps me young, being the girl in the painting, and if you're not young, Mr. Charbonnet, you're no one in this town. When

I told Mr. Smallwood about how Levette smelled, he told me the sweetest thing. 'I'd have washed for you, Mrs. Dalrymple.' Then he kissed the back of my hand."

※

I left the museum and drove directly to Central City and the Guild's studio on Martin Luther King. I hoped to tell Rhys in person about Smallwood's claim of having arranged to buy an Asmore, but I was equally determined to see the work she'd done on the mural. While the possibility existed that Smallwood had succeeded in persuading a collector to sell, it was easier to presume that he'd reached an arrangement with Gail Wheeler. This presented more potential scenarios for disaster than I would ever attempt to sort out alone.

I rang the bell and Joe Butler let me in. "How's the weather?" he said.

"It's beautiful. I don't think it can get any prettier."

"I thought you might say that."

Under loupes lighted with fluorescent tubing the retouch specialists, Sarah and Morgan, were busy at their easels, and not far away the cleaning specialist, Leland, worked on a canvas on a table heretofore used only for gilding frames. A moment passed before it occurred to me that the artists were now downstairs, rather than on the second floor at their usual posts. Joe signaled for me to follow him.

We walked to the other side of the room and stood next to the portrait of the instant ancestor known as "Jack," or the one formerly known as such. The name tag had been removed.

Joe was cleaning his glasses on the tail of his shirt. "She said if you called or came by to give you a message. She said she owes you a lot, you're still good friends and everything, and please don't take this wrong."

"What's going on around here, Joe?"

"She wants some time to finish the job before letting anyone see it."

"And why is that?"

"It's personal with her, bro. Haven't you figured that out yet?" He put the glasses back on but the lenses were as hard to see through as before. "The thing is," he said, "she decided she was going to do the restoration herself—all of it, every step, and every square inch. The paint removal, the retouch, the consolidation, the whole damn deal. A couple of days ago she banished everybody to the first floor."

"Banished? She actually said you were banished?"

" '*Banished!* Everyone's *banished!*' More like that."

I leaned against the wall next to him. "If that isn't some shit."

"Tell me about it. I really wanted to get my hands on that son-ofabitch—the mural, I mean. I'm good with old Levette. I understand the dude's moods, his rhythms, his strokes, his colors, his likes and his dislikes, his dos and his don'ts. I can get in his head, you know what I'm saying? But she's locked me out. She wouldn't even let me in this morning to get the coffeepot."

"Any idea why Rhys is doing this?"

"I think you know." He leaned in closer and tugged on his goatee. "For somebody like Rhys," he said, "this is as good as it gets and as good as it will ever get. It's the Holy Grail, my brother. She's a temporary Jesus up there saving what was lost, healing it with the magic and the power in her hands." I had to fight off an impulse to laugh. The guy was spastic. I wondered how long it had taken him to come up with such crap. "She'll save other great paintings," he went on. "Sure, she will. But she'll never have a chance to save this one. It was his masterpiece. It's got to be hers, too."

"I appreciate what you're saying, Joe. I really do."

"Thank you, bro."

"But what I've got to tell her is important." I was trying to sound reasonable. "It's urgent. It can't really wait."

"It's *got* to wait. You should see her up there, man. She doesn't go home. She's sleeping on an old army cot, having us bring her food. It's like she's in her own desert fighting her own devil. It's biblical. You think I'm full of shit, don't you?"

"I didn't until you mentioned the devil. Okay, Joe. Listen to me. Tommy Smallwood has negotiated to buy Levette's mural."

"But we already got the mural."

"Exactly."

He seemed to understand finally. "I'll tell her."

"One other thing," I said, and pointed over his shoulder at the portrait of the instant ancestor. "Thanks for taking my name off that ugly thing."

"Don't thank me, bro. It was Rhys. She's the one that did it."

❉

She didn't call until later that night, hours after I'd gone to bed. As I reached for the phone I glanced at the dial of the clock on the bedside table. "It's almost two in the morning," I said, by way of greeting.

"Is it?" I could hear her scrambling around for proof. "Wow, you're right, it is almost two. Forgive me, Jack. I shouldn't be calling this late."

"What are you wearing?" I said.

"Huh?"

"It's a joke. 'What are you wearing?' A man gets a call from a woman at this time of night and it's often about . . . well, it's probably *never* about a painting, let me put it to you that way."

"How interesting," she said, in a not-so-subtle dismissal. "Now what did that monster Smallwood go and do?"

I didn't bother to turn on the lamp. There was an edge to her voice, a hint of agitation, and I knew it wasn't going to be a long conversation. I told her what I'd learned during my visit to the State Museum, and she yelled out a laugh that forced me to move the phone from my ear. "I only wish I could be there when they take down our replacement mural and Hairy Mary wipes away the fake yellow paint and finds a blank canvas underneath. This is good. Oh, this is wonderful. Either Smallwood will think she overcleaned the painting and damaged it or he'll realize he's been had and it'll make him want the mural more."

"He'll suspect you, Rhys. He'll figure it out. And that's what has me worried. Smallwood broke into Patrick's apartment and tried to steal *Dorothy*. The guy's dangerous. Who can guess what he'll do to get the mural?"

"Who can? Let me try." She fell silent and I could hear the sound of liquid being poured into a cup. "Nah, it doesn't matter," she said. "I just wish I'd left something for Hairy Mary on the replacement mural. A stick figure shooting the bird. A rat nibbling on Tommy Smallwood's toes. Yes, that would've been nice. Am I being mean tonight?" Now she sipped the liquid. "I have to tell you something, Jack, I have to say it. I can't let Tommy Smallwood own Levette's mural, not at any price. I just can't let that happen."

"He'll own it if he outbids everybody else."

"I know you're right. And it would be a mistake not to invite him to the auction. But I'd almost rather die than let him take actual possession of it."

"Don't you need him, Rhys?"

"Yes, I do need him. If I were to keep Smallwood from pursuing the painting, I would undermine our chances of scoring big. He has to be there. And it'll be his if he buys it, I guess. But I can't fathom the idea of his actually owning it. . . . Oh, God, why am I suddenly obsessing on Smallwood when there's still so much work left to do? I'm tired, obviously. I mean, I'm *really* tired." She sipped again. "Jack, if you want to dig around and find out how he got Mrs. Wheeler to agree to sell him the mural, you have my blessing to do so. Me, I have work to do."

I could hear her chair squeak and I pictured her seated in the one without casters, there in her office with books and pottery and paintings all around. Through the door at her back I could see a splash of golden light from the studio holding the four Asmore panels, now unfurled on tables and the floor. "Tell me about the painting," I said.

She was quiet but for the rustling of papers.

"Rhys? Come on now, tell me what you've found under all that old paint."

I'd barely finished when she put the phone down, ending the call.

※

Classes were done for the day, and after the last of the students had left the school grounds I went inside and found Rondell Cherry mopping the floor of the lobby where the mural had been. He pushed the knot of sudsy red rags between the chairs and over the bases of the heavy chrome platforms. He worked it under the sinks and the racks holding hair-care products. Because he was wearing headphones and listening to music, he didn't hear me when I entered the room, nor did he notice when I tracked a few steps back into the hall, stood in the shadows against the wall and had a careful look at the replacement mural. Tacks driven into the edges appeared to be in place, and the seams that ran between the panels remained glued to the wall. The corn-yellow surface was perfectly hideous. It had been no small accomplishment, matching the appearance of the copy to the original, and yet she'd pulled it off. I felt a flood of admiration for Rhys and wished she were with me now to view her marvelous handiwork. "It's you who's the real artist," I said under my breath, then walked into the room headed straight for Cherry.

"Government man," he said, coming up to his full height, which in boots put him at no less than six feet seven inches. He tipped the mop handle against one of the chairs and removed the headphones, and we shook hands like old friends. "Where's Miss Goudeau?" he said, throwing a glance in the direction of the hallway.

"Rhys had to work. I'm afraid it's just me today, Rondell."

He did a lousy job of hiding his disappointment. "And what brings you back, Jack? You're not looking for another three-dollar haircut, are you?"

I told him I was hoping for a word with Mrs. Wheeler and he led me to her office down a corridor smelling sharply of Pine-Sol, its tiled overlay still damp and shining. He knocked on the door and nudged it open when the old woman told him to come in. "Miss Wheeler, you remember Jack Charbonnet from a few weeks ago?"

"Come in, Rondell."

"Jack Charbonnet," he said again. "Used to write for the *T-P.*"

"The *T-P*? What is that, Rondell?"

"The newspaper. The *Picayune.*"

"How you doing today, Mrs. Wheeler?" I said, stepping around Cherry's large, sweaty form and showing myself.

She was sitting behind a desk with a shopping catalog open in front of her. There were other catalogs on the desk, along with a small lamp, a telephone and an ashtray holding a smoldering cigarette.

"Jack Charbonnet," she said. "Help me out here, Jack."

"I came on Wednesday with Rhys Goudeau and got a haircut. We met afterward out in front."

"You were with Rhys Goudeau," she said, still not certain. "Come in, young man. Come in." Rondell Cherry started to leave and Gail Wheeler said, "Isn't it your boy's ball game this evening, Rondell?"

"Just about got it done, Miss Wheeler."

"You don't want to miss his ball game, Rondell."

"I won't miss it. See you tomorrow, Miss Wheeler."

After Cherry was gone she leaned forward with her forearms resting on the desk. She was wearing another polyester number, this one with a scarf around her neck instead of the usual sweater. Drifts of cigarette ash clung to the front of her blouse and the air above us was blue with smoke. "Them blacks sure do love their sports," she said, in a conspiratorial whisper.

I wasn't sure how to respond. I glanced out the window before looking at her again. She nodded and cocked her head back as she dragged hard on the cigarette. "Nothing they like better than playing ball." She exhaled through her nose, the smoke coming hard from her nostrils. "I can put it out," she said, and showed me the cigarette.

"That's okay, Mrs. Wheeler. It's your office."

"You remember that song 'Smoke Gets in Your Eyes'? Somebody sang it. My husband Jerry used to change the words. He would say, 'Smoke gets in my clothes.' I'd say, 'You can't give me a better hint than that?' He didn't smoke, you see."

"When it came on the radio?"

"What's that?"

"He'd change the words when the song came on the radio?"

"The radio? No, I think that was one we put on the record player."

"That's a funny story."

"Something I like," she said, "I like that Rhys. I think she's got a lot on the ball." She put her hand on the base of the lamp, where the switch was, but she never did turn it on. "What is it I can help you with today, Jack?"

"It's about Tommy Smallwood, ma'am. I wanted to talk to you about him."

"Tommy Smallwood?" she said, then gave her cigarette such a hard suck that the end flared and crackled. "You're going to have to help me with that one, Jack. Do I know him? No," she said. "I don't think I know a Tommy Smallwood. *Smallwood?* That sounds like one of them Indian names. Is he an Indian?"

"I don't think so. He doesn't look Indian."

"Most Indians don't look Indian anymore, but they're still Indian. Same with your blacks. Or a lot of your blacks."

"Ma'am?"

"I'm a man I sure the hell don't want my name to be Smallwood. It has some negative connotations that could lead to what you might call self-esteem issues, you understand?"

"So you have no memory of ever having met Tommy Small-wood?"

"You see there. You mention it and I like to crack up. Bigwood, I could see. Now I could live with Bigwood." She sucked again.

"You didn't meet him?"

"No, I didn't," she said. "Well, not to my knowledge, I didn't. I met you before, hadn't I, and I didn't remember. You never can say for sure with Gail Wheeler, whom she's met and whom she hasn't met. Am I saying that right? Or is it 'who'?"

"You said it right."

"Whom I've met and whom I haven't met," she said. "I need to buy me a dictionary, that's what I need to do."

"Well," I said, and patted my thighs with my open hands, "I guess I'll go now and let you get back to what you were doing."

"You'll do what?" She crushed her cigarette in the tray and came out from behind the desk. "Listen here, Jack, you got something to get off your chest you don't have no reason to hold back with Gail Wheeler."

"It's a delicate situation, Mrs. Wheeler. Tommy Smallwood's a powerful man, and he's a rich man, and I don't want any legal problems. Besides, it's not my habit to go around slandering people."

"Doing what, now?"

"Slandering people. Saying things about them that might hurt their reputations."

"Of course not. Now what did that sonofabitch go and do?"

"Mrs. Wheeler, let me just say this: If Tommy Smallwood comes around the school, you might want to keep an eye on him."

"Oh, don't tell me."

"The man has problems. He's a known . . . well, don't make me say it."

Past the dirty lenses I could see her eyes squeeze tight and burn with sudden purpose. "That no-good sonofa . . . What was his name?"

"Smallwood. Tommy Smallwood."

"Oh, Jack," she said. Her mouth started to tremble and she brought a hand up against it. "You were right to warn me. Thank you."

"Yes, ma'am."

She left about half an hour later, picking trash off the ground as

she descended the steps. I was parked on the side street, slumped behind the wheel. On the sidewalk she stood gazing at the building, first
at the roofline, then at the battered façade and the peeling broadsheets
over windows with cracked panes. She flicked her cigarette out onto
the lawn where grass had probably once grown and the hedges had
leaves. When she brought her dusty little car around to Magazine
Street she braked in front of the building and leaned down low in the
seat. That look came over her face again.

I wondered if it had something to do with her late husband. Had
he always made a point to stand at a window upstairs and wave down
at her? Was that a little love game they played?

A truck came up behind her with a sharp horn blast, and she
sped off.

I was tempted to walk out in front of the building and have a look
for myself, but I knew there was nothing to see that I hadn't seen before.

❋

Almost an hour went by before Rondell Cherry emerged from the
building. He pulled at a fist of keys on his hip, found the ones he
needed and locked the doors. He was carrying his lunch pail and a
newspaper, and as he started for the bus stop I rolled up beside him
and let the passenger window down. He bent low at the waist and his
face showed surprise when he saw who it was. "You got yourself a nice
ride there, Jack."

"Can I give you a lift home, Rondell?"

He shook his head. "I'm fine with the bus."

He walked on and I came up beside him, having to brake to keep
the car moving at his pace. "Rondell, I need to talk to you."

He kept walking. "You need to talk to me?" He stopped and bent
over again. "A man in a car like that needs to talk to *me*? What about,
Jack?"

Horns sounded behind me and I said, "I think you know."

"You think I know what?"

A car sped by me and then another; more horns wailed. "Tommy Smallwood," I said. "You and Tommy Smallwood. How much money did he give you for the mural, Rondell? However much he gave you I can assure you it wasn't enough."

"You don't know me to talk like that, Jack," he said. "Now you and your fancy car can get on out of here. You're going to make somebody wreck."

"It isn't enough, Rondell. I know Smallwood and it isn't enough."

"Go home, Jack. Go home if you know what's good for you."

"Listen to me, Rondell. I'm going to park on the next block over. Meet me at the restaurant across from the school, will you? The pizza place . . ."

"I got me a bus to catch. I got a wife and kids waiting at home."

"The pizza place," I said again. "Meet me."

By the time I reached the restaurant he'd already seated himself at a table by the window. A waitress had taken his order. Presently she brought a couple of draft beers in cold mugs. He sat with his big shoulders slumped forward and his hands folded together. His headphones, silent at last, formed a collar around his neck. A nervous twitch worked at the corner of his mouth. "Ten grand isn't enough?" he said. "How can ten grand for that thing that's already ruint not be enough?"

I sipped the beer and tried to communicate understanding in how I looked at him. "It's not even close," I said.

"Not even close," he repeated. "Then tell me how much is close, Jack?"

"A conservative estimate?" I said, silently issuing an apology to Rhys Goudeau even before I provided an answer. "On a bad day when it's raining cats and dogs outside and the stock market is taking a tumble and there's talk in the air of an economic recession? Even on a day like that—on the worst of days—in New Orleans at auction that painting would bring at least a million dollars."

"A million dollars," he said. He rocked a fist against the table and sent beer tippling over the rim of his mug. "A million dollars? You have got to be kidding me."

"I said at *least* a million. It could bring more, maybe a lot more. I suppose you have your reasons, Rondell. I suppose you've thought this through. I don't have a wife and kids myself, but I know it must be hard. Add to that Mrs. Wheeler's problems and those inspectors coming around and I can't say I blame you."

"You don't blame me, do you?" he said, and his voice cracked. "You think that money's for me? Jack, you think it's for *me*?" He was so angry his hands were shaking. He pulled his wallet out of his back pocket and removed a business card and slid it across the table. Scripted on the face was the name of a New Orleans lawyer. I knew the name. He'd recently represented a former governor of the state who'd been prosecuted in federal court for peddling influence. "You went to college," he said, "then you bound to know what a retainer is? That money went to a retainer to make sure Miss Wheeler has herself a real lawyer. I met with the man today. That girl Miss Wheeler's had working for her—this so-called niece? She might know her way around Lakeside Mall but I doubt she knows it around the legal system. I can't let Miss Wheeler go to jail. No way."

"I owe you an apology."

"You apologizing, then?"

"Yes, I am. I'm sorry, Rondell."

He lowered his head and scratched one of the scars on top, then he laid his hand flat against his skull, as if to quiet the commotion inside. "You think you and Rhys Goudeau were the first to come around looking for that old painting? You think the first day I met you I didn't know what you were looking for? What about when I saw her crying? And what about later when she came back and stood in the lobby taking pictures and pretending they were of the light. *Of the light, Jack?* You must think I'm some kind of ignorant motherfucker."

"Hey, now, come on, Rondell, that isn't fair."

"Rondell," he said in a quiet voice. "Listen to you. I'm *Rondell* to you. Why am I Rondell to you and Miss Wheeler isn't Gail? Rhys

Goudeau doesn't call me Rondell." He shook his head. "I'm old enough to be your daddy, boy. I ever tell you it's okay to call me by my first name? I don't remember telling you shit, Jack." He took a long swallow of the beer, then raised a hand and called the server over. "I'll take the ticket when it's ready," he said.

She made a notation, put the bill on the table and walked back around the counter.

"I'm sorry, all right?" I said. "I'm sorry for everything today."

He placed a ten-dollar bill under the saltshaker and picked up his lunch pail and newspaper and hugged them close to his chest. He was staring at what remained in his mug. "You couldn't know this, you wouldn't, but I had the chance to play for Eddie Robinson at Grambling State University."

"Who's that?"

"He came to see me once on a recruiting trip."

The statement was so far off subject that I was taken aback and couldn't think of how to respond. "Eddie Robinson?" I said. "You mean the football coach?"

"He met my mama and my daddy. He sat at the kitchen table showing brochures with pictures of the campus and the weight room and where they practiced. He had this twinkle in his eye. He told Mama she made the best potato pancakes he ever ate in his life. He told Daddy it was okay to call him Coach Rob. We had ourselves a good time."

"Can I say something now?"

"Let me finish, Jack, then I'll go. You'll let me finish?" I nodded and he said, "I remember he was someone who combed his hair just so, and who kept his shoulders straight and up like this here even when he was sitting down. He was young then, but he had a presence. 'You have what it takes,' he told me. He looked me right in the eyes and told me that. '*You have what it takes.*' I was six foot five and two hundred and seventy-three pounds and I wasn't yet eighteen years old. When he left, the little boys in the neighborhood chased after his car, ran all the way up South Rocheblave. I stood out in the yard and looked at the taillights of his Olds Ninety-eight and got the shivers where I never had them before." A faraway look came to his eyes and he pushed his beer to the side and leaned back in his chair. "Two weeks later I blew out my knee against Saint Aug and never played football again. Coach Rob said I could come up and be on the team as a manager or trainer but I pouted and hung my lip and made every excuse and never left New Orleans. I would get wasted and show all the brothers the train tracks running along the side of my leg, from where the doctor cut me. I had what it takes, I told everybody. This went on for years. You don't want to know how many. I was on the damn street, Jack. Then I met my wife and she got me in the Bridge House? You know about Bridge House?"

"It's a place down on Camp Street."

"That's correct. They help addicts and alcoholics there, people who are down on their luck. I ain't mad at you, Jack. You can't help it."

"I don't know what to say. I'm embarrassed, I feel like shit."

"Telling you about Coach Rob. Like that's going to make you see I'm somebody that deserves your respect." He pushed the beer even farther away and when he looked at me I could see that the anger had gone out of him. "You know why you can't help it? You can't help it because you never really stopped to consider what it's like to be a black man in America. You come at me without the benefit of the motherfucking doubt. You think to yourself, *Look at this ignorant brother with the mop.*"

"I don't think that at all."

"The words might not be there, but the feeling is. I don't like the patronizing, you know what I'm saying? You know what else I don't like? I don't like some boy nearly half my age calling me *Rondell.*"

"What if I called you Mr. Cherry from here on out?"

"You haven't heard a word I'm telling you." He shook his head, then opened his lunch pail and dug around inside and removed a handful of the tacks Rhys had used to hang the replacement mural.

He dropped them in my beer, letting one fall after the other. "I'm going home to my family now," he said and rose to leave. "What are you going home to?"

"Wait. Please, wait." I reached out and put my hand on his arm. "At least let me try to explain."

He stared down at my hand until I moved it away. "I got a feeling this is something I'd rather not know about," he said.

He brushed by me and walked to the door, and I ran outside after him. Something came to me in the moment before I spoke. "You knew we'd taken it out of the building and yet you sold it to him, anyway."

He took a few more steps before stopping and turning around. He brought his shoulders up in a shrug, the lunch pail dangling from one hand, the newspaper in the other. "What do you expect for ten grand? A masterpiece? Come on, Jack."

His laughter was lost in the roar of a truck moving past.

❋

When the call came, I was sleeping and lost in yet another dream of Rhys Goudeau. I reached for the phone and glanced at the clock, hardly surprised by the hour. Dreams are fine, especially when they're the kind I was having, but give me real. Give me the girl who naps on a cot in her office when she should be at home in bed. Give me coffee and a squeaky chair and a voice thick with exhaustion. It was 3:00 A.M., but I snapped awake. For days I'd slept in hopeful anticipation of the interruption, and with a script prepared. I waited long enough to hear her breathing, the delicate silence between each exhalation. "What are you wearing?" I said.

In rehearsal the question was met with rich, heartfelt laughter. She remembered. But tonight the response was the last thing I could've imagined. "Jack, it's Isabel. I'm sorry, sweetheart. You were expecting someone else."

She was quiet, waiting for me to speak. In times of boredom and stress, I recalled, Isabel had the irritating habit of clicking her finger-nails against her teeth, and this was what I heard now. "Jack . . . Jack, I do apologize. This is so—"

"Isabel?"

"Yes. Yes, it's me, darling: Isabel Green, your beloved former editor and one-time fuck buddy. And, no, I'm not calling with an assignment, if that's what you're wondering."

I should've put the phone down, right then. "Is something wrong?" I said instead.

"No one in your past life has died, if that's what you mean. Jack, I'm calling to ask if you would meet me tomorrow at the Sazerac."

"Have you been drinking again, Isabel?"

"Oh, shit. Oh, shit, Jack. Don't you start on that, too."

"I was sleeping, Isabel."

"I keep remembering that Christmas we went there after the office party and rented the room upstairs with the view of the rooftops. God, that was nice."

"That was four years ago."

"I loved that night. When I die I want to be remembering that night."

"To be honest, I'd rather forget it. I'm not proud of any part of the memory. It was a stupid thing we did and I regret it."

"No more sex for Jack with Jack's married boss. Is that what you're saying? Jack has changed. Jack has *grown*."

"I like to think I have."

"Jack has become a *good* man." She laughed in the loud, obnoxious way I probably deserved. "You were good, too, then, Jack. You were very good. God, boy, you went at it like a jackhammer. Jack the jackhammer."

"Why did I have to answer the phone? Isabel, please don't call here again. And if you insist on calling, at least show me the courtesy of doing so at a decent hour."

"Please, Jack. Just meet me in the goddamn bar, will you?" I didn't answer and she said, "Freddie left me, baby. The little bastard . . . he *left* me. Do you know the woman they brought in to help edit the section? She's fourteen years older than he is."

I sat up in bed and turned on the lamp. It was hopeless: there would be no more sleep for me tonight. I wondered if she could hear my teeth grinding together. "Freddie and the new editor," I muttered. "Tell me, Isabel: what am I supposed to do about it?"

"Help me. You're supposed to help me. You're supposed to help me because you're supposed to be my friend." And now she was crying, bawling into the phone.

"I am your friend," I said. "But I wonder if you're my friend, Isabel."

"Then meet me there, Jack. Be my friend and meet me there."

"By tomorrow," I said, "do you mean later today or do you mean tomorrow, as in Saturday?"

"I mean like in fifteen hours from now, so tonight. I guess I mean tonight. By the way," she continued, "to answer your question—you want to know what I'm wearing, Jack? I'm not wearing anything."

"I'll see you later, Isabel."

"You'll be there? Oh, thank you, sweet Jack."

"One drink," I said. "That's it."

After she hung up I lay in bed looking at the ceiling and trying to calm myself. My stomach hurt. Why hadn't I just told her to go to hell and slammed the phone down? Why couldn't it have been Rhys calling with an invitation to meet her at a hotel bar? I got up and put on some clothes and walked out to the gate. A light shone in one of the windows and I brought my face against a pane of wavy glass and looked in and saw Lowenstein asleep in his chair, a single gooseneck floor lamp burning at his shoulder. His mouth had fallen open. At his feet were piles of books such as those I'd come to favor and on top of one of the piles was a bottle. Would that be me in fifty years? I wondered. All alone with my art tomes and my booze and my stuffy fat chair? I was tempted to rap on the glass and ask him if he'd ever done dumb, regrettable things when he was young, but he looked too peaceful to disturb. His face lacked its usual grip of pain and anger and I saw in it the man he might've been once. *No, that won't be you,* I said to myself. *No way will that be you.*

I left the bayou and Moss Street and went for a drive. I cruised the French Quarter where the neon had gone dark on Bourbon Street and yet tourists continued to roam. I passed under the oaks of Saint Charles Avenue and followed the path of the Mississippi until I was at Riverbend. I had breakfast at the Camellia Grill and when I left it was still dark, the streetlamps abuzz under the palm trees.

My mother's house was only a couple of blocks away, and I drove there and parked across the street and waited for about an hour until she came out for the paper. Somehow seeing her in a robe and padded slippers, and reaching down for the sack in the grass as she had each morning for as long as I could remember, gave me the lift I needed. She was the good, pure thing that made the bad, corrupted ones tolerable. But I wasn't entirely comfortable spying on her this way; I felt as if I were cheating her out of something. She paused at the door and looked back at the street. Her eyes seemed to drift to my car parked in front of the Berteaus'. I thought she'd spotted me, but then she turned and went back in the house, into rooms with empty squares and rectangles on the walls. I started the engine and shifted to Drive, and suddenly there Mom was standing at the door again. She walked to my side of the car and I let the window down. She bent forward at the waist, holding the robe together at her chest, and peered inside. "Everything okay, Jack?"

"Yes, ma'am."

"Would you like to come in and join your mother for coffee and the paper?"

I shook my head. "I was just out driving and ended up here."

"It's your home, Jack. You can always come here. No matter what."

"Yes, ma'am."

"Will you bring your friend over sometime, Jack?"

"Sure, Mom."

"If she's anything like her name, she must be really beautiful."

"Rhys is black, Mom."

"Yes, I know, sugar." She reached in the car and put her hand on my face. "You just bring her whatever color she is."

I waited until she'd gone back in the house before I left, and before I let the tears start to fall. I hadn't cried when my dad died, nor had I cried since, but I really made up for it now. I cried so hard I thought I was going to hurt myself. My whole body was involved. I had to pull over on the side of the road.

When I finished, I drove to Martin Luther King and the old firehouse that was home to the Guild. By now it was almost six o'clock in the morning, way too early to be feeling so much. Central City was coming awake in the spinning gray light. Pigeons fed in the street; a woman in raggedy clothes pushed a shopping cart holding a collection of cans and other found objects. I don't know why I was surprised, finding the studio lights on upstairs. At some other time I might've sat on the horn and forced Rhys to come outside and talk to me. But this morning I was content to wait. A couple of hours went by before I caught a glimpse of a shadow moving across one of the windows, and then in an instant Rhys was standing there, staring out at me. She wore a lab coat and her hair was pulled back in a loose arrangement. I stepped out of the car and stood in the street and waved up at the building. She lifted the window and thrust her head out. "He used casein paint," she called out.

"He did what?"

"Levette. He used casein paint. He covered the surface with casein paint. To protect it. He saved the painting, Jack."

"That's great," I yelled up at her.

She wrapped her arms around her chest and hugged herself.

I started to ask if I could come up for a look, and then I thought it might be the right time to tell her that I was in love with her. But suddenly the window came down and Rhys disappeared back into the studio.

＊

Isabel stood as I approached the table, and tugged at the body of a blazer that had never fit her properly. There were tears in her eyes, a tremble at the flesh beneath her chin. "Don't say anything," she began. "Obviously I'm going through a bad time."

"Did I say anything?"

We sat in chairs directly across from each other and she immediately began to drum her teeth with her nails. I reached out a hand and stopped her. "Don't do that," I said. "And don't be so hard on yourself."

"I'm fat," she said. "I've put on fifteen pounds in the last six months."

"I think you look great."

"We really miss you, Jack. We really do."

"I miss you, too. But that doesn't matter for anything."

She looked at me for a long while. She started to drum her teeth again but then stopped herself. "I've decided to start Sugar Busters tomorrow," she said. "That's the diet where you cut out carbohydrates and eat only protein?"

"I've heard about it."

"Steaks and chicken and fish are fine. Peanut butter's fine. No bread, though. And no pasta. Bread and pasta turn to sugar in the body, and sugar's poison, it's absolute poison. That's why they call it Sugar *Bust*ers."

"You bust the sugar?"

"That's it, yes."

To the wall on my right, curving with the rounded corner, was one of four Paul Ninas murals in the lounge. It was a typical, Depression-era scene celebrating the American everyman. This one showed black laborers working a dock on the Mississippi River waterfront. Like the other paintings in the room, decades of exposure to cigar and cigarette smoke had yellowed the surface and softened the palette. I might've mentioned the mural, and Levette Asmore's connection to Ninas, had doing so not raised the possibility of intruding on any one of the many confidentiality agreements I had with Rhys. Instead I feigned interest in the wine list wedged between a basket of sugar packets and the salt and pepper shakers.

"How many times did we actually make love?" Isabel said.

"A couple, I think."

"It was more than that."

"It was a mistake no matter how many times it was."

"Why didn't it last, Jack?"

"You were married. And you said you still loved Freddie."

The server brought a basket of breadsticks and took our order: for Isabel a glass of Merlot, for myself a Scotch. As soon as the woman left, Isabel selected one of the sticks, snapped it in half and generously lathered an end with butter. Her mouth was full when she said, "The last time I saw Freddie he said I was a dead lay."

"Freddie says a lot of things, Isabel."

"Was I dead with you, too?"

"You were wonderful with me."

"Why would he tell me that, Jack?"

"Freddie's full of baloney."

"I might drink too much but there are still some things I won't do, not for any man." She bit off another piece of bread and leaned forward to make sure she had my attention. "I should write a book about the whole Barnett clan, or at least threaten to write one. It's terrible to admit but I don't think I'm above blackmail." She made a pistol of her hand and pretended to be sticking me up. " 'Give me ten grand a month for life or I tell all your rich, fancy friends what kind of weird sex Freddie likes.' Yep, that might work with old Fred. Anything to avoid displeasing Big Rodg." She meant Freddie's father—the paper's publisher, Rodger Barnett. She placed her bread in a dish and reached over and ran a hand through my hair. "Handsome Jack. How are you, my darling? How are you *really?*"

"I'm well, thank you, Isabel."

"You look well," she said. "You look wonderful, in fact. Healthy, even. What have you been doing with yourself? Working out? Eating your veggies, for heaven's sake?"

"I keep busy. I've fallen in with a new group of friends. . . . Well, actually with one friend, a woman named Rhys Goudeau. She repairs damaged art objects—paintings, mostly. Ever hear of the Crescent City Conservation Guild?"

Isabel cocked an eyebrow and finished off the breadstick. "She's the new girlfriend, isn't she?"

"I told you I don't have a new girlfriend."

"Good. Because I've heard enough about this Rhys Goudeau for one lifetime. I edited the takeout David Charles wrote about the old painting they found in that haunted house on Ursulines. *Beloved Emily.* Is that what it was called?"

"Beloved Dorothy."

"Yes, that's the one. David came back from reporting the story and this Rhys Goudeau was all he could talk about. And David's gay, for God's sake."

Our server arrived with the drinks. As she was setting them on the table Isabel said, "Speaking of discoveries, Jack, David made a damned-sure interesting one when he was out foraging for his feature about Levette Asmore."

"Did he really? And what was that?"

"First a little back story, to set it up. I made a slip of the tongue earlier, when I referred to the haunted-house painting as *Beloved Emily.* In actual fact there was a *Beloved Emily.* But for years it hung in a house at Audubon Place. It was a portrait of Freddie's grandmother, Emily Weeks Barnett."

"Okay."

"Asmore gave her the treatment. She was an eighteen-year-old

debutante studying at Newcomb College and running with the bo-
hemians of the French Quarter, when she met the artist and sat for
the portrait. They were lovers for a time, or they were alleged to be,
anyway. Rodger as a rule avoided advertising the fact that his mother
was a randy little tart before she married his father, but pump a few
drinks in him and he would stand on the baby grand crowing about
how Dear Old Mom used to get it on with the great Levette. Emily
died years ago, before I ever entered the scene, and the painting didn't
survive either. It was lost in a fire that took out the kitchen and a back
section of the house. I have seen pictures of the painting, though.
Photographs. And it's just like all the others. When the news of
Dorothy broke, Big Rodg naturally became interested. In editorial
meetings it was all he could talk about, and he had David check
around to see if any of Asmore's relatives were still alive. He came
from a town near Opelousas—"

"Melville."

"What was that?"

"Melville. Asmore came from a town closer to Melville."

She nodded. "Yes. You're right. It was Melville."

"Asmore was orphaned as a child and sent to a home here in New
Orleans."

"Yes, that's what David said. But Asmore first was placed with a
relative, an uncle, as I understood it. Well, David decides to find out
if this person, this uncle, or any other relatives are still around and so
he drives out to Saint Landry Parish and starts asking people on the
streets. 'No,' everyone says, 'never heard of anyone named Asmore.'
David's about to give up when he thinks to check with the clerk of
court's office, so he drives over to the courthouse in Opelousas. They
pull up records showing that an Asmore has indeed owned property
in the parish. And upon his death this man's only child, a daughter,
had inherited the land, and she'd married and taken her husband's
name. Anyway, according to the records the lady is still paying taxes
on the property, so she's still alive, right? Still in Palmetto. Don't you
just love that name, Jack? Palmetto?"

"It's a kind of plant, isn't it?"

"It's a kind of palm with leaves shaped like a fan. Palmetto covered the stones and the dirt of the roads that Jesus walked on his way to Gethsemane."

"That might be more detail than I need at the moment. Why don't you finish?"

"Well, David gets directions and heads out to the old Asmore homestead for a visit. At long last he comes to this little house up on pilings with a chinaberry tree in front and chickens rooting around in the yard. David said it wasn't a place you'd even notice when you drove by, because it was like so many other houses out there where poor and hardworking people live. A wood fence surrounds the lot, and he goes through the gate and walks up a dirt path to the front door. He knocks and steps back and waits and nobody answers. And so he knocks again. Still no one. He's about to give up when he decides to walk out around back and there he finds an old woman sitting under a tree fanning herself and drinking a glass of Kool-Aid. He says, 'Ma'am, I'm looking for Annie Mae Asmore,' I think that's what he said her maiden name was. The woman puts her glass down and says, 'You with a collection agency?' He says, 'Does she owe somebody money?' And she answers, 'I don't owe nobody nothing but love and tenderness.'" Isabel twirled the stem of her wineglass and started to laugh. "Isn't that beautiful, Jack? All she owes anybody is love and tenderness."

"It's good. Go on."

"Well, David's stunned and for a minute he can't say anything."

"Why is David stunned?"

Isabel held up a hand. "He's stunned because she's nothing like he was expecting to find."

"And why is that?"

"Are you going to let me tell my story?" She sipped her wine and reached for another breadstick before deciding against it. "So David's standing there in this old woman's backyard. He's confused by what he's found, and he says, 'Ma'am, are you really Annie Mae Asmore?'

She looks at him and must decide that he's not there to take her money, and she says, 'I used to be, before I got married to that no-account Milo Toussaint.' He says, 'Ma'am, are you the daughter of So-and-so and So-and-so Asmore?' 'Yes, I was their little girl,' she says. David says, 'Was the artist Levette Asmore related to you?' 'Levette? Levette was my first cousin,' she answers. 'His daddy was my daddy's half brother. His folks, both of them, drowned in the flood of 1927 when the levee broke in Melville.' David puts his reading glasses on and walks up closer to get a better look at the woman. 'Ma'am,' he says, careful to be polite, 'ma'am, was Levette Asmore black?' The lady looks David in the eye and says, 'Yes, Levette was black, all the way until he died.' "

Now Isabel tapped my arm with one of the breadsticks. "Jack, what is wrong with you all of a sudden? Was someone in your family a *Beloved* girl, too?"

"Nothing like that," I said.

"Then take it easy, will you?"

The Scotch had burned my throat, and I coughed into a fist. My eyes were watering and I felt cold all over. "Why didn't David write it?" I said, and coughed again. "How could the paper sit on a story as important as that one?"

"What? Are you kidding me? Levette Asmore was a Negro, Jack, passing as a white. Good God, imagine the scandal if that piece of news hit the streets. Do you think Rodger Barnett would allow such a thing to be printed in his paper—that as a teenage girl his mother, future matriarch of one of the city's most prominent families, was screwing a black man? Now, Freddie's been with black women—he's claimed to, anyway—but that's different. While it might be cool to picture Freddie with sassy colored chicks, it ain't cool imagining a black man putting the wood to Miss Emily."

"But this black man looked white enough to pass as white. He assimilated into white society."

"Don't give me that assimilation shit. You really think that mat-

ters? It's not how the man *looked*, Jack, it's what he was. I don't care if
he could pass as Brad Pitt's long-lost identical twin. There was no way
in hell that little nugget was ever going to make it to print."

Isabel seemed pleased with herself: pleased that her revelation had
sparked such a response in me, and pleased to have such juicy dirt on
the family of her ex-boyfriend. "If David's reporting is accurate—and
he did admit that he wasn't able to substantiate much of what he
got—Asmore nailed more than just young Emily Weeks. He cut a
swath through the whole social registry. Uptown New Orleans would
do more than simply cancel their subscriptions to the paper if David's
discovery hit the press, they'd run out to the Huey P. and leap from it
just like Asmore did."

"As far as we've come, we're still not even close."

"Are you talking about race in this country?" Isabel laughed. "Tell
me something I don't know. The same day David came back with his
big scoop, Rodger Barnett called the 'Living' staff together and swore
us to secrecy. 'This does not leave the building,' he said, in that phony,
high-pitched drawl of his. He later pulled me aside and told me to
figure out a way to get David to shut up. He gave me two options: fire
him or send him on vacation. There was no way I would agree to fire
him—since you left the paper, he's the only real writer I've got. And
it wouldn't have worked to send him on vacation, because he'd just
come back from one. So this was Rodger's solution: He dispatched
David to the Gulf of Mexico to work on a story about the danger of
life on offshore drilling rigs. And I really think Rodger's hoping
David experiences the danger firsthand, that he gets stuck in a hurricane or something. Short of learning that he's vanished at sea,
Rodger's hoping that David gets hit real hard in the head and loses
his memory, especially the area where he stored his file on Levette Asmore."

I summoned our server. I needed another drink. I needed two
drinks. "My God," I said to Isabel, "Levette Asmore was black."

"He was black."

The rest of the evening felt like an out-of-body experience. I would hang around just long enough to offer a comment in response to something she said, and to keep from having her think I was a total catatonic, then I'd flee to a space in the celestial haze above the old hotel where I could look down on the world and try to understand it. If nothing else I'd learned that Levette Asmore now had a motive for killing himself. He'd lied to so many people by presenting himself one way when in fact he was another that he'd probably suffered from a gangrenous case of self-hatred. Was that too simple? People have wasted themselves over lesser crimes than deceit. Another possible explanation came to mind. Maybe some white guy, the Rodger Barnett of his day, had learned that his ex-girlfriend was having an affair with the artist. After checking out Asmore's background, much as David Charles had done, he'd discovered the truth about the artist's phony racial identity. And maybe this guy had personally seen to it that Asmore took a leap from the Huey P.

Perhaps I'd read too many stories and seen too many movies about black men being persecuted by whites for tinkering with their women. But whatever currents had come together to bring about Asmore's death, I now was more intrigued than ever. His was more than a story about a tortured artist who couldn't handle having his precious work rejected. Levette Asmore truly might've been the most important artist ever to come out of the American South, but the man also had been a fraud.

"You seem distracted," Isabel said.

"I didn't go back to sleep after you called. I'm tired, that's all."

"This was a terrible idea, wasn't it?"

I put some cash on the table, then leaned forward and took her hands in mine. "Listen to me, Isabel. I'm truly sorry things went so badly for you with Freddie. But I want you to know something. I'm a great fan of yours and I always will be. You're a lovely woman, when you let yourself be, and you surely deserve better than that spoiled little prick. Will you always remember I told you that?"

"Which part, Jack? The one about Freddie being a prick or the one about me being lovely?"

"You'll forget Freddie," I said. "Never forget how lovely you are."

"Will you rent a room with me, Jack? Let's make it how it was."

"I can't, Isabel. We won't do that ever again. We shouldn't have done it before. I'm sorry. You do understand?"

She gave her head a shake, sending tears down her face.

"I need to go now. Good-bye, Isabel."

"Good-bye, Jack."

Near the doors leading out of the bar I paused and had a look at another of the Ninas murals. This one showed tourists cavorting at Jackson Square. In the corner a black woman, seated on the ground like a beggar, and wearing a tignon, peddled pralines to white people. Next to her a young black boy gave a man a shoeshine. I turned back and took in all four of the paintings. In each of them blacks were depicted as subservient to whites. Blacks picked cotton or toted baskets and heavy sacks; whites either gave them orders or stood around in fashionable clothes talking to each other.

It would be a mistake not to care about race, Rhys had told me weeks ago. I could hear her speaking these words now, and suddenly something came clear to me: if Levette Asmore was black, then maybe we all were black.

It was Annie Rae, not Annie Mae, and the tree in the front yard wasn't a chinaberry but a sycamore. There wasn't a chicken in sight, although a white cat lounging in the sun did meow when I climbed up on the porch. I looked back at the fence and rickety gate, wondering how barbed wire could be confused with wood. I also wondered what other facts Isabel, quoting David Charles, had got wrong.

"Mrs. Toussaint, it's Jack Charbonnet," I said through the screen.

"The one who called me on the telephone?"

"Yes, ma'am."

She looked to be in excellent health for an eighty-year-old. We shook hands and though her skin felt as soft as eiderdown her grip was sure and strong. On the drive over it had occurred to me that Annie Rae Toussaint, being a cousin of Levette Asmore's, also was a relation of Rhys Goudeau's; but the two looked nothing alike. The old lady had a dark complexion and dark eyes and she wore her hair short and close to the scalp. There was no mistaking her race. "It wants to scare me how everybody's been looking at me lately," she said, pushing the door open and letting me in the house.

"I didn't mean to stare, ma'am. I apologize."

"It makes me want to put some tissue paper up to my nose. Like there's something there I should know about."

"No, ma'am, everything's fine."

The living room was outfitted with a sofa, a recliner and a bentwood rocker. An oval rug lay on the floor. Plants stood on pedestals in the windows and hung from ceiling chains. It was a comfortable space, cooled today by a box fan and a small window unit that, roaring away together, sounded like an approaching freight train. She'd been reading a book; it lay open on one of the end tables. "I poured you a Kool-Aid," she said, and gestured to the place where she wanted me to sit. A glass running with condensation was waiting on a coaster. "You like Kool-Aid, Charbonnet?"

"Yes, I do."

"You want some cookies?"

"No, ma'am, thank you. The Kool-Aid's plenty."

I recognized the dust jacket of the book. The title was a personal favorite, and one in my collection at home: *Art in the American South: Works from the Ogden Collection.*

"I went I don't know how many years and nobody even brought up the name Levette Asmore. Now they got him in a library book. If you wait long enough, I suppose they always come and find you. Well, maybe I should say if you've got something to give to the world they come and find you. If you got only memories, like I do, they tend to leave you alone, not wanting to hear more talk. I wish I'd saved his doodles. I bet I could get something for his doodles."

"Do you own any of his paintings?"

"No, I don't, sad to say."

"So this is the house where he lived after his mother and father died?"

"Yes, this is it, and it was a new house then, no more than ten years old. They call it a cottage nowadays, the real estate people do, but I remember not many years ago when everybody just called it a shack."

"How long was he actually here, Mrs. Toussaint?"

"For three months, until the state came and took him. He was the saddest little boy in the world. He wouldn't want to leave the house for anything. Wouldn't go with us to church on Sunday. Wouldn't talk but to say a few words every now and then. He stayed inside and drew pictures of his mama and daddy, most of them showing them being swept away with the cows and other animals. There was an old hotel in Melville, the Able Hotel. It went up two stories and he would draw it, with the water from the river up to the roof and all the people inside trapped. He would keep his pictures hidden under the bed. One time I remember Mama tried to get him to take his bath. It was a Saturday, when they would put the washtub in the kitchen and everyone took a turn. And when it was time for Levette he started screaming about the snakes in the water and they never did get him to bathe. He used to clean himself with a wet cloth and a bar of soap. I remember that. That's all Mama could get him to use."

"The poor child."

She nodded. "I also remember I asked him once to color me a flower and he made me a magnolia. There was a big magnolia tree used to grow in front of his house—his real house, where his mama and daddy lived—that the flood took with it."

"Mrs. Toussaint," I said, trying to stay on track, "I read somewhere that your father couldn't afford to keep him. Is that true?"

"True about halfway, not true the other half."

"Tell me what you mean."

"My daddy farmed like Levette's daddy did. Corn and cotton mostly. Look out the window at the land around the house, that was it. Just a small patch that he bought from the white people who owned it before us. There wasn't any money anywhere, it was the Depression. Not a lot of food, either, except what you could grow. Sometimes Levette wouldn't eat his supper and Daddy would take exception. He'd tell Levette to go outside and get him a switch from the camellia bush."

"You remember him, Mrs. Toussaint? I mean, how he looked and dressed and how his voice sounded and everything?"

"Of course I remember Levette."

"What was he like?"

"Well, he was very light-complected, if that's your way of getting me to say it."

"Complected? Are you saying he had fair skin?"

"He was bright, his skin was bright, his hair was bright. He was kind of golden, yes, he had a shine about him. His daddy and my daddy were only half brothers, you see. They had the same father, Oscar Asmore, but different mothers."

"How much older was Levette than you?"

"Two years older. That doesn't sound like much, but when you're a child it's a lot. He didn't pay me much mind. When I was in high school he sent me a Christmas card from New Orleans saying he thought about me and wanted to wish me a happy holidays. That surprised me, because by that time I thought for sure I'd be the last thing on his mind. The card had a little picture of a French Quarter patio on the front, a little watercolor he'd done. We had a pipe burst and water got on everything and that's what happened to it."

"The card was destroyed?"

"Yes. Levette came back only once to my knowledge and he had somebody with him. They came and parked up by the road but they never got out. I was in the yard hanging clothes on the line. Levette had grown up by then. I could see him, sitting in his seat, and just looking with that other person."

"Was it a man or a woman he was with?"

"A man."

"Was the man a white man or a black man?"

"A white man. He looked white to me, anyway."

"And that day he came, Levette didn't talk to you?"

"No, he didn't. He didn't talk to anyone. I heard Mama come through the front door, and she called out for Daddy, that Levette had come back. But then the car started up and roared off down the road. Maybe he was afraid Daddy would get the switch after him again. My daddy was a good man, but when he drank, he could be mean. It was a disease with him. I remember when they came and told us Levette had jumped from the bridge. Daddy put on his coat and his hat and he walked to town. It was a hot night, and he went to the bar where they had the white entrance and the colored entrance. It was like that in those days. Daddy kept trying to get in the white entrance and the white men kept throwing him out. They liked my daddy, the white men did. He liked them, too. But that was a line you didn't cross, not in them days. After a while they had enough of him trying to get in the white side and they beat him so bad we had to get Mr. Leroy Guidry, he was our neighbor, he's dead now . . . we had to get Mr. Leroy to load him in the back of the truck and bring him home. It was like he was in pieces. It was what he wanted, for the white men to beat him up. I guess he was feeling guilty about Levette."

"Because he'd abused him when he lived here as a boy?"

"Nobody said abused in those days, Charbonnet. They said spanked."

"Spanked? That's treating it a little lightly, calling it spanked."

"To me, too."

She pulled herself up out of her chair and went through a swinging door into what I presumed was the kitchen. I used the time alone to have a look at a cluster of photographs hanging on the wall. None showed Levette Asmore, but there was one of Mrs. Toussaint, housed in a vintage frame behind bubble glass, that showed her as a teenage girl standing with a middle-aged couple that likely was her parents. The woman had light skin and straight hair, the man was dark and handsome, although his features were obscured by a shadow cut from his snap-brim hat. Behind them stood Mrs. Toussaint's house. The sycamore in the yard looked like a twig stuck in the ground.

Hanging in matching frames next to the photographs were a high school diploma and a certificate from the University of Southwestern Louisiana commending Annie Rae Toussaint for completing a correspondence course in agriculture.

"At one time I wanted to learn if there was more to planting than just planting," she said, as she walked past me carrying a silver service tray. The tray held a glass pot containing coffee, bowls with sugar and cream, and cookies on a plate. The cookies were covered with cellophane, which she proceeded to remove. "You know what I found out, Charbonnet? I found out the books knew less about how to farm than Daddy had taught me before I got to first grade."

"Mrs. Toussaint," I said, "I'm really not hungry. You didn't have to go through all that trouble."

"See that lady there? That one in the picture you were just looking at? She taught me to be polite, so I'm being polite." She poured a cup of coffee. "You like cream and sugar, Charbonnet?"

"No, ma'am. I like it regular."

"Black?"

The way she said the word made me look up. "Yes, please."

She removed the glass of Kool-Aid and the coaster from the end table next to my chair and replaced them with the coffee and cookies. "You saw my little white kitty outside on the porch?" she said.

"Yes, I did. It's a cute little thing."

"Nature's funny how it works. That little cat's mama was black, black on every inch of her body. I don't know who the daddy was, but the mama used to stay around here. I'd leave her scraps on the back steps. She and I got along like family. She delivered her litter under the house and in the morning I crawled under there with my flashlight to have a look. She had herself a place kind of dug out in the soil, where it was cool, and the kittens were feeding on her, and I put the light on them and every last one of them was black. Black from the tip of their nose to the tip of their tail, just like she was. They were all getting their milk, doing fine. I started to leave but then I heard a little meow. I moved the light around and I saw this little pink thing off to itself with some white hair on it. It was a baby kitty that the mama cat had pushed off to the side so it couldn't get any milk. She had put it there to die. And it would have, too, if I hadn't gone to check."

"Was this the little cat I saw out on the porch?"

"Yes, it was. It was the only one of the litter I decided to keep. I gave all the others away and I kept the one the mama didn't want."

"What happened to the mama cat?"

"She left. I guess somebody gave her better scraps." Mrs. Toussaint nibbled the edge of a cookie and gave me a smile. "How did that black cat have all black babies except for one, and how did that one come out *white*?" She lifted her eyebrows as if in expectation of an answer. "And why," she continued, "did the mama treat the little white kitty like it did when the little white kitty was innocent and pure and had never done it anything. I forgot to tell you there were only four other kittens in the litter, so the mama had plenty of milk to go around. She just wasn't going to have anything to do with that white cat, was she, Charbonnet?"

"I guess she wasn't."

"Nature," she said, pronouncing the word *"Nay-chuh."* "Nature made her act like that."

"It was nature, was it?"

"Another thing I forgot to tell you is that the mama cat was a good cat. She was friendly, she liked everybody. She'd rub up against your ankles, sleep in your lap. She wasn't even mean to other cats, these strays that come around. But then she had that little white one and all of a sudden she's trying to kill it."

"I guess there's a lesson to be learned. Are you telling me this story because it has something to do with how your father treated Levette?"

"Nature," Mrs. Toussaint said again. "Daddy didn't want him. And Daddy always had the door open to everybody. He would feed the hoboes when they got off the trains looking for food. Whenever he butchered a hog he would bring some of the meat to the neighbors and whoever else was hungry. What does that tell you?"

"I wonder if your father and Levette's father got along."

"I told you they were half brothers, Levette's daddy and my daddy?"

"Yes. What were their names, Mrs. Toussaint?"

"My daddy was Simon. Levette's was Anthony. Simon and Anthony Asmore. Their father was Oscar. They had different mothers, like I said. Simon and Anthony were either nine or ten years apart. Simon came first. After his mother, Josie, ran off to Opelousas, then Oscar got remarried and Anthony was born. I don't think Oscar ever got over his first wife leaving him like that. Did I tell you it was with a white man?"

"No, ma'am."

"Well, it was. It was a white man from Opelousas."

"That must've hurt Oscar."

"Hurt him? It like to kill him. He would hear about it everywhere he went. People would be laughing at him. The whites would be laughing, the blacks would be laughing. I'm told this, anyhow. I grew up hearing about it, even though it had happened years before. How many black women run off with white men in those days?"

"I couldn't say, Mrs. Toussaint. Probably not many."

"That was my grandmother. It's hard to believe. She left her husband, left her son. When Oscar would come in from the fields in the evening, who do you think got the worst of it?" The smile had left her face. She seemed to have forgotten about the coffee and cookies. "It only got worse for Simon after Anthony came along. Oscar had a pretty new wife, he had a new baby boy. But he still had Simon, too, and Simon looked enough like Josie to remind him."

I wondered about the woman, Josie, and her legacy. While she might've gone on to important things—such as working to help make life better for the disadvantaged, or volunteering to serve at her area hospital, or saving souls at a church—in Annie Rae Toussaint's house, in Palmetto, she would always be identified with one event only. She had run off to Opelousas with a white man.

"Simon was different complected than Anthony," Mrs. Toussaint said. "He wasn't nearly as bright as Anthony because his mama hadn't been as bright as Anthony's mama. So Oscar had his black son in Simon and his white one in Anthony, that's what people would say. Anthony was the family favorite, the little pet, while my daddy got the spankings. Simon would come in with dirt on his clothes, Oscar spanked him. He'd sleep a little too late on a Sunday morning, Oscar spanked him for that. All the while Anthony, Levette's daddy, is the little prince, you see? The black son caught hell and got the switch. The white son got treated like he was somebody special. Memory, Charbonnet. It will go a long way if you let it."

"So then Anthony dies along with his wife in the flood, and Simon, being the only relative left alive, has no choice but to take in Levette?"

"That's what happened. I don't think my daddy wanted to be mean to Levette, but nature made him do it. Maybe he remembered how his daddy had always favored Anthony, and maybe this had built up in him over the years. Jealousy? Resentment? I'm sure there's a name for it. And now here comes little Levette, and Levette looks like Anthony, only he's even whiter. He's the white son, the lucky son. And poor Simon, it's not as if he doesn't have enough troubles already. He's barely able to feed his wife and daughter—that's me. He can barely afford to put clothes on their backs. And because of the flood he has this nephew to raise who reminds him, every time he looks at him, that his mother was a tramp who went to Opelousas with a white man, and that Oscar Asmore, his own daddy, didn't love him right. It all comes back, you see? He can't help himself, even though he's grown up and made a life for himself. He's a responsible adult, like they say. But something comes over him and he has a drink and the next thing you know he's taking it out on Levette, treating Levette just like Oscar treated him."

"Nature," I said.

"Human beings have more going on inside than cats. But cats remember, too. That black mama cat pushed that white kitten aside for reasons that were probably a mystery even to herself. Something in the past, Charbonnet. Something in the past that just wouldn't fix itself."

I asked her for a pen and a piece of paper, and together we drew a sketch of the family tree. Oscar and Josie begat Simon, who with Lonna begat Annie Rae. Simon and Lonna were the couple depicted in the old photograph hanging on the wall. Branching off on the other side of the tree was Levette's family. Oscar and Mary Beth begat Anthony, who with Camille begat Levette. Anthony and Camille perished in the flood, then Levette, their only child, was dead fourteen years later. "Did you have any children of your own, Mrs. Toussaint?" I said.

"No, I never did. My husband, by the way, was Milo, Milo Toussaint." She pointed to the place on the tree where his name belonged. "He and I were married eleven years when he got hit by a train on the tracks that run through town."

"Through Palmetto?"

"I can't say it was the worst thing that ever happened. On the other side of the tracks where he was going was the house where his girlfriend lived. It must've been good, because he was in a hurry to get there. He was trying to beat the train." Her humor had returned, as had her appetite. She dipped a cookie in her coffee and took a large bite. "We always heard about Levette passing for a white," she said. "I'm not sure it surprised anybody, and I'm not sure anybody held it against him, either. You have to remember how things were in them times. Well, you won't be able to remember, Charbonnet, because you weren't born yet to see it." She inhaled deeply, then let out a long exhalation. Her face now looked troubled. "The thing that makes me saddest when I think about Levette," she said, "is how he never really had a place. His uncle Simon didn't want him because he was white, and the whites in New Orleans wouldn't have wanted him had they known he was black. Dear Lord in heaven forgive me for saying this, but I used to think the only real peace he must ever have known was in those seconds when he jumped from the bridge and went falling toward the water."

She asked me to make her a copy of the family tree. As I was working on the sketch she returned to the kitchen and came back in a few minutes with a paper bag. Inside were cookies wrapped in aluminum foil and paper towels. "Don't want you to go getting hungry on the drive home."

I included Levette's name on the tree, along with other names that now seemed all but official. Levette Asmore and Jacqueline LeBeau had begat Beverly, who with Robert Goudeau had brought Rhys into the world. My heart got tight in my chest as I wrote out Rhys's name.

"I'm not familiar with these people," Mrs. Toussaint said. "It looks like Levette was way more busy than we knew about."

"He liked his women," I said. "I've read that there were only a dozen of his *Beloved* portraits known to exist, and that doesn't seem like many until you take into account how old he was when he died. Twenty-three. I don't know about you, Mrs. Toussaint, but I didn't have a dozen girlfriends by the time I was twenty-three."

"I knew only one man in my life. Ask me that was one too many."

We walked out on the porch and the cat was still there, asleep in the sun. Mrs. Toussaint put her lips together and made a sharp kissing sound, and the animal looked up and meowed. "Well, Charbonnet, you sure had me reflecting. I hope I was helpful."

"You were, ma'am. And I'm grateful. Thank you."

I stepped into the yard and she dropped to her haunches and began to stroke the cat, whispering as she used both hands to massage its back. She lifted it in her arms and held it close to her chest. "I gave him a name. It came to me the other night in a dream. Until then I just called him 'Cat.' "

"It wouldn't be Levette, would it?"

"Levette? Oh, no, it's not Levette." She didn't seem to mind when the cat clawed her dress and climbed up on her shoulder. It sat curled up with its face pressed close to her neck. I could hear it purring from ten feet away. "It's Casper," she said. "After the ghost in the cartoon."

"Casper," I said. "I like that."

"We all have them. Ghosts, I should say. Somebody told me the place where Levette used to live was famous because they had a ghost that lived there."

"I heard that, too. In a book it said the house had a sinister aspect."

"What is that?"

"I don't know for sure."

"You mean, you never went to see where he lived?" She put the cat back on the ground and stood quietly watching as it cleaned itself. "He'll run off eventually when somebody gives him better scraps," she said. "Until then, at least we'll know who he is."

NINE

 The house on Saint Philip Street where Asmore once lived didn't look like the sort of place a ghost would appreciate much. It was clean and tidy, with fresh paint, new copper gutters and a wooden flower box with pansies by the stoop.

Imagining the young artist in this neighborhood took almost as much effort as it had to picture him bounding up the steps of the forlorn Wheeler Beauty Academy, because now the artist's former home, recently refurbished, ranked as an architectural treasure bound in every direction by some of the most valuable real estate in the southern United States. In little more than half a century Asmore's low digs had been Disney-fied.

Only minutes before the rain had stopped, and now the black streets smoked in the late-summer heat. For a second time I brought my fist against the wood, and for a second time I tried to construct an introduction that might win favor with the current occupant. After I knocked a third time I began to wonder what to say if Asmore himself, back from the grave, pulled open the door and stepped out with a hand to shake. Had he lived, he would be eighty-three years old now. "May I have a moment of your time, please?" I might've begun. No, better to skip the formality and get right to the point: "Spoke to your cousin earlier today. Remember Annie Rae, do you? Well, Levette, she tells me you're black . . ."

"May I help you?"

He appeared not from the house but the sidewalk, a small man of about fifty with a dense cloud of silver hair and a paunch, shambling up with a collection of plastic sacks bulging with groceries. While I met him with a phony smile, he fixed on me with the kind of gaze peculiar to French Quarter homeowners tired of unwelcome visits from inebriated tourists randomly searching for a bathroom.

"Do you live here, sir?" I said, smile broadened now to the point of parody.

He eyed me again. "How can I help you?"

"My name is Jack Charbonnet. I was doing some research and I found this address in an old book—"

"So you're Charbonnet, are you?" Unable to free a hand, he stuck out an elbow and I answered the gesture by giving the bony thing a shake. "Tell me, then," he went on, "how is Uncle Charlie getting along these days? Still miserable? Still watching the dust collect on all those old paintings?"

My God, I thought, it was Lowenstein. It was Lowenstein who'd shared the cottage with Asmore. "You're the other one listed in the White Pages," I said, "the one I spoke to on the telephone? You're the nephew."

"Well, the *great*-nephew," he said. He handed me a couple of bags and extracted keys from a pocket. "Lawrence is the name, but my friends call me Larry, as I expect you to do. Why don't you come in, Charbonnet? I suppose this is about my uncle."

"Actually it's about the artist Levette Asmore."

"Then it's about Uncle Charlie." He shifted a bag from his left to his right hand. "I've got some cold Abitas in one of these somewhere. Let's sit out in the courtyard and see if we can't kill a few."

I followed him into a living room that adjoined a small dining area and kitchen. The floors were longleaf pine covered with thread-bare rugs. The furnishings, though spare, fit the architectural period of the house, which made them not a day less than two hundred years old. Asmore had once brought his work into these rooms, stacking his burlap and canvas creations on chairs and tables, hanging them, and yet the walls today had not a single painting on them, nor was there a print or a poster. Each wall was a grid of brick and mortar, old posts black with age.

"Tell me," Lowenstein said, "ever track down that fellow you were looking for?"

"Which fellow was that?"

"Wiltz, I think it was."

"Wiltz Lowenstein was a law firm. It went out of business many years ago."

"Oh, so law firms go out of business, too, do they? I thought all they did was proliferate." He handed me a bottle. "Thanks for the good news."

He led me past French doors into the shade of a small courtyard. We sat on rusting iron chairs beneath a sweep of banana trees tower-ing fifteen feet high. Except for his mismatched collection of clothes he bore little resemblance to his uncle, although I did wonder if his current mood had some genetic connection. Even as he guzzled beer he was bemoaning how his neighborhood market, once a wonderful place, had become little more than a water supply for tourists. Chief among his complaints was that people stood in line to pay three dol-lars for a small bottle when, if they only bothered, they could find a faucet against any one of a number of buildings and drink for free. "The world has gone mad," he said. "Absolutely insane."

And over water, I thought.

When he quieted down, I began to speak, glad for the opportunity to settle at least this one issue. "The cottage," I said, "is it really haunted?"

"I haven't seen the ghost," he answered, "but I have encountered the strange and unusual in the old place, most recently last Mardi Gras when a tourist let himself in after I opened a window for the breeze. I went after him with a frying pan. I took a couple of swings, in any case. I went for his head. He might've ended up a ghost had my aim been better." He liked this story. It made him laugh. He swigged his beer. "You didn't answer me earlier, Charbonnet. How's Uncle Charlie getting along?"

"Uncle Charlie," I said. "I might be talking out of school here, Larry . . . no, I'm sure I am, but your Uncle Charlie seems depressed to me."

"Yeah? Well, what else is new?"

"He tells me he intends to sell the house. He's made some poor financial moves and he now finds himself in a hole."

"He's not alone in that hole," Larry Lowenstein said. "Why doesn't he sell the collection of Newcomb pottery he keeps upstairs, or the Mallard suite in his bedroom, or some of those pictures by his former teachers and friends? He could begin with the Drysdales and the Kinseys. Am I asking the obvious when I wonder how many swamp and courtyard pictures one man honestly needs?"

"Your uncle lived here, didn't he? With Asmore?"

"Yes, long ago. They were like brothers, nailing chicks left and right, doing everything together. I've never explored the story in detail, but I know the basics from conversations with my parents—my late father, mainly. And then there are the visitors who show up asking for a peek inside. Their grandmother was a *Beloved* girl, or they own a painting that looks like an Asmore and hope that someone at this address can authenticate it. Every one of them seems to have another tale to add to the Asmore legend. You can't imagine how impatient I've grown with the whole silly mess. I quit trying to debunk the myth a long time ago."

"A myth, is it?"

"However you wish to call it, Charbonnet, you end up with the same result. Granted, the guy painted some nice pictures, especially those portraits. But he made them a lot prettier by dying the way he did, and as young he did."

"I'm not sure I get your point."

"Let me try it this way: If people believe they need to buy water in a bottle, they will believe anything. Does that explain it?"

I shook my head. "The reason people buy water in a bottle, Larry, is because it's safe and handy that way. They like art on their walls because they want to look at pretty things. One might argue they also want to be challenged, enlightened and inspired, but I think for most people it's much simpler than that."

"You think so, do you?"

"Yes, I do."

"Ever stop and really look at a painting? There ain't a whole lot to it. Basically what you have is a sheet of paper or some other material with paint smeared on the surface. That's all it is. Why are Levette Asmore's smears so much more valuable than the smears of other talented artists?" He washed back more of the beer, then exhaled a gassy belch before answering his question. "He knew how to market himself, is why. And what's the best way to market yourself? If you're an artist it's to check out young. Look at Van Gogh. He knew it, too, didn't he?"

"So you're saying that the secret to success in the arts is to kill yourself?"

"Very well put, Charbonnet. My sentiments exactly."

I considered leaving at this moment. He was gracious to have invited me in, and the beer was good, but I couldn't tolerate his ignorance. "I don't share your opinion, Larry, I'm sorry."

"Nah, don't be sorry. And don't listen to a goddamn word I'm saying. I'm just talking. I'm still pissed for having to wait in line at the market. Maybe Asmore really was a genius, but my thoughts about the man have always been colored by my love for Charlie Lowenstein.

He was with him when he died, you know? Uncle Charlie was with Asmore. He was there on the bridge. He saw him jump."

I was growing impatient. I let out a long sigh and sat forward on the chair. "I don't think I believe you. It's too . . . I don't know, implausible."

"You don't believe me? Well, you should believe me. Because you can take what I'm telling you to the bank. Uncle Charlie was on that bridge when Asmore killed himself. And it ruined him. Why do you think he never amounted to anything?"

"I don't know that he didn't. He has a beautiful historic home, filled with valuable paintings. In the estimation of most people your uncle amounted to quite a lot."

"Most people? Most people are idiots, Charbonnet." He laughed in his ugly way and drank again. "You ever have a best friend? You know, somebody in your life you care about more than any other? Somebody you share everything with?"

"Sure."

"For Uncle Charlie that person was Levette. So let's pretend for a second you're Uncle Charlie, and it's 1941. One day you and your buddy go out for a drive and end up parked at the foot of the big new bridge they've put over the river. You start walking up that thing, it rises like a mountain out of the goddamn swamp. You reach the top and you look out and see the river and the land and it puts a lump in your throat, it's so beautiful. You're happy. But then you glance over at your friend—you love this person, okay?—and he's climbed up on the guardrail. 'Oh, Levette. Get down from there, Levette.' I mean, what are you going to do? Then before you know it he's catapulted off the side into the longest swan dive anyone's ever seen."

"A swan dive?"

"That's the story."

"I don't see Asmore doing a swan dive."

"You're probably right. He probably just jumped, huh? Uncle Charlie never told me any of this, he refuses to talk about it. But I grew up hearing the story. What made him go crazy? Why is he such a hermit? How come he never shows up at any family get-togethers? You'd ask any one of those questions and that was the answer you got: the story of Levette doing the dive from the bridge."

"And your uncle saw it all?"

"He saw it. After Pearl Harbor he tried to enlist but the Army wouldn't have him because he was F-something. In other words, so certifiably nuts that he couldn't pass the medical. I think about that sometimes. The world is at war, all these thousands and thousands of young people are sacrificing their lives trying to stop Hitler and the Japs, and Uncle Charlie's here in the French Quarter still hanging his lip over his weird friend. Talk about your priorities being fucked up." He pointed at me with the bottle. "Something had to happen."

He excused himself, went back into the house and returned with two more beers. He offered me one and I waved it away, and this seemed to please him. He rubbed a hand over his belly before sitting back down.

"You said something had to happen. Do you mean you think something happened between the two of them that prompted Asmore to kill himself?"

"Yeah, that's always been my guess. Why else would Uncle Charlie become a hermit the way he did? It's like he was guilty, he had blood on his hands."

"How long did he live here in the cottage?"

"All the way up until his mother died and they divided her estate and he got the house. That would've been around '48, '49. My grandfather got this place and an office building on Canal Street, and that explains how I eventually ended up living here. We always tried to involve Uncle Charlie in family events. My sisters got married and they invited him. He didn't show. We'd send him invitations to things and he wouldn't even RSVP. Uncle Charlie was all about Uncle Charlie. He did his own thing. Know what that was, Charbonnet?"

I waited as he brought a beer to his mouth and finished it off. He belched again. "Uncle Charlie's thing," he said, "was always to sit there and wonder why he couldn't stop his friend from jumping off the bridge."

※

She came to the door in her usual jeans, T-shirt and lab coat, hair pulled back and tied with a slip of scarlet ribbon. I'd punched the bell only once, expecting to be met by Joe Butler if anyone at all. I was so surprised to see her there in the trap of iron bars, and not a glowering scarecrow, that my head went blank and I could not think to speak. "It's you," I managed to mutter.

"Jean Rhys Goudeau, restoration girl." She took a step back, pulling the door with her. "And you are?"

"John Francis Charbonnet, Junior, prematurely retired newspaper hack. But you can call me Jack."

"Nice to meet you, Jack."

"Pleasure is mine."

It now was almost six o'clock in the evening, some three hours after I'd left Larry Lowenstein at his cottage in the French Quarter. I'd spent the better part of the afternoon at a tavern on the corner of Saint Charles and Martin Luther King, and just a block away from the Guild's studio. I'd had more beer while seated at a table watching the streetcars rumble by. Levette Asmore was black, and my landlord had been with him when he died. That said it in a nutshell, and yet I was at a loss as to how to relate this information to Rhys. Asmore's connection to Lowenstein, a former client of hers, would be stunning but welcome news. Perhaps we could get him to talk. What I wasn't sure about was how well she would take the revelation that the artist had not been white, as she'd long presumed. Apparently Rhys's racial identity, which seemed to place her in a subgroup that was neither white nor black, and added to a perception that she was different and apart, a breed unto her own, needed some tweaking. She was blacker than she knew. In the tavern I'd gone from laughing to nearly crying at the bleary absurdity of it all. Although I was as confused as ever about most things, it was clear to me now that the whole business of classifying a human being by the color of his skin, let alone its tone or degree of color, was a lot of crazy horseshit.

"May I see the painting?" I said.

She bit her lip and studied my face. She was going to send me away, I was certain, but then she added to the day's load of surprises. "Follow me."

In the studio upstairs there were four large worktables standing next to each other, spaced a few feet apart, so that there was enough room to walk between them. Each table held a panel, and she'd arranged the panels in their proper order, as they'd hung on the wall at Wheeler. The panel on the second table from the left actually had two pieces of canvas: a large rectangle and the narrow strip that had fallen to the ground and colored me gray with residue. In two of the panels you could see the rectangular-shaped holes cut to accommodate the air-conditioning vents. Because Rhys had spent more time working at the center tables, the center of the mural was well on its way to being cleaned while the edges still remained hidden beneath layers of paint. Imagine a window so densely coated with dust and condensation that you can't see through it. In the middle of the window, now, wipe clear an area in the shape of a circle, allowing a view.

"Stand here, Jack," she said, holding my waist with both hands and guiding me to a spot at the foot of the tables. She then lifted the ends of the second and third tables and brought them flush against each other. This matched up the edges of the middle panels, and gave the painting a narrative form that it didn't possess when the panels were separated. "Tell me this isn't the most amazing thing you've ever seen in your life."

In the painting a beautiful man, dressed as a swashbuckling pirate, embraced a beautiful woman in the middle of a French Quarter street, while all around them Carnival was in full swing. The man had white skin; the woman, who wore the crown and frilly clothes of a fairy princess, had a darker complexion. I recognized the lovers: Asmore had painted himself in the arms of Jacqueline LeBeau. As many as a hundred other faces populated the scene. They were black and white, yellow, red and brown, and every combination and shade in between. Each figure was presented in colors even bolder than those in the Ninas murals at the Sazerac Bar, and each wore a costume, some with feathered masks, others with tall, pointed hats wrapped in brightly colored ribbons. The figures danced together, kissed and hugged each other, conversed in pairs and in groups, shared smokes and bottles of alcohol, and howled or pointed at a smiling caricature of the moon. Above the party a costumed black man on stilts reached for the hand of a costumed white woman on stilts, the tips of their fingers touching. A yellow man, tall and thin, whispered in the ear of a red one, who was short and heavyset. A young brown woman swooned in the arms of an older black one. In the distance stood town houses with still more revelers, arranged several deep on the balconies. These people, too, appeared to be of every race and sexual orientation. In the foreground a black child and a white one held hands as they navigated the crowd. Sprawled on the ground next to them was a group of rough characters shooting dice. It was hard to distinguish each man's race, but the joy they seemed to find in their illicit game was shared equally among them. As I studied their faces one of them struck me as being familiar. Something about the shape of the jaw, and the owlish contours of the eyeballs, triggered the recognition. It was none other than Lowenstein, with his hair a thick patch standing on end, a pack of cigarettes screwed into the sleeve of his shirt.

The scene was both an orgy and a celebration. *"Look at me,"* each of the figures might have been saying. *"Look. I am alive."*

"It could be this year's Carnival," I said. "Or next year's."

"Have we really come that far, Jack? I'm not sure we have."

"It reminds me of that line from Martin Luther King's 'I Have a Dream' speech, the one about little white boys and white girls joining hands with little black boys and black girls and walking together as sisters and brothers."

"Yes, it does, but ratcheted upward exponentially. Those little kids there at the bottom are indeed holding hands, but most of the other figures seem to have more serious contact in mind. Now consider that Levette made this picture more than twenty years before Reverend King gave his famous speech. This might've been Levette's idea of utopia, but you can't overstate how shocking the scene must have been to your average white-bread American in the Deep South in the year 1941. It's a defiant renunciation of Jim Crow and segregation. It throws every sexist and racist taboo on its head. And while the image might fit today's idea of America as a melting pot, sixty years ago this kind of integration would've been greeted with hysteria. See all these happy people in the painting, Jack? Most of them would've had their asses tossed in jail. Others would've had their skulls cracked, and I promise some would've been lynched. In that respect, Levette's mural is asking for it. The man wasn't stupid. He had to know he would be pissing people off."

She stepped in front of me and, using a fingernail, carefully removed a fleck of something from the canvas. "Do you remember the story I told you about the artist from Mississippi who depicted whites and blacks swimming together in a public pool? For that the man was dragged out of his house and beaten. Levette's message is a helluva lot more incendiary than that guy's. Levette has blacks and whites actually touching each other, Jack. The two on stilts are obviously a couple, and other interracial pairs look like they're about to go at it in the street. No wonder city officials and the WPA ordered the painting destroyed. What's more surprising is that Levette himself wasn't tarred and feathered the moment anyone had a look at this thing."

I kept returning to the portrait of a dog in the middle ground, its coat a quilt of colors. The dog had a superior expression on its face. "Even the mutt is telling people to go to hell," I said.

"Yes, even the mutt."

"It's kind of corny."

"I suppose it is. But a lot of art is corny without an historical context. Even I can remember when people in this town called any dog that wasn't purebred a nigger dog. Didn't matter if it was a good dog, if it was a dog that did tricks or saved people from house fires. If it wasn't a certain type, with papers, it was a nigger dog. Well, that little dog right there is happy, he's happy with his place in the world, and it doesn't matter what anybody calls him."

Now she pointed to the figure of Jacqueline LeBeau. "Levette gave her the *Beloved* treatment, didn't he? The poor girl looks like she just tumbled out of the sack. She's the virgin princess who's been de-flowered, and by a rogue! Look at her expression, Jack. It's almost ex-actly like that of the little colored dog. You think she cares what anyone thinks of her and her handsome pirate?"

"Pirates are rebels," I said, glancing at Rhys for confirmation. "That's why Asmore presents himself as one, isn't it?"

"Very good, Jack." She was standing close behind me; I could hear her breathing. "I'll need a few more weeks to finish. But I also need to sleep—real sleep in a real bed. The cot in my office has done a job on my back."

"You should go home, Rhys. Give it a break. But first let me buy you dinner. There are some things I need to tell you."

She stood looking at me, then found another fleck to remove from the painting. "Some things, are there? That sounds rather ominous. Are they bad things, Jack?"

"No, I wouldn't call them bad. But they are significant. They're things about Asmore I think you should know."

"In that case let's get moving. Know what I have an *envie* for? Red beans and rice—a big, messy plate of the stuff. How about Mother's on Poydras?"

"Mother's is good if we don't have to stand in line with all the tourists."

"Let's go see."

As she was locking the building she said, "Oh, I hate to leave the painting. This is the first time it's been out of my sight since we . . . ?"

"Stole it?"

"Right." Now she blew a kiss and started across the street. "Bye, Levette. Be good, sugah. Mama will be back soon."

We drove downtown in my car. Rhys clapped her hands at the sight of an open parking slot on the side of the restaurant. Business was slow tonight, without a wait in line. We placed our orders, paid at the register, and claimed a table in the middle of the room. My name was called and I went up for our food. I placed Rhys's plate in front of her and she forked up some beans and rice even before I'd had time to sit down. "Sorry, Jack. Obviously I'm starving."

"Eat," I said. "That's why we're here."

"It's not pizza, it's not a burger in a sponge box, and it's not indefinable chicken parts. Okay, Jack. Now let me hear what I need to know. I promise I can handle it."

"This isn't easy for me," I said. "I've debated whether to tell you, because I'm not really sure what it means yet." I paused and waited for her to look at me. "Levette Asmore was black, Rhys—he was an African American. He started passing as a white sometime after he moved to New Orleans. I interviewed his last surviving family member yesterday in a little town in Saint Landry Parish, a place called Palmetto. Her name is Annie Rae Toussaint. She was his first cousin."

"That would make her my cousin, too."

"Yes, it would. You're related, the two of you."

"Does this upset me?" She put her fork down and sat up tall in her chair. Her head moved on a swivel. "I don't think it does. Do I look upset to you, Jack?"

"Maybe you're chewing faster than you should. That's the only thing I can see."

"I'm chewing faster because the food is so good."

"What about the tears in your eyes? What would that indicate?"

"That I'm sleep-deprived? Yes, I'm sure that's it." She reached across the table and placed a hand on top of mine. "What's important, Jack, is not how your discoveries inform Rhys Goudeau's story, but how they inform Levette Asmore's. It's his drama we've set out to understand, and his mystery we need to solve." She pulled her hand back. "It was Levette's masterpiece that got lost, not mine."

I'd ordered onion rings and a Ferdi poboy, a sandwich combining a long list of improbable ingredients, a chunky beef gravy called "debris," made from roast leftovers, most prominent among them. I took a few bites out of the thing and watched Rhys's eyes for clues to how she was feeling. "Why are you looking at me like that?" she said.

"You're sitting right in front of me. Where the hell else am I supposed to look?"

She gave me a wad of paper napkins for the debris that was running down my arm now. "What else?" she said. "I hope there's more. That can't possibly be the best you can do."

"Levette was rooming with Lowenstein when he jumped from the bridge."

She stared at me and continued chewing. Her head moved up and down. "When he killed himself. From here on out let's call it what it is. Saying he jumped from the bridge sort of sanitizes what happened. Levette Asmore was a suicide."

"He and Lowenstein were sharing a cottage in the French Quarter at the time. Lowenstein apparently witnessed everything that day on the bridge."

"Did Mr. Lowenstein tell you this?"

"His nephew did."

"Have you confirmed this with Mr. Lowenstein yet?"

"No, but only because I haven't approached him with it. He's a tough one, and I'm not sure he'll be accommodating to more of my questions. He'll talk about the past, but only in trade for something he wants. As we were driving over here I thought of a way to get him to open up about Levette. He told me once that he saw the mural before it was destroyed. I bet he'd give up a lot for another look, including the story of what happened that day on the bridge. Will you let him see it, Rhys?"

She was a while before answering. "It's risky, but I'd do it. Sure, I

would. Soon enough others will have to see the painting, too, if we intend to sell it. Nobody can be expected to offer a dime until they see it
in person." She put down her fork and leaned back in her chair. "You
can probably guess that having others experience the painting isn't
something that excites me in the least. The fact is, I loathe the
thought. Right now Levette's mural is mine. When others come to inspect it I give up that sovereignty. Does that sound selfish? I suppose it
does. But having the painting to myself has been nothing short of
magical. I would tell you it also was a spiritual, life-altering experience
but you probably wouldn't buy that. The last couple of weeks have been
the most intense and gratifying of my life, Jack. It's almost been like
having a lover, a secret lover, who no one else in the world knows about
but me." She smiled and ate more of the red beans. "Okay," she said,
"now it's my turn to tell you something. Remember back, if you would,
to the night when you and I met at Patrick Marion's dinner party. I
told you then about repairing one of Mr. Lowenstein's paintings."

"A Drysdale. The old man put a foot through it."

"Yes. Jack, I think Mr. Lowenstein intentionally damaged the
painting to arrange a meeting with me. Only a week before his accident, the Guild was featured in a story in *New Orleans Magazine*.
There were pictures—pictures of our work in studio, and close-up
shots of me as well. Portraits, you know? Mr. Lowenstein mentioned
the article when he called and asked me to come by and give an estimate for a repair. The moment I walked through his door and introduced myself he became extremely nervous. The way he looked at
me—I can't describe it. He gave me the creeps. Usually when somebody calls about a painting their concerns are whether I'll be able to
fix a cherished family heirloom or whether they'll be able to afford the
cost of restoration. Neither concerned Mr. Lowenstein. He kept apologizing, although I never knew for what exactly. He was trembling
when I thanked him for the job and shook his hand good-bye.
Stranger still, he followed me out to the van and stood in the street as
I drove away—he just stood there watching."

"It was about Levette."

"Of course it was."

"He saw your picture in the magazine story and saw the face of an old friend."

"You know everything," she said. "Now finish your Ferdi before it gets cold."

❊

When we were done she asked me to take her for a drive up Saint Charles Avenue. She hadn't been out in weeks, and she was starved for fresh air and a view. We lowered the windows and let the wind blow in, and she sat with her head thrown back on the padded rest. The great homes and gardens flashed by one after another, but her eyes were closed for most of the trip. We went up past Riverbend and stopped at a confectionery on North Carrollton and she stayed in the car while I went inside and bought small cups of pistachio ice cream. As I walked back outside I glanced at Rhys past the wind-shield. She was asleep, head lolling against the seat. Even when I closed the door she didn't wake up. "It's pistachio," I said. "Aren't you hungry, Rhys?"

Still nothing.

Like any wise man presented with the dilemma of having two servings of ice cream and only one mouth to consume them, I ate my cup, then hers, before driving back to the Guild's studio.

I parked on the boulevard across from the old firehouse. I consid-ered taking her to the garçonnière and putting her up in my spare room, but there was no bed in that room. The only bed was in my room, and it likely would've made for trouble to bring her there. What a perfect beauty Rhys was. Even her silent, sleeping form let off a sex-ual power that made me crazy. I studied the slow pace of her breath-ing, the golden down on her thinly muscled forearms, the shadows created by the angles of her cheekbones. Sometimes it was hard to be a man. I also studied the shape of her lips and wondered if I should just go ahead and kiss her and see what happened. I wished I knew how to paint. I would've painted her mouth, on a large, perfectly shaped canvas. That would've been my masterpiece.

I looked over at the firehouse and tracked backward to the few minutes when Rhys had closed the building before we left for dinner. She'd turned out the lights and locked both doors. I'd watched her takes these steps, and yet lights clearly shone now in the windows upstairs. How was that? I wondered.

I nudged her with the heel of my hand. "Rhys? Rhys, wake up, sweetheart."

She recoiled in her seat and stared at me past fluttering lids.

"Do you have timers set on the lights upstairs in the studio?"

Confused, she gave no answer. She waved a hand in front of her face, either to get rid of me or to dismiss the possibility that someone had let himself in the building. "Do I have . . . what did you say?"

"Do you have timers set on the lights upstairs?"

She bent forward and peered up at the building, then in an instant she was out of the car and running across the boulevard. I caught up to her at the entrance, where she fumbled for keys even though both doors were unlocked and partially opened. She let out a groan, then unloaded with a string of obscenities. I stepped around her and led the way inside, pulling her by an arm. "Does Joe Butler have the keys?" I whispered.

"It isn't Joe."

"How can you be sure?"

"Joe had to go out of town. It isn't him. Trust me."

"What about the others?"

"No. Joe and me, we're the only ones who have keys." She still wasn't fully awake. I crossed the floor and stopped at the foot of the stairs. When she joined me she said, "And I'm the only one with a key to *that* door." She pointed to the one on the second-floor landing. It was standing open, with a block of light shining through.

"Let me get something to hit him with," I said, searching the floor for a brick or a piece of wood. Where was my Pete Rose when I needed it?

Rhys grabbed two fistfuls of my shirt and pulled me close against her. "The painting has been damaged enough," she said.

"I know that."

"You will not be throwing things or hitting anyone. Do you hear me?"

"Not even Tommy Smallwood? Can't I hit him? Because that's who it is, Rhys. I would bet anything that's who's up there."

She raced up the stairs making noise and I followed her into the studio where Smallwood stood at the foot of the tables holding the panels. He shot a look in our direction, smiled at Rhys, then ran his hands over his face and made a blubbering sound with his lips. "Nice to see you again, Miss Goudeau," he said.

"Mr. Smallwood?" Rhys's voice was calm. "Mr. Smallwood, you shouldn't be here. I'm going to have to ask you to leave."

"Levette really liked his coloreds, didn't he? God, there must be fifty of them here." He turned back to Rhys. "You think there's a signature in a corner somewhere, under the house paint? I like an autograph on my pictures."

"Mr. Smallwood?"

"Y'all count the blacks yet?"

Rhys walked to within a few feet of where he was standing. "Mr. Smallwood, you're giving me no choice but to call the police."

Smallwood's laughter dissipated to a slow, steady rumble and he moved back from the painting. "Now why would you want to go and do that?"

"You're trespassing. You broke and entered without permission."

"I broke and entered?" An injured look came to his face as he dug in a pocket and removed a ring of keys. He placed them in the palm of his hand and held them out for Rhys to inspect. "This is my property, Miss Goudeau. I own this building."

"You don't own it."

"I've owned it since 1992. Bought it at public auction. Stood outside in the cold and the rain and raised my hand and *fetched* that sonofabitch."

"But I have a lease with a real estate company, sir."

"Yes, you do and you've been a good tenant," Smallwood said. "That company takes care of all my rental properties. And that lease, if you care to read it sometime, stipulates that the lessor—that's me—has the right to enter the premises for inspection at any reasonable hour, provided the lessor—me again—doesn't interfere with the tenant's business. In other words, Miss Goudeau, I can come in here any time I feel like it, so long as I don't make a nuisance of myself." He raised an arm and consulted the diamond-encrusted dial of his Rolex. "It's almost ten o'clock at night. You closed shop hours ago. How am I bothering you?"

"That painting—"

"That painting doesn't belong to you." Smallwood was having fun now, and even from a distance of ten feet away I could smell the alcohol on his breath. "Is that what you were going to say? That you are in possession of stolen government property? Looting the American taxpayer, are we, Miss Goudeau?" He pointed a finger at her. "Maybe I'm the one who should be calling the police."

Rhys leaned back against one of the worktables and crossed her arms at her chest. "What do you want?"

"What do I want? I'm the one who should be asking what you want. You want a check? A bank draft? *Cash?* Tell me what it's going to take, Miss Goudeau."

"I need you to leave now."

"You're going to agree to sell me this painting first."

"I won't do that."

"The way I see it, you don't have much choice but to place it with a private individual such as myself. So sell it to me."

"You'll have your chance, Mr. Smallwood. But you'll have to outbid the others."

"Are you telling me you're planning an auction?"

"That's exactly what I'm saying."

"Oh, I do love an auction." He clapped his hands, then fell into a dance that sent him shuffling backward.

"I'm dialing 911," Rhys said, and held up a portable telephone.

"She's calling 911," Smallwood said to me, his compatriot, with a throaty roar.

Rhys punched numbers and brought the receiver to her ear. "Hello, Operator? Operator, this is Rhys Goudeau, calling from the studio of the Crescent City Conservation Guild. Yes, ma'am. Martin Luther King and Carondelet . . . You got it." She winked at Smallwood. "Well, yes, we do have a problem, a big problem. I just came by to check my office and the doors were open. Someone broke into the building, I'm afraid. Could you send officers right away? Yes, ma'am . . . Thank you."

Smallwood stood looking at her for a time. He laughed. He ran both hands through his hair, then he stepped over to the foot of the tables and surveyed the painting again. Against the banks of fluorescent light overhead his florid face shone purple. "My, God, it's beautiful," he said.

"She said it would only be a few minutes," Rhys told him.

"It is some kind of beautiful." He shook his head and started for the stairs, and as he moved past me I thought I saw a glint of tears in his eyes. "I remember you," he said.

"Jack Charbonnet."

"What's the name again?"

"Charbonnet."

"You think you saved my life, don't you?"

"All I saved was the door at the auction house. You were about to fall through it."

"Miss Goudeau, will I be hearing from you? About the auction?"

"Yes, you will, Mr. Smallwood."

"Fine," he said, seeming satisfied.

We followed him downstairs and out to the boulevard. A police cruiser was pulling up at the curb. The cops got out of the car and Rhys walked up to greet them. "False alarm," she said. "Maybe I left the door unlocked by mistake when I went out earlier for dinner."

The officers had a look around inside, anyway. They walked the

length of both floors and peered into closets shelving supplies. They
checked the rear patio and the alleys that ran on either side of the building. Neither commented on the mural or seemed to notice it, for that
matter. Each of them had coffee on his breath and carried an attitude of
extreme boredom. I was standing downstairs in the framing gallery
when one of them said to Rhys, "Do you usually work this late?"

"Not usually."

"I would recommend a big dog, maybe like a Doberman?"

After they were gone, Rhys and I trudged back upstairs. She
stood at the tables studying the mural for any evidence that Smallwood had tampered with it. I sat on the floor with my back to the wall
and my legs splayed in front of me. I was nervous and I felt as if the
wind had been knocked out of me. "Let me ask you a question," I said.
"How did you know Smallwood would leave if you called the cops?
How did you know that? I mean, that painting really does belong to
the government. And he was in his rights to be here, if it's true he
owns the building."

"I think you know the answer," she said. She walked over and sat
next to me. "Smallwood tells the police about the mural and he
threatens to forfeit any chance to own it himself. He can't let them
know it's here. The government surely would claim ownership, and he
would be without his precious Asmore, the one great southern artist
who's eluded him."

"And the cops walked right by it?"

"That can't surprise you either."

"Smallwood had tears in his eyes as he left. He actually had tears."

"That's not all he had," she said.

I revisited the image of Smallwood moving past me, headed for
the stairs. And something about it did strike me as being unusual.
What were the names of the neurotransmitters that made a collector
a slave to desire? I saw the asymmetrical knot of his necktie, the wide
lapels of his suit coat, the combative expression. But I also saw details
particular to the lower half of his body. When it came to Asmore, the
man had it bad.

I don't think I've ever left Rhys's company without her initiating my departure, and I certainly would've stayed with her longer had she not suddenly announced it was time for me to leave. She got up off the floor and went into her office and started brewing a pot of coffee. I stood in the doorway and looked in at the little sleeping cot shoved against one of the vitrines crowded with pottery. On the floor under the cot was a Ken Follett paperback, titled *The Modigliani Scandal,* open to the page where she'd left off. "Aren't you going home?" I said.

She shook her head. "Too risky. Besides, I feel like working."

"I'll stay here the night, if you're worried about Smallwood coming back."

"No, but thank you, Jack. It's kind of you to offer. I don't think I'll be leaving the studio again until I finish bringing the mural back. Obviously he's been watching the building, waiting for a chance to come in, and I wouldn't rest if I went home now."

She walked with me downstairs and stood just outside the entrance on the sidewalk with her arms loosely folded at her chest. "Come here," she said.

I moved toward her and she kissed the side of my face, then wiped the spot, I supposed to remove a lipstick smudge. "Jack, you're wonderful," she said. And then she kissed me again and wiped me off again.

I headed back to Moss Street under assault from my own private store of neurotransmitters. At one of the traffic lights there was a streetlamp burning bright and illuminating the interior of the car and I checked in the rearview mirror to see if any of her lipstick was still on me. I touched the spot on my face where she'd kissed me. "Serotonin and something else," I said out loud, still trying to remember.

※

After coffee at the shop on Esplanade I walked home, covered in a slicker to keep dry. I paused to look at the black curving plain of the bayou dimpled with rain, ducks paddling along the bank, an abandoned toy boat floating upside down near the bridge. It was an ugly morning, and almost too humid to endure. The weather was a perfect reflection of how I was feeling today. Last night when I got home, still reeling from Rhys's kiss, I encountered a for-sale sign on the front gate. High Life Realty was offering the property, and phone numbers for Patrick Marion were provided. I also encountered a note torn from a memo pad taped to my door. "Call me," it said in a simple, straight-forward hand. "The ghost faces immediate eviction. Please let's cele-brate soon around the Chambers."

Sally answered my knock and brought her face up close to the screen. "What kind of fool but Jack Charbonnet goes walking in the rain?"

"May I come in, Sally?"

"You have to ask me that? You know you can't come in. Even if you could come in I wouldn't let you in all wet like that."

"Please give him a message, in that case, if you wouldn't mind. Tell him Levette's mural—"

"Levette's *what?*"

"His mural, his painting . . . ?"

"All right."

"Tell Mr. Lowenstein I can show it to him, if he's interested. But he'll have to answer a few of my questions afterward."

"I'll tell him," she said, then pressed her mouth flush against the screen and proffered a kiss. "That's for helping me that time."

I walked back to the garçonnière, thinking about it, and called Patrick. He seemed to have a hard time reining in the phone; it banged around awhile before he said anything. "You get my note?" He sounded hung over.

"Unbelievable," I told him.

"He wants two million for it. He should get every penny, too, the way the market's been going lately."

"Did he tell you what his plans are, Patrick? He's lived at the place for more than fifty years. I wonder where he'll move to."

"I didn't ask him. He's not the sort of man who invites personal questions of that sort, and I didn't want to give him any excuse to reconsider and change his mind. Can you keep a secret, Jack?"

"I think you know the answer to that one."

"I've talked to Elsa about buying the property—about our doing it together. Most of her accounts originate in New Orleans as it is, and for months she's been talking about opening an office here. She makes a good living, far better than I do, and if we shop for a mortgage together we might get lucky and find someone willing to do the loan. It's a long shot, but well worth our investigating."

"Would you marry her, Patch?"

"Let's not put the cart before the horse, old boy. We don't want to be hasty. Elsa and I have been dating for only seventeen years now. Why rush things? You know," he said, "I'm rather overwhelmed that I even find myself in a position to make a run at a place like Lowenstein's. Before *Beloved Dorothy* entered the picture, I didn't have two nickels to rub together. Not to overstate it, but I feel a great debt of gratitude to this Asmore character. He's changed my life, and only sixty years after he ended his. Too bad he's no longer around to thank, isn't it?"

"Too bad," I said.

"One day I'll have to place a wreath on his grave. I owe him that much. By the way, Jack, you wouldn't know where he's buried, would you?"

⁂

Less than an hour later I was standing at the spot in a corner of Saint Louis Cemetery Number One, just across Basin Street from the French Quarter, and hard by a housing project built on the former site of Storyville, the city's infamous red-light district. Rain fell in sheets from the black sky and raked against my slicker, and I couldn't stop shaking, although it wasn't the weather that had my body in spasms.

Like others in the cemetery, Asmore's tomb was raised above-ground to protect the coffin inside from being disinterred in the event of flooding. I recalled from my reading that the artist's remains did not reside in the low, rectangular structure of brick and mortar, but to stand on the sod where his friends, teachers and admirers had once stood and grieved over his empty coffin had no small impact on me. I'd become one of them, I supposed, and suddenly I felt a closeness to the man that no amount of research had been able to provide. In the graveyard he was more real to me than he had been anywhere else, including the beauty school, the small rooms of Annie Rae Toussaint's house and his home in the French Quarter. While locating his tomb had been significant, it was the dark poetry of the legend carved on its face that made my heart pound. I reached out a hand and felt the words with my fingertips. BELOVED ASMORE, it said.

It wasn't until I started to walk away from the tomb that other unanticipated details registered. I turned back and leaned against the rain surveying the mausoleum again as well as others in the area. At least three of them, including those to the left and the right of Asmore's, were inscribed with the same family name: Lowenstein. "You again," I muttered, although I can't say it came as a surprise.

It should have ended there. But I happened to cast my eyes downward, to the foot of Asmore's tomb, where a single flower lay on the cement slab that formed an apron under the bricks, its petals bruised from exposure, the spray of leaves around it beaded with raindrops. It was a magnolia. On the path leading up to the tomb were parallel tracks running a few feet apart and cut into the wet sod. They might've been put there by a gardener's cart. But more likely they were marks left by a wheelchair.

We drove to the studio in silence. I reached to turn on the radio but he tapped the back of my hand, stopping me. He smelled of analgesic rub, urine and other odors that I thought best not to acknowledge lest they discourage me and send me back home. As usual, his shirt was clean and stiffly starched, immaculate, while his pants were rumpled, stained and filthy. Over his clothes he wore a raincoat even though the storm was long gone. He also wore leather brogans without laces and without socks and I could see the bruises and broken blood vessels at his ankles. He was unshaven and sparse white whiskers pebbled his jaw, but at least he'd taken the trouble to comb his hair. It was good hair for an old man. I considered telling him that, but saying anything about a man's hair felt unnatural and I couldn't get it out. I also considered starting with the questions about Asmore, now that he was stuck in the car with me and couldn't escape. Instead I said, "Where will you go, Mr. Lowenstein, once you find a buyer?"

He stared at me but never did answer.

It had stopped raining and now a breeze blew and tunneled down the streets. Light from the streetlamps lay in pools on the asphalt and colored the air a greenish yellow. It felt like fall was coming even though the temperature outside was probably over seventy degrees and midnight had come and gone an hour ago. I felt a loneliness I couldn't place or make sense of. It was the loneliness, I figured, that came with the changing of the seasons, and it made me want out of my body. I wished I'd stayed at home and gone to bed. I would be sleeping now like everybody else in the world. That was how I felt: like I was the last person awake in the world, even with Lowenstein beside me and Rhys Goudeau waiting for us on Martin Luther King.

I parked and got out and from inside the car he said something. I walked around to his side and opened the door and lowered my head to hear him better. "You say something, Mr. Lowenstein?"

"Goddamned arthritis," he said.

"No, it was something else."

"I said that's where I went to temple."

"Where?"

"That building there. When I was a boy." He looked off in the direction of an old church that now was home to an African-American congregation, Baptist probably. "I grew up in this neighborhood," Lowenstein said. "It's all black now but I grew up here."

"It isn't all black," I said.

"No, it's all black, trust me."

"But I know for a fact that not all the businesses are black."

"The businesses?" And he laughed. "What businesses? The businesses on Dryades Street? The ones on Carondelet? They all left. They left a long time ago."

"Uglesich's Restaurant is still here. There's a dairy still here. The Crescent City Conservation Guild is here."

"The what?" He grabbed the doorframe and put a foot out. "Take my word for it," he said. "I know what I'm telling you."

I offered a hand but he pushed me away. I stood back and watched him. What had Levette Asmore seen in the man to keep him around as a friend? Had he ever been anything but rude and condescending? What about *old*? Was it truly possible that he'd been young once? A look of pain aggravated his face as he extricated himself from the car and stood on the sidewalk and rose to as tall as he could make himself. "I remember when the fire department came and saved my grandmother's house," he said.

"The *what*?" I said it the same way he had said it earlier, to show that it didn't matter, that *he* didn't matter.

He was looking across the boulevard at the firehouse. "The whole back of it was in flames. They were Irish, the firemen."

"They were Irish? How'd you know that?"

"I remember their blue eyes."

I was still thinking poorly of him, still wondering if he might've been different once. "I could give a damn what they were," I said.

He nodded as though he understood. He looked at me awhile. "It started in the kitchen," he went on. "They stopped it before it could move to the rest of the house."

"Why did they have to be white firemen? Irish boys?"

"They didn't have to be," he said. "That's what they were."

"Sometimes I hate the world, I swear I hate it. I hate the way God made it."

"So do I," he said. "But I didn't hate it as much back then."

We walked to the building and Rhys opened the doors and I went in first and Lowenstein followed. The two of them stood just inside looking at each other. She helped him off with his raincoat. "Can I get you something to drink?" She was talking to Lowenstein. "How about a cup of coffee? I think I have Coke, too. Would you like a Coke?"

"I'm not thirsty."

"I'm glad you came," she said.

"I thought it might be worth another look."

He refused our help getting up the stairs, and for a while I thought we'd have to carry him. With each step he paused for breath and, using a badly disfigured index finger, counted the number remaining before he reached the top. "Only nine left," he said near the halfway point.

"You're doing great," Rhys said.

"Eight," he said, five minutes later when he'd made it to the next step.

He reached the landing and asked for a chair and Rhys dragged one over and he sat with his elbows on his thighs and his upper body taking in and letting out air. A film of sweat glistened on his face. Rhys gave him a glass of water and when he drank some spilled on his shirt and exposed wisps of curly white hair against the pink of his sunken chest. "I'm used to spilling on myself," he said.

"You should never get used to that," Rhys said.

"It'll dry. Give it a half hour."

She came back with a towel and patted the wet spot on his shirt. She put the glass away, then she placed a hand on his shoulder and stooped down until her face was almost even with his. "Can I help you back up to your feet, Mr. Lowenstein? Why don't we walk the rest of the way together?"

He glanced upward, eyes rimmed red and blinking as they met the lights overhead. He looked confused, as if he'd momentarily forgotten who Rhys was or who he was himself. "Mr. Lowenstein?" Rhys said in a sweet voice.

"I want you to know how well I thought of your grandmother," he told her. "She was a sweet, dear girl."

Rhys moved her hand over to the back of his neck. Her face was right in front of his. "Thank you. Thank you for saying that. That means a lot to me."

"A dear, sweet girl," he said again.

He got up and shuffled over to the middle of the room and stood at the foot of the tables with the mural. His gaze went first to the lovers, then to the group of men shooting dice. He tapped a hand against his flank and a strange, clumsy grin came to his face. He threw his head back and seemed to laugh, but except for a kind of wheezing no sound came out. After a minute I understood that he was crying, sobbing as he choked on the air he was trying to breathe. "I'm there," he said, pointing his crooked finger at the painting now. "I'm still there."

"Jack thought that might be you," Rhys said.

"What a . . . what an ugly boy I was."

"You weren't ugly."

"I was *ugly*."

"Here," and Rhys brought the chair back over.

He sat as upright as he could, pushing with his hands against his thighs to keep from pitching forward, and fighting the thing that had taken control of him. "Oh Levette," he said. "Oh Levette oh Levette . . ."

It was hard to watch and when I looked at Rhys I saw that she was fighting it, too. You would think it goes away at some age and doesn't hurt so much anymore. That it fades from memory or is forgotten or scars over so that when you visit it again there is none of the wound left. But it doesn't go away. As long as we're alive it never goes away. "Mr. Lowenstein," I said, "do you want me to take you home? It's no problem if you want to go home."

He didn't answer and Rhys said, "Mr. Lowenstein?"

"No," he said. He started to stand again and Rhys held him under an arm. "I need a softer chair. Is there a softer chair?"

"We can go in my office," Rhys said.

Together we helped him get there. "Jack? Bring that chair here for Mr. Lowenstein, please." She nodded at a Mission chair with back and seat cushions upholstered in leather. I pulled it over and she and I lifted against his arms as he fell backward.

She leaned down and put her arms around him and whispered in his ear, asking again if he wanted something to drink.

"Have you nothing stronger than coffee and Coke?" Lowenstein said.

"We might have something."

"Pour me a glass and I'll tell you about Levette."

Rhys seemed reluctant to leave him, even for that.

TEN

It was difficult to believe, he said, but in those days the French Quarter was still a neighborhood, a real one. One didn't find all the nastiness on Bourbon Street, the strip clubs and transvestite bars, the T-shirt and sex shops with blow-up plastic genitalia in the windows. In those days the only place that sold whips was the hardware store, and they were used for spanking animals, not people. Oh, there were bars, and plenty of them. But one found none of the perversion and seediness, out-of-towners being sick in the gutters, many of them yelling, on any day of the week, and at any hour, for women on the balconies to show their breasts. The tourists, in other words, hadn't ruined it yet.

On Saturdays ladies dressed when they came downtown and did their shopping on Canal Street. They came with their hair done or else wearing little hats with flowers. This, he said, might border on cliché. Surely it was nothing Miss Goudeau and I hadn't heard before, that the Quarter was once a real place, or that women actually went there wearing clothes, but he thought it worth repeating, if only to build a picture of a world entirely different from the one in which we now found ourselves. "It wasn't all better in those days," Lowenstein said. "God, no, it wasn't. But I'll get to that."

He sipped from his glass of whiskey. His eyes were closed, I suspect as much to keep from having to look at Rhys and me as to see through his window on the past.

It was on a streetcar on Carondelet Street, he said, headed toward the Quarter on a Monday morning in August of the year that he saw him for the first time. The front of the car was crowded, but the rear, where the Negroes sat, still had seating available. Asmore was riding in front, in the middle of a crowd of passengers, busily filling in the page of a sketchbook open on his lap. Lowenstein stood in the aisle grasping a handhold overhead. Because he admired fine bones and great hair, and the general appearance of someone beautifully made, Lowenstein found that he could not keep his eyes off the young artist. Asmore's long, slender fingers were making quick studies of unsuspecting fellow travelers, and drawing them in caricature. He was like that, always having to keep his hands busy. In fact, he smoked because he couldn't stand to have his hands idle. It was not the nicotine he craved but rather intimacy with the cigarette itself.

"Did he chain-smoke?" Rhys asked.

"Did he chain-smoke?" Lowenstein opened his eyes. I, too, recognized the question as being odd, and hardly significant. "No," he answered, seeing that she sincerely wanted to know. "I don't think you could describe his smoking that way. We mostly rolled them back then. It took too much time for a busy young person to chain-smoke."

"It's just that I want to see him as best I can."

"I understand," he said.

The car stopped to load more passengers, almost all of them white, and Asmore, finding his range of motion restricted, and thus being unable to continue sketching, stood up and casually walked to the rear of the car. Nobody said anything, but several passengers turned back and stared, including blacks scattered on the benches. Asmore sat next to a dark-skinned woman—a Negress, they would've called her—and began drawing again, not the least mindful of what he'd done. The only other white people Lowenstein had ever seen sitting among blacks on a streetcar were a bunch of drunks in devil costumes riding home after a Mardi Gras parade.

They got off at Canal Street and Lowenstein followed him into the French Quarter. As it happened, they were both bound for the Arts and Crafts Club Building. Asmore politely held the door open, seeing Lowenstein striding up behind him. "You rode with the Negroes," Lowenstein told him.

"Did I?" Asmore seemed either distracted or uninterested, Lowenstein couldn't tell which. "Well, I should consider myself lucky to have survived in one piece."

What an odd bird, Lowenstein remembered thinking. Later someone told him who he was.

They were the same age, but they never had a class together. Asmore already had established himself as a star at the school, while Lowenstein was a pretender posing as a bohemian to avoid having to fulfill his parents' expectations and enroll at Tulane. "I told my father I wanted my independence and my own place to live," Lowenstein said. "I was stubborn and hardheaded even then. Against my mother's wishes he let me have the cottage on Saint Philip. It was a dump, filled with antiques my mother no longer wanted. It had two bedrooms, and this pleased me because I saw an opportunity to make beer money. Without my parents ever knowing, I posted a note on a bulletin board at school advertising a room for rent. Levette was the only one who answered it."

Asmore showed up with a cardboard suitcase containing toiletries and clothes, a large toolbox in which he stored painting supplies and an army-issue duffel bag stuffed with painted canvases. His disastrous show at the Arts and Crafts Club gallery was now a few months behind him. A girl drove him over in an old Ford and stood around twirling her hair and trying to look mysterious. Her pose failed when she began to glare at Asmore with the kind of sexual hunger that Lowenstein heretofore had associated with men only. Soon another girl was knocking at the front door, this one an Uptown debutante whose social calendar was often reported in the papers. While the two girls argued in the kitchen, Asmore slipped outside and went for a bottle of whiskey. The girls were still arguing when he returned. Lowenstein recognized that life with his new housemate was going to be interesting.

"Besides his obvious good looks," Rhys said, "why do you think women found him so attractive?"

"It wasn't only women, dear girl."

"Let me rephrase that, then. Besides how he looked, why did people find Asmore so attractive?"

"It's a fair question, and one I've often wondered about myself, because if truth be told, Levette was a reluctant lover. I can tell you his reputation as a libertine is exaggerated and largely undeserved. He was many things—an alcoholic, for example; a terrible alcoholic—but he was not sexually promiscuous. Oh, he might've had dalliances with a few of them, but not nearly as many as the years have piled on him. He was more interested in making their picture than making love to them."

"Yes," Rhys said, "but what made him so desirable, Mr. Lowenstein? What made them *want* him?"

"Precisely what I just told you. His indifference, I do believe, combined with a shyness or humility that one finds attractive in a boy. There also was about his nature a wounded thing that every woman who met him presumed she could help him to heal. His drinking wasn't attractive, no, but it did add to the impression that there was something deep and troubling at work beneath the surface. He had an air of being unknowable, and of having secrets. He was the sort of person people whispered about. And of course he was brilliant. Levette was truly brilliant. When I tell you there was no one like him I mean he was not how other people are—other artists, I should say. Technically he was superior to the rest of the crowd. He could paint a complicated architectural view as easily as a human face, and he understood that women liked sitting for him. Rather than show them exactly as they were, he presented them as they secretly hoped to look. He appealed to their vanity. Women may deny this, or some may, but after a woman's made love . . . well, these are the moments when she believes herself to be most beautiful and alive. Levette aimed to capture that. In most cases he succeeded."

They lived together for two years, although Lowenstein left the art school after only a semester and began his studies in business at Tulane. Asmore, on the other hand, remained at the school as a part-time instructor of painting and took on various odd jobs in the Quarter. He waited tables and did carpentry and roofing work. For a while he contracted with a dealer named Harmanson, who had him decorate plates with New Orleans scenes for the tourist trade. All of Asmore's plate paintings—and there were hundreds—were distinguished by their banality; he often painted two of them at a time, using both hands, a brush in each. Lowenstein once watched Asmore paint a view of the Brulatour Courtyard with his eyes closed, to prove a point. "Have you ever seen those plates?" Lowenstein asked.

"I've seen plates from that period decorated with city scenes," Rhys said, "but never one that I can say looked like his work or came with his signature."

"Oh, he never would've signed one of those dreadful things, and he intentionally painted them all to look like something the worst street artist might've done. I'm a little uncomfortable bringing up the subject of the plates, because his legacy is secure and I don't want to detract from it. He never advertised the fact that he was painting plates. Outside of Mr. Harmanson, I was probably the only person who knew it. Levette was paid ten cents for each plate, if I recall correctly. You could always tell when his funds were depleted because he would say, 'Well, Low . . .'—he called me Low—'well, Low,' he'd say, 'my plates await.' " Lowenstein laughed. " '*My* plates await,' as if he cared about them."

One night in his room Lowenstein was awakened to the sound of a woman's laughter. It wasn't the first time, but he checked his wristwatch and saw that it was 4:00 A.M., late even for Asmore. Lowenstein covered himself with a robe and walked into the living room. There was no one. He looked around and saw empty wine bottles standing on the floor, a saucer serving as an ashtray covered with butts, pillows arranged in a stack at one end of the sofa only. The doors leading to the courtyard were open, and when he walked outside he saw Asmore sitting on a bench with a young woman. Moonlight sent their shadows in sprawling puddles on the flagstones. A wind rustled the leaves of the banana trees and blew the girl's hair in her face, and when she raised a hand and pulled the hair back Lowenstein saw that the girl was a light-skinned Negro. Levette and the girl rose to their feet, and Levette, who was so drunk he had a hard time standing, introduced her as "Jacqueline, not Jackie, LeBeau."

Had he grown up in any southern city but New Orleans, Lowenstein might've been shocked to find his housemate involved with a black woman. When Lowenstein was a teenager his uncle Teddy, a bachelor with a wily, concupiscent nature, had often regaled him with stories about the Quadroon Balls of old at which moneyed white men, most of them French Creoles with wives and children at home, had courted beautiful women of color to keep as paramours. Perhaps Asmore was pursuing such an arrangement. "But, no, this didn't add up," Lowenstein said. "Levette wasn't married and he barely had enough money to keep himself, let alone a woman."

They carried on their love affair largely in the confines of the cottage, venturing out in public together after hours when there were few people to observe them. They went for walks along the river or borrowed Lowenstein's car and took drives in the country. When Asmore painted plein-air in the old district, Jacqueline occasionally accompanied him, but she made certain to keep a distance, slipping in doorways or blending in crowds. None of Levette's contemporaries knew about the relationship, although he seemed less reticent to talk about Jacqueline with his teachers at the school, primarily Alberta Kinsey and Paul Ninas. "Like them, I thought it was an infatuation that would end after a few weeks," Lowenstein said. "But it didn't end. Levette continued to pursue Jacqueline for no reason but the obvious one. He was in love with her."

From his bedroom Lowenstein could hear the sounds of their lovemaking. One night he listened as Jacqueline pleaded with Asmore to stop drinking. "I heard her say, 'Please, Levette, you are my heart,' over and over. She was weeping, and to hear her that way almost made me weep myself. It probably sounds maudlin now, but she was begging him not to kill himself."

Other times, better times, Lowenstein endured their giggles as they played like clumsy puppies on the living room floor. When Asmore got the WPA commission to paint the post office mural, the couple took over the kitchen and Jacqueline prepared a huge dinner in celebration. They had porterhouse steaks, Lowenstein recalled. "It was a happy day. We played jazz on the phonograph and took turns dancing across the floor, the three of us did. When Jacqueline left off to tend to her cooking, Levette and I came together and danced as well. We were both three sheets to the wind and there was no suggestion of intimacy. He and I had roughhoused before, as young men do, but this night was the only time I ever actually held him in my arms. I remember how strong and powerful he felt. His body might've been cut from rock."

Jacqueline lighted candles on the table and served the meal. "Here's to the history of transportation in America," said Asmore, lifting a toast with his wineglass. Lowenstein noticed a tight edge of sarcasm in his friend's voice.

"To the history of transportation in America," Lowenstein and Jacqueline answered in unison, and raised their own glasses.

Asmore brought the glass up higher. "And here's to its history of discrimination against the Negro," he said, suddenly turning serious.

"To the Negro," Lowenstein shouted out, and nodded at Jacqueline, who'd lowered her glass and sat without responding.

Later that night Lowenstein, watching through his half-open door, saw them lying together on a blanket on the floor of the living room, their naked bodies bathed in candlelight. They seemed oblivious to his presence, but then Jacqueline's gaze turned to Lowenstein and she seemed to smile at him in the moment before she came to orgasm. "It was too much to bear," Lowenstein said. "I turned over and put my back to them."

In the early days Lowenstein had enjoyed the spectacle. But by now the couple's passion for each other, ever on display, gave him reason to wonder if they meant to taunt him. Were they intentionally trying to hurt him? They truly seemed to enjoy making him miserable. Ever since Jacqueline entered the scene he'd begun to feel alienated from Asmore, whom he'd regarded as his closest friend and confidant. But he and Asmore never talked anymore. They never went out on the town together, never shared meals at home alone, never did anything without Jacqueline being with them. Lowenstein felt abandoned and betrayed.

" 'Night, Low," Jacqueline said, standing in the doorway to his bedroom. Against the soft light of the living room he could see her shapely form, the dense weight of her breasts barely contained by the light fabric of her dress. She was holding a shoe in each hand. Her lips were dark and full from kissing and her hair hung loose past her shoulders. Lowenstein lay still, willing himself not to move. " 'Night," she said again. He wondered if he was losing his mind.

In the weeks that followed, he stopped attending class and rarely got out of bed before noon. On dates of his own, he began to act differently than he ever had before. He pawed at the girls when they clearly had no romantic interest in him, and forced kisses on them when they didn't want to be kissed. One of them, Jennifer Vaden, a judge's daughter, slapped him so hard he thought she'd ruptured his eardrum. He started visiting a house on Toulouse Street, finding there the sexual intimacy he craved, if not the affection.

"It went beyond jealousy," Lowenstein said. "I began to resent them. I can recall waking up one day and finding candle wax on a table in the living room. The table was nothing special, and it was only candle wax, for heaven's sake. But I exploded in a rage and carried on as if some terrible crime had been committed."

One night Jacqueline arrived at her usual hour and Lowenstein let her in. Asmore had not returned home yet. He was still working at his studio, trying to meet a deadline for the post office mural.

"I remember what your grandmother was wearing," Lowenstein said to Rhys. "It was a blue silk dress with an Oriental design, probably straight off the rack at D. H. Holmes. It was cut rather low, which was unusual for Jacqueline, who was quite modest. She'd had her hair done; it was piled on top of her head. She was such a gorgeous girl, and tonight she smelled of a strong, fancy perfume. Around her neck was a Spratling creation. Do you know who Bill Spratling was?"

"Yes."

Lowenstein looked at me. "And do you, Mr. Charbonnet?"

"He was the artist from here in the twenties who moved to Mexico and became a silversmith."

"And famous for his jewelry," Lowenstein said. "I think it was Alberta Kinsey who introduced Levette to Bill, when Bill had returned to New Orleans from Taxco one year and lectured at the art school. They hit it off and the two of them exchanged letters for years. When Levette wrote to Bill that he'd met the woman of his dreams in Jacqueline LeBeau, Bill sent him a silver necklace to give to her. He knew, of course, that Levette couldn't afford such a thing. That's the kind of man Bill Spratling was." Lowenstein coughed into a fist and a splash of red came to his face. "Anyway, your grandmother was wearing her Spratling piece this day. I invited her to sit down, and she thanked me and pulled up a chair from our little dining table, and I sat across from her and stared without speaking until she began to feel uncomfortable."

"I have something important to tell Levette today," she said. "I'm nervous, Low." Lowenstein didn't comment and she said, "What is it?" She glanced down to make sure she was covered. "Low, is something wrong?"

"Yes," he answered. "There's a lot that's wrong."

"What is it?" Now she reached up and felt her hair, to make sure it was in place. "Did I do something?"

He was tempted to reach over and grab the necklace and rip it off her neck. His anger boiled to a point where he could feel the color rise in his neck. "Did you do something?" he said. "You better believe you did something."

"What, Low? What did I do?"

"You're a goddamned nigger bitch, that's what you did."

She sat for a while, then stood and walked to the door, a hand covering her mouth. Lowenstein remained seated in his chair wondering where the words had come from and feeling such shame that he thought he'd rather die than face either Jacqueline or Asmore again. "I hated myself," he said. "I'd never intentionally been so vicious to anybody before in my life."

He left the cottage and walked to the house on Toulouse Street and satisfied himself in the rough fashion that had become his release. As he was leaving, a boy came outside and said, "Hey, aren't you Charlie Lowenstein, from Tulane?" He didn't answer and the boy said, "We have a business class together." Lowenstein put his head down to avoid contact with the boy. "How about a drink, Charlie. What's the hurry?"

"I'm not who you think I am," Lowenstein said.

"You're Charlie Lowenstein. Don't worry," the boy said. "I won't tell anyone." He looked around and laughed. "You're not here alone, are you?"

Lowenstein slowly backed away from the boy, then ran back to the cottage as fast as he could, his sobs seeming to grow louder with every stride.

He found them waiting outside on the courtyard. "I'll be out as soon as I finish hanging the mural," Asmore said when Lowenstein passed through the French doors.

"Jacqueline, I'm sorry, darling. Please forgive me." He was winded, his hair and face lathered with sweat.

"What the hell is wrong with you?" Asmore flicked his cigarette in Lowenstein's direction. "And what are you doing, calling her 'darling' now?"

"Jacqueline, I apologize. I'm sorry. I don't know what came over me. Forgive me. You must forgive me."

"Get away from her," Asmore shouted.

"Tell me you forgive me," Lowenstein said to Jacqueline.

She was sitting on the bench under the banana leaves, in a different, more conservative suit of clothes now, and without the Spratling necklace. She'd also let her hair down, he noticed. She hugged her arms to her chest and lowered her chin. "I forgive you, Low," she whispered.

"I should cut your tongue out of your mouth," Asmore said to Lowenstein.

"I forgive you, Low," she whispered a second time.

In Rhys's office Lowenstein paused and drank from the whiskey. Rhys walked across the floor without any apparent direction, then returned to her chair and sat on the edge leaning forward. "Did she ever tell you what it was that was so important?"

"She didn't have to tell me."

"Jacqueline was pregnant, wasn't she?"

"I'm certain that was it. She was radiant that night, when she first came over. She'd dressed up for him. I think that's what set me off. I just couldn't take it another minute. I despised her." He closed his eyes again. "She was carrying his child. I'd lost him forever now."

Early the next morning he awoke to find the artist standing in his room. Asmore reeked of cigarette smoke and his eyes were bloodshot. He was wearing canvas coveralls, the ones from work, and paint colored his fingers. After leaving the cottage the night before, he'd gone to the studio to complete work on the mural. But he obviously had also found time to drink. Asmore's expression was so severe that Lowenstein covered his face, in anticipation of being struck. "Get up," Asmore told him. "It's time you saw something."

"What is it?"

"You'll see when we get there."

They left the city in Lowenstein's car headed west on the state highway. They drove past swamp bottoms and vast areas of farmland and stopped for fuel in Baton Rouge. They'd been traveling for more than two hours. Asmore, though hardly in any condition to drive, had manned the wheel the entire distance, refusing to answer Lowenstein's pleas for forgiveness or questions about their destination. They crossed the river on a ferry, then drove for another hour, the latter part of it on dirt and shell roads. It was late afternoon when they motored into a small railroad town, dust coming up like a hurricane in their wake. They stopped finally before a shack where a girl was removing clothes from a line that stretched between trees in the yard. The girl shielded her eyes with a hand as she gazed up at them.

"There," Asmore said, pointing. "You see her?"

"See who?"

"That girl there?"

Lowenstein sat up in the seat and peered through the dusty glass. "Yeah, I see her. Jesus, Levette. We came all this way to look at a colored girl?"

"That's not just any colored girl."

Lowenstein looked again. He gave her a closer inspection this time. "I don't see how she's any different."

"That girl's my first cousin, Low. Her name is Annie Rae Asmore. Her father and my father were brothers. You want me to call her up to the car?"

Lowenstein didn't answer and Asmore reached over and placed a hand against the back of his head and held it there, forcing him to look again. "Look at her, Low. Drink it all in. She's a goddamned nigger just like I'm a goddamned nigger."

"You're not a god—" Lowenstein muttered.

"I'm not?"

"You're drunk. You're a drunk is what you are."

Lowenstein wouldn't look again at the girl. He wouldn't talk, either.

Asmore began to laugh then, even as tears filled his eyes and his voice broke. "Sure, I'm a nigger," he said. "Or I was a nigger until they moved me to New Orleans and somebody decided I was too pale and pretty to be placed in a home with them. That's when I became like you, Low."

Lowenstein slipped lower in his seat. His eyes were closed. "I wish you'd take me home now," he mumbled.

"Let me call Annie Rae on up here."

Lowenstein shook his head. "Take me home."

"Take me home, nigger," Asmore said.

"What?"

"Take me home, nigger. Say it like that. Say, 'Take me home, nigger.'"

Through clenched teeth Lowenstein said, "Take me home, Levette."

"Take me home, nigger," Asmore said, raising his voice. "We don't leave until you say, 'Take me home, nigger.'"

"Take me home."

"Take me home, nigger."

"Take me home, nigger."

Asmore started the engine and pushed the stick into gear. "I'm going to tell you what we're going to do," he said. "It's simple, Low. It's simple what we're going to do. I'll be moving out soon but until then you're going to be nice to my girlfriend. You're going to treat her with kindness and respect. If you don't treat her with kindness and respect . . . well, Low, I'm going to have to do something."

"What are you going to do?"

"I'm going to tell everyone who'll listen that Charlie Lowenstein went and fell in love with a nigger. Worse, with a goddamned nigger."

"I'm not in love with Jacqueline," Lowenstein said.

"You're not?"

"I'm fond of her. She's lovely. But I'm not in love with her."

Asmore laughed again, then set the car in motion. "Jacqueline isn't the nigger I meant," he said.

❄

It now was after two o'clock in the morning. Lowenstein held his glass high as Rhys poured more whiskey. His hand was trembling when he brought the glass to his mouth. "I didn't see him again," he said.

"No?"

"Well, no, of course I saw him again. What am I saying?" He glanced over at me. "Be a gentleman and have a drink with me, Mr. Charbonnet."

I'd been sitting on the floor. I stood up and went for a glass.

"You, too, Miss Goudeau. Don't let me go through the rest alone."

After we'd poured our whiskeys Lowenstein said, "He moved out and never lived with me again. That's what I should have said. I'm afraid I've lost my ability to think straight. Maybe we should finish this some other time."

"You can do it," Rhys said.

"It's too hard."

"You can do it. We're here with you, Mr. Lowenstein."

He looked at the place on his shirt where he'd spilled earlier. It was dry now. "What Levette had done," he said, "well, he'd come to the cottage while I was in class and packed his things, to avoid having to see me. I learned later that he'd moved in with Knute and Colette Heldner, the artists, blocks away on Saint Peter. When I got home that day—it was just after one o'clock—I sat in his empty room with my back against the wall and I stayed there for hours. I got up finally and checked the furniture in his room for anything he might have left behind. I'm not completely sure why I felt compelled to do this, but I think I wanted proof that I'd known this man. Even then I was certain that no experience in my future would equal the one of my time with Levette."

In the room there was a tall chest with drawers and he combed over it from top to bottom but found nothing. Next he went through the armoire. It was a huge thing, one of those pieces made in the state a hundred years before, with double doors and a drawer on the bottom and moulding fashioned as a cornice on top. Asmore had emptied it out as well. Two years together and there was no trace of the man. It was as though Asmore had never lived there. "I decided to show him," Lowenstein said. "I would kill myself. I went to the bathroom and took my razor from the medicine cabinet."

He ran the water in the tub and while it was filling up he used the razor to shave his face—the same razor with which he intended to slit his wrists. How could he be serious about suicide if he was concerned about keeping his face clean? He turned off the water and started to remove his clothes. From outside came the bell of a bicycle passing by and the thud of newspapers against nearby house fronts. It was the delivery boy, making his afternoon rounds. Although he wasn't a subscriber, Lowenstein went out half-dressed and picked a paper off the ground. It was a beautiful afternoon, the coolest day yet of the season. He would have to remove his winter clothes from storage, he thought. And he would have to pay his neighbor for the paper when he saw him again.

He glanced at the headlines on the front page. Does a man who intends to kill himself care about the news of the world in the last moments of his life? Does he notice the weather? Does he wonder if moths have eaten holes in his favorite sweaters? Does he care that his neighbor is paid for his missing paper?

Lowenstein sat in the living room with a cold cup of coffee. As he read, he could hear the dripping of the tub faucet in the bathroom. It seemed to beckon him to get on with it. The story about Levette's mural, describing it as an outrage, appeared on the last page.

"I pulled the plug, letting the water out of the tub, and I put the razor away," Lowenstein said. "At last I had a way to win him back. I could predict the mob that would be awaiting him at the post office in the morning. I would prove myself to Levette by defending him against them."

"So that was you," Rhys said.

"Who was I?"

"Levette had a friend who was arrested that morning for coming to his support. I read about it in an old newspaper clipping."

Lowenstein raised his hand. "Present and accounted for."

Typical of New Orleans, the crowd that morning was making a party of it, chanting to be let in. There was no one he recognized. They didn't seem particularly angry until he pushed his way up to the front and yelled for them to go home.

"Jew boy," someone shouted.

"Lousy queer," said another.

He was glad he'd decided against killing himself with the razor. He would let them do it. "There was a window in each of the doors, shaped like a star, not very big," Lowenstein said. "I looked in one and I could see down a short hallway to the lobby where he'd hung the painting. It was up above tiers of scaffolding. At one time Levette had placed tarpaulin all around the mural to keep people from seeing, but now the tarps had been removed. The morning light was on the painting, and the colors were in full riot. I could see Levette and Jacqueline embracing at its center. I also saw others whom I recognized, people from the art school. He had Ninas fondling a girl who wasn't his wife. He had Alberta Kinsey dressed like a nun. Miss Kinsey was a Quaker, but he'd made her out to be a Catholic Sister of Charity, with a big habit. He'd had fun with them, none more than me."

"Why do you think he depicted you shooting dice, Mr. Lowenstein?" Rhys said.

"He meant to show I was a gambler, I suppose, Miss Goudeau. There I am with a collection of boys, prepared to lose it all for the sake of some fleeting pleasure." He hesitated, as another idea seemed to come to him. "Levette had to know. He must have followed me on one of my trips to the house on Toulouse Street."

Lowenstein could see Asmore huddled on the lobby floor with a group of older people, administrative types. One of them repeatedly pointed a finger in his face. Asmore stood calmly by before finally erupting in anger. He became so animated that two of the men grabbed his arms and pulled him back. When they released him he came striding up the hall toward the entrance, a look of determination fixed on his face. He pushed through the doors and the crowd moved back to let him out. Lowenstein wondered if Asmore was asking for his own death, but then it occurred to him that none of these people knew who he was. The paper hadn't run his photo with the story. "Let me through," he said, lowering a shoulder as he made his way into the crowd. "Let me through, please. Let me through . . ."

Lowenstein wanted to call out to him but he knew better than to speak his name. "Let me help you," he said instead. "Please let me help you."

Asmore pushed past him, broke free of the mob and ran across the street to a lot where a house was going up. When he returned he was carrying a five-gallon bucket in each hand. The buckets were filled with a milky paint that slopped against his legs and splashed to the ground. "He's going to whitewash it," somebody shouted. The mob responded with wild cheers and let him move forward. Asmore entered the building and locked the doors behind him, and the people realized they were going to be denied a look at the painting. A panic seemed to come over them. Even as Lowenstein shouted for calm they began to press forward and push against the doors.

"Something snapped in me and I started throwing punches, mimicking the motion of a windmill. I struck a few of them before being hit myself. One got me here—" Lowenstein indicated a small, crescent-shaped scar on the side of his head, just above the eye—"and I went down so fast whoever hit me must have thought I was dead. It stopped the crowd. I was conscious but I pretended to be out cold. I lay without moving. The area around the eye is very vascular, and I could feel blood pouring over my face and taste it in my mouth. I was sure I looked a mess, but I wasn't badly hurt. I could've got up and walked away."

"You wanted to give him time to cover the painting, didn't you?" Rhys said.

"Yes. That crowd would have ripped the mural to pieces. At the art school they'd taught us how to make our own paints, casein among them. It was popular on house projects because it was inexpensive to produce. People used it more then than they do today. Levette probably knew the carpenters and crew on the construction site. Remember, he'd worked for a time in the building trade himself, and he'd often gone to these workers for materials to use for his easel paintings. I'm sure he'd cadged cigarettes off them, too, during breaks from his work hanging the mural."

The police arrived and suddenly Lowenstein was being lifted to his feet. As voices nearby argued their innocence and blamed the incident on him, Lowenstein got a final glimpse in the window past a burning film of blood. Asmore was high on the scaffolding now, painting the top of the mural with broad strokes that ran in streaks. "He looked like a god up there. His body glowed in the sunlight. He was absolutely radiant. I experienced something then that might be called a premonition, but it was more profound than that. Would that make it a revelation? Yes, I suppose it could be called a revelation. Because I knew he wouldn't be with us much longer." He paused for more whiskey. "What I couldn't have imagined, however, was the role I would play in his death."

Lowenstein spent the day at Central Lockup, where a doctor administered to the cut on his face with fourteen stitches. Released the next morning, he returned to the cottage on Saint Philip and the empty room that had been Asmore's. Once again he searched for evidence that his friend had ever lived there. He would've been pleased to find strands of hair in the bristle of a brush. But, as before, there was nothing to be found. He began to wonder if he'd imagined the last two years.

After a few days alone Lowenstein forced himself to put on clean clothes and leave the house. He walked the streets of the French Quarter, hoping that fresh air and exercise might help clear his head. It was useless. Stopping in front of the house on Toulouse Street, he needed only to hear muffled laughter past the door to be lured inside.

In minutes it would be his laughter they heard from the street. He stayed for the remainder of the day, drinking whatever was handed to him, only too willing to disclose his identity to anyone who asked for it. He met a colleague of his father's named Shaw, whose wedding band remained on his finger even as the older man thrust his tongue deep in Lowenstein's mouth. As he moved from one room to the next, Lowenstein was visited by an echo that seemed to increase in volume the more he tried to convince himself it wasn't there. "Please, Levette, you are my heart," a voice kept saying.

The boy from Tulane who'd recognized Lowenstein on a previous visit appeared in the house. They went into a room already crowded with men. As he was finishing Lowenstein could bear it no longer. He shouted out the words that had been beating around in his head all afternoon. Others in the room began to laugh and point at him. The boy pushed Lowenstein off of him. Lowenstein repeated the words, this time with a sob.

"Crazy goddamned faggot," the boy said.

Lowenstein spent the next week alone in the cottage, sleeping on a pallet of blankets on the floor of Asmore's room. One morning he walked to the market for fruit and a meat sandwich but he couldn't eat more than a few bites before becoming ill. As he napped later that day he heard the front door being opened. He sat up and waited, the wood beneath him vibrating as someone stepped through the house. It was Asmore. He stood in the doorway staring at Lowenstein on the floor. "What in God's name are you doing?" Asmore walked over and knelt beside him. "You've bled all over yourself."

He helped Lowenstein to the bathroom and wet a cloth and brushed off the scabby black blood on his face. "I'm sorry, Levette," Lowenstein said.

"You're sorry, are you?"

"I'm really sorry, Levette."

"Low, hasn't anybody told you to clean yourself? Jesus Christ, man, you're filthy."

"Will you be coming back? Please come back."

"I don't think it's a good idea."

"Come back. Please come back."

"You can't share your home with someone like me, now can you, Low? No, that wouldn't be good." There was no passion in his voice. He spoke in a direct, matter-of-fact tone. "What would people say?"

It was devastating to hear how casually Asmore dismissed him. "I told you I was sorry," he said. "I told Jacqueline I was sorry. Why won't you forgive me?"

"Clean your face, Low."

"I don't understand. Why? Why can't you forgive me?"

Asmore didn't answer. He returned to the bedroom and opened the double doors of the armoire. Lowenstein, coming in from the bathroom, could hear him whistling a popular song of the day as he stepped up on the floor of the cabinet and reached over the top of the cornice. He removed a rolled-up canvas and tossed it to the floor. He then tossed a second canvas. Lowenstein sat on the floor and spread the first canvas open. It was a portrait of a young woman, signed by the artist in the upper-left corner, and titled *Beloved Stephanie*. He checked the other paintings. Many of them were *Beloved* portraits, as well.

"The canvases rained down," Lowenstein said. "He'd been storing them there all this time. About twenty of them were left over from his show two years before, but most were older than that. I'd pulled the house apart searching for the smallest wisp of the man, and all along about fifty of his paintings lay hidden on top of the armoire. The best of them were portraits, but there were city views as well. One of the last he pulled out was about half-finished. It was on burlap primed with a kind of gelatin he often used. One could see where he'd sketched the image with pencil. It showed a bridge spanning the river. The sky was filled with blackbirds. It was the one he'd come for."

Asmore stepped down from the armoire and took the painting out of Lowenstein's hands. "I got a letter yesterday at the school from Will Henry Stevens. You remember Will Henry, Low?"

Stevens was an art instructor. Lowenstein nodded. "Sure."

"He's up in North Carolina where he goes to paint the mountains. He says he'll trade me a mountain picture for this one of the bridge, plus he'll throw in a hundred dollars. You know what I think, Low? I think somebody told Will Henry about the post office mural and he means to help out a friend."

"How would he have known about your painting of the bridge?"

"We were out there together when I started it—out there at the bridge. It isn't bad. It's sketchy yet, but it's better than I remembered."

"Why didn't you finish it before?"

"It started to rain." He looked up from the painting. "I'm going out there now."

"I wish you'd let me go with you," Lowenstein said. "I don't want to impose or interfere, but I would really like that. We can go in my car."

"Thanks." And he shook his head. "I've already arranged to borrow a car."

"I'm going mad in this house. Let me drive you. I won't be in the way." Even as he spoke, Lowenstein could sense how he must've sounded to Asmore: the pathetic, mortally wounded victim of his own bad behavior trying to put a good face on a situation from which he would never recover.

Somehow, after more pleading, he got Asmore to agree. As they motored west from the city Asmore sat with the painting unfurled in his lap, running his fingers over the blue streak of paint that represented the river. He also had a whiskey flask from which he took long drinks. He showed no interest in the passing scenery and kept his head down as they traveled from Orleans to neighboring Jefferson Parish. "He seemed mildly irritated with himself for being alone with me again," Lowenstein said. "I didn't dare speak. I was afraid the sound of my voice would trigger a memory and prompt him to order me to turn back around."

They parked near the bridge's approach and walked to a spot on the riverbank. He'd brought his toolbox packed with supplies, but he'd neglected to stretch the burlap or to bring materials with which to do so now. Asmore laid the material flat on a piece of packed, sandy ground and bent over it and worked on the painting in this fashion, Lowenstein watching from nearby.

When Asmore was done Lowenstein held the finished painting out in front of him and studied it as he walked back to the car. Lowenstein laid the burlap on the backseat and it occurred to him that Asmore could import meaning to a picture without trying to, so great was his power as an artist. By now he realized that Asmore hadn't followed him to the car. Lowenstein scanned the riverbank but he wasn't there. Eventually he spotted him walking up the side of the bridge.

"I started up after him, but it wasn't easy going. It wasn't a walkway built to encourage pedestrian use. It was extremely narrow, only a few feet wide at most. I guess the bridge builders had emergencies in mind when they included it, but I can tell it wasn't there to invite sightseeing. It seemed every other car that whooshed by me blew its horn. The draft from a couple of tractor-trailer trucks was so strong I almost went over the guardrail, which came up to only about waist-high. I was scared out of my wits and hoping the police would arrive and arrest us both."

Until now Lowenstein had carefully avoided peering over the side, afraid that he'd get dizzy or lose his courage to continue. But presently he allowed himself to look and he saw the full sweep of the Louisiana low country, the nearby woods thick with old-growth cypress, tupelo and hardwood trees and the distant plantations etching geometric patterns in the earth. But most impressive of all was the river itself. Huge and dark, it seemed to Lowenstein to have no concern but for its own slow journey. Lowenstein opened his mouth and the cool air belled out his cheeks and made his eyes water. Asmore was standing a few paces ahead of him, with his hands on the rail, the wind blowing his clothes tight against his body and throwing his hair back. "I should've come up here a long time ago," he said. "Why didn't I come up here before, Low?"

"Why?" Like Asmore, he had to shout to be heard above the buffeting roar of the wind. "Because it's crazy to be up here. People don't do this."

Asmore took the flask out of his pocket and drank from it. "You don't see that?" he said, looking over at his friend.

"Don't see what?"

"You don't see how beautiful it is? Damn, Low, it's beautiful."

Lowenstein looked out again and it truly was beautiful, but it was hard to appreciate the beauty because he was so terrified. He began to see things he hadn't seen the first time he looked. Ships docked at a port, for instance. And in the near distance in front of them great clouds of blackbirds moving in the sky. The blackbirds seemed to hover effortlessly in the wind.

"How do they fly like that?" Asmore said, gazing out at them, too, and drinking. "I just wish somebody would answer me that. How do they do it?" He took another swallow from the flask and set it on the pavement at his feet.

"I think we should be getting down from here," Lowenstein said.

Asmore kicked the flask with his boot and sent it past the guardrail, tumbling out a ways and then dropping toward the water. "It's beautiful. All of it is."

"It's dangerous," Lowenstein said. "Come on, Levette. Let's go back."

"I mean the river," Asmore told him. "I mean the river's beautiful. I never thought so before, I always feared it before, but now I see it's beautiful."

He laughed and spread his arms out on either side of him. His hair whipped behind him and his eyes were closed and Lowenstein saw him sway ever so slightly.

"Levette? Please . . ."

Asmore glanced over at Lowenstein and a smile came to his face. He lowered his arms and leaned forward against the rail to regain his balance.

"I'll take you home," Lowenstein said.

"I am home," Asmore told him. "Dammit, Low, I am home." Somehow Lowenstein understood that he meant the river. "I need to clear something up," he said. "Will Henry never wrote me no letter."

"What did you say?"

"I said he never wrote to me. Will Henry? I made that up. I never had another way to get out here, either. I meant for you to take me." The smile was gone from his face now. He turned away from Lowenstein and stared out in the distance, out past the blackbirds. And it came to Lowenstein that his friend meant to kill himself.

"I forgive you," Asmore said. "You couldn't help it, Low."

"What are you saying, I couldn't help it?"

"I forgive the others, too," he said. "I forgive them all."

Lowenstein stepped up closer with the half-formed intention of grabbing him by an arm and guiding him down from the bridge, but Asmore moved to avoid him and seemed to lose his footing—he might've tripped on a shoestring, the way he suddenly got tied up. He fell backward hard against the guardrail. "Low," he said and gave a quick laugh to show his surprise. A spark of recognition flashed in his eyes and he reached out for Lowenstein's hand and they touched briefly before Asmore followed the pull of his weight and went over the side without a sound.

"I couldn't watch it," Lowenstein said. "I didn't see him hit the water. I was so traumatized that I sat at the foot of the guardrail clinging to it. I remember looking around and the cars were still coming and blowing their horns and out over the river the blackbirds still hung suspended in a swarm. The world was exactly as it had been a minute before except for the presence of that one man, and yet I knew that without him in it the world would never be the same again. After a while I was able to stand and I stumbled out into the road. I should've been killed then myself, I wanted to be, but somehow I succeeded in stopping traffic. A man out for a drive with his family was the first to offer help. The passenger door fell open and I looked in

and there must have been six or seven of them and they were all gazing out at me with the same expression.

"The man said, 'You weren't planning to jump, were you, son?' I
said no and his wife squeezed up closer to him, to make room for me
on the seat. 'Come sit,' the man said. 'We'll drive you to the other
side.' "

ELEVEN

We were waiting when she arrived in the U-Haul and parked on the driveway that ran under the old hotel. Joe Butler raised the rear door and we unloaded the panels and lighting equipment and she gave the keys to one of the garage attendants and told him she wouldn't need the truck again until later tonight. Each of the panels was fitted taut over wood stretchers and covered with butcher paper, and we carried them into a service elevator, then up past the lobby with its liveried door staff, Italian-inspired ceiling frescoes and crystal chandeliers, and stopped finally on the floor where she'd rented adjoining suites with four-poster beds in the bedrooms and Louis XIV furniture arranged on the fancy rugs. In advance of our arrival Rhys had asked the hotel to clear out the furniture in one of the living rooms. We removed the paper and stood the panels against the wall and Rhys set up a photoflood lamp on each side and one directly in the middle, and when she turned them on we stood back and stared past the heat and the glare.

"It blows my mind," Rondell Cherry said. "It really blows my mind this was there all that time."

"Hiding," Joe Butler replied.

Asmore's signature, painted black, was in the upper-left corner. On opposite sides of the painting, positioned along the edges, I could see Paul Ninas with the girl and Alberta Kinsey in the nun's habit. I had another close look at Lowenstein as a young man gambling his life away while all around him the Carnival celebration was going full steam.

"Tell me this dude's name again," Cherry said.

"Asmore," Rhys said. "His name was Levette Asmore."

"A black man?"

"Yes, he was black, as a matter of fact."

"You can see that," Cherry said, although he never did explain how.

Cherry had a butterfly bandage covering a closed wound on his face where he'd taken a punch thrown by one of two thugs who'd attacked him outside the Wheeler Beauty Academy the week before. In his fifteen years at the school it was the first time he'd been the target of a crime, and even after he'd pummeled the boys senseless, neither would admit that it wasn't his wallet they were after but retribution for his having sold Tommy Smallwood a worthless piece of canvas.

Like Joe Butler and me, Cherry was wearing a suit with a clean shirt and necktie, as per Rhys's instruction. It was strange to see him out of his usual canvas coveralls and I wondered where a man that large went to buy clothes.

"You look sharp, Mr. Cherry," I said.

He shook my hand, the second time today. "I *feel* sharp."

As for Joe Butler, his transformation was even more dramatic. He'd had his hair cut and his shirt collar covered the tattoos that usually were visible on his neck. Most surprising, though, was the tan that browned his skin. He'd had so much sun that his forehead was flaking. "Have you been vacationing at the beach or something?" I said.

"Yes, I have. Did Rhys tell you?"

I had a good laugh at the thought, Joe Butler the scarecrow wearing a swimsuit and stretched out in the sand. "You're a strange man, you know that?"

"Thank you, bro."

Rhys opened the door adjoining the two suites and called for a meeting in the other living area. This room had furniture. I sat between the two men on a sofa and Rhys sat across from us in a wing chair with her legs crossed, a yellow writing tablet propped on a knee. She was wearing a tailored jacket with a velvet collar, a black skirt, hose and shoes that looked new. Her hair hung down and fanned out over her shoulders and her face held subtle touches of makeup that sharpened her bones and brightened the shine in her eyes. She glanced at her watch and I checked my own, somehow succeeding in pulling my eyes away from her for a moment. It was eight o'clock in the morning.

"Okay, listen up," she said. "The first of them arrives in less than an hour. His name is Cedric Anderson. Mr. Anderson is the only visitor we'll have coming today from Texas. He owns a computer software design company in Austin. Mr. Anderson collects American regionalist paintings and is reputed to own three excellent examples by Thomas Hart Benton, all of them bought privately in New York. He also owns a Levette Asmore cityscape, a view of Canal Street in the rain, for which he paid a dealer three hundred thousand dollars. He bid on *Beloved Dorothy* by phone, one of the last of the phone bidders to drop out. Like the others, Mr. Anderson will have thirty minutes to inspect the painting. He'll be accompanied by his wife, Julie."

Joe Butler raised his hand. "Should we be taking notes?"

"No notes. Just listen. I thought you might like a brief introduction to the collectors we'll be meeting today."

"Cedric Anderson," Rondell Cherry said. "He's not black, is he?"

"I can't answer that," Rhys said. "I spoke to him on the phone and we've exchanged e-mail. But I've never asked him his race."

"Because his name sounds black," Cherry said. "I grew up in Pigeon Town with this boy, name of Cedric Williford. Now he was black."

"We need to move on, Mr. Cherry."

He pushed back deeper into the sofa. "I just thought you'd like some input."

"Thirty minutes after the Andersons leave, Taylor Dickel of Columbia, South Carolina, will be our guest. Mr. Dickel inherited his money and hasn't worked a day in his life. His wealth is estimated at a hundred and fifty million. His mother is reputed to have sat for Asmore in 1938, but the painting's whereabouts is unknown. Mr. Dickel attended the *Beloved Dorothy* sale but did not bid because he said he wasn't feeling well after eating bad oysters at dinner the night before. Witnesses, however, observed Mr. Dickel drinking Hurricanes at Pat O'Brien's that Friday evening, and in fact he failed to attend dinner with friends. Mr. Dickel has long included Asmore on a wish list left with Lucinda Copeland at Neal. He is an erratic but engaging personality, and a faithful client of the Guild's. He will be alone today, and, I hope, sober. Joe?"

"Yes, boss?"

"I'm putting you in charge of serving beverages. If Mr. Dickel asks for a drink, please limit the amount of liquor you serve him to a jigger."

"Will do."

"Now he's white," Rondell Cherry said. "He is definitely white."

Rhys ignored him. "After Mr. Dickel we'll have Amanda Howard and her husband, David," she said, referring to her notes. "The Howards, who live in Miami, own several hundred fast-food restaurants in the state of Florida and will be traveling to New Orleans this morning by private jet, their own. They collect southern art, mostly images of black people. They've been redecorating their home and need 'something large, busy and dramatic,' as Mrs. Howard said it, to hang in a hallway. Mrs. Howard already owns a *Beloved* portrait, *Beloved Molly*. She's hoping the mural's colors will match those of the runner she and her husband intend to use in the hall."

"I don't have any idea what those two are," Cherry said.

"Mr. Cherry, am I going to have to put you out in the hall?"

"But I was just saying . . ."

Rhys provided profiles for five other potential buyers, all of whom were coming from out of state but one, Tommy Smallwood, the last of the group scheduled to view the painting. His appointment was set for six o'clock.

"In summary," she said, "there are several common denominators among these collectors. The first, obviously, is wealth. The second is an impulse to spend this wealth on things that are important to them. The third might be called greed if that word didn't carry such a negative connotation. These buyers are all competitive individuals whose motivation to spend money often is driven by their desire to possess things simply so that others of their financial stature can't have them. Any questions?"

"What about the issue of provenance?" I said. "Might they be dissuaded from bidding on the painting without some record of previous ownership? For all they know, the mural could've been stolen from a private collection or, worse, a post office."

"Good one, Jack. I failed to mention a fourth common denominator, that being a disdain for the federal government. When I spoke with these collectors, I explained the history of Levette's mural in detail. I then followed up these calls by overnighting them packages containing photocopies of old stories about the mural. I also included a batch of eight-by-ten color photographs documenting every step of the restoration, from the start when the surface was yellow with house paint to its current state. None seemed opposed to taking possession of an object that was produced for and then discarded by the government. In fact, to a collector they seemed excited by the prospect."

"Eight collectors, that really isn't so many, is it?" Joe Butler said.

"You would think for something as important as Levette's mural there'd be more."

"You're right. But for obvious reasons I couldn't involve the museums or those private collections that offer access to the public, such as the Historic New Orleans Collection. And after consulting with Lucinda, I also decided against involving potential buyers who, to put it simply, were straight arrows. I didn't want anyone who conceivably could take issue with buying an object that might be considered stolen property."

"What about dealers?" I said.

"I eliminated them, too."

"All of them? What about the guy in Charleston, the one who was supposed to be such a player? West, was it?"

"I couldn't risk it," she said. "Dealers have big mouths, and some of them can be difficult, not to mention stingy, jealous and hateful. Competition has made them that way. If a dealer were to be the winning bidder, other dealers would be bad-mouthing him and the purchase before he could get the painting out the door. The losing dealers would then be on the phone reporting us to the General Services Administration. Also, why sell to a dealer when we can sell directly to a collector? The dealer's interests begin and end with himself. Any dealer who bought the painting would only turn around and try to place it—at a profit, a great profit—with one of the collectors visiting us today."

"The people who are coming," Rondell Cherry said, "they sound a little different to me. They might have the money, they might know what kind of pictures they like, but they sound like they're not right in the head, you know what I'm saying?"

"You're right, Mr. Cherry, they're eccentrics, all of them. But most serious, committed collectors are flawed personalities. Most of them feel a sense of duty to the things they buy. They feel they have a responsibility to their collections, and that responsibility compels them to continue growing their collections. It's like feeding a monster whose appetite can never be satisfied. These people are as addicted to buying what they like as heroin addicts are to shooting up. But you know what I say? I say thank God for them. Without them I wouldn't have a job, and we wouldn't be here today in these lovely rooms in the Hotel Monteleone."

"Boss?" Joe Butler raised his hand again. "Boss, do I have to keep my tie on?"

"Sweetie, if you knew how cute you looked, you wouldn't be asking me that."

Both Rondell Cherry and I turned to him and nodded.

Over the last few days Rhys had contacted each collector and given him the suite number and his appointed time for viewing the painting. As Rhys had drawn up the rules, no one was to be more than fifteen minutes early or fifteen minutes late, and no one could inspect the mural for more than his allotted time. If anyone did arrive more than fifteen minutes early or late, he would forfeit his chance to inspect the mural. The auction itself was scheduled for the next day at three o'clock in the afternoon. It would be held in the same suite. To protect the integrity of the auction and avoid against any possible allegations of phantom shill bidding, buyers had no option but to attend the sale in person; there would be no phone bidding allowed. Payment in full was to be made within twenty-four hours after the hammer came down. Rhys would accept a wire transfer only, and the painting would be released to the winning bidder as soon as the deposit registered in her bank account.

"What about a reserve?" I said. "What's the minimum you would take for the painting?"

"I haven't set one. But, as I told the collectors, I reserve the right to stop the auction at any time and withdraw the painting."

"And they went for that?"

"It's a twenty-foot-long oil painting by Levette Asmore, Jack. It's the single greatest thing he ever did and it's likely to be the greatest southern painting these people see in their lifetimes. Most of these

collectors would travel around the world for a chance to see newly discovered *sketches* by Asmore. They can't expect me to give the mural
away and, believe it or not, they wouldn't want me to."

"And why is that?" Cherry said.

She carefully considered the question. "It's like love, I guess. If it
doesn't hurt a little, and if you don't bleed for it, then it somehow
doesn't feel right. They need to know that what they're buying is
unique, special and historically significant. The best gauge of that is
how much they have to pay for it."

Not wishing to intimidate any of our visitors, Rhys asked the
three of us to remain secluded in the second suite. She would leave the
door unlocked in the event of a problem. We were welcome to leave
the building one at a time, as long as two of us stayed behind. She also
green-lighted room service orders and gave us permission to eat and
drink anything we wanted from the concessions bar. "Last but not
least," she said, minutes before the Andersons were scheduled to arrive, "I want to thank you all for being here today. Mr. Cherry, thank
you, sir. Joe? Thank you, sweetheart. Jack, you've been amazing.
Thank you for everything."

And that was how she left it, before quietly pulling the door
closed. Joe Butler went back to the bedroom and lounged on his
stomach, grazing TV channels with the remote, while Rondell Cherry
sat by a window in the living room and read the morning paper. I
stood next to the door between the two suites smelling the quiet
residue of Rhys's cologne, and replaying her last words to me. "It's going to be a long day, Jack," Cherry said. "Maybe you should come have
a seat."

"Rhys called me amazing, Mr. Cherry. You caught that, right?"

He was wearing drugstore reading glasses and his shaved head
glowed a rich copper in the block of sunlight. He didn't look up from
the paper. "I was wondering about that myself," he said. "Miss
Goudeau knows a lot, she's smart about that art, especially. But I guess
she doesn't know everything."

"Thank you for the vote of confidence."

"No problem."

I was listening with my ear against the door when Cedric and Julie Anderson arrived promptly at 9:00 A.M. Rhys welcomed them and Mr. Anderson weighed in with an ominous weather prediction, but after they moved off in the direction of the painting their conversation became too muffled to make out. I pulled a chair up to the door and sat there until their voices were clear again. By now thirty minutes had passed and Rhys was thanking them and saying good-bye. "I'm glad you'll be coming tomorrow," she said. "We open at two, and you're welcome to inspect the painting again at that time."

After they were gone she rapped on the door and I opened it. Joe Butler had left the bedroom and come up behind me and Rondell Cherry was standing there, too. None of us had to ask Rhys how it went. You could see the answer in her face.

"Was it really that good?" I said.

"I don't think they were quite prepared," she replied. "Mr. Anderson cried. Mrs. Anderson asked if she could touch the figures of Jacqueline and Levette. I told her she could grope them if she liked. This got her to laugh, but her hands were trembling when she reached to place them on the canvas."

"They liked it, huh?" Rondell Cherry said.

"Yes, Mr. Cherry. They liked it."

Taylor Dickel came next. He was easier to hear than the Andersons had been because he was a shouter, and a drunken one. "Oh, shit, will you look at that!" he said. Dickel had one of those voices with the old, benighted South in it. The old, benighted South was in short supply these days, but it had a foothold in him. "You knew he had a thing for my mama, didn't you, Rhys? Yes, he did. Old Levette had a thing. Hey, well, lookee here. Is that Mama? Hell, Rhys, that ain't Mama. . . . Who is that? That's him, all right. That's Levette. But who on earth is *that*? Who's he with? Jesusgodawmighty! Will you look at all them *homos*!"

Rhys opened the door and stuck her head inside. Her cheeks were burning red. "Where's Joe Butler?"

"Watching TV in the bedroom."

"Jack, will you please pour Mr. Dickel a drink. He wants bourbon. Forget I said only a jigger. Give him a glassful in a plastic cup."

"Why don't I pour it in a regular glass?"

"No, I'm about to run him out of here. Make sure it's plastic."

I did as instructed and five minutes later she'd succeeded in escorting him out into the hall. As he stumbled away I could hear him conversing with the same invisible man all hard-core drunks seem to converse with. "Get me out of this place! Where's the elevator? Hey, hombre, you call that art? Come here. That's right, come here. I'll show you . . . I'll show you some art . . ."

Although doing so broke one of Rhys's rules, I looked outside and saw Dickel staggering down the hall. The cup lay in the middle of the floor, with ice cubes scattered on the carpet. Dickel moved on to the elevators, beside which stood several houseplants. "Hang on a minute!" he yelled to his invisible friend, then chose the rhododendron on which to relieve himself.

⁂

At noon we ordered club sandwiches and chocolate cake from room service. In the other suite Rhys was showing the mural to Sam Horowitz of Greenville, Mississippi, a plantation owner with a helicopter pad on the edge of one of his cotton fields. Joe Butler excused himself and toted his tray to the bedroom. Even though three hours had now passed, Rondell Cherry was still reading the paper, his glasses poised at the end of his nose. With his left hand he dipped French fries in a puddle of ketchup; with his right he made circles around listings in the Classifieds. "You shopping for something in particular, Mr. Cherry?" I asked, past my own mouthful of deep-fried potato.

"Just a job," he answered.

The room became quiet again. I watched as he ate, read and circled, all at once.

"I wish I was a registered nurse. I'd have me some benefits and paid vacation time." He put down the fries and the pen and touched the bandage on his cheek. "I'm not going to work at no Taco Bell, I can promise you that."

"You should've kept that money Tommy Smallwood paid you for the mural, Mr. Cherry. I don't think anyone would've said anything."

"That money wasn't mine to keep, Jack. I thought we already been through that." He lowered the paper and looked at me over his glasses. "I guess you heard, huh?"

"Heard what?"

"About that money."

"You paid it to a lawyer for Mrs. Wheeler. His retainer, you said."

"I did pay the man. But Miss Wheeler went behind my back and let him go and got back with this so-called niece."

"She rehired Alice O'Neil?"

"That's it. She rehired Alice O'Neil. The man called me last week and was real nice but said Miss Wheeler had told him his services were no longer needed. He said he tried to talk her out of it but she wouldn't listen to reason. I told him I understood completely. You know what I think? I think she went and hired herself a shopping partner in this Alice because what those two women do together has nothing to do with the law, I can promise you that. Dillard's, Bombay Company, Adler's Jewelry, Chick-fil-A. That's always last, the Chick-fil-A. They sit in the food court with their cigarettes and waffle fries and look at the hairdos and the clothes the other women are wearing. I'll tell you what else I think. I think she's tired of the aggravation and ready to give up the school."

"Maybe she should."

"My wife says the same thing. Maybe she should."

"If she doesn't go to jail first for taking all that grant money."

Cherry laid the paper down on the coffee table and pushed his glasses up to the bridge of his nose. "You didn't hear about them applications from me, Jack."

"No, it came from the horse's mouth, actually. Mrs. Wheeler told Rhys about it the first time they met. You remember when I got my hair cut?"

He nodded.

"It was then, while I was outside waiting on the steps."

"All right," he said. "I guess Miss Wheeler misspoke. Or maybe it was Rhys that didn't hear her right."

"I'm not sure I understand what you mean."

"She filled out the applications, Miss Wheeler did. And she sent a bunch in. But to my understanding the goverment never gave her any money. They caught her red-handed at the start. Miss Wheeler's a good lady, she's real good. But she's getting on in years now and her mind tends to wander. Turns out she went and put her own signature on every one of them applications."

"She did what?"

He nodded again. "Let's say it was one for Tammy Rideau—Tammy was at the school a few years ago. . . . After Miss Wheeler filled in all the information for Tammy they had a place that said 'Sign Here' or 'Your Signature' or something like that. Well, instead of 'Tammy Rideau' Miss Wheeler signed her own name. 'Gail Wheeler,' she put. It was easy to catch, even for the government. Hey, Jack?"

"Yeah?"

"You want the rest of your fries?"

"No."

"What about your cake?"

I brought my tray over and placed it on the edge of the coffee table. "Mr. Cherry, you know how Mrs. Wheeler turns around and looks up at the building every day after work when she comes down the stairs and reaches the sidewalk?"

"You caught that, too, huh?"

"What's she doing? Was that something she did when Mr. Wheeler was alive?"

"Do what, now?"

"I just wondered if that was their little love thing. You know, would he be watching from a window upstairs? It's kind of sad. She seems to look at the windows as if searching for his face or something."

"Searching for his face? For Mr. Wheeler's face?" He shook his head, then forked up a piece of cake. "You ever see Mr. Wheeler's face? It wasn't a face you looked for. It was a face you looked away from."

"Then why does she stare at the building that way?"

He took another bite and smiled, and I could see the chocolate icing coating his teeth. "Curtains. She's been talking about curtains. Says the sun from the windows hurts her eyes. I guess that's one of the things they look for at the mall, Miss Wheeler and this so-called niece. JCPenney, Sears. They carry curtains, don't they?"

❄

Between her four o'clock and her five o'clock I asked Rhys to join me downstairs in the lobby for a talk. She refused, saying she'd come this far and didn't want to leave the mural yet. "Why can't we talk here, Jack?"

I glanced at Cherry. "I was hoping for some private time with you, Rhys."

"Private time," she said with a look of impatience, then waved me over to the suite with the painting.

We walked back to the bedroom. She closed the door and sat on the edge of the bed and removed her shoes and started rubbing her feet. The bed had a mirrored canopy and I could see Rhys massaging her feet in the ceiling of smoky glass.

"If you're too tired," I said, "I don't mind waiting until later."

"No. I'd rather you told me now. Something obviously is bothering you."

"It's more like a few things," I said. "Like three things, to be precise." I was standing against the wall, with my hands behind my back, palms flat against the textured paper. "It's probably nothing, Rhys, I hope so, anyway. But one day when I visited Mrs. Wheeler she said something that's stuck with me ever since. Mr. Cherry was leaving to go to his son's ball game, and she said, 'Them blacks sure like their sports,' or something like that."

She cocked an eyebrow. "And?"

"It sounded like something a real cracker would say. And it made me wonder, yet again, why we're taking such risks for this person we don't really know. I didn't respond to what she said, but I wish now that I'd asked her what other things blacks liked. Or where sports ranked behind watermelon and fried chicken."

"What else, Jack?" She was still running her hands over her feet. "You said there were three things."

"Well, Mr. Cherry just told me she didn't actually receive any grant money for those phony applications. She sent them off and not long after the agents from Baton Rouge started coming around. They caught on to her right at the start."

"And?"

"And it made me wonder, Rhys, can these people all be cruel and heartless? They can't be, can they? She's an old woman with a crappy little hair school nobody wants to go to anymore. You would think they'd recognize that. You'd also think they'd be smart enough to leave her alone and let time and her own ignorance determine the fate of Wheeler Beauty Academy. To my knowledge she hasn't been indicted and charged with anything yet. But here we are peddling off the greatest thing either of us has ever seen and we're doing it for the sole purpose of raising money to throw at a situation and a woman that should be left alone. Or I think that's why we're doing it."

Rhys put on her shoes and leaned back with her arms propped behind her. She glanced up and saw herself in the mirror and immediately turned away. "And the third, Jack? You said there were three things."

"The third came to me this morning, as I watched Taylor Dickel water a potted plant down the hall. I don't know how to say this except to say it. I can't be polite about it. But I don't see why someone like that asshole should have the mural."

"The high bidder wins the auction. It's not always fair, but that's how it works. Do you think the lowest bidder should get the painting?"

"I didn't finish," I said. "Rhys, for weeks now I've listened patiently to your rants against the government as if it were the army of
the devil. You've made it out to be evil and corrupt, without a care for
anybody. But it was always my understanding that the government
belonged to the people. Hell, I was even gullible enough to believe
that it *was* the people. We've been showing these rich collectors Levette's mural, but how can we let only one of them have it? It's so beautiful, Rhys, and we both know how important it is. Maybe Asmore
didn't die for his painting, but he died because he couldn't tolerate a
world in which a picture such as the one he created had no place. I
don't want to sound sanctimonious here, and forgive me if I sound like
Jimmy Stewart in some old piece of thirties corn pone . . . but, Rhys,
dammit, that mural doesn't belong to any one man. It belongs to all
men and to all women and to all the little children, and it belongs to
them equally, without prejudice whether they're black or white or gay
or straight or rich or poor. What I'm saying is, you need to stop this
sale. You need to stop it and tell those collectors to go on home, because you, Rhys Goudeau, granddaughter of the artist, have changed
your mind."

"I should, should I?"

"Yes. Yes, you should. And you should then donate the painting
to a place where people can come and see it and learn from it. You owe
that to Levette. How do you think he would feel watching his mural
being sold off to some bigot just because the man has more money
than everybody else? 'It's not about what they're worth,' you told me
once. 'It's about what they are.' But look at where we are today."

She opened the door and stood gazing out for a moment, then she
closed it again behind her. "You finished, Jack?"

"Yeah, I'm finished."

"Was that your three things?"

"Three, maybe three and a half."

"Because I intend to kiss you now, Jack Charbonnet." And that
was what she did, pressing up against me as I kept close to the wall,
the feeling of her mouth willingly given to mine better than I ever

dreamed it. Even after she pulled away, it felt like a while before my heart started to beat again. "Trust me, Jack," she said. "Always trust me."

"Trust you?"

"Trust me." Then she walked out to greet her five o'clock.

❊

Tommy Smallwood arrived fourteen minutes late for his scheduled viewing. Accompanied by Mary Thomas Jones, he was the only visitor who threatened to break one of Rhys's rules. Positioned in the hallway outside the door, Rhys was studying the minute hand of her wristwatch when he and the conservator stepped off the elevator and came loping toward her.

"Ten seconds later and I'd have had no choice but to lock you out," Rhys said.

"Go on," said Smallwood, pretending to doubt her.

Until now Rhys had kept us quarantined next door, but for Smallwood's visit she'd insisted we stand close to the mural and effect poses meant to appear menacing. Smallwood strode past Joe Butler and me without saying anything and approached Rondell Cherry. "What happened to your face, my man? Cut yourself shaving?"

Cherry's body tensed and knots worked at the points of his jaw, but he somehow managed to keep his temper in check. From his nostrils came a noisy exhalation, like a bull about to charge. "I hope it didn't hurt," Smallwood said.

"Leave the man alone," Joe Butler said, stepping up between them.

"Go stand there," Rhys said, shoving Smallwood to the other side of the room.

We stood back and watched as Mary Thomas Jones ran her fingers over the painting's surface and studied it under a loupe. Next she produced a black light and asked Rhys to close the blinds and curtains and to shut off the photoflood lamps. Once the room was dark she held the glowing purple light an inch or two from the surface and swept it over the image from left to right, rather in the motion of a windshield wiper. Even from where I stood several feet away I could see areas that appeared dark purple against the light. "So it's required considerable retouch, has it?"

"Not considerable, Mary. That's an exaggeration."

"But here on this section I find in-painting on parallel lines from the top to the bottom of the canvas. Was there damage?"

"Yes, there was. The canvas tore away in a strip before I got it in studio."

"Oh, that's too bad." Now she turned her attention to the back of the painting. "And you relined it, each panel?"

"I lined each panel, yes."

"And you *re*lined the old way. Why didn't you use a Beva lining, if you don't mind my asking?"

"You should know why, Mary."

"Edify me. Please. I'm all ears."

"I prefer wax lining for several reasons," Rhys said. "To start, it's been good enough for the Europeans for five hundred years, so why shouldn't it be good enough for me now? Also, it's stable and organic, and it's easily reversible. Beva lining, on the other hand, requires a synthetic adhesive and a polyester fabric in a process that dates back only about twenty years, if that long. I've seen other conservators— you, for instance, Mary—seriously damage a paint layer because the solvents you used to correct a Beva lining were too strong. Lastly, Mary, Beva lining stinks. It smells like chemicals. And it costs too much." Rhys glanced at her watch. "Mr. Smallwood, you have twelve minutes left. Shall I continue to take this woman's obnoxious questions or do you want to examine the painting?"

"Mary, move over," Smallwood said.

She stumbled away and Smallwood dropped to a crouch and positioned his face close to the painting. His nostrils flared and his eyes fluttered closed as he sniffed the surface, and I was reminded of

Patrick Marion's story about the intruder in his apartment who'd seemed as eager to smell the painting as to see it. In this case Small-wood inhaled a warm scent of honey from the beeswax lining. He huffed and puffed like a man on the verge of orgasm, then gave his head a violent shake and instantly came out of it. "Sweet Jesus," he muttered, and removed a pair of white gloves from an inner pocket of his jacket. He put them on and began to caress the figures of the lovers at the mural's center. I turned to Rhys and registered the edge of pain on her face. One might've thought that she herself was being violated. "Mary, did you count the coloreds?" he said.

The conservator, already humiliated, smiled weakly at him. She shook her head.

"If you're counting the coloreds, don't forget me," Rondell Cherry said from his corner ten feet away. "I'm a colored. Born and raised a colored."

Smallwood wheeled around and stared. "I meant the ones in the painting, Rondell. The Negroes *in the painting*."

"Me, too," Joe Butler said. "If you're counting the Negroes count me in, too. I'm a Negro and always have been a Negro, long as I can remember."

"You ain't no goddamned—"

"And me," said Rhys, cutting him off. "You shouldn't forget me, either, Mr. Smallwood, if you insist on counting them."

"What the hell is going on around here?" he shouted, glaring at each of them. "I was talking about the painting!"

"Or me," I said, shouldering up next to Rhys. "I'm colored, too, Mr. Smallwood. Don't leave me out."

The room was quiet but for his labored breathing. He gave his head a shake and removed the gloves from his hands. "Bunch of lu-natics," he said. "You're a bunch of crazy people."

"Colored ones," Rondell said. "Yeah, you right."

Rhys walked to the door and pulled it open. "Mr. Smallwood, if you intend to bid tomorrow please make sure to come on time. And remember you won't have a fifteen-minute cushion like you did today. We start promptly at three o'clock."

Mary Thomas Jones slipped past Rhys into the hall, and Small-wood followed as far as the door. He looked back at the painting and sniffed one more time, seeming to find what he was after even for the distance.

An hour or so later, after Joe Butler and Rondell Cherry had unknot-ted their ties and left for home, Rhys ordered dinner from the room service menu and we ate by candlelight with the curtains pulled open to a view of the river. "I'm rooting for the Andersons." I said. "I don't like that they're from Texas, but I like that he cried and she wanted to touch Jacqueline and Levette."

"What's wrong with Texas?" Rhys said.

"Nothing. I'd just like to see the painting stay in the South."

"Texas isn't part of the South?"

"Texas isn't part of anything but Texas."

She forked up another piece of New York strip. "I'm for the An-dersons, too. No matter where Texas is on your map, Jack, I'd much rather see the mural go there than to Smallwood's mansion on Pryta-nia Street. But we both know who's going to get it and it's no use pre-tending."

"Why can't someone else win the auction?" I said. "The Ander-sons have almost as much money as Smallwood, and so do some of the other collectors. Why can't one of them win out for a change?"

She poured more wine in my glass and I watched the light from the candles in her eyes. "It's not always about money," she said. "Win-ning at auction is as much about moxie. In a situation where every-thing is equal—everything meaning personal wealth—moxie is what triumphs. Every one of the collectors asked me the same question to-day: Is Tommy Smallwood going to be bidding? They deflated like balloons when I said he would be. Watch him tomorrow, Jack. Every aspect of the man's persona will be an exaggeration carefully thought out. The clothes he wears, the way he walks, the things he says when he first enters the room, the type of woman he likely will have on his arm. He wants you to think he's an ignorant bubba, but every detail is calculated to intimidate the opponent and build on his projecting invincibility."

When we were done we stood at the window looking out at the water and the ships and small lights along the bank and we kissed again and it was as powerful as before. She started to laugh, feeling me tremble in her arms, and she pulled me even closer and made a shushing sound in my ear. It had been a while since a woman shushed me and I'd forgotten how nice it was to be shushed. "Do that again," I said.

"I can't hold you any tighter," she said.

"No, I mean shush me again. That sound you made."

She did it and I trembled and she laughed, precisely in that order. I was rusty and out of practice, and I didn't know how to talk to a woman except to say exactly what was on my mind. "Let me stay with you tonight."

"You can't, Jack."

"We don't have to do anything. Let me just stay in the suite with you. I'll sleep on the floor. I'd really like to be with you."

"You can't. I'm sorry."

"Is it still because I'm not like you? Not black like you?"

"Black like me? What are you talking about?"

"That day after we had oysters at Casamento's you said you wanted 'somebody like me,' and I quote you on that."

"Yes, I did say that. But I meant somebody who thinks like me, and who shares my values, and who cares about what I care about, and whose passion for art is as great as mine is. I didn't mean somebody who is the same race as I am. The reason you can't stay tonight," she said, "is because I have a few things to take care of yet. And I've already committed to Levette tonight."

"So my rival is a dead man?"

"Right," she said with an exaggerated nod. "Who happens to be my grandfather. Now come on, Jack. I'll walk you to the elevator."

She held my hand and escorted me down the hall. I punched the Down button and the car arrived. "Rhys, what about taxes?" I said suddenly.

When the door started to close she stuck a hand out and stopped it. "That's an odd question. What about them?"

"You make a bank deposit of ten grand or more and the bank automatically notifies the IRS? It's the law. Deposit a million and the government will probably send a Brinks truck to take its share."

"Why don't we talk about that after the auction?" she said. She let go of the door and it started to slide closed again. "One more thing," she said.

This time it was I who stuck a hand out and forced the door back open.

"I've invited Mr. Lowenstein to be here tomorrow," she said. "I thought you should know."

"Why on earth would you invite him, Rhys?"

"I thought he could use the lift."

"A lift? Are you kidding? Seeing Tommy Smallwood walk off with his friend's mural is going to give Lowenstein a lift? I can't imagine a worse form of torture. It would be like having to watch Levette die twice."

"That's a bit of an overstatement, wouldn't you say?" She shrugged at the same time I did. "He's put the house up for sale, you know?"

"Of course I knew. But how did you know?"

"Trust me," she said, then pushed my hand away, letting the door close.

※

Breaking with tradition, Tommy Smallwood was the first of the bidders to arrive. He did not storm in like a proud champ with a title to defend but rather calmly entered the suite and led his date to the front of the room. They crouched beside the painting and studied the scene, Smallwood's face arranged in an attitude of bliss. He was wearing a suit and his gumbo smell had been replaced today with one of after-shave. Against the small chandelier overhead the top of his head re-sembled the meringue of an icebox pie. I stared at him and asked myself the same questions that always came up at a Smallwood sight-ing: Why art? Why not souped-up muscle cars or trucks with big tires? Why not customized fishing rigs, for heaven's sake?

"I didn't pass out," he said, when he'd seen enough of the paint-ing. "How about that, Charbonnet? I didn't pass out."

I smiled at him.

"Where do we get our paddles?" he said to Rhys.

"We won't be using paddles," she answered.

"No paddles?"

"Not counting yourself, there will be five bidders in the room to-day. Since I know everyone, I didn't think paddles were necessary."

"But how will I bid?"

"You bid by raising your hand."

"I'd still like to have one," he said. "I'd really like a number."

"Mr. Smallwood, it isn't necessary. We know who you are."

"Yes, but I want one anyway."

Rhys wrote "00" on a sheet from her writing pad and handed it to him.

"Is that a number?" he said. "I don't think it is. You're trying to trick me."

She snatched the paper from his hand, crossed out the "00" with her Sharpie pen, and wrote "01" next to it. "How's that?" she said.

"I'll take it."

Even before Cherry and I had arrived at noon, Rhys and Joe But-ler had arranged two rows of chairs in a semicircle facing the mural, in all about twenty chairs, although fewer than half would be occu-pied today. Smallwood and the woman selected seats in the exact cen-ter of the front row.

The rest of the bidders arrived in short order, the last of them,

Taylor Dickel, enjoying surreptitious sips from a whiskey flask. He sat one chair away from Smallwood.

"Okay, then, that looks like everyone," Rhys said. She opened the door to the adjoining suite. "Sally, darling," she said.

They came in together, Lowenstein in his wheelchair, Sally pushing him. The old man might've been another collector, judging from the reception he received. Each bidder inspected him closely as if to take stock of his strengths and weaknesses. Deciding he had only weaknesses, they quickly turned away from him.

Sally wheeled the old man to the rear of the room close to where I was standing and maneuvered him into a corner. When she saw me she puckered her lips and kissed the air, but soundlessly. I kissed the air back.

"I'd like to thank you all for being here today," Rhys began. She was standing behind a lectern without a microphone. "I'm not a professional auctioneer, so bear with me, please. So as to avoid confusion, mostly to myself, the bidding will be increased by increments of no less than ten thousand dollars. You're free and encouraged to bid higher than ten thousand, but you can't bid less than that. Now before we start, I'd like to reiterate a few of our rules. The first is, when the gavel sounds today the sale is final. Under no circumstances will there be a return, not that I expect anyone who wins the bidding to ever consider parting with this wonderful painting. If the winning bidder is from out of town he must arrange his own shipping. If the winning bidder is local I can deliver the painting myself or arrange for the buyer to pick it up at the studio of the Crescent City Conservation Guild. As I've notified each of you before, there will be no taxes and no buyer's premium. The price you pay is the hammer price. If there are any questions please don't hesitate to ask them. It's now or never."

Tommy Smallwood raised his hand. "Will you take cash?"

"Cash?" It was Dickel, shouting out the word. "Did he say *cash*?"

"No, Mr. Smallwood," Rhys said, "I will not accept cash. The only payment I'll accept, as I've stated before, is a wire transfer. Immediately after the sale I'll meet with the winning bidder and provide further details. Anything else?" She glanced around the room, her gaze moving from one collector to the next. "Is everyone ready?" When nobody said anything Rhys took in a deep breath. "Up for bids now is the Levette Asmore Magazine Street post office mural of a Mardi Gras fantasia, circa 1941. Do I have a bid?"

Several hands shot up and from his chair to the right of where I was standing Cedric Anderson called out, "Five hundred."

"Five hundred," repeated Rhys. "Five hundred dollars? Five hundred thou—"

"Five hundred *thousand*," said Anderson, to scattered laughter.

Good God, I thought. The record for a southern painting at auction had been shattered with the maiden bid.

"Five hundred thousand dollars, then," Rhys said. "Very good, Mr. Anderson. We have five hundred thousand dollars bid. We have five hun—"

Smallwood raised the sheet of paper to the side of his head and gave it a shake.

"Five ten," Rhys said and pointed at him.

"Five twenty," countered Cedric Anderson.

"Five thirty," said Amanda Howard.

"Five forty," answered Rhys, for Smallwood.

"Six hundred thousand," crowed Taylor Dickel, hopping forward in his chair.

"Six ten," said Rhys, once again for Smallwood.

Cedric Anderson thrust his hand over his head. "Seven hundred thousand," he said, in a voice an octave higher than the one he'd used previously.

"And seven ten to Mr. Smallwood," came Rhys's reply.

"*Eight* . . . eight hundred thousand!" shouted Amanda Howard.

A silence fell over the room but for the rattling of the paper in Tommy Smallwood's thick right hand. "Eight ten," Rhys said.

"Eight twenty."

"Eight thirty."

Smallwood's left hand went up now, the index finger pointing skyward, as he mouthed the figure he was prepared to pay. "One million dollars," Rhys said. "I have one million dollars. Thank you, Mr. Smallwood. Do I have—"

"One million ten thousand," Amanda Howard said.

Smallwood's left index finger beat twice against the air. "One million one hundred thousand," Rhys said.

"One million two hundred thousand dollars," came a bid from the collector in the chair directly behind Smallwood.

"One million three hundred thou—"

"And one million four to Mr. Smallwood," Rhys said, cutting off Amanda Howard, who lowered her head on her husband's shoulder. She began to weep silently.

The Howards were out now. Faced with his own end moments later, Taylor Dickel reached for his flask and mumbled a single obscenity under his breath. The last two buyers were Cedric Anderson and Tommy Smallwood, and then it appeared to be only Smallwood.

Rhys raised her gravel in plain sight of everyone in the room. "I have two million and fifty thousand dollars," she said. "Do I have two million and sixty thousand dollars? Do I have two million and sixty, anyone? *Anyone?* Do I have it, anyone? In that case it's going once . . . going *twice* . . . ?"

"Two million sixty," cried David Howard, to the apparent surprise of his wife, who clutched his arm to keep from falling off her chair.

"Two million seventy thousand," replied Rhys, on Smallwood's cue. "I have two million seventy. Do I have—"

"Yes. Two million eighty," came a voice from the rear of the room. It was Lowenstein, clearing his throat now with a wet cough. He thrust his hand in the air to make sure he had Rhys's attention. "Did you get that, Miss Goudeau? I bid two million and eighty thousand dollars."

Smallwood craned his neck for another appraisal of Lowenstein. "Two million ninety," he said out loud, abandoning his sheet of paper.

"Two million one hundred—nah, I'm out, I'm out." Lowenstein waved both hands to signal defeat. "I'm out, Miss Goudeau. *Out . . .*"

And so that ended it. The painting was Smallwood's.

I sat for a while waiting for Rhys's reaction, but she gave none. She didn't leap to her feet and pound a fist in the air. She didn't shout out or come to us for hugs and high-fives. There was no crying jag, either, at the prospect of having to turn over the painting to Smallwood. Instead she took a seat and waited for the room to clear out.

I walked up and put a hand on her shoulder. "You okay?"

She smiled and grabbed one of my fingers and gave it a tug. "Just tired. I have a new respect for my auctioneer friends. I feel like I've run a marathon."

"You did a fine job up there today, Rhys. I'm proud of you."

"I'm not." She tugged at my finger again. "I'm not proud at all. All I feel is shame. Overwhelming shame. I can't breathe for it. I think I'm going to suffocate."

The Howards came over and pulled her away before I could flesh out an explanation. As they were thanking her for including them in the auction, a loud voice sounded behind me, and I wheeled back in time to see Taylor Dickel attempt to shake Tommy Smallwood's hand. Smallwood slapped him away. "But Mr. Smallwood?" Dickel was saying. "Mr. Smallwood, will you think of me if ever you change your mind about the—"

"Leave me alone," Smallwood muttered, and slapped at him again.

"I was only—"

"Leave me alone, Dickel. Do you hear? Leave me alone."

"But I was—"

Smallwood knocked over chairs as he sidestepped Dickel on his way to the window. He stood staring out at the river below, then put his face in his hands and began to sob. His girlfriend remained seated, watching after him with a pretense of concern. I couldn't presume to understand what motivated Tommy Smallwood to do anything, but I thought I knew why he was crying. It had something to do with why the truly rich and the truly beautiful always seem unhappy, if not altogether miserable. When it's all been given, and it's all been had, what use is there in dreaming any more? Smallwood had his Asmore now. He might as well be dead.

"But I don't understand," Dickel complained, ostensibly to the woman. "He's won it, the fool has won it. Why the damned hell is he acting as if he's lost?"

Rhys ushered Dickel into the hall, nearly shoving him out when he tried to resist. "But he won, the bloody fool won . . ."

After he was gone Rhys joined Smallwood at the window. He nodded when she spoke to him and after a time followed her into the neighboring suite. Having come to feel halfway sorry for his date, I was tempted to sit with the woman and give her company. But on second thought she seemed fine. Maybe Smallwood was paying her by the hour, it occurred to me.

The Howards left, with the bidder whose name I never got fast behind them. Then Sally began to roll Lowenstein toward the door. "Excellent job, sir," I whispered as they rattled by.

"Excellent, was it?" said Lowenstein.

He looked up at me and I gave him a wink.

"Did you see that, Sally? Mr. Charbonnet just winked at me because I was excellent. I was excellent," he went on, "although I have no idea what for."

I dropped to my haunches and checked around to make sure Smallwood and his girlfriend weren't listening. "It's called shill bidding, what you did. There's no way you could afford to buy the painting and yet you drove up the price, presumably to fetch more for the consignor. It's unethical, Mr. Lowenstein, not that I care. In fact, I was glad to see the bastard have to bleed a little more."

"So I'm a shill, am I? And what does that make you? A *thief*? Yes, I think it does. If I'm a shill, then you're a thief. Let's go, Sally."

"You can never be nice, can you?" I shot a look at Sally and she stepped back as if to reject any possibility of being brought into the conversation. "There's something I feel compelled to tell you, sir. I hope you'll forgive the sentiment, but I admire you for being here today. I can't imagine how difficult it must've been."

"How's that?" He cupped a hand around the back of his ear.

"I said, it must have been very difficult for you, not to say painful, to sit back here this afternoon and watch your friend's painting being sold. I admire your courage. It came to me during the auction that you've come full circle with the mural. It must feel like completing a journey."

He stared at me. "What did I tell you about making assumptions as far as I'm concerned? Don't do it, Mr. Charbonnet. You make a mistake."

He swiveled in his seat and patted Sally's hand where she gripped the chair. She pushed him out into the hall.

TWELVE

To complete the deal, Tommy Smallwood wired his payment to an offshore bank account in George Town, Grand Cayman, an island in the West Indies south of Cuba. I was sitting in Rhys's office when a representative with the bank called and spoke to Joe Butler, confirming the deposit. I was also there when, moments later, after Joe had left the room, Rhys reached Smallwood on his cell phone and told him she would drop off the painting within the hour.

"Start over at the beginning," I said, when she put the phone down. "I'm still not clear about some of the details."

"Pay attention this time. You're supposed to be such a great reporter."

"I never claimed that."

Only weeks before, Rhys said, she had dispatched Joe to Grand Cayman strictly for the purpose of exploring options that would allow her to conceal a large deposit from the U.S. government. After a few days Joe had called from his hotel room. "You wouldn't believe this place," he had said. "They've got a total of five, maybe six, traffic lights, and there's all of twenty-five thousand people living here. But they have more than five hundred banks. I shit you not, boss. They got more banks than New Orleans has daiquiri stores and strip joints put together."

Later in the conversation Joe had said, "So what you do, you wire the money to this account, okay? And then the bank does two things. First, it gives you Visa platinum cards with basically unlimited credit lines and lets you access the money using these cards. The bank doesn't inform the IRS that you own the account or that it even exists. The second thing it does, you ever hear of a Dutch corporation? Well, basically, that lets you secretly borrow mortgage funds from the money you deposit. In other words, this Dutch corporation lets you withdraw whatever you want but makes it look like you're actually *borrowing* the money. You get caught," Joe had told her, "and that's our ass. Tax evasion, wire fraud. They'll fine us, throw us in jail, make us suck our thumbs and say we're sorry over and over for a very long time. But I don't think we will get caught." When Rhys didn't say anything, Joe Butler had added, "Not any more than I think Tommy Smallwood will catch us."

I squinted at her now across the piles of paper on the desk. "Repeat that last part again, would you, please?"

"He said the U.S. government wouldn't catch us any more than Tommy Smallwood would catch us."

"I thought that's what you said. Now what do you mean?"

She switched on the episcope, and even before she projected the first image on the wall I felt myself sliding back in my chair, anticipating her next revelation. An image of the mural came up. She gave me time to look at it. She then removed the photo from under the projector and replaced it with a second photo. What appeared to be the same image flashed against the screen.

"There's no way I could let that evil sonofabitch have it," she said.

"So you sold him a fake?"

"I sold him a copy."

"Which one was at the hotel? Was it the real Asmore or the copy?"

"Both," she said. "The one Hairy Mary and the others inspected at the preview was the original. I switched them out after you and I had dinner in the room. That meant coming back here to the studio in the U-Haul and picking up Joe and the copy. We didn't finish getting everything in place until almost five o'clock in the morning. That's one reason why I was so tired yesterday. When I finally brought the hammer down I thought I'd collapse from exhaustion."

"Was it Joe who made the copy?"

"Yes, it was. For some reason that's beyond me Joe has the ability to get inside Levette's head. It's uncanny. It's as though he gets into character, say, as an actor would, and the part he's playing is Asmore. For the weeks when he was painting the copy he insisted I call him 'Levette.' I told him to let me know if ever he had a sudden urge to jump from a bridge."

"Funny, Rhys."

"No, it wasn't. It wasn't funny at all. But I've been going on fumes for weeks. Both of us have. We used an old canvas, circa 1940, that we pulled out of a restaurant that had closed in Mid-City. Joe stripped it, then primed it with gesso. Next we made a tracing to work from. We used slides and a projector and the episcope to get the color and the brushstrokes right and all the subtle variations. If Hairy Mary happens to black-light the copy, she'll see the same areas of retouch fluoresce that she saw on the original. Making the copy was time-consuming but a lot easier than you might think—easy for a professional conservator. The best fakes in the history of art were made by painting restorers."

"So if it's the copy that's waiting outside in the U-Haul, where's the original?"

"You'll have the answer soon enough. Better yet, I'll show you. Why don't you drive with me to Prytania Street? I'm sure Tommy Smallwood would love nothing more than an opportunity to collapse in your arms again."

❋

Past the tall iron fence the black gardeners cut grass, whacked weeds and watered flower beds still sprouting color from the summer planting. On the lower gallery black maids in uniforms used straw brooms to remove cobwebs from the corners of the ceiling. On the upper gallery a black butler wearing white gloves served coffee from a silver pot. When the cup was filled, the man bowed and left Tommy Smallwood alone under the baskets of impatiens and lipstick vine swaying in the breeze.

"What year is this?" I said.

"The same one we've been living for too damned long," Rhys answered.

As she squared the truck against the curb, Smallwood stood and welcomed us with a wave, then disappeared in the house. In minutes he was in the garden, striding toward us, his body naked but for a white Speedo swimsuit, a towel draped around his neck and a pair of flip-flops. Past the suit's polyester weave one could see the stubborn knot at his crotch. "Lift your feet up off the floor, Jack. I think I'm going to be sick."

"Come on," I said and opened my door. "You're almost done."

Smallwood had just finished his daily regimen of laps in the pool, and he smelled pleasantly of chlorine and cocoa butter. He was both polite and solicitous, inviting us to join him on the gazebo, where he would have sandwiches and lemonade served. One of his girls, he said, made the best cucumber sandwich in town.

"No, thank you," Rhys said. "I have appointments at the studio."

She raised the truck's rear gate and Smallwood put a couple of fingers in his mouth and let out a whistle. The men in the yard looked up. "You think I have all day?" he shouted. Before I could offer to help, six of them were removing the panels and carrying them to the house.

"I had to let Mary go," Smallwood said to Rhys, as she was pulling the gate back down. "It'd been coming for a long time. You remember the William Aiken Walker I bought at Neal a while back? It was one of his cotton kingdom paintings, showing all your Africans in the fields. Well, I asked Mary to make the half-breed a little blacker. I call him a half-breed, but he could of been a Mexican. All she had to do was paint the man's face and arms. Give him a black dab here, a black dab there. She refused to do it. I told her she was being unreasonable and fired her on the spot."

Rhys didn't say anything. She stared up at him, blocking the sun with the flat of her hand.

"So I need somebody to look after my paintings and my pottery," Smallwood continued. "And, seeing the job you did restoring my Levette, I thought I'd offer you the position, Miss Goudeau. Conservator of the Thomas Smallwood Collection. It's yours, dear, if you want it."

"It's mine?" She touched her chest.

"All yours. What do you say?"

Rhys was slow to respond, and when she did, it surprised Smallwood no more than me. She began to laugh so hard that tears tracked down her face and she lost her breath and seemed to have a hard time getting it back. She fell against the truck and let out a shout that scattered pigeons from the eaves of the garage and drove the doves from the olive trees. The gardeners dropped their tools and stood staring. The maids lowered their brooms. By now Smallwood was laughing, too. It was the laugh of a man who couldn't decide what was so goddamned funny.

"No," Rhys said.

"No? No what?"

"No," she said again, and lunged at him.

I managed to grab her and pull her away before she could connect with more than a couple of blows. They were roundhouse punches, coming from way up high, both of them landing squarely against Smallwood's head. He stumbled backward, tripped on the curb and fell to the sidewalk, skinning his knees when he met the bricks. A look of terrible confusion was on his face. Leaves and debris from the ground clung to the thick slab at his waist. I went to help him up but Rhys yelled for me not to touch him. "Get in the truck," she said. I didn't move for a second and she said, "Jack, in the truck."

She was standing over him now, hands balled into fists. A thin rope of mucus hung from her nose and her mouth was distorted in an angry shape. She seemed to be trying to decide her next move. Her eyes grew large and she snorted as she suddenly seemed to understand what she'd done. But rather than leave then or help Smallwood off the ground, she raised her hand and slapped him once hard across the face. Her open palm meeting his cheek sounded like a rifle shot. Tommy Smallwood crawled back against the fence and wrapped his head in his arms.

"That last one was for Levette," she said.

❋

Toward the end of the year the Wheeler Beauty Academy closed. The few students who were left enrolled in other hair colleges in town and Rhys hired Rondell Cherry to work a variety of jobs at the Guild's studio. At first she had him answering the phone, cleaning up and making deliveries, but soon he was apprenticing in the frame department. Under Joe Butler's direction, he learned how to repair antique frames and how to carve and gild moulding. Rhys paid him more than double his previous salary and gave him a lab coat with his name scripted in red thread on the chest. When she finally decided to buy the company a new vehicle—a black SUV with tinted windows to keep people from seeing inside—she sold Cherry the Guild's old van for less than book value, which was all of five hundred dollars. Since he liked them, Rhys let him keep the magnetic signs on the doors advertising the Guild.

"Do you ever miss the school?" I asked Cherry one day at the studio.

He was applying small squares of gold leaf to rabbit glue lathered on the surface of a frame. "I miss the kids," he said. "They were great. That's about it."

"What about Mrs. Wheeler?"

"I don't miss her cigarette smoke, that's for sure."

"But do you miss Mrs. Wheeler the person?"

"I don't *not* miss her, let me put it to you that way."

"You'll have to explain that to me, Mr. Cherry. How one doesn't *not* miss a person."

He'd been listening to music, and presently he put his headphones back on. "You don't miss them, you don't *not* miss them," he explained. "Look, Jack, that's the best I can do." There was a look in his eyes that reminded me of the one I saw when Rhys and I first met him, when he was cleaning the floor and it seemed he could've made us both disappear with his mop. "You might not have nothing to do," he said, "but this frame won't get done by itself. Let me back to my work, government man."

Patrick Marion removed the High Life for-sale sign a few days after we auctioned off the mural, just as another sign was going up in front of the beauty school. Rhys and I checked on the old place whenever we traveled to Riverbend and visited my mother, taking Magazine Street to make sure the property hadn't sold yet. "Every time I see it the crack in my heart gets a little deeper," Rhys said one day, as we drove by.

Sometime later, when I was alone, I surrendered to a spirit of nostalgia and pulled over by the curb and had another long look at the building, rather as Mrs. Wheeler used to do. Its façade was in worse shape than ever, with the broadsheets hanging like tree bark in the process of shedding, and more gaps in the roof layer where shingles had come off. The electric sign by the curb had been turned off for good, and the one over the door had been removed. The only positive change was the grass growing on the front lawn. There were more weeds than grass, but at least it was green.

The windows upstairs, I noticed, were still black holes without curtains, dead eyeballs staring out at the world. Kids with rocks had broken more of them.

I'd thought Gail Wheeler was seeing the ghost of her husband past the dusty panes, and for a moment as I stood there I had an unsettling feeling that I was being watched. It wasn't Jerome Wheeler, however. "You know how we know things?" Rhys had said months before. "How as human beings we just know things or at least intuit them?" It came to me who was looking out at me from a window upstairs. I *knew*.

"You're dead," I called out. "You've been dead."

Cars moved past on the street and I looked around to see if anyone had heard me. I was glad Rhys wasn't there. She surely would've thought me insane. But then I shouted out again, and for the same reason as before. I *knew*.

"What else, Levette? What else do you want?"

I never did see his face, and I left wishing I hadn't stopped. But somewhere on the drive home, down where you leave the dense clutter of houses on Orleans Avenue and arrive at the old bayou, I heard a voice in my head. It wasn't the voice Rhys had heard telling her to save Levette's mural. And it wasn't my own voice, reminding me the way it does when I need to stop at the store and pick up sandwich meat and a loaf of bread. It was the voice the world gives to people when they really need to hear something. *"I don't want you to forget me,"* the voice said. *"Jack, don't forget."*

A few days later Rhys and I were having dinner at my mother's house. "My lease for the firehouse is up in May," Rhys said between bites of crawfish étouffée. "If the old post office station is still available, I'm going to buy it and move the Guild there. I can't see continuing to pay rent to that jerk on Prytania Street."

"Why, that sounds wonderful, darling," my mother said.

I waited until I'd swallowed my food before letting her know what

I thought of the idea. "Hasn't buying one old place cured you of ever wanting another?"

"No," she said. "Just as I'm sure that owning two old places won't keep me from wanting a third. This is who I am, Jack. And it's what I do." She put her fork down and extended her hands across the table and shook them in my face. "I fix things."

"She fixed me," I said to my mother.

"You . . . ?" And my mother laughed. "No, Jack, you remain a work in progress."

Rhys gave her a wink. "Give me time, Mrs. Charbonnet. Just give me time . . ."

I saw Mrs. Wheeler only last week outside Canal Place, a shopping center on the edge of the French Quarter. She was there with a woman who looked to be about my age, the two of them seated at a Starbucks patio table with shopping bags collected at their feet. Each had a coffee in a big paper cup, and a cigarette burning in a tin tray. Everything Mrs. Wheeler was wearing this day looked new. Her blouse still had fold lines and creases, as though she'd pulled it off a store shelf only minutes before. She reminded me of the late comedian Minnie Pearl, who kept the price tag hanging from her hat to make sure everyone saw what she'd paid for it. When Mrs. Wheeler didn't pick me out in the crowd, I thought about moving on and going about my business. But then as I was crossing the street I said to myself, "And where have your manners run off to?" I decided to see how she was doing.

"Oh, sure," she said when I told her who I was. "I remember you. You're that cop with NOPD that came looking for the child molester."

"Actually, ma'am, I'm Rhys Goudeau's friend."

"Rhys Goudeau," said the other woman, perking up. "Isn't she the one who hired Rondell Cherry in that bad neighborhood? Oh, I love Rondell. I hope they don't shoot him. They shoot people over there, you know?"

It was Alice O'Neil, the niece who'd represented Mrs. Wheeler when the government came to investigate her phony grant applications. Like me, they'd traveled to the Quarter to shop for Carnival costumes. They'd veered off track when they saw the sale signs posted in the mall. Saks had some real bargains in cosmetics, and they recommended I poke my head in Mignon Faget, if I needed any jewelry. Maybe tomorrow they would shop for costumes; they'd spent all the money the budget would allow for today.

I finally got Mrs. Wheeler on the subject that, if I were to be honest, was the real reason I'd stopped by their table. "Whatever happened to the case the government was building against you?" I said, employing the Rhys Goudeau approach to interviewing, that being to bluntly come right out and ask the question. "Did they ever bring charges?"

"Charges?" And now Alice O'Neil dragged hard on her cigarette. "I think one of them lectured her once. Pointed a finger. Didn't one of them get smart with you, Nanny?"

"Yes, one did. Real smart."

"They liked an excuse to leave Baton Rouge and come visit New Orleans, I think," Alice O'Neil continued. "They would stop by the school for half an hour and poke around then drive to the Quarter for a poboy and lap dances on Bourbon Street. Make a real day of it." Alice sucked on her cigarette, and Mrs. Wheeler did the same. "They were *men*, in other words," Alice said with a note of finality.

"They were *men*," Mrs. Wheeler repeated, with her own note. She flicked a cone of ash in the tray and looked at me. "What are you going to be?" she said.

"Ma'am?"

"You said you were shopping for a Mardi Gras costume."

"Oh. Well, it's not definite yet, I'm still trying to find the right one. But I thought I'd go as a pirate."

❄

We stand in the crowd with arms raised and yell for throws as Endymion rolls by, the great parade of floats and marching bands and dancing girls twirling batons. This night in February is cold and breezy, gumbo weather, but we're warmed and shielded by the masses that have gathered all around us and press in close. I am Jean Lafitte, or "Jack the Feet," as Rhys takes pleasure in calling me. And while she was supposed to dress as a fairy princess, in my opinion she better resembles an angel. She wears a frilly pink tutu over a leotard and tights, the layers of diaphanous netting reaching to her ankles and the soft satin shoes of a ballet dancer. She wears a rhinestone tiara and, harnessed to her back, wings made with goose and ostrich feathers. Glitter and smears of paint mask her face, and in the orange light of the flambeau carriers she burns for me as brightly as their torches do.

Because she is beautiful, Rhys attracts the attention of the riders on the floats, who deluge her with plastic beads and toys, and who gawk at her through the black holes of their masks long after the procession has moved past. One of them, high up on a throne, stands and bows at the sight of her. If not the king, he certainly is royalty. He wears a gold suit and a flowing red robe trimmed in animal fur. He, too, wears a mask.

He steps down to the edge of the passing float and the other riders move to let him through. He reaches out with his scepter and hands it to Rhys, who recognizes him before I do. "God bless the Hurricane," she says. "Love you, Patch."

"Love you, too, Rhys Goudeau, even if you did buy my house."

It is midnight when we return to the old house on the bayou and embrace under the crape myrtles. Although Rhys has owned the property for several months now, she still treats it as though it belonged to Lowenstein, never entering the grounds without his or my permission. If she owns a key, I haven't seen it and she's never used it. We clear the gate and gently close it behind us so as not to wake him. Hand in hand, we tiptoe to his library window. A bulb is burning in the gooseneck lamp at his shoulder, and he sits with a book open in his lap and a snifter of cognac balanced on the arm of his chair. Rhys hesitates at first, then raises a fist and lightly raps on the glass. "Mr. Lowenstein, I brought you some beads."

He sits up, startled, and glares in our direction.

"It's Rhys Goudeau, Mr. Lowenstein. If it's not too late, I brought you some beads. Some Mardi Gras beads."

He is a long time coming to the door, and I am grateful for the chance to pull her close again and put my mouth on hers. The lights come on and Lowenstein is at the screen inviting us in. "I thought we might share the wealth," Rhys says, removing a fat cord of beads and putting it around his neck.

"Oh, dear girl," he says.

"We just caught them at the parade. Aren't they beautiful?"

"Oh, they are . . . they are beautiful . . . oh . . ."

We move to the library and Rhys tells him about our night, this strange, eternally tormented old man in a perfectly pressed dress shirt and raggedy pajama bottoms, hands shaking as he reaches to wipe tears from his face. It doesn't seem to register with him that Rhys is costumed as Jacqueline and I Levette, but then he remembers something and his voice lifts an octave. "I have a gift for you, too," he says to Rhys.

Crossing to the rear of the house, we pause in the center hall, where on one side Levette's mural has replaced the many Drysdales. In silence we enjoy another look, then move on to his bedroom. A lamp burns on a bedside table, illuminating more paintings and books and furniture, the furniture deriving from antebellum Louisiana cabinetmakers. He tells me to bring over the chair standing in the corner and to place it next to the armoire across from the foot of his bed. "Now reach your hand up there, Jack, up over the crown. See what you find."

I take them down one at a time and place them on the bed, in all some fifty rolled-up canvases. Rhys is overcome. The angel wings prevent her from sitting in a chair, so she clears out a spot on the edge of the bed and leans forward with her elbows resting on her thighs and sobs so hard that glitter and paint cloud her tears and drip to the floor.

When I'm done, Lowenstein goes through them all and finds the one of the bridge.

"It can't match your gift of the beads," he says, shuffling over with the painting and handing it to her. "But I thought you might like to have this, Miss Goudeau."

Acknowledgments

 When my uncle, Joe Bradley, completed his long, distinguished career in the U.S. Marine Corps, he put the wars
behind him and became an artist. Uncle Joe was the first
Louisiana painter whose work I collected, and without him I doubt
that I ever would've discovered the other artists whose stories inspired
this book. I owe a huge debt to Uncle Joe and I wish to thank him.

I also would like to thank John Sanderford for introducing me
to the paintings of his uncle, Edward Schoenberger, who as a young
man made a significant contribution to the Federal Art Project in
Louisiana. I spent several wonderful days with Eddie and his wife,
Sylvia, at their home in Wausau, Wisconsin, and I'm grateful to Eddie for his willingness to entertain my many questions about his life
and work.

I'm indebted to Jack and Frankie Kinsey of Dayton, Ohio, for helping me gather information about the great but vastly underappreciated Alberta Kinsey. I also want to acknowledge other family members of WPA-era artists from Louisiana who allowed me to interview them, most notably Franz Heldner and Paula Ninas. The artist John Clemmer and his wife, Dottie, made an important contribution to my research and have become dear friends; I thank them both. Clemmer's recollection of his years as an instructor and administrator at the Arts and Crafts Club of New Orleans made me wish I could travel back in time and walk the streets of the French Quarter that he knew as a young man. Another painter, William Arnold of Wakefield, Louisiana, welcomed me into his home and generously shared his memories of making pictures for more than sixty years. He and his wife, Doris, could not have been kinder or more gracious to me.

I thank the many collectors and dealers who told me stories about their favorite southern artists and contributed to my profile of Levette Asmore. Denise Berthiaume and Christy Wood of LeMieux Galleries were a tremendous help, as were Cindy Nicholas of Taylor Clark Gallery, Allain Bush of Bush Antiques, and Daria Atwell of the Charleston Renaissance Gallery.

The archives of the Historic New Orleans Collection, housed in the Williams Research Center, were an important resource, and I learned a lot by attending sales at the New Orleans Auction Galleries, the Neal Auction Company, and Hampshire House Auctions. The Ogden Museum of Southern Art mounted several excellent shows that featured works by WPA artists from Louisiana and provided valuable insight. In addition, my research assistant, Stephanie Boris, and my friend Robin Miller have my eternal gratitude for helping me run down many of the historical details that went into telling Levette's story.

Finally, I wish to thank the conservator Blake Vonder Haar for being such a devoted and patient teacher. Like Rhys Goudeau, Blake can fix anything. Without her help I could not have written this book.